THE BLUE SWORD

ROBIN McKINLEY

THE BLUE SWORD

Julia MacRae Books
A DIVISION OF FRANKLIN WATTS

First published in the United States of America 1982 by Greenwillow Books. First published in Great Britain 1983 by Julia MacRae Books, a division of Franklin Watts Ltd, 12a Golden Square, London W1R 4BA

British Library Cataloguing in Publication Data
McKinley, Robin
   The blue sword
   I. Title
   813'.54[J]   P27
   ISBN 0 86203 123 0

Reproduced from copy supplied
Printed and bound in Great Britain by A. Wheaton & Company, Exeter

CHAPTER ONE

S HE SCOWLED AT HER GLASS of orange juice. To think that she had been delighted when she first arrived here—was it only three months ago?—with the prospect of fresh orange juice every day. But she had been eager to be delighted; this was to be her home, and she wanted badly to like it, to be grateful for it—to behave well, to make her brother proud of her and Sir Charles and Lady Amelia pleased with their generosity.

Lady Amelia had explained that the orchards only a few days south and west of here were the finest in the country, and many of the oranges she had seen at Home, before she came out here, had probably come from those same orchards. It was hard to believe in orange groves as she looked out the window, across the flat deserty plain beyond the Residency, unbroken by anything more vigorous than a few patches of harsh grass and stunted sand-colored bushes until it disappeared at the feet of the black and copper-brown mountains.

But there was fresh orange juice every day.

She was the first down to the table every morning, and was gently teased by Lady Amelia and Sir Charles about her healthy young appetite; but it wasn't hunger that drove her out of bed so early. Since her days were empty of purpose, she could not sleep when night came, and by dawn each morning she was more than ready for the maid to enter her room, push back the curtains from the tall windows, and hand her a cup of tea. She was often out of bed when the woman arrived, and dressed, sitting at her window, for her bedroom window faced the same direction as the breakfast room, staring at the mountains. The servants thought kindly of her, as she gave them little extra work; but a lady who rose and dressed herself so early, and without assistance, was certainly a little eccentric. They knew of her impoverished background; that explained a great deal; but she was in a fine house now, and her host and hostess were only too willing to give her anything she might want, as they had no children of their own. She might try a little harder to adapt to so pleasant an existence.

She did try. She knew what the thoughts behind the looks the servants gave her were; she had dealt with servants before. But she was adapting to her new life as best as her energetic spirit could. She might have screamed, and hammered on the walls with her fists, or jumped over the low windowsill in her room, clambered to the ground by the ivy trellis (special ivy, bred to withstand the desert heat, carefully watered by Sir Charles' gardener every day), and run off toward the mountains; but she was trying her best to be good. So she was merely first to the breakfast table.

Sir Charles and Lady Amelia were all that was kind to her, and she was fond of them after a few weeks in their company. They had, indeed, been far more than kind. When her father died a year ago, Richard, a very junior military adjutant, had laid the difficulty of an unmarried sister and an entailed estate before Sir Charles, and begged for advice. (She heard all this, to her acute embarrassment, from Richard, who wanted to be sure she understood how much she had to be grateful for.) He and his wife had said that they would be happy to offer her a home with them, and Richard, too relieved to think hard about the propriety of such a godsend, had written to her and said, Come out. He had not specifically said, Mind your manners, but she understood that too.

She hadn't any choice. She had known, because her father had told her five years ago when her mother died, that she would have no inheritance; what money there was was tied up very strictly for the eldest son. "Not that Dickie will mistreat you," their father had said, with the ghost of a smile, "but I feel that, with your temperament, you had best have as long as possible a warning to resign yourself to it. You'll like being dependent on your brother even less, I fancy, than you like being dependent on me." He tapped his fingers on his desk. The thought that lay silent between them did not need to be spoken aloud: that it was not likely she would marry. She was proud, and if she had not been, her parents would have been proud for her. And there is little market for penniless bluebloods of no particular beauty—especially when the blueness of the blood is suspected to have been diluted by a questionable great-grandmother on the mother's side. What the questionableness exactly consisted of, Harry was not sure. With the self-centeredness of childhood she had not thought to ask; and later, after she had realized that she did not care for society nor society for her, she had no desire to ask.

The shipboard journey east on the *Cecilia* had been long but uneventful. She had found her sea legs almost at once, and had made friends with a middle-aged lady, also traveling alone, who asked no personal questions, and loaned her novels freely to her young companion, and discussed them with her upon their return. She had let her own mind go numb, and had read the novels, and sat in the sun, and strolled the decks, and not thought about the past or the future.

They docked at Stzara without mishap, and she found the earth heaved under her strangely when she first set foot ashore. Richard had been granted a month's leave to meet her and escort her north to her new home. He looked younger than she had expected; he had gone overseas three years ago, and had not been Home again since. He was affectionate to her at their reunion, but wary; they seemed to have little in common any more. I shouldn't be surprised, she thought; it's been a long time since we played together every day, before Dickie was sent off to school. I'm an encumbrance now, and he has his career to think of. But it would be nice to be friends, she thought wistfully. When she pressed him to give her some idea of what she could expect of her new life, he shrugged and said: "You'll see. The people are like Home, you know. You needn't have much to do with the natives. There are the servants, of course, but they are all right. Don't worry about it." And he looked at her with so worried a face that she didn't know whether to laugh or to shake him. She said, "I wish you would tell me what is worrying *you*." Variations of this conversation occurred several times during the first days of their journey together. At this point there would be a long silence.

Finally, as if he could bear it no more, he burst out: "You won't be able to go on as you did at home, you know."

"But what do you mean?" She hadn't thought much about native servants, or her position, yet; and obviously Richard knew her well enough of old to guess that now. She had written him letters, several each year, since he had gone overseas, but he had rarely answered. She had not minded very much, although she had thought occasionally, as when his six hastily scrawled lines at Christmas arrived, that it would have been pleasant if he were a better correspondent; but it hadn't troubled her. It troubled her now, for she felt that she was facing a stranger—a stranger who perhaps knew too much about her and her accustomed way of life.

She blinked at him, and tried to rearrange her thoughts. She was excited, but she was frightened too, and Richard was all she had. The memory of their father's funeral, and she the only family member standing beside the minister, and of the small handful of servants and tenants whom she had known all her life and who were far away from her now, was still raw and recent. She didn't want to think about her new life; she wanted time to ease into it gradually. She wanted to pretend that she was a tourist. "Dickie— Dick, what do you mean?"

Richard must have seen the homesick bewilderment on her face. He looked back at her unhappily. "Oh—er—it's not your house, you know."

"Of course I know that!" she exclaimed. "I appreciate what the Greenoughs are doing for you and for me by—by taking me in." And she added carefully: "You explained all that to me in your letter."

He nodded.

"Do you think I don't know how to behave myself?" she said at last, goaded, and was rewarded by another long silence while she felt the blood rising in her face.

"It's not that I don't think you know *how*," he said at last. She flinched, and he began: "An—"

"Harry," she said firmly. "It's still Harry." He looked at her with dismay, and she realized that she was confirming his fears about her, but she wasn't going to yield about that of all things. The realization that she would insist on being called Harry seemed to silence him, because he did not try to reason with her further, but withdrew into his corner seat and stared out the window.

She could tell by his voice that he did not want to hurt her, but that he was truly apprehensive. She and Richard had been wild animals together as small children; but when Dickie had been packed off to school, their mother had dragged her into the house, mostly by the ears or the nape of the neck, and begun the long difficult process of reforming her into something resembling a young lady.

"I suppose I should have started years ago," she told her sulky daughter; "but you were having such a good time, and I knew Dickie would be sent away soon. I thought it hardly fair that your lessons should start sooner." This lifted the cloud a little from her daughter's brow, so she added with a smile, "And, besides, I've always liked riding horses and climbing trees and falling into ponds better myself." After such an open avowal of sympathy from the enemy, lessons could never be quite awful; on the other hand, they were not perhaps as thorough as they might have been. On particularly beautiful days they often packed a lunch and rode out together, mother and daughter, to inspire themselves—the mother said—with a little fresh air; but the books as often as not stayed in the saddlebags all day. The daughter learned to love books, particularly adventure novels where the hero rode a beautiful horse and ran all the villains through with his silver sword, but her embroidery was never above passable; and she only learned to dance after her mother pointed out that such grace and balance as she might learn on the dance floor would doubtless stand her in good stead in the saddle. She learned the housekeeping necessary in an old ramshackle country house well enough to take over the management of theirs successfully during her mother's last illness; and the first horrible months after her mother's death were made easier by the fact that she had something to do. As the first pain of loss wore away, she realized also that she liked being useful.

In the shock five years later of her father's death, and with the knowledge that she must leave her home, and leave it in the indifferent hands of a business manager, it had occurred to her to be relieved that the little eastern station at the farthest-flung border of the Homelander empire where Richard had been posted, and where she was about to join him, was as small and isolated as it was. Her mother had escorted her to such small parties and various social occasions as their country neighborhood might offer, and while she knew she had "conducted herself creditably" she had not enjoyed herself. For one thing, she was simply too big: taller than all the women, taller than most of the men.

Harry could get nothing more useful out of her brother about his private misgivings as the small rickety train carried them north. So she began to ask general questions—a tourist's questions—about her new country; and then she had better luck. Richard began visibly to thaw, for he recognized the sincerity of her interest, and told her quite cheerfully that the town at the end of their journey, where Sir Charles and Lady Amelia awaited them, was the only town of any size at all within three days of it. "There's a wireless station out in the middle of nowhere where the train stops—it exists only for the train to have someplace to stop—and that's all." The town's name was Istan, after the natives' Ihistan, which was deemed too hard to pronounce. Beyond Istan was a scattering of small depressed cottages in carefully irrigated fields where a tough local tassel-headed grain called korf was grown. Istan had been a small village before the Homelanders came, where the farmers and herders and nomads from the surrounding country came to market every fortnight and a few pot-menders and rug-weavers kept shops. The Homelanders used it as an outpost, and expanded it, although the native marketplace remained at its center; and

built a fort at the eastern edge of it, which was named the General
Leonard Ernest Mundy.

Istan had lately become a place of some importance in the gov-
ernmental network the Homelanders had laid over the country
they had conquered eighty years before. It was still an isolated
spot, and no one went there who didn't have to; for it was at the
edge of the great northern desert of the peninsular continent the
Homelanders called Daria. But thirteen years ago the Aeel Mines
had been discovered in the Ramid Mountains to the northwest,
and in the last eight years the Mines had been officially declared
the most profitable discovery on the entire Darian continent, and
that was saying a great deal. The profits on oranges alone paid the
wages of half the civil servants in the Province.

"The Mines are awful to get to, though; the Ramids are very
nasty going. Istan is on the only feasible route to the Mines, and is
the last town large enough to re-supply any caravan or company
going that way or coming back out again. That's why we got the
railroad, finally. Before that we were the only reason anyone would
want to come so far, and our attractions are limited. But the Mines
are the big thing now. They may even figure out a way to dig a
road through the Ramids. I wish them luck."

Istan also remained tactically important, for while south of it the
boundary to Homelander territory swung rapidly east, the Homelanders failed to push it back any nearer the mountains of the
north and east. The natives, perhaps from learning to cope with
the desert to survive at all, had proved to be a tougher breed than
their southern cousins.

Some of this Harry had read at Home when she had first heard
of Richard's posting three years before. But she felt the reality of it
now, with the western wind blowing down on her from the rich
Aeel Mines, and the odd greenish-bronze tint in the sky, and the
brilliant red of the sunsets. She saw the dull brown uniforms of
the Homelander soldiers stationed here, with the red stripe ver-
tically drawn over the left breast that indicated they served in the
Darian province of the Homelander sovereignty. There were more

soldiers, the farther they traveled. "It's still a sore point that Istan is the eastern frontier; we can't seem to bear the idea that the border doesn't run straight, north to south, because we would like it to. They keep threatening to mount new offensives, but Colonel Dedham—he's in charge of the old Mundy—says that they won't do it. And who wants to own a lot of desert anyway? It's the farmland in the south—and the Mines—that make it worthwhile to be here."

She encouraged him to talk about Her Majesty's Government of the Royal Province of Daria, and if she did not listen as closely as she might to the descriptions of the ranks and duties of the civil servants Richard had the most contact with, she arrived at Istan at last with some small idea of how Homelanders in general were expected to respond to Daria. And she had seen korf with her own eyes, and a band of the wandering tinkers known as dilbadi, and the changing color of the earth underfoot, from the southern red to central brown to northern yellow-grey. She knew a broad-leafed ilpin tree from the blue evergreen torthuk, and when Lady Amelia met her with a corsage of the little rosy-pink pimchie flowers, she greeted them by name.

Lady Amelia was a small round woman with big hazel eyes and curly grey hair and the wistful look of the fading beauty. Her husband, Sir Charles, was as tall as Richard and much broader; he must ride sixteen stone, Harry thought dispassionately as she shook his hand. He had a red face and white hair and a magnificent mustache, and if his blue eyes were a little shallow, there were laugh lines generously around them, and his smile was warm. She felt as if they had looked forward to her coming, and she relaxed a little; there was none of the loftiness she was expecting toward a poor relation—someone else's poor relation at that.

Sir Charles during the first evening gave her a complete history of Daria, its past, its conquest by the Homelanders, its present, and its likely future, but most of it she was too tired to follow. Lady Amelia's occasional quick comments, when her husband stopped to draw breath, about Harry's present comfort were much more welcome, although she tried not to show it. But midway through the evening, as Sir Charles was gesturing with his liqueur glass and even Richard was looking a bit glassy-eyed, Lady Amelia caught her new charge's eye for a long moment. A look of patience and affection passed between them; and Harry thought that perhaps all would be well, and she went up to bed in good spirits.

For the first few days in Istan she unpacked, and looked around her, and only saw the newness of everything. But the Homelanders of Istan were a small but thriving community, and she was the latest addition to a society which looked forward to, and welcomed, and cross-examined, and talked about, its additions.

She had always suffered from a vague restlessness, a longing for adventure that she told herself severely was the result of reading too many novels when she was a small child. As she grew up, and particularly after her mother died, she had learned to ignore that restlessness. She had nearly forgotten about it, till now. She wondered sometimes if her brother felt that impatience of spirit too, if something like it had had anything to do with his ending up at a small Border station, however tactically important, although his prospects, when he graduated from university, had suggested something better. This was one of the many things she did not ask him. Another question she did not ask was if he ever missed Home.

She set down her empty orange-juice glass, and sighed. They'd missed the orange groves, coming north from Stzara, where her ship put her ashore. She picked up her fork from its shining white, neatly folded linen napkin, and turned it so that the sunlight that had glittered through her orange juice now caught in tiny star-bursts across its tines. Don't fidget, she told herself.

This morning she was to go riding with the two Misses Peterson, Cassie and Elizabeth. They were near her own age, and the admitted beauties of the station; the entire 4th Cavalry, stationed at the General Mundy, were in love with them. But they were also cheerful and open-hearted, and she was fond of them. She had never much cared for beauty, although she was aware that she lacked it and that her position might have been a little easier if she had not.

They would return from their ride by midmorning, because the sun would be growing too hot for anyone to brave it for pleasure. She planned to ask Lady Amelia if they might all come back here for lunch. She already knew what the answer would be: "Why, of course! We are always delighted to see them. I am so pleased, my dear, that you should be so clever as to attach the two most charming girls we have here to be your particular friends." Harry caught herself playing with her fork again, and laid it down emphatically.

This evening there was to be another dance. Richard had promised to escort her; she had to acknowledge that, however little they found to say to one another now, he was very good about escorting her to parties, and dancing with her—which meant that there was at least one man present whom she did not tower over. Her gratitude was not at all dimmed by the suspicion that he was nursing a secret passion for Cassie, nor by the thought, not even a real suspicion, that he might not want himself made a fool of by his sister's unpopularity. No, his kindness was real; he loved her, she thought, in his silent and anxious way. Perhaps simply being a very junior military adjutant with an unmarried sister suddenly thrust on one's hands inevitably made one a bit of a prig.

It never occurred to her to speculate whether any of the young men in their shining regimentals that Dickie painstakingly introduced her to, and who then painstakingly asked her to dance, presented themselves from any motive outside a willingness to do their friend Crewe a favor by standing up with his oversized sister. It would have surprised her very much to learn of her two or three admirers, who so far resisted the prevailing atmosphere of the barracks as to incline to an altar less populated than that of either Miss Peterson. "But she's just like her brother," one of them complained to his best friend, who listened with a friend's patience, although he was himself incapable of seeing the charms of any woman other than Beth Peterson. "So damned polite. Oh, she's nice enough, you know. I don't suppose she actually dislikes me," he continued, a bit uncertainly. "But I'm not at all sure she even recognizes me from one day to the next, so it hardly counts."

"Well," said the friend good-humoredly, "Dick remembers you well enough."

The admirer threw a boot at his friend—the one he hadn't polished yet. "You know what I mean."

"I know what you mean," agreed the friend. "A cold fish." The admirer looked up from the boot-blacking angrily and the friend held up the extra boot like a shield. "Dick's stiff with honor. I daresay his sister's like that. You just don't know her well enough yet."

"Balls, dinner parties," moaned the admirer. "You know what they're like; it could take years." The friend in silent sympathy (thinking of Beth) tossed the boot back, and he began moodily to black it.

The object of his affections, had she known of this conversation, would have agreed with him on the subject of balls and dinner parties. In fact, she would have added the rider that she wasn't sure it could be done at all, getting to know someone at any succession of such parties, however prolonged. And the friend was right about Dick Crewe's powerful sense of honor. He knew well enough that at least two of his friends were falling in love with his sister; but it never crossed his mind to say anything about them to her. He could not compromise the privileged knowledge of friendship in such a way.

And Dick's sister, oblivious to the fact that she had won herself a place in the station hierarchy, chafed and fidgeted.

Lady Amelia arrived at the breakfast table next. They had just settled the question of Cassie and Beth coming to lunch—in almost the precise words anticipated—when the door to Sir Charles' study, across the hall from the breakfast room, opened; and Sir Charles and his secretary, Mr. Mortimer, entered to breakfast. The two women looked at them in surprise; they had the unmistakable air of men who have been awake several hours, working hard on nothing more than a cup or two of the dark heavy local coffee, and who will rush through their meal now to get back to whatever they

| 11

have been doing. Neither of them looked very happy about their prospects.

"My dear," said Lady Amelia. "Whatever is wrong?"

Sir Charles ran a hand through his white hair, accepted a plate of eggs with his other hand, and sat down. He shook his head. Philip Mortimer glanced at his employer but said nothing. "Richard's not here yet," said Sir Charles, as if his absence explained everything.

"Richard—?" said Lady Amelia faintly.

"Yes. And Colonel Dedham. I'm sorry, my dear," he said, a few mouthfuls of eggs seeming to restore him. "The message came quite out of the blue, in the middle of the night," he explained through his metaphors as well as his mouthful. "Jack—Colonel Dedham—has been out, trying to find out what he can, and I told him to come to breakfast and tell us what he's learned. With Richard—that boy knows how to talk to people. Blast them. Blast *him*. He'll be here in a few hours."

His wife stared at him in complete bewilderment, and his young guest averted her eyes when he looked at her, as it was not her place to stare. He laid down his fork and laughed. "Melly, your face is a study. Young Harry here is going to be a fine ambassador's wife someday, though: look at that poker face! You really shouldn't look so much like your brother; it makes you too easy to read for those of us who know him. Just now you're thinking: Is the old man gone at last? Humor him till we're sure; if he calms down a bit, perhaps we'll get some sense out of him even now."

Harry grinned back at him, untroubled by his teasing, and he reached across the table, braving candlesticks and an artistically arranged bowl of fruit, to tap her cheek with his fingers. "A general's wife, on second thought. You'd be wasted on the diplomatic corps; we're all such dry paper-shufflers." He speared a piece of toast with his fork, and Lady Amelia, whose manners with her own family were as punctilious as if she dined with royalty, looked away. Sir Charles piled marmalade on his toast till it began to ooze off the edges, added one more dollop for good measure, and ate it all in three gulps. "Melly, I know I've told you about the difficulties we're having in the North, on this side of the mountains with our lot, and on the far side with whatever it is they breed over there—a very queer bunch, from all we can gather—and it's all begun to escalate, this last year, at an alarming speed. Harry, Dick's told you something of this?"

She nodded.

"You may or may not know that our real hold over Daria ends just about where this station stands, although technically—on paper—Homeland rule extends right to the foot of those mountains north and east of here—the Ossanders, which run out from the Ramids, and then that far eastern range you see over the sand, where none of us has ever been . . . those mountains are the only bits of the old kingdom of Damar still under native rule. There used to be quite a lot of fighting along this border—say, forty years ago. Since then their king—oh yes, there's a king—more or less ignores us, and we more or less ignore him. But odd things—call them odd things; Jack will tell you what he thinks they are—still happen on that plain, our no-man's-land. So we have the 4th Cavalry here with us.

"Nothing too odd has happened since the current king took the throne around ten years ago, we think—they don't bother to keep us up to date on such things—but it never does to be careless. Um." He frowned and, while frowning, ate another piece of toast. "Everything has been quiet for—oh, at least fifteen years. Nearly as long as I've been here, and that's a long time. Ask Jack, though, for stories of what it was like up and down the northern half of this border before that. He has plenty of them." He stood up from the table, and went across the room to the row of windows. He lifted the curtain farther back as he looked out across the desert, as if breadth of view might assist clarity of thought. It was obvious his mind was not on the explanation he was giving; and for all his assumed cheerfulness, he was deeply worried. "Damn! . . . Excuse me. Where is Jack? I expected he would have at least sent young Richard on ahead before now." He spoke as if to himself, or perhaps to Philip Mortimer, who made soothing noises, poured a cup of tea, and took it to Sir Charles where he stood squinting into the morning sunlight.

"Trouble?" said Lady Amelia gently. "More trouble?"

Sir Charles dropped the curtain and turned around. "Yes! More trouble." He looked down at his hands, realized he was holding a cup of tea in one of them, and took a swallow from it with the air of a man who does what is expected of him. "There may be war with the North. Jack thinks so. I'm not sure, but—I don't like the rumors. We must secure the passes through the mountains—particularly Ritger's Gap, which gives anybody coming through it almost a direct line to Istan, and then of course to the whole Province. It may only be some tribal uproar—but it could be war, as real as it was eighty years ago. There aren't many of the old Damarians left—the Hillfolk—but we've been forced to have a pretty healthy respect for them. And if King Corlath decides to throw his chances in with the Northerners—"

There was a clatter in the street below. Sir Charles' head snapped around. "There they are at last," he said, and bolted for the front door and threw it open himself, under the scandalized eye of the butler who had emerged from his inner sanctum just too late. "Come in! I've been in high fidgets for the last hour, wondering what's become of you. Have you found out anything that might be of use to us? I have been trying to explain to the ladies what our problem is."

"Would you care for breakfast?" Lady Amelia asked without haste, and with her usual placid courtesy. "Charles may be trying to explain, but so far he has not succeeded." In response to her gesture, a maid laid two more places at the table. With a jingling of spurs the two newcomers entered, apologized for their dirt, and were delighted to accept some breakfast. Richard dropped a perfunctory kiss on his sister's cheek on his way to the eggs and ham.

After a few minutes of tea-pouring and butter-passing, while Sir Charles strode up and down the room with barely suppressed impatience, it was Lady Amelia who spoke first. "We will leave you to your business, which I can see is very important, and we won't pester you with demands for explanations. But would you answer just one question?"

Colonel Dedham said, "Of course, Melly. What is it?"

"What is it that has suddenly thrown you into this turmoil? Some unexpected visitor, I gather, from what Charles said?"

Dedham stared at her. "He didn't tell you—? Good God. It's Corlath himself. He's coming. He never comes near here, you know—none of the real Hillfolk do if they can help it. At best, if we want badly enough to talk to him, we can catch one of his men as they pass through the foothills northeast of here. Sometimes."

"You see," broke in Sir Charles, "it makes us hope that perhaps he wishes to cooperate with us—not the Northerners. Jack, did you find out anything?"

Dedham shrugged. "Not really. Nothing that we didn't already know—that his coming here is unprecedented, to say the least—and that it is in fact him. Nobody had any better guesses than ours about why, suddenly, he decided to do so."

"But your guess would be—" prompted Sir Charles.

Dedham shrugged again, and looked wry. "You know already what my guess would be. You just like to hear me making an ass of myself. But I believe in the, um, curious things that happen out there—" he waved the sugar spoon—"and I believe that Corlath must have had some sort of sign, to go to the length of approaching us."

A silence fell; Harry could see that everyone else in the room was uncomfortable. "Sign?" she said tentatively.

Dedham glanced up with his quick smile. "You haven't been here long enough to have heard any of the queer stories about the old rulers of Damar?"

"No," she said.

"Well, they were sorcerers—or so the story goes. Magicians. They could call the lightning down on the heads of their enemies, that sort of thing—useful stuff for founding an empire."

Sir Charles snorted.

"No, you're quite right; all we had was matchlocks and enthusiasm. Even magic wanes, I suppose. But I don't think it's waned quite away yet; there's some still living in those mountains out there. Corlath can trace his bloodlines back to Aerin and Tor, who ruled Damar in its golden age—with or without magic, depending on which version you prefer."

"If they weren't legends themselves," put in Sir Charles.

"Yes. But I believe they were real," said Jack Dedham. "I even believe they wielded something we prosaic Homelanders would call magic."

Harry stared at him, fascinated, and his smile broadened. "I'm quite used to being taken for a fool about this. It's doubtless part of the reason why I'm still a colonel, and still at the General Mundy. But there are a number of us old soldiers whose memories go back to the Daria of thirty, forty years ago who say the same thing."

"Oh, magic," said Sir Charles disgustedly, but there was a trace of uneasiness in his voice as well. "Have you ever seen lightning come to heel like a dog?"

Dedham through his politeness looked a little stubborn. "No. I haven't. But it's true enough at least that the men who have gone up against Corlath's father and grandfather were plagued by the most astonishing bad luck. And you know the Queen and Council back Home would give their eyeteeth to push our border back the way we've been saying we would for the last eighty years."

"Bad luck?" said Lady Amelia. "I've heard the stories, of course—some of the old ballads are very beautiful. But—what sort of bad luck?"

Dedham smiled again. "I admit it does begin to sound foolish when one tries to explain it. But things like rifles—or matchlocks—misfiring, or blowing up; not just a few, but many—yourself, and your neighbor, and his neighbor. And their neighbors. A cavalry charge just as it reaches full stretch, the horses begin to trip and fall down as if they've forgotten how to gallop—*all* of them. Men mistake their orders. Supply wagons lose their wheels. Half a company all suddenly get grit in their eyes simultaneously and can't see where they're going—or where to shoot. The sort of little things that always happen, but carried far beyond probability. Men get superstitious about such things, however much they scoff at elves and witches and so on. And it's pretty appalling to see your cavalry crumple up like they're all drunk, while these madmen with nothing but swords and axes and bits of leather armor are coming down on you from every direction—and nobody seems to be firing at them from your side. I assure you I've seen it."

Richard shifted in his chair. "And Corlath—"

"Yes, Corlath," the colonel continued, sounding still as unruffled as when he thanked Lady Amelia for his cup of tea, while Sir Charles' face was getting redder and redder and he whuffled through his mustache. It was hard not to believe Dedham; his voice was too level, and it rang with sincerity. "They say that in Corlath the old kings have come again. You know he's begun to reunite some of the outlying tribes—the ones that don't seem to owe anyone any particular allegiance, and who live by a sort of equal-handed brigandry on anyone within easy reach."

"Yes, I know," said Sir Charles.

"Then you may also have heard some of the other sort of stories they've begun to tell about him. I imagine he can call lightning to heel if he feels like it."

"This is the man who's coming here today?" said Lady Amelia; and even she now sounded a little startled.

"Yes, Amelia, I'm afraid so."

"If he's so blasted clever," muttered Sir Charles, "what does he want with us?"

Dedham laughed. "Come now, Charles. Don't be sulky. I don't suppose even a magician can make half a million Northerners disappear like raindrops in the ocean. We certainly need him to keep the passes through his mountains closed. And it may be that he has decided that he needs us—to mop up the leaks, perhaps."

Lady Amelia stood up, and Harry reluctantly followed her. "We will leave you to discuss it. Is there—is there anything I could do, could arrange? I'm afraid I know very little about entertaining native—chieftains. Do you suppose he will want lunch?" She spread her hands and looked around the table. Harry suppressed a smile at the thought of proper little Lady Amelia offering sandwiches, with the crusts neatly trimmed off, and lemonade to this barbarian king. What would he look like? She thought: I've never even seen any of the Freemen, the Hillfolk. All the natives at the station, even the merchants from away, look subdued and . . . a little wary.

"Oh, bosh," said Sir Charles. "I wish I knew what he wanted—lunch or anything else. Part of what makes all this so complicated is that we know the Free Hillfolk have a very complicated code of honor—but we know almost nothing about what it consists of."

"Almost," murmured Dedham.

"We could offend them mortally and not even know it. I don't know if Corlath is coming alone, or with a select band of his thousand best men, all armed to the teeth and carrying lightning bolts in their back pockets."

"Now, Charles," Dedham said.

"We've invited him here—"

"—because the fort is not built for receiving guests of honor," Dedham said easily as Sir Charles paused.

"And," Sir Charles added plaintively, "it doesn't look quite so *warlike* here." Dedham laughed. "But four o'clock in the morning," Sir Charles said.

"I think we should be thankful that it occurred to him to give us any warning at all. I don't believe it's the sort of thing he's accustomed to having to think of." The colonel stood up, and Richard promptly took his place behind him. Sir Charles was still pacing about the room, cup in hand, as the ladies prepared to leave. "My apologies for spoiling your morning to no purpose," said Colonel Dedham. "I daresay he will arrive sometime and we will deal with him, but I don't think you need put yourselves out. His message said merely that he desired an audience with the Homelander District Commissioner—not quite his phrase, but that's the idea—and the general in command of the fort. He'll have to make do with me, though; we don't rate a general. The Hill-kings don't go in much for gold plate and red velvet anyway—I think. I hope this is a business meeting."

"I hope so too," murmured Sir Charles to his teacup.

"And—at the moment—we can't do much more than wait and see," said the colonel. "Have some more of this excellent tea, Charles. What's in your cup must be quite cold by now."

CHAPTER TWO

HARRY AND LADY AMELIA TOOK THEIR LEAVE, and the older
woman closed the breakfast-room doors with a sigh. Harry smiled.
Lady Amelia turned back to her in time to see the smile, and returned it ruefully. "Very well. We will leave the men to do their
uncomfortable waiting alone. I am going to visit Mrs. McDonald,
you are going to go riding with Beth and Cassie and bring them
back here for luncheon."

"Perhaps under the circumstances—" began Harry, but Lady
Amelia shook her head.

"I see no reason why you should not. If he is here, those girls
have very pretty manners, and are just whom I would invite if we
were to give a formal dinner. And—" here her smile broadened
and became as mischievous as a girl's—"if he has brought his
thousand best men, we shall be terribly short of women, and you
know how I dislike an unbalanced table. I shall have to invite Mrs.
McDonald as well. Have a pleasant ride, dear."

Harry changed into her riding-clothes, mounted her placid pony,
already bridled and saddled and held for her by one of the Residency's many servants, and rode off in a thoughtful mood toward
her meeting with her two friends. She wondered first what and
how much she should tell Cassie and Beth; and, second, found
herself hoping that this Corlath would stay at least long enough for
her to see him. Would a witch-king look any different than any
other man?

The sun was already hot. She pushed her hat back long enough for a cautious squint at the sky. It was more dun-colored than blue, as if it, like everything else near Istan, were faded by the fierceness of its sun. It looked as hard as a curved shell overhead, and brittle, as if a thrown lance might pierce it. The placid pony shuffled along, ears flopping, and she stared out over the sands. The woods to the west of her father's house were old, hundreds of years old, tangled with vine and creeper. Ancient trees had died and, not having room to fall, crumbled where they stood. No landlord had thought the old forest worth clearing and the land put to use; but it had made a wonderful jungle for herself and Dickie as children, to be bandits in, and hunt dragons through. Its twisted shadows had always been welcome to her; when she grew older she liked the feeling of great age that the forest gave her, of age and of a vast complicated life that had nothing to do with her and that she need not try to decipher.

The desert, with the black sharp-edged mountains around it, was as different from what she was accustomed to as any landscape could be; yet she found after only a few weeks in Istan that she was falling by degrees in love with it: with the harsh sand, the hot sun, the merciless gritty winds. And she found that the desert lured her as her own green land never had—but what discovery it lured her toward she could not say.

It was an even greater shock to realize that she was no longer homesick. She missed her occupation; and even more she missed her father. She had left so soon after the funeral that it was difficult to believe that he was dead, that he was not still riding around his estate in his shabby coat, waiting for her to return. Then she found that she remembered her parents together again; as if her mother had died recently, or her father five years ago—or as if the difference, which had been so important, no longer mattered. She didn't dream of honeysuckle and lilac. She remembered them with affection, but she looked across the swirled sand and small obstinate clumps of brush and was content with where she was. A small voice whispered to her that she didn't even want to go Home again. She wanted to cross the desert and climb into the mountains in the east, the mountains no Homelander had ever climbed.

She often speculated about how other people saw the land here. Her brother never mentioned it one way or another. She was accustomed to hearing the other young people refer to "that hateful desert" and "the dreadful sun." Beth and Cassie didn't; they had lived in one part or another of Daria for most of their lives— "except the three years our mother took us Home, to acquire polish, she said"—and to both of them, Darian sun and Darian weather, whether it be on the fertile red earth of the south, with the eternal fight against the jungle to keep the fields clear, or the cool humid plateaus of the orange plantations, or the hot sand of the northeast Border, were simply things that were there, were part of their home, to be accepted and adjusted to. Harry had asked them how they liked the Homeland, and they had had to pause and think about it. "It was very different," Cassie said at last, and Beth nodded. Cassie started to say something else, stopped, and shrugged. "Very different," she repeated.

"Did you like it?" pursued Harry.

"Of course," said Cassie, surprised.

"We've liked all the places we've lived," said Beth, "once we made some friends."

"I liked the snow in the north," offered Cassie, "and the fur cloaks we had to wear there in the winter."

Harry gave it up.

The older people at the station seemed to put up with the land around them as they would put up with any other disadvantage of their chosen occupation. Darian service, civilian and military, bred stoicism in all those who didn't give up and go Home after the first few years. The Greenoughs' making-the-best-of-it attitude was almost as tangible as mosquito netting.

Harry had once won an admission from Mr. Peterson, Cassie and Beth's father. There were several people to dinner at the Residency that evening, among them the Petersons. Mr. Peterson had been seated across from her at dinner, and had not appeared to pay any attention to the conversation on the other side of the table. But later in the evening he appeared at her side. She was surprised; he spoke rarely enough at social gatherings, and was notorious around the station for avoiding young unattached ladies, including his daughters' friends.

They sat in silence at first; Harry wondered if she should say anything, and if so, what. She was still wondering when he said: "I couldn't help hearing some of what that young chap next to you was saying at dinner." He stopped again, but this time she waited patiently for him to continue and did not try to prompt him. "I wouldn't pay too much attention, if I were you."

The young chap in question had been telling her about the hateful desert and the dreadful sun. He was a subaltern at the fort, had been there for two years and was looking forward to his escape in two more. The subaltern had continued: "But I wouldn't want you to think we have no change of seasons here. We do: we have winter. It rains steadily for three months, and everything gets moldy, including you."

Mr. Peterson said: "I rather like it here. There are those of us who do." He then stood up and wandered away. She had not spoken a word to him.

But she remembered what he said later as she realized that she too was becoming one of those who liked it here. She pondered who else might belong to their select club. It was a game, and she amused herself with it when she ran out of polite conversation. She took mental note of all those who did not complain of the heat, the wind, the unequal rainfall; and then tried to separate those like herself who actually enjoyed being scratchy with blown sand and headachy from glare, from those like Cassie and Beth who were merely cheerfully adaptable.

Harry at last settled on Colonel Dedham as the most likely member of her club, and began to consider if there was any way to broach the subject with him. She thought that perhaps there was a club rule that read, Thou shalt not speak. But her chance came at last, less than a fortnight before Corlath's messenger arrived at the Residency at four a.m.

It was at another small dinner party at the Greenoughs'. When the gentlemen brought themselves and an appalling reek of Sir Charles' finest cigars into the drawing-room to join the ladies, Colonel Dedham came across the room and tossed himself down on the window-seat beside Harry. She had been looking out at the mysterious white pools the moon poured across the desert.

"Open the window a bit," he said, "and let some of this smoke out. I can see poor Amelia being brave."

"Cigars should be like onions," she said, unfastening the catch and pushing back the pane. "Either the whole company does, or the whole company does not."

Dedham laughed. "Poor Melly! She would spoil many a party, I fear. Have you ever smoked a cigar?"

She smiled, with a glint in her pale eyes, and he reflected that some of the young men had labeled her cold and humorless. "Yes, I have: that is how I know. My father was used to giving dinners for his hunting friends, and I would be the only woman there. I was not going to eat in my room, like a punished child, and I liked to stay and listen to the stories they told. They permitted themselves to become accustomed to my presence, because I could ride and shoot respectably. But the smoke, after a few hours, would become unbearable."

"So your father—?" prompted Dedham.

"No, not my father; he taught me to shoot, against his better judgment, but he drew the line at teaching me to smoke. It was one of his friends—Richard's godfather, in fact. He gave me a handful of cigars at the end of one of these very thick evenings and told me to smoke them, slowly and carefully, somewhere that I could be sick in private. And the next time the cigars went around the table, I was to take one for myself—and he'd help me stand up to my father. It was the only way to survive. He was right."

"I shall have to tell Charles," said Dedham, grinning. "He is always delighted to find another cigar-lover."

Her gaze had wandered again to the moonlight, but now she turned back. "No, thank you, Colonel. I am not that. It was the stories that made it worth it. I only appreciate smoke when I'm seeing things in it."

"I know what you mean, but you must promise *not* to tell Charles that," he replied. "And for heaven's sake call me Jack. Three months is quite long enough to be called Colonel more often than business demands."

"Mmm," she said.

"Cassie and Beth do it very nicely. Say 'Jack.'"

"Jack," she said.

"There, you see? And for your next lesson I will walk across the room and ask you to say it again, and you will see how quickly I turn around and say 'Yes?'"

She laughed. It was hard to remember that Dedham was a few years older than Sir Charles; the latter was portly and dignified and white-haired. Dedham was lean and brown, and what hair he had left was iron grey. Sir Charles was polite and kind; Dedham talked to one like a friend.

"I see you staring out of the windows often, at our Darian wilds. Do you see yew hedges and ivy-grown oak and, um, cattle and sheep in green pastures?"

She looked down at her lap, a little uneasily, because she had not thought she was noticed; but here was her chance. She looked up. "No. I see our Darian wilds."

He smiled a little at the "our." "You're settling in, then? Resigned to too much sun all of the time—except for when there is too much rain? But you haven't seen our winter yet."

"No—no, I haven't. But I'm not resigned." She paused, surprised at how hard it was to say aloud, and her club's first law floated across her mind. "I like it. I'm not sure why, but I like it here."

The smile disappeared and he looked at her thoughtfully. "Do you?" He turned and looked out of the window himself. "There aren't many of us who do. I'm one—you must have guessed that I love the desert. This desert. Even in winter, and the three weeks of jungle after the rain stops and before the sun gets a good hold again. Quite a lot of my griping about being the oldest colonel still

24 |

active is noise only; I know that if they promoted me they'd almost certainly promote me away from here—to one of the more civilized parts of this uncivilized land. Most of Daria is not like this, you know." He paused. "I don't suppose that means very much to you."

"But it does."

He frowned a little, studying her face. "I don't know whether to say you're very fortunate or very unfortunate. We're strangers here, you know—even I, who've been here forty years. This desert is a little piece of the old Damar. It's not even really under our jurisdiction." He smiled wryly. "Not only can we not understand it, we are not able to administer it." He nodded toward the window. "And the mountains beyond. They stand there, looking at you, and you know you'll never climb them. No Homelander ever has—at least to return to tell the tale."

She nodded. "It is not a comfortable passion."

He chuckled. "No; not a comfortable passion."

"Is that why no one ever mentions it? One hears enough for the other side."

"God! Don't I know it. 'Only four hundred and ninety-six days till I get out of this sand pit.' Yes, I suppose so. It's a strange country, especially this corner of it, and if it gets too much in your blood it makes you strange too. And you don't really want to call attention to it."

She recalled that conversation as she rode; and now she saw Cassie and Beth jogging toward her. She was thinking again of Corlath, and trying to recall what little she knew of the Free Hillfolk. Jack had been reluctant to talk about them, and his evasiveness led her to believe that he knew quite a lot about them, because he was always open about saying he didn't know something. He was trying to spare her, perhaps, from her uncomfortable passion.

Oh, glory, she thought, and with a quick leap her curiosity transformed itself into excitement: I do hope he's there when we get back.

The question of what to tell her friends died painlessly. As soon as their ponies came abreast Beth said: "Is he here yet?"

Harry was expecting a good-morning-and-how-are-you and for a moment didn't know who was meant.

"Corlath," said Cassie. "Jack came to our house to see Daddy before breakfast, told him to go up to the Residency, that they would need him there." Mr. Peterson and Jack Dedham were the only people in the station who knew Hill-speech even passably fluently. Most Darians who had much contact with Homelanders learned Homelander. Harry had picked up a few Darian words, but only a few; no Homelander had thought to write a Darian grammar for general use, and when she inquired further was told that there was no need for her to learn it. The only person who encouraged her, and who had taught her the words she did know, was Jack Dedham, and he had not the time to spare for more. Sir Charles was reasonably articulate in Darian speech, but uncomfortable about it. He felt a responsible commissioner should know the language of those he oversees, but it made him no happier to fulfill his own expectations. He kept an interpreter near at hand.

"Corlath," breathed Beth, as if the name were a charm. "Daddy says that the Hillfolk have never liked us much—"

"We've always known that," put in Cassie.

"—so he'll probably slip in and out again and we'll never even see him."

"I've permission to invite you to lunch," said Harry. "If he's there at all, we'll see him."

"Oh, how wonderful!" said Beth. "Surely even he won't have finished his business before lunch. Let's not ride far; we should see something when he comes, and then we'll know when to ride back. It's very tiresome to have a real king come to visit and not even have an excuse to meet him."

"Do you know anything of the Free Hillfolk?" said Harry. They rode at an angle away from the Residency, where they could keep an eye on it over their shoulders. "I don't. No one will tell me anything."

They both laughed. "The Hillfolk are the best-kept secret in

Daria," said Cassie. "I mean, we know they exist. Some of them come here—to the station, I mean—for the spring Fair." Harry looked at her. "Oh, surely Lady Amelia has told you about our Fair," Cassie said. "After three months of the rains we come out of hiding and work off our foul temper by holding a Fair—"

"—where we sell to each other all the ridiculous little bags and bonnets and dolls and footstools that we've made during the rains to keep from going mad because we couldn't go out," Beth continued.

"Yes, most of it is nonsense. But everyone is very gay for the first two or three weeks after the rain stops. The weather is cool enough—the only time all year you can go out even at midday; and there're *green* things growing up from the ground, and everything you own is spread on the roofs and hanging from the windowsills, and they're green too," Cassie added with a grimace. "We decorate the streets and the square with paper flowers and real flowers, and banners and ribbons, and the whole town looks like it's on holiday, with the dresses and blankets hanging out everywhere. We do have real flowers here—besides the eternal pimchie—although nothing like what you're used to at Home, I daresay. Everything grows tremendously for two weeks, so for the third week, Fair week, everything is green and blossoming—even the desert, if you can believe it."

"Then of course the sun kills everything again. That's the fourth week. And you know what it's like here the rest of the time."

"Yes, but the Fair—everyone comes to the Fair. The Hillfolk too, a few of them, although never anyone very special. Certainly never the king. And it's not all the bead purses that our sort has been making in despair. There are always some really lovely things, mostly that the Darians themselves have made. Even the servants aren't expected to do as much, you know, during the rains. After the first few weeks you're far too cross yourself to give many orders to anyone else."

"But mostly the best things come up from the south. It's only way up here that the weather's so ridiculous, but the south knows about our Fair, and the merchants know that when we break out of winter prison we're so mad with our freedom that we're fit to buy *anything,* so they come up in force."

"There are Fairs, or celebrations of spring of one kind or another, all around here, but ours is the biggest."

"Well," said Beth, "we've the biggest in things to buy and so forth; and we're the only Homelander station up here. But there're quite a number of Darian villages around here, and they take spring very seriously. Lots of singing and dancing, and that kind of thing. And they tell the most beautiful stories, if you can find someone to translate into Homelander. Which isn't often."

"We have singing and dancing too," said Cassie.

"Yes, I know," said Beth slowly; "but it's not the same. Our dancing is just working it off, after being inside for so long. Theirs means something."

Harry looked at her curiously. "You mean asking the gods for a good year—that kind of thing?"

"I suppose so," said Beth. "I'm not quite sure."

"No one will talk about anything really Darian to Homelanders," said Cassie. "You must have noticed it."

"Yes—but I'm new here."

"You're always new here if you're a Homelander," said Cassie. "It's different in the south. But we're on the Border here, and everyone is very aware that Freemen live in those Hills you see out your windows every day. The Darians that do work for you, or with you, are very anxious to prove how Homelander they really are, and loyal to all things Homelander, so they won't talk; and the others won't for the opposite reasons."

"You're beginning to sound like Daddy," said Beth.

"We've heard him say it all often enough," Cassie responded.

"But the Hillfolk," said Harry.

"Yes. The one thing I suppose we all have in common is a joy in those three short weeks of spring. So a few Hillfolk come to our Fair."

"They don't act very happy, though," said Beth. "They come in those long robes they always wear—over their faces too, so you can't see if they're smiling or frowning; and some of them with those funny patched sashes around their waists. But they do come, and they stay several days—they have the grandest horses you've ever seen. They pitch camp outside the station, and they always set guards, quite openly, as if we weren't to be trusted—"

"Maybe we aren't," murmured Cassie.

"—but they never sell their horses. They bring the most gorgeous tapestries, though, and embroidered sashes—much nicer than the cut-up ones they wear themselves. These they sell. They stalk around the edge of the big central square, the old marketplace, carrying all this vivid stuff, while the rest of us are laughing and talking and running around. It's a bit eerie."

"No it's not," said Cassie. "You listen to the stories too much."

Beth blushed. After a pause she said, "Do you see anything at the Residency?"

"No," said Harry. "What stories?"

There was another pause while Cassie looked at Beth and Beth looked at her pony's mane. "My fault," said Cassie presently. "We're not supposed to talk about them. Daddy gets really annoyed if he catches us. The stories are mostly about magic. Corlath and his people are supposed to be rotten with it, even in this day and age, and Corlath himself is supposed to be more than a little mad."

"Magic?" said Harry, remembering what Dedham had said earlier. "Mad?" He hadn't said anything about madness. "How?"

They both shrugged. "We've never managed to find out," said Cassie.

"And we can usually wring what we want to know out of Daddy eventually," said Beth, "so it must be something pretty dreadful."

Cassie laughed. "You read too many novels, Beth. It's just as likely that Daddy won't talk about it because he refuses to admit it might be real—the magic, I mean. Jack Dedham believes it—he and Daddy argue about it sometimes, when they don't think anyone else is around. The madness, if that's what it is, is tied up somehow in the king's strength—in return for having power beyond mortal men or some such, he has to pay a price of some kind of mad fits."

"Who reads too many novels?" said Beth, and Cassie grinned. "It does rather catch the imagination," she said, and Beth nodded.

"No wonder you're so eager to set eyes on him," said Harry.

"Yes. I know it's silly of me, but I feel maybe it'll show somehow. He'll be eight feet tall and have a third eye in the middle of his forehead," said Beth.

"Heavens," said Harry.

"I hope not," said Cassie.

"Well, you know how the legends go," said Beth.

"No, not really," said her sister repressively. "Even when Daddy is willing to translate some, you can tell by the pauses that he's leaving a lot out."

"Yes, but even so," persisted Beth. "The old kings and queens were supposed to be taller than mortal—"

"The Darians are mostly shorter than we are, at least the ones we see," interrupted Cassie. "A king could look quite ordinary to us and be very tall for them."

"—and you can tell the royal blood by something about the eyes."

There was another pause. Harry said, "Something?"

Again they both shrugged. "Something," said Beth. "That's one of the things Daddy always leaves out. Like the madness."

"You're hoping he'll froth at the mouth," said Cassie.

Beth threw a peevish look at her sister. "No. I'll settle for the third eye."

This conversation had taken them well away from the outlying houses of the station, and the dust kicked up by their ponies' feet was giving up even the pretense of being anything other than desert sand. A silence fell; Cassie suggested a canter, which was duly accomplished. The sun was hot enough that when they pulled up again, after only a few minutes, the ponies' shoulders were dark with sweat. Harry sent another of her long looks across the desert, and had to squint against the shivering light.

"Do you think we might turn back now?" Beth asked wistfully, shading her eyes with an elegantly white-gloved hand.

Harry grinned. "We can spend the rest of the morning in my sitting-room, if you like. It overlooks the front door, you know."

Beth gave her a grateful look, Cassie chuckled; but they all three turned their ponies' heads with dispatch and sent them jogging homeward as quickly as the heat would allow.

By the time they reached the suggestion of shade offered by the thin determined trees marking the outskirts of the station proper, Harry was hot and slightly headachy, and cross with herself for rushing back for no reason. Nothing could have escaped their notice; the Residency stood a little apart from the rest of the station, in its own grounds, and the road that ended at its front door had been under their eyes for the entire ride. They had been gone only a little over an hour. Harry considered suggesting that they meet again after another hour, time enough to change and have a bath; in her present condition she didn't feel like meeting any kings, mad or otherwise.

But she stole a glance at Beth and saw how anxious she was not to miss anything; and she thought, Oh well, I can wash my face at least, and we can all have some cold lemonade, and watch the front door in comfort.

The horses walked slowly up the street to the Residency. Cassie pulled off her hat and fanned herself with it. Harry shut her eyes for a moment. An execrable habit, she told the insides of her eyelids. What if this fat sleepy fourposter with ears and a tail should bolt, or shy suddenly? What if the sky should fall? responded the insides of her eyelids.

The fourposter stopped dead in the road and raised its head a few inches just as Beth said in a strangled whisper: "Look."

Harry and Cassie looked. They had come nearly to the end of the road; what was left was the broad circle in front of the Residency, suitable for turning carriages in, or forming up half a regiment. Off to one side, where the tall house cast a little shade, seven horses and one man stood. The horses stood in a little semicircle around the man, who sat cross-legged near the wall of the house. They stood quietly, stamping a foot now and then, and occasionally one would put out its nose to touch the man; and he would stroke its cheek a moment, and it would raise its head again. The first thing Harry noticed was the beauty of these animals; not a one was less than sixteen hands high, with long clean legs and tails that nearly touched the ground. Three were chestnuts, their coats shining even in the dusty shadow; one grey, one dark bay, one golden dun; but the finest horse stood farthest from three fat ponies standing foolishly in the carriage drive. He was a blood bay, red as fire, with black legs and tail; he stood aloof from the other horses and ignored the man at his feet. He stared back at the newcomers as if it were his land he stood on, and they intruders. As the other horses slowly swung their heads around to see what their leader was looking at, Harry noticed something else: they wore no bridles.

"He's here," said Cassie flatly.

Beth drew a deep breath. "How?" she said.

"Look at those *horses*," said Harry, and the longing in her voice was so clear that even she heard it.

Cassie looked away from the impossible sight of seven horses that had made their way invisibly across a bleak desert right in front of three people who were looking for them, and smiled with sympathy at her friend. "Haven't you ever seen a Hill horse before? They're supposed to be the finest in Daria."

"And they never sell them," said Harry, remembering.

Cassie nodded, although Harry's eyes never left the horses. "Jack Dedham would give an arm even to ride one once."

"No bridles," said Harry.

"No stirrups, either," said Cassie, and Harry saw that this was true. They wore saddles that were little more than padded skins, cut and elegantly rolled; and she could see the gleam of embroidery on girths and pommels. Not a horse moved from its place in the semicircle, although all now, with the man, watched the three ponies and their riders.

"Horses," said Beth disgustedly. "Don't you understand what they mean? They mean that he's here already, and we never noticed a thing. If that's not magic, what is?" She prodded her pony forward again. Cassie and Harry followed slowly and stopped before the steps. Three stable boys appeared, ready to take the ponies back to the stable behind the house.

Harry's feet had only just touched the ground—the boy hovering anxiously to one side, since he had learned through bitter experience that this Homelander did not wish to be assisted while dismounting—when there was a commotion at the entrance to the house. Harry turned around in time to see the heavy door thrown violently open, so that its hinges protested; and out strode a man dressed in loose white robes, with a scarlet sash around his waist. Several more figures darted out in his wake, and collected around him where he paused on the verandah. He was the axis of a nervous wheel, moving his head slowly to examine the lesser people who turned around him and squeaked at him without daring to come too near. With a shock Harry recognized four of these small mortals: Sir Charles and Mr. Peterson, Jack Dedham and her own brother, Richard. The man in white was tall, though no taller than Richard or Sir Charles. But there was a quivering in the air around him, like the heat haze over the desert, shed from his white sleeves, cast off by the shadows of his scarlet sash. These who stood near him looked small and pale and vague, while this man was so bright he hurt the eyes. More men came quietly out behind the Homelanders and stood a little to one side, but they kept their eyes on their king. He could be no one else. This must be Corlath.

Harry took a deep breath. He didn't look insane or inhuman. He did look uncooperative. He shook his head and frowned at something someone said, and Sir Charles looked very unhappy. Corlath shrugged, and made a sweeping movement with his arms, like a man coming out of a forest gratefully into the sunlight. He took a long step forward to the edge of the verandah. Then Dedham took two quick steps toward him and spoke to him, a few words only, urgently; and Corlath turned again, as it seemed unwillingly, and looked back. Dedham held out his hand, palm down and fingers spread; and so they stood for a long minute. Corlath dropped his eyes to the hand stretched toward him, then looked into the face of its owner. Harry, watching, held her breath without knowing why.

With a nasty feeling in the pit of her stomach she saw a look of terrible strain cross Dedham's face as the Hill-king held his gaze; and the outstretched hand trembled very slightly. Corlath slowly reached out his own hand and touched the back of Dedham's wrist with two fingers; the hand dropped to Dedham's side once more, but as if it were heavy as stone, and the man slumped in relief like a murderer reprieved at the scaffold. The look of strain slid off his face to be replaced by one of great weariness.

Corlath swung around again, and set his foot on the top stair, and no one moved to stop him. Five men in the loose robes of the Hillfolk separated themselves from the verandah shadows and made to follow. Harry found she could not take her eyes off the king, but from the corners of her eyes she noticed that the other men too wore vivid sashes: gold and orange and green and blue and purple. There was nothing to indicate the king but the glitter of his presence.

Harry stood only a few feet from the bottom step, holding her pony's bridle. Cassie and Beth were somewhere behind her, and the stable boy stood frozen a few steps from her elbow. Corlath still had not noticed them, and Harry stared, fascinated, as he came nearer. There seemed a roaring in the air that beat on her eardrums and pressed against her eyeballs till she blinked. Then he looked up abruptly, as if from some unfathomable depth of thought, and saw her: their eyes met.

The man's eyes were yellow as gold, the hot liquid gold in a smelter's furnace. Harry found it suddenly difficult to breathe, and understood the expression on Dedham's face; she almost staggered. Her hand tightened on the bridle, and the pony dropped its head and mouthed the bit uncomfortably. The heat was incredible. It was as though a thousand desert suns beat down on her. Magic? she thought from inside the thunder. Is this what magic is? I come from a cold country, where the witches live in cool green forests. What am I doing here? She saw the anger the man was holding in check; the anger stared at her through the yellow eyes, and swept through the glistening white robes.

Then it was over. He looked away; he came down the last steps and past her as if she did not exist; and she cowered out of his way so that no corner of his white sleeve should touch her. The man with the horses emerged from the shade, riding one of the chestnuts; and the six others went up to their riders and nuzzled them. The blood bay reached the king first, and greeted him with a low whinny. Corlath mounted with an easy leap Harry could not even follow with her eyes, although she could see anger informing the set of his legs against the great stallion's sides. The horse felt it too; without moving, all its muscles were suddenly taut, and its stillness was the quiet before battle. The other men mounted. Corlath never looked at them, but the red stallion plunged forward at a gallop, and the other men followed; and the sound the horses' hooves made on the hard earth suddenly reminded Harry how unnaturally silent everyone had been since Dedham's last words. The inaudible thunder faded with the sight of the colored sashes and the bright flanks of the Hill horses. Harry woke up to who she was, and where; Sir Charles and Jack and Mr. Peterson looked their normal size again, and she had a raging headache.

CHAPTER THREE

C ORLATH STARED AT HIS HORSE'S black-tipped ears. The Hill-folk passed through the gate of the Residency and Corlath lifted his gaze to rake angrily across the dusty station street, the little dun-colored houses and shops, the small straggly trees. At a slight shift in his rider's weight the red horse turned off the road. The harsh clatter of hooves on the packed-dirt road changed to the duller sound of struck sand. He could hear his men turning off the road behind him; he shook his head in a futile attempt to clear a little space for thought amid the anger, and leaned back in his saddle, and the horse's pace slowed. There was no sense in charg-ing across the desert at midday; it was hard on the horses.

The six riders closed up behind him; the two who came forward to ride at his side stole quick looks at him as they came near, and looked away again as quickly.

Outlanders! Involuntarily his hands, resting lightly on his thighs, curled into fists. He should have known better than even to try to talk to them. His father had warned him, years ago. But that was before the Northerners had come so near. Corlath blinked. The heat of his own anger was hard to contain when there wasn't some use he could put it to; anger was splendidly useful on the battlefield, but he was not facing any regiments just now that could be tangled in their own feet and knocked over in companies. Much as he would like, for example, to set fire to the big stupid house—an absurd building for the desert: it must be the sort of thing they lived in in their own country—and watch it crash down around the ears of the big soft creature who called himself commissioner . . . but spite was for children, and he had been king for thirteen years, and he bit down on his anger and held it.

He remembered when he was young and before the full flowering of his *kelar,* of the terrible strength known ironically as the "Gift," his father had told him that it would often be like this: "We aren't really much good, except as battle machines, and even there our usefulness is limited. You'll curse it, often enough, far more often than you'll be glad of it, but there you are." He sighed, and looked wryly at his son. "They say that back in the Great Days it was different, that men were made big enough to hold it—and had wit enough to understand it. It was Lady Aerin, the story goes, that first knew her Gift and broke it to her will, but that was long ago, and we're smaller now."

Corlath had said, hesitantly: "They say also that the Gift was once good for other things: healing and calming and taming."

His father nodded sadly. "Yes; perhaps it once was; but no more. Luthe knows, if he will tell you, for he has the old *kelar,* and who his parents are even he has forgotten; but Luthe is himself. You and I are of duller blood.

"And it is duller blood that has brought us to what we are, what we remain—what remains to us. Avoid the Outlanders, if you can. They can't, or won't, understand us; they don't recognize horses from oxen, and will try to put the yoke on you that they have hung on the rest of our land. But their strength is the strength of numbers and of stubbornness and persistence; do not underestimate it."

He could see his father standing in one of the inner courtyards of the City in the mountains, staring at one of the fountains, water running shining over the colored stones of the Hills, talking half to himself. Then the picture faded, blotted out in another swift sweep of anger; and he found himself looking at the girl again, the girl he had seen standing in front of the Outlander house. What had she to do with anything?

He frowned, and his horse's ears and black mane reappeared

before him. He looked up; it was still a long ride to their camp. He had not, somehow, wished to sleep too near the Outlanders; it was not that he suspected deliberate treachery, but that the air that hung over an Outlander station sent bad dreams to Hillfolk.

His anger kicked him again like a spurred heel; he flinched. It had a life of its own, the Gift, damn it. What indecipherable object did it desire of him this time? He knew by now that the idiosyncrasies of kings, and others whose blood carried much *kelar,* were viewed with more alarm by the victims themselves than by their friends and subjects. Not that the alarm did any good. If one was king, one could not explain away one's more impenetrable actions by saying that one just couldn't help it.

Woven into his anger there was a pattern. Occasionally he understood it. He waited, gritting his teeth; and he saw the girl again. This time, as long as she was there, he looked at her.

When he had seen her first, at the foot of the steps, just a few minutes ago, he had been surprised into looking at her. He knew what his glance could do when he was angry, and tried to be careful about whom it rested on, and for how long. But this girl had, unfortunately for her, somehow caught his attention, and he had looked longer than he meant.

She was tall, as tall as most men, tall even by Outlander standards. Her hair was yellow, the color of sun on sand, and almost as bright. His people, the Hillfolk, were usually smaller than the Outlanders, and dark of skin and hair. But it wasn't her size or her coloring that held him beyond the first startled flick of notice; nor was it her beauty. There was too much strength in that face and in the long bones of the body for beauty. Something about the quietness of her, perhaps? Or her self-contained straightness; something about the way her eyes met his, with more thought behind them than the usual half-hypnotized, half-fearful look he had learned to expect if he held anyone's gaze too long—even when his *kelar* was quiet. Something, he thought suddenly, like the controlled straightness he himself had learned, knowing well what could happen if he relaxed. But that was nonsense. She was an Outlander. While there were still wild sports among his own peo-

38 |

ple, where a few drops of royal blood from many generations past would suddenly burst into full *kelar* in the veins of some quiet family's child, there had never yet been an Outlander with any Gift to contain.

This train of thought took him far enough from the center of anger that he had begun to relax a little; his hands uncurled, and the black mane swept against his fingers. He looked ahead; he knew, although he could not yet see it, that his camp lay just beyond this next bit of what looked like flat bare impartial desert and was in fact a little rise in the land, enough of a buffer from sand and storm to allow a small well of sweet water, with a little grass and low scrub, to live behind a protecting shoulder.

As he looked out across his desert, almost calm again, or at least finding the beginnings of calm, the *kelar* suddenly produced a picture of Sir Charles' foolish white face anxiously saying, "My dear sir—hmm—Your Majesty" and explaining why he could not help him. The picture was thrust before his eyes, and he took his breath in sharply between his teeth. Having caught his attention, the single-minded *kelar* snatched Sir Charles away and presented him with the girl again.

What *about* her? he shouted silently, but there was no answer. It was rare that the Gift ever made it easy for him by explaining what it wanted. Sometimes he never did find out, and was left to muddle through like any other mortal—with the added disadvantage of inscrutable messages banging inside his skull.

His patience gave way; he leaned forward in the saddle, and the big stallion leaped into a gallop. The six riders, who knew their king's moods, and hadn't been very happy at their reception at the Outlanders' hands themselves, let him go. He swerved away from the line that would take him directly to the camp.

The man on the golden dun, who had been riding on the king's right, soothed his mount with one hand. "Nay, we do not follow him this time."

The man at his left glanced across at him and nodded briefly. "May the Just and Glorious be with him."

The youngest of the riders snorted with laughter, although it was not pleasant laughter. "May the Just and Glorious be with all of us. Damn the Outlanders!"

The man on the dun frowned and said, "Innath, watch your tongue."

"I am watching it, my friend," replied Innath. "You may be glad you cannot hear what I am thinking."

The king had disappeared in the heat glaze rising from the sand by the time the little group topped the rise and saw the pale tents of their camp before them, and resigned themselves to telling those who awaited them what had occurred during the meeting with the Outlanders.

Harry blinked and recognized the boy at her elbow. "Thank you," she said absently, and he led the pony away, looking anxiously over his shoulder at the way the desert men had gone, and evidently grateful to be leaving himself. She shaded her eyes with her hand a moment, which only served to throw the fire of her headache into greater relief. She looked up at the men on the verandah and saw them moving uncertainly, as if they were waking up, still half under the influence of unpleasant dreams. She felt the same way. Her shoulder creaked when she dropped her arm again. At least it will be a little cooler inside, she thought, and made her way up the steps. Cassie and Beth, their mounts led away after Harry's, followed her.

Luncheon was a quiet meal. All those who had played a part in the morning's performance were there. Rather, Harry thought, as if we can't quite bring ourselves to separate yet, not because we have any particular reason to cling to one another's company. As if we'd just been through . . . something . . . together, and are afraid of the dark. Her headache began to subside with the second glass of lemonade and she thought suddenly: I don't even remember what the man looks like. I stared at him the entire time, and I can't remember—except the height of him, and the scarlet sash, and those yellow eyes. The yellow eyes reminded her of her headache, and she focused her thoughts on the food on her plate, and her gaze on the glacial paleness of the lemonade pitcher.

It was after the meal had been cleared away—and still no one made any move to go—that Jack Dedham cleared his throat in a businesslike manner and said: "We didn't know what to expect, but by the way we're all sitting around and avoiding one another's eyes—" Harry raised hers, and Jack smiled at her briefly—"we don't have any idea what to do with what we've got."

Sir Charles, still without looking up, said, as if speaking his thoughts aloud: "What was it, Jack, that you said to him—just at the end?"

Harry still had her eyes on Dedham, and while his voice as he answered carried just the right inflection, his face did not match it: "It's an old catch-phrase of sorts, on the let-us-be-friends-and-not-part-in-anger-even-though-we-feel-like-it order. It dates from the days of the civil war, I think—before we arrived, anyway."

"It's in the Old Tongue," said Sir Charles. "I didn't realize you knew it."

Again Dedham's eyes suggested something other than what he said: "I don't. As I said, it's a catch-phrase. A lot of ritual greetings are in the Old Tongue, although almost nobody knows what they mean any more."

Peterson said: "Good for you, Jack. My brain wasn't functioning at all after the morning we'd spent. Perhaps you just deflected him from writing off the Outlanders altogether." Harry, watching, saw the same something in Peterson's face that she had wondered at in Dedham's.

Sir Charles shrugged and the tension was broken. "I hope so. I will clutch at any straw." He paused. "It did not go well at all."

The slow headshakes Dedham and Peterson gave this comment said much louder than words could how great an understatement this was.

"He won't be back," continued Sir Charles.

There was the grim silence of agreement, and then Peterson added: "But I don't think he is going to run to the Northerners to make an alliance, either."

Sir Charles looked up at last. "You think not?"

Peterson shook his head: a quick decided jerk. "No. He would not have listened to Jack at the end, then, if he had meant to go to our enemies."

Jack said, with what Harry recognized as well-controlled impatience, "The Hillfolk will never ally with the Northerners. They consider them inimical by blood, by heritage—by everything they believe in. They would be declaring themselves not of the Hills if they went to the North."

Sir Charles ran his hand through his white hair, sighed, and said: "You know these people better than I, and I will take your word for it, since I can do nothing else." He paused. "I will have to write a report of this meeting, of course; and I do not at all know what I will say."

Beth and Cassie and Harry were all biting their tongues to keep from asking any questions that might call attention to their interested presence and cause the conversation to be adjourned till the men retired to some official inner sanctum where the fascinating subject could be pursued in private. Therefore they were both delighted and alarmed when Lady Amelia asked: "But, Charles, what happened?"

Sir Charles seemed to focus his gaze with some difficulty on the apprehensive face of his wife; then his eyes moved over the table and the girls knew that they had been noticed again. They held their breaths.

"Mmm," said Sir Charles, and there was a silence while the tips of Beth's ears turned pink with not breathing.

"It hurts nothing but our pride to tell you," Dedham said at last. "He was here less than two hours; rode up out of nowhere, as far as we could tell—we thought we were keeping watch so we'd have some warning of his arrival."

The girls' eyes were riveted on Dedham's face, or they might have exchanged glances.

"He strode up to the front door as if he were walking through his own courtyard; fortunately, we had seen them when they entered the gates in front here and were more or less collected to greet him; and your man, Charles, had the sense to throw open the door before we found out whether or not he would have walked right through it.

"I suppose the first calamity was that we understood each other's languages so poorly. Corlath spoke no Homelander at all—although, frankly, I don't guarantee that that means he couldn't."

Peterson grunted.

"You noticed it too, did you? One of the men he had with him did the translating, such as it was; and Peterson and I tried to talk Darian—"

"We *did* talk Darian," Peterson put in. "I know Darian almost as well as I know Homelander—as do you, Jack, you're just more modest about it—and I've managed to make myself understood to Darians from all sorts of odd corners of this oversized administration—including a few Free Hillfolk."

Harry thought: And the Hill-king stopped dead, as angry as he was, when Dedham addressed him in the Old Tongue?

"In all events," Dedham went on, "we didn't seem able to make ourselves understood too readily to Corlath."

"And his translator translated no faster than he had to, I thought," Peterson put in.

Dedham smiled a little. "Ah, your pride's been bent out of shape. Be fair."

Peterson answered his smile, but said obstinately, "I'm sure of it."

"You may be right." Dedham paused. "It wouldn't surprise me; it gave them time to look at us a little without seeming to."

"A little!" Sir Charles broke out. "Man, they were here less than two hours! How can they—he—conclude anything about us in so little time? He gave us no chance."

The tension returned. Dedham said cautiously: "I daresay he thought he was giving us a chance."

"I am not happy with any man so hasty," said Sir Charles sadly; and the pompous ridiculousness of his words was belied by his tired and worried face. His wife touched his hand where she sat on his right, and he turned to her and smiled. He looked around the table; both Peterson and Dedham avoided his gaze. He said, lightly, almost gaily, "It's simple enough. He wants arms, men, companies, regiments—help to close the mountain passes. He, it would appear, does not like the idea of the Northerners pouring through his country."

"Which is reasonable," said Dedham carefully. "His country would be turned into a battlefield, between the Northerners and . . . us. There aren't enough Hillfolk to engage the Northerners for any length of time. His country would be overrun, perhaps destroyed, in the process. Or at least annexed by the victor," he added under his breath.

"We couldn't possibly do as he asked," Sir Charles said, lapsing back to speaking his thoughts aloud. "We aren't even sure what the Northerners mean toward us at present."

Peterson said shortly: "The Hillfolk's attitude toward the North being what it is, I feel certain that Corlath's spy system is a good one."

"We offered cooperation," Sir Charles said.

"Capitulation, you mean," Peterson replied in his blunt way. "His." Sir Charles frowned. "If he would agree to put himself and his people entirely under our administration—"

"Now, Bob," Dedham said.

"That's what it amounts to," Peterson said. "He should give up his country's freedom—that they've hung on to, despite us, all these years—"

"It is not unusual that a smaller country should put itself under the protection of a larger, when the situation demands it," Sir Charles said stiffly.

Before Peterson had a chance to reply, Dedham put in hastily: "What it comes down to is that he is too proud to hear our terms, and we are—er—we cannot risk giving—lending—him troops on his terms."

"The Queen and Council would be most displeased with us if we precipitated an unnecessary war," said Sir Charles in his best commissioner's voice, and Peterson grunted. "We know nothing about the man," Sir Charles continued plaintively.

"We know that he wants to keep the Northerners out of Daria," Peterson muttered; but Dedham moved in his chair in a gesture Harry correctly translated as bestowing a swift kick on Peterson's ankle; and Peterson subsided.

"And he would not stay to parley," Dedham finished. "And here we are, feeling as if we'd all been hit in the head."

Corlath paced up and down the length of his tent as his Riders gathered. He paused at one end of the tent and stared at the close-woven horsehair. The wall moved, for the desert wind was never still. There were so few of the Hillfolk left; in spite of the small hidden tribes who had come out of their fastnesses to pledge to Damar's black-and-white banner after generations of isolation. Corlath had worked hard to reunite the Free that remained—but for what, when one thought of the thousands of Northerners, and eventually the thousands of Outlanders who would meet them?— for the Outlanders would learn soon enough about the Northern-ers' plans for southern conquest. Between them they would tear his country to shreds. His people would fight; he knew with a sad sore pride that they would hold on till the last of them was killed, if it came to that. At best they would be able to continue to live in the Hills: in small secret pockets of their Hills, hiding in caves and gathering food in the darkness, slipping away like mice in the shadows, avoiding those who held their land, claimed it and ruled it. The old Damar, before the civil wars, before the Outlanders, was only a wistful legend to his people now; how much less it would be when there were only a few handfuls of the Free living like beggars or robbers in their own Hills.

But he could not submit them to the Outlanders' . . . practical benevolence, he called it after a moment's struggle with himself. For his army to be commanded by Outlander generals . . . The corners of his mouth turned up. There was some bitter humor in the idea of the pragmatic Outlanders caught in a storm of *kelar* from both their allies and their opponents. He sighed. Even if by some miracle the Outlanders had agreed to help him, they would have refused to accept the *kelar* protection necessary—they didn't believe *kelar* existed. It was a pity there was no non-fatal way to prove to them otherwise.

He thought of the man who had spoken to him last, the grey-haired man. There had almost been a belief in him—belief in the ways of the Hills, that Corlath had read in his face; they might have been able to speak together. That man spoke the Hill tongue understandably at least—although he may not have known quite what he was offering in his few words of the Old Tongue. Poor Forloy: the only one of his Riders who knew even as much of the Outlander tongue as Corlath did. As an unwelcome envoy in a state far more powerful than his own, he had felt the need of even the few minutes a translator might buy him, to watch the faces of those he wished to convince.

Why wasn't there some other way?

For a moment the heavy cloth before him took on a tint of gold; the gold framed what might have been a face, and pale eyes looked at him—

She's nothing to do with this.

He turned away abruptly and found his Riders all seated, watching him, waiting.

"You already know—it is no good." They bowed their heads once in acknowledgment, but there was no surprise on their faces. "There never was much chance—" He broke off as one of his audience dropped his head a little farther than the seriousness of the occasion demanded, and added, "Very well, Faran, there wasn't *any* chance." Faran looked up, and saw the dawn of a smile on his king's face, the nearest thing to a smile anyone had seen on the king's face for days past. "No chance," Corlath repeated. "But I felt, um, obliged to try." He looked up at the ceiling for a minute. "At least it's all over now," he said. Now that any chance of outside assistance had been eliminated, it was time to turn to how best to guard their mountains alone.

The Northerners had tried to break through the mountains before, for they had always been greedy and fond of war; but while they were cunning, they were also treacherous, and trusted nobody because they knew they themselves were not to be trusted.

46 |

For many years this had been a safeguard to the Hillfolk, because the Northerners could not band together long enough or in great enough numbers to be a major threat to their neighbors. But in the last quarter-century a strong man had arisen from the ranks of the petty generals: a strong man with a little non-human blood in him, which granted him a ruthlessness beyond even the common grain of Northern malice; and from whatever source he drew his power, he was also a great magician, with skills enough to bring all the bands that prowled the Northlands, human and non-human alike, under his command. His name was Thurra.

Corlath knew, dispassionately, that Thurra's empire would not last; his son, or at most his son's son, would fail, and the Northerners break up and return to their smaller, nastier internecine quarrels. Corlath's father, and then Corlath, had watched Thurra's rise through their spies, and Corlath knew or could guess something of the cost of the power he chose to wield, and so knew that Thurra would not himself live much longer than an ordinary man. Since the Hill-kings lived long, it might be within Corlath's own lifetime that, even if the Northerners won the coming war, he would be able to lead his people in a successful rebellion; but by then there might not be enough of the country left to rebel, or to live off of after the rebellion was finished. Not much more than five hundred years ago—in Aerin's day—the desert his tent was pitched on had been meadow and forest. The last level arable land his people had left to them was the plain before the great gap in the mountains where the Northern army would come.

Sir Charles might beg off now while the Northerners had not yet attacked any Outlander-held lands. But once they had cut through the Hillfolk they would certainly try to seize what more they could. The entire Darian continent might fall into the mad eager hands of Thurra and his mob, many of them less human than he; and then the Outlanders would know more than they wished of wizardry.

And if the Outlanders won? Corlath did not know how many troops the Outlanders had to throw into the battle, once the battle was engaged; they would learn, terribly, of *kelar* at Thurra's hands. But even *kelar* was limited at last; and the Outlanders were stubborn, and, in their stubbornness, courageous; often they were stupid, oftener ineffectual, and they believed nothing they could not see with their eyes. But they did try hard, by their lights, and they were often kind. If the Outlanders won, they would send doctors and farmers and seeds and plows and bricklayers, and within a generation his people would be as faceless as the rest of the Outlander Darians. And the Outlanders were very able administrators, by sheer brute persistence. What they once got their hands on, they held. There would be no rebellion that Corlath would ever see.

It was not pleasant to hope for a Northern victory.

His Riders knew most of this, even if they did not see it with the dire clarity Corlath was forced to; and it provided a background to Corlath's orders now. King's Riders were not given to arguing with their king; but Corlath was an informal man, except occasionally when he was in the grip of his Gift and couldn't listen very well to anything else, and usually encouraged conversation. But this afternoon the Riders were a silent group, and Corlath, when he came to the end of what he had to say, simply stopped speaking.

Corlath's surprise was no less than that of his men as he heard himself say: "One last thing. I'm going back to the Outlander town. The girl—the girl with the yellow hair. She comes with us."

CHAPTER FOUR

S HE STARED OUT OF HER BEDROOM WINDOW at the moonlit desert. Shadows drifted across the pale sand, from one shaded hollow to the next clump of dry brush. Almost she could pretend the shadows had direction, intention. It was a game she often played. She ought to be in bed; she heard two o'clock strike. The location and acoustics of the big clock that stood in the front hall were such that it could be heard throughout the large house it presided over—probably even in the servants' quarters, although she had never had occasion to find out and didn't quite dare ask. She had often wondered if it was perversity or accident—and for whatever reason, why wasn't it changed?—that the clock should so be located as to force the knowledge of the passing of time upon everyone in the Residency, every hour of every day. Who would want to know the time when one couldn't sleep?

She had had insomnia badly when she was fresh from Home. It had never occurred to her that she would not be able to sleep without the sound of the wind through the oak trees outside her bedroom at Home; she had slept admirably aboard the ship, when apprehensions about her future should have been thickest. But the sound of the ceaseless desert air kept her awake night after night. There was something about it too like speech, and not at all like the comfortable murmur of oak leaves.

But most of that had worn off in the first few weeks here. She had had only occasional bad nights since then. Bad? she thought.

Why bad? I rarely feel much the worse the next day, except for a sort of moral irritability that seems to go with the feeling that I ought to have spent all those silent hours asleep.

But this last week had been quite as bad—as sleepless—as any she had known. The last two nights she had spent curled up in the window-seat of her bedroom; she had come to the point where she couldn't bear even to look at her bed. Yesterday Annie, when she had come to waken her, had found her still at the window, where she had dozed off near dawn; and, like the placid sensible maid that she was, had been scandalized. Apparently she had then had the ill grace to mention the matter to Lady Amelia, who, in spite of all the alarums and excursions of the week past, had still found time to stop at Harry's room just at bedtime, and cluck over her, and abjure her to drink some nice warm milk (*Milk!* thought Harry with revulsion, who had given it up forever at the age of twelve, with her first grown-up cup of tea), and make her promise to try to sleep—as if that ever had anything to do with it—and ask her if she was sure she was feeling quite well.

"Very well, ma'am," Harry replied.

Lady Amelia looked at her with concern. "You aren't fidgeting yourself about, mmm, last week, are you?"

Harry shook her head, and smiled a little. "No, truly, I am in excellent health." She thought of the end of a conversation she had heard, two days past, as Dedham and Peterson left Sir Charles' study without noticing her presence in the hall behind them. ". . . don't like it one bit," Peterson was saying.

Dedham ran his hand over the top of his close-cropped head and remarked, half-humorously, "You know, though, if in a month or a year from now, one of those Hillfolk comes galloping in on a lathered horse and yells, 'The pass! We are overwhelmed!' I'm going to close up the fort and go see about it with as many men as I can find, and worry about reporting it later." The front door had closed behind the two of them, and Harry proceeded thoughtfully on her way.

"I hope you are not sickening for anything, child," said Lady Amelia; "your eyes seem overbright." She paused, and then said in a tone of voice that suggested she was not sure this bit of reassurance was wise, as perhaps it would aggravate a nervous condition instead of soothing it: "You must understand, my dear, that if there is any real danger, you and I will be sent away in time."

Harry looked at her, startled. Lady Amelia misread her look, and patted her hand. "You mustn't distress yourself. Sir Charles and Colonel Dedham will take care of us."

Yesterday Harry had managed to corner Jack when he came again to closet himself with Sir Charles for long mysterious hours. Harry had lurked in the breakfast room till Jack emerged, looking tired. His look lightened when he saw her, and he greeted her, "Good morning, my dear. I see a gleam in your eye; what bit of arcane Damarian lore do you wish to wrest from me today?"

"What was it exactly that you said to Corlath that morning, just as he left?" replied Harry promptly.

Jack laughed. "You don't pull your punches, do you?" He sobered, looking at her quizzically. "I don't know that I should tell you—"

"But—"

"But I will. In the days of Damar's civil wars, a man pledged himself so, to his king, or to the particular claimant he wished to support. It was a particularly dangerous and unsettled time, and so the ritual swearing to one's leader meant rather a lot—more, for example, than our Queen's officers taking an oath to her, as we all must do. The phrase still carries weight in Hill tradition . . . but you see, my giving it to Corlath was a trifle, hmm, unprofessional of me, as Homelander protecting the Homelander Border from Corlath. A calculated risk on my part. . . ." He shrugged. "I hoped to indicate that not all Homelanders are . . . unsympathetic to the Free Hillfolk, whatever the official attitude is."

Harry lay down in her detestable bed after Lady Amelia left her, and dozed, after a fashion, till midnight; but then the darkness and peacefulness wakened her, and she came again to her window-seat to watch the night pass.

Two-thirty. How black the sky was around the stars; nearer the horizon were longer flatter glints in the darkness, unsuitable for stars, and these were the mountains; and the desert was shades of grey.

Without realizing it, she drifted into sleep.

There was the Residency, stolid and black in the moonlight. Faran and Innath would stay here, with the horses; it was not safe to take them any nearer. He would go the rest of the way on foot. Safe! He grinned sourly behind the safety of the grey hood pulled over his face, and slid into the shadows. The adventure was upon them, for good or ill.

"Sola, not an Outlander," Faran had begged, almost tearfully; and Corlath had flushed under his sun-darkened skin. There had been certain romantic interludes in the past that had included galloping across the desert at night; but he had never abducted any woman whose enthusiastic support for such a plan had not been secured well in advance. Corlath's father had been a notorious lover of women; unsuspected half-brothers and half-sisters of the present king still turned up occasionally, which kept the subject in everyone's mind. Corlath sometimes thought that his own policy of discretion in such matters only made his people nervous because they didn't know what was going on—or if anything was. For some time now there hadn't been, but by the gods, did his own Riders really expect him to break out by making an ass of himself over an Outlander—and now of all times?

But, on the other hand, he could not well explain his reasons— even to himself—although his determination was fixed, as he had unhappily realized the moment the words were out of his mouth. But he hated to see his people unhappy—because he was a good king, not because he was a nervous one—and so, while he could rightfully have told Faran to let it be, he had given as much of an answer as he could.

"This is an affair of state," he said slowly, because he could not quite bring himself to say that his *kelar* was concerning itself with an Outlander, even to his Riders, who were his dearest friends as well as his most trusted subjects. "The girl will be a prisoner of honor, treated with all honor, by me as well as by you."

No one had understood, but they were a little soothed; and they avoided thinking about the unwritten law of their land that said that a kidnapped woman has been ravished of her honor, whether she has been actually ravished of anything beyond a few uncomfortable hours across somebody's saddlebow or not. It was generally accounted an honor for a Hillman or woman to be seduced by a member of the royal family—which was why *kelar,* originally a royal Gift, continued to turn up in odd places—if a somewhat uncomfortable honor, for who could be entirely at ease with a lover who must never quite meet one's eyes? And Outlanders were peculiar, as everyone knew, so who did know how they might react?

"Sola," Faran quavered, and Corlath paused and turned a little toward the man to indicate that he would listen. "Sola, what will happen when the Outlanders find her gone?"

"What of it?"

"They will come after her."

"Not if they do not know where she has gone."

"But—how could they not know?"

Corlath smiled grimly. "Because we shall not tell them." Faran, by his own choice, had not been one of those who accompanied his king to the council with the Outlanders; Forloy and Innath and the others who had gone were wearing smiles to match the king's. The Outlanders could not see what happened under their very noses. "You shall leave here at once, and travel, slowly, toward the mountains; and set up camp again where the Leik spring touches the surface. There you will wait for me. I will return the way we came, in secret, in three days' time, so that the girl will not disappear too soon after the Hillfolk were seen in the Outlander station. Then I shall take the girl from her bed as she sleeps in the big house, and ride back to you."

There was a meditative silence; at last Faran said: "I would go with you, Sola. My horse is fast." His voice was still unhappy, but the quaver was gone; and as he looked at the faces of the six Riders who had been with Corlath when he spoke with the Outlander commissioner, he began to feel curious. He had never seen an Outlander, even from a distance; never looked upon an Outlander town.

After three restless days at the deserted campsite, Corlath, Faran, and Innath rode swiftly back toward the Outlander town. Corlath thought: They can't see us even in broad daylight when we gallop toward them with cloaks flapping and horses whinnying. We creep like burglars to an empty house, pretending that it has an owner because we can't quite believe it is this easy.

Faran and Innath knelt down where they were and did not look as their king left them, for they knew they would see no more than he wished them to. The horses waited as silently as the men, but the king's bay stallion watched him go. The only sound was the wind whispering through the low brush and the horses' long manes.

Corlath reached the house without difficulty; he had expected none. Watchdogs ignored him, or mysteriously counted him a friend. There were several black-and-brown furry shapes lying about sullenly snoring in the Residency garden. Outlander dogs did not like the northeast Border of Daria; and Hill dogs, who would have awakened at once and watched him silently, did not get on well with Outlanders. He passed the stables, but the grooms slept as heavily as the dogs. He couldn't see in the dark, but even in the places where the moonlight was no help he knew where things were.

He reached the wall of the house and laid a hand on it. Depending on what sort of a mood the *kelar* was in, he could occasionally walk through walls, without knocking them down first, or at least see through them. And then again, sometimes he couldn't. It would be tiresome if he had to break in like the common burglar he felt, and wander from room to room looking at faces on pillows. There was even the remote chance he could get caught at it.

No. This wasn't going to be one of those times: the *kelar* was with him—since it had gotten him into this dilemma, he thought, at least it was going to help to get him out of it—and he knew almost at once where she was. His only bad moment was when that damned clock in the front hall tolled like a call for the dead, and seemed to reach up the stairs after him like cold pale hands.

She was curled up, drooping and asleep on a cushioned shelf built out from a curved window; and for a moment pity struck him and he hesitated. What good will pity do me? he thought almost angrily; I'm not here by choice. But he wrapped the cloak around her with unnecessary tenderness as he breathed a few words over her head to make sure she would sleep.

Harry struggled out of some of the oddest dreams she'd ever had into a dim and foggy reality full of bumps and jolts. Was she ill? She couldn't seem to make out what was happening to her, save that it was very uncomfortable, and it was not like her to have difficulty waking up.

She opened her eyes blearily and saw something that looked like dawn behind something that looked like hills, although she was a long way from them. . . . Where she was, she then realized, was slung sideways across a horse's withers with her feet sliding across his shoulder with every stride—no more comfortable for him than me—and she was held sitting upright by an arm round her middle that clamped her arms to her sides, and her head appeared to be bouncing against a human shoulder.

Her only clear notion, and it wasn't very, was that she was perfectly capable of riding a horse herself, and resented being treated like a bundle or a baby: so she struggled. She raised her head with a gasp and shook her face free of the deep hood pulled over it; tried to sit up a bit farther and turn a bit more to the front.

This caused the rider to rein his horse in abruptly; except she realized there were no reins. The rider seized her a little more firmly and then there were two other men on horseback beside her, and they dismounted and came toward her at once. They were dressed like Hillfolk, with hoods pulled low over their faces; and quite suddenly, still not understanding what had happened to her, she was afraid. The rider who held her handed her down to the men beneath; and she noticed that the shoulder her heels were knocking was bright bay, and the mane long and black. Then as the two men caught her by the arms, her feet touched the ground, and she fainted again.

She woke once again in twilight, but this time the red glow came from the opposite direction. This time she awoke feeling more like herself; or she thought she did, but her surroundings were so unlikely she wasn't sure. She sat up and discovered she could; she was lying on a blanket, still wrapped in a dark hooded cloak that wasn't hers; and underneath she discovered she was still wearing her nightgown, and the dressing-gown over it. She was barefoot; she spent a light-headed minute or two trying to remember if her slippers had disappeared or if she'd never put them on—last night, or whenever it was—caught herself here, and looked around.

She was in a bit of a hollow, with a scrub-covered dune behind her. Over her was a sort of tent roof, pegged out in a square, but with only one side let down. The other three offered her a view of the dune; the sunset, if that was what it was; and three men crouching over a tiny smokeless fire, built against the opposite arm of the same dune. Around its edge she could see the black hills fading in the last light, and three horses. Three lumps that might be saddles lay near them, but the horses—a grey, a chestnut, and a blood bay—were not tethered in any way.

She had only just looked at these things with a first quick glance, and had not yet begun to puzzle over them, when one of the men stood up from the fire and walked over to her. The other two appeared to pay no attention, remaining bent over their knees and staring into the small red heart of the fire. The third man knelt down near her and offered a cup with something in it that steamed, and she took it at once without thinking, for the man's gesture had been a command. Then she held it and looked at it. Whatever it was, it was brown, and it smelled delicious; her stomach woke up at once, and complained.

She looked at the cup, and then at the man; he was wrapped in a cloak and she could not see his face. After a moment he gestured again, at the cup she held, and said, "Drink it."

She licked her lips and wondered how her voice was going to sound. "I would rather not sleep any more." That came out pretty well.

There was another pause, but whether it was because he did not understand her—his accent was curious and heavy, although the Homelander words were readily recognizable—or was choosing his answer carefully, she could not tell. At last he said: "It will not make you sleep."

She realized that she was much too thirsty to care whether or not she believed him; and she drank it all. It tasted as good as it smelled, which, she thought, gave it points over coffee. Then she realized that she was now terribly hungry.

"There is food if you wish it."

She nodded, and at once he brought her a plate of food and some more of the hot brown drink. He sat down again, as if with the intention of watching each mouthful. She looked at him, or rather at the shadow beneath the hood; then she transferred her attention to her plate. On it, beside the steaming hump of what she took to be stew, was an oddly shaped spoon; the handle was very arched, the bowl almost flat. She picked it up.

"Be careful," he said. "The sleep you have had makes some people sick."

So I was drugged, she thought. There was a peculiar relief in this, as if she now had an excuse to remember nothing at all about how she came to be where she was. She ate what she had been given, and felt the better for it, although the meat was unfamiliar to her; but the feeling better brought into unwelcome prominence all her questions about where she was, and why, and—worst— what next. She hesitated, looking at her now-empty plate. It was a dull grey, with a black symbol at its center. I wonder if it means anything, she thought. Health and long life? A charm against getting broken or lost? Or a symbolic representation of Death to Outlanders?

"Is it well?" the man beside her asked.

"I would—er—be more comfortable if I could see your face," she said, trying to strike a clear note among reasonable timidity, dreadful cowardice, and politeness to one's captor.

He threw back his hood, and turned his head so his face was clearly visible against the fading light behind him.

"My God," she said involuntarily: it was Corlath.

"You recognize me, then?" he inquired; and at her startled nod—Yes, Your Majesty, she thought, but her tongue was glued to her teeth—he said, "Good," and stood up. She looked dazed; he wished he might say something to reassure her, but if he couldn't explain to his own people why he was doing what he was doing, he knew he would be able to say nothing to her. He watched her gathering her dignity about her and settling it over her stricken expression. She said nothing further, and he picked up her plate and cup and took them back to the fire, where Innath scrubbed them with sand and put them away.

Harry was too busy with her own thoughts to suspect sympathy from her kidnapper. She saw him as a figure in a cloak, and watched him join his men at the fire; neither of them looked her way. One stamped out the fire and packed the cooking-utensils in a bag; the other saddled the horses. Corlath stood staring at the hills, his arms folded, his cloak shifting in the evening breeze; the light was nearly all gone, and she soon could not discern his still figure against the background of the black hills.

She stood up, a little shakily; her feet were uncertain under her, and her head was uncertain so far from the ground. She walked a few steps; the sand was warm underfoot, but not unbearably so. The two men—still without looking at her—slid past her, one on each side, and dismantled the tent, rolled it up, and stored it away so quickly it seemed almost like magic; and as the last bag was fastened to a saddle strap, Corlath turned, although no word had been spoken. The red bay followed him.

"This is Isfahel," he said to her gravely. "You would say perhaps . . . Fireheart." She looked up at the big horse, not sure what response was required; she felt that patting this great beast would be taking a liberty. To do something, she offered him the flat of her hand, and was foolishly gratified when he arched his neck and lowered his nose till his breath tickled her hand. He raised his head again and pricked his ears at Corlath; Harry felt that she had just undergone some rite of initiation, and wondered if she'd passed.

The other two men approached them; the other two horses followed. Am I about to be slung over the saddlebow like a sack of meal again? she thought. Is it more difficult to do the slinging when the sack in question is standing and looking at you?

She turned her head away, whereupon the other two men were found to be looking intently at the sand around their boots. The baggage was all tied behind their saddles, and the hollow they stood in looked as bare and undisturbed as if it had never sheltered a campsite. She turned her head back to Corlath again. "I can ride—at least a little," she said humbly, although she had been considered an excellent horsewoman at Home. "Do you think I might sit . . . facing forward, perhaps?"

Corlath nodded and let go the horse's mane. He adjusted the leather-covered roll of fleece at the front of the saddle, then turned back to her. "Can you mount?"

She eyed the height of the horse's back: Eighteen hands if he's an inch, she thought, and that may be conservative. "I'm not sure," she admitted.

Then, to the horror of the other two men, the puzzlement of Fireheart, and the surprise of Harry herself, Corlath knelt in the sand and offered her his cupped hands. She put a sandy foot in the hands, and was tossed up as easily as if she were a butterfly or a flower petal. She found this a bit unnerving. He mounted behind her with the same simple grace she'd seen in the Residency courtyard. The other two horses and their riders came up beside them; they wheeled together to face the hills, and together broke into a canter; Harry could detect no word or gesture of command.

They rode all night—walk and canter and brief swift gallop—and Harry was bitterly tired before the line of hills before them began to emerge from a greying sky. They stopped only once; Harry swung her leg over the horse's withers and slid to the ground before any offer of help could be made; and while she didn't fold up where she stood, there was a nasty moment when she thought she might, and the sand heaved under her like the motion of a horse galloping. She was given bread, and some curious green fruit, and something to drink; and Corlath threw her into the saddle again while his men bit their lips and averted their eyes. She wound her hands in Fireheart's long mane, stiffened her back, and blinked, and willed herself to stay awake. She'd said she could ride, and she didn't want to be carried . . . wherever they were going . . . but she wasn't going to think about that. Just think about sitting up straight.

Once when they slowed to a walk, Corlath handed her a skin bag and said, "Not much farther now," and the words sounded kindly, not scornful. She wished she could see his face, but it was awkward to twist around to peer at someone who was just behind one's shoulder, so she didn't. The contents of the bag burned her mouth and made her gasp, but she sat up the straighter for it.

Then as she stared at the line of hills, and squeezed her eyes shut and opened them again, and was sure that the sky was turning paler, she was not imagining things, the three horses pulled up to a walk, then halted, ears forward. Corlath pointed; or to Harry it seemed that a disembodied hand and arm materialized by her right cheek. "There." She followed the line his finger indicated, but she saw only waves of sand. The horses leaped forward at a gallop that appalled her with its swiftness at the end of such a journey; the shock of each of Fireheart's hoofs striking the ground rattled her bones. When she raised her eyes from the lift and fall of the black mane over her hands, she saw a glint of white, and of grey shapes too regular to be dunes. The sun broke golden over the hills as the three horses thundered into the camp.

CHAPTER FIVE

C ORLATH WAS ON THE GROUND AT ONCE, calling orders that sent long-robed figures scurrying in all directions. Harry sat alone on the big bay horse, who stood quite still; to her tired and befuddled gaze there were dozens of tents and hundreds of people. Men came forward from the mouths of tents and out from shadows, to make their bows to their king—to congratulate him on the success of his venture? Harry thought. Was it successful? Some were sent at once on errands, some faded back into the darkness from which they had emerged. The two men who had ridden with the king dismounted also, and stood a little behind him as he looked around his camp. Harry didn't move. She didn't quite believe that they had arrived—and besides, where was it they were? She didn't feel that she *had* arrived—or didn't want to. She thought wistfully of her despised bed far away in the Residency, and of fat dull busybody Annie. She wished she were home, and she was so tired she wasn't sure where home was.

When Corlath turned back to her she woke up enough to slither down from the horse's tall back before he tried to help her; this time she did no fancy sliding, but turned to face the horse's shoulder, and kept her hands on the saddle till her feet touched the ground. It was a long way down. She was sure it had gotten longer since the last time she dismounted. Fireheart stood as patiently as the fourposter pony as she leaned against him, and she patted him absently, as she might have patted her own horse, and his nose came round to touch her forearm. She sighed, and thought of Jack Dedham, who would give an arm to ride a Hill horse, even once. Perhaps it didn't count if you were riding double with a Hillman.

Harry had her back toward Faran and Innath as they led the horses away. Faran said, "That was a longer ride than I enjoy, at my age," and Innath replied laughing: "Indeed, Grandfather, you had to be tied to your saddle with your long white beard."

Faran, who was a grandfather several times over, but looked forward to being a king's Rider for many years yet, and wore his dark-grey beard short, grinned and said: "Yes, I long for a feather-bed and a plump young girl who will admire an elderly warrior for his scars and his stories." His eyes slid round, and he looked straight at Harry for the first time since Corlath had carried her, a black-wrapped bundle lying so bonelessly quiet in his arms that it was difficult to believe it contained anything human, to the shadow where two men and three horses awaited him. But Harry was frowning at her dirty feet and did not notice.

"The Outlander girl," Faran said slowly, with the air of an honest man who will be just at any cost. "I did not know the Outlanders taught their children such pride. She has done herself honor on this ride."

Innath considered. To do yourself honor is high praise from a Hillman; but as he thought of the last two days, he had to agree. He was almost a generation younger than his fellow Rider, however, and had viewed their adventure differently. "Do you know, I was most worried that she might weep? I can't bear a woman weeping."

Faran chuckled. "If I had known that, I would have advised our king—strongly—to choose another Rider. Not that it would have mattered much, I think: she would merely have had the sleep laid on her again." He pulled a tent flap aside, and they and the horses disappeared from Harry's sight. She had recognized the Hill word for "Outlander," and wondered dejectedly what Corlath's companions, who had so pointedly ignored her during their journey together, were saying. She wiggled her grubby toes in the sand.

She looked up and noticed that she was standing only a few feet from the—what does one call it on a tent? *Door* implied hinges and a frame—front of the grandest tent of all. It was white, with two wide black stripes across its peak from opposite directions, meeting and crossing at the center, and extending to the ground like black ribbons. A black-and-white banner flew from the crossed center, the tallest point in the camp, as the tent was the biggest. "Go in," said Corlath at her side again; "they will take care of you. I will join you presently."

As she approached, a man held aside the golden silk rectangle that served the great tent for a door. He stood to attention with as much dignity as if she were a welcome guest, and perhaps a queen in her own country. This amused her, with a stray thought that the Hill-king seemed to have his followers well schooled, and she smiled at him as she went inside; and was gratified by the startled look that crossed his face when she managed to catch his eye. At least they aren't all inscrutable, she thought. One of Dedham's subalterns might have looked like that.

It was also comforting to have succeeded at last in catching someone's eye.

What she did not know was that the honor guard at the door, who stood to attention because he was an honor guard and it would have been beneath him to be less than courteous to anyone who had the king's grace to enter the king's tent, was saying to himself: She walks and smiles at me as if she were a grand lady in her own home, not a prisoner of—of— He stumbled here, since neither he nor anyone else knew exactly why she had been made a prisoner, or an involuntary guest, or whatever it was that she was, except that it was the king's will. And this after a journey that made even old Faran, who was not flesh at all but iron, look a little weary. This was a story he would tell his friends when he was off duty.

Inside Harry looked around her with awe. If the camp from the outside was white and grey and dun-colored, as dull but for the black-and-white banner flying from the king's tent as the sand and scrub around it and brightened only by the robes and sashes some of the men wore, inside this tent—she was sure it was Corlath's own—there was a blaze of color. Tapestries hung on the walls, and between them were gold and silver chains, filigree balls and rods, bright enameled medallions—some of them big enough to be shields. Thick soft rugs were scattered on the floor three or four deep, each of them gorgeous enough to lie at the foot of a throne; and over them were scattered dozens of cushions. There were carved and inlaid boxes of scented red wood, and bone-colored wood, and black wood; the largest of these were pushed against the walls. Lanterns hung on short chains from the four carved ribs that crossed the high white ceiling to meet at the center peak, above which the banner flew outside, and below which a slender jointed pillar ran from floor to ceiling. Like pillars stood at each of the four corners of the tent, and four more braced the ribs at their centers; and from each pillar a short arm extended which held in its carven cupped hand another lantern. All were lit, bathing the riot of deep color, shape, and texture in a golden glow which owed nothing to the slowly strengthening morning light outside.

She was staring up at the peak of the roof and feeling impressed at the smooth structure of the tent—her own knowledge of tents was limited to stories of the Homelander military variety, which involved ropes and canvas and much swearing, and leaks when it rained—when a slight noise behind her brought her back again to her presence in a Hill camp. She turned around, nervously, but not so nervously as she might have; for there was a graciousness and—well, humanity, perhaps, if she tried to think of a word for it—to the big white-walled room that set her at ease, even against her own better judgment.

Four white-robed men had entered the tent. They brought with them, carrying it by handles set round the rim, an enormous silver basin: bath-sized, she thought. It had a broad base and sides that flared gently. The metal was worked in some fashion, but the play of the lantern light over the patterns prevented her from deciding what the designs might be.

The men set the great basin down at one end of the tent, and turned to leave, one after the other; and each, as he passed her standing uncertainly near the center, bowed to her. She was made uneasy by the courtesy, and had to stop herself from taking a step or two backward. She stood with her arms at her sides, but her hands, invisible in the long full sleeves of her battered dressing-gown, closed slowly into fists.

As the four men passed in front of her on their way out, several more were coming in, with silver urns on their shoulders; and the urns, she found when the carriers emptied them into the silver bath—it had to be a bath—were full of steaming water. No drop was spilled; and each man bowed to her as he left. She wondered how many of them there were engaged in water-carrying; there were never more than a few in the tent at once, yet as soon as one urn was empty the man behind was there to pour from another.

It took only a few soft-footed minutes, the only sound that of the water falling into the basin, for it to be full; and the stream of men stopped likewise. She was alone a moment, watching the surface of the water glint as the last ripples grew still; and she saw that some of the design on the bath was simply the presence of hinges, and she laughed. This was a traveling camp, after all. Then four men entered together and ranged themselves in a line—like horse-herders, she thought, presented with an animal whose temper is uncertain—and looked at her; and she looked at them. She rather thought these were the four who had brought the bath in to begin with; but she wasn't sure. What she did notice was something else, something that hadn't quite registered while the steady shuffle of men and urns had gone past: that each of these men had a little white mark that looked like a scar on his forehead, in the center of the brow, above the eyes.

She wondered about this; and then she wondered about what looked like towels lying over the shoulders of three of the men; and then the fourth one came toward her with a motion so swift and polite, and somehow unthreatening, that he slipped the Hill cloak off her shoulders and folded it over his arm before she reacted. She spun around then and backed away a step; and was almost certain that the look on this man's face was surprise. He laid the cloak down very gently on a wooden chest, and motioned toward the bath.

She was grateful that at least he didn't bow to her again, which probably would have made her leap like a startled rabbit. It wasn't, she thought, that the gesture held any unpleasant servility. But it felt like an indication that she was somehow in command of the situation—or ought to be. The lack of servility was therefore alarming, because these men were too capable of observing that she didn't feel in the least as if she were in command.

They looked at one another a moment longer. She thought then incredulously: Surely they're not expecting to *give* me a bath?— and noticed with the sides of her eyes that the other three men were standing behind the bath now, and one of the towels when unfolded was revealed as a robe, with a braided gold cord at the waist.

The man directly in front of her, who had removed her cloak, reached out and laid his hands on the belt of her dressing-gown, and she suddenly found that she was angry. The last two days had been one indignity after another, however politely each had been offered; and to preserve what self-respect she could—and what courage—she had preferred not to think about them too closely. But that she wasn't even to be allowed to bathe without a guard— that she should be expected to submit tamely to the ministrations of four men—*men*—like a—like a— Her imagination chose to fail her here, far from home, with the terror of the unknown, and of the captured, only barely kept at bay. She threw off the man's polite fingers with as much violence as she could and said furiously: "No! Thank you, but *no.*" There are enough of them, for God's sake, to stand me on my head if they want to force the issue, she thought. But I am *not* going to cooperate.

There was a ripple of golden silk at the sound of her voice, and a new shadow appeared in the lantern light. Corlath, who had been hovering just outside to see how his Outlander was going to behave, entered the tent. He spoke two or three words and the men left at once; each bowing, first to her and then to their king. A corner of Harry's mind, which refused to be oppressed by the dreadfulness of the situation, noticed that the bows were of equal depth and duration; and the same mental corner had the impertinence to think this odd.

There was another little silence after the four men had left, only this time it was the king she was facing down. But she was too angry to care. If she said anything she would say too much, and she hadn't quite forgotten that she was at the mercy of strangers, so she bit her tongue and glowered. Why was this all happening? The bit of her mind which had commented about the equality of bows presently observed that anger was preferable to fear, so the anger was encouraged to carry on.

Evidently Corlath had already had his bath; his black hair was wet, and even his sun-brown skin was a few shades lighter. He was wearing a long golden robe, stiff with elegant stitching, open at the front to show a loose cream-colored garment that fell almost to his sandaled feet. In her own country she would have been inclined to call it a nightshirt under an odd sort of dressing-gown—although nobody ever wore a scarlet cummerbund over one's nightshirt—but it looked very formal here. She mustn't forget to glower or she might feel awed. And then, inevitably, afraid.

She recognized the quality of his silence when at last he spoke: the same feeling she had had when she first spoke to him, at the small campsite between the arms of a sand dune, that he chose and arranged his words very carefully.

"Do you not wish to bathe, then? It is a long ride we had." He was thinking, So I have managed to offend her immediately. It is done differently where she comes from; she can't know and must not be able to guess—but how could she guess?—that in the Hills it is only the men and women of the highest rank that may be waited on by household servants of both sexes. I feared—but for what good? We know nothing of each other's customs, and my household men have only done as they ought: treated the king's Outlander with the greatest honor.

Harry in her turn had unbent slightly at the "we." It was friendlier than the accusatory "you" she'd been expecting. She hadn't unbent so far, though, as to prevent herself from saying coldly, "I am accustomed to bathe alone."

Ah. Yes. I don't suppose I should mire myself with involved explanations at this point? She doesn't look to be in the mood for them. He said, "These are men of my household. It was to do you . . . courtesy."

She glanced away and felt her anger begin to ebb; and so she was unprepared when he took a sudden stride forward as she dropped her eyes. He grabbed her chin and forced it up, turning her face to the light and staring down at her as if amazed. Her abrupt reversion to existence as an object to be bundled about, turned this way and that at another's will, made the anger boil up again at once; and her eyes glittered back at him without a trace of fear.

He was staring into those eyes, as the light played full across them, and thinking, That's why. I don't understand it, but this must be why—the first step to why. He had just caught a glimpse, a suspicion, when she turned her head, the way the light fell, and he had put his hand out before he thought. Her eyes, under his gaze, shimmered grey to green with bubbles of amber that flickered like lightning in the depths and floated up to break like stars on the surface: bottomless eyes, that a man or beast fool enough to look at long would fall into and drown. He knew—he was one of the very few who need have no fear—that she did not know. She met his eyes too clearly: there was nothing in her eyes but simple and forthright fury—and he couldn't blame her for that. He wondered if she'd learned by accident not to focus her anger, or whether people she hated had a habit of falling downstairs or choking on fishbones—or if perhaps she had never hated. One doesn't generally look into mirrors when one is especially angry; one has better things to do, like pace the floor, or throw things. Perhaps no one had ever noticed, or been in a position to notice. And the thought came to him vaguely, for no particular reason, that she couldn't ever have been in love. If she had ever turned the full intensity of her *kelar*-brilliant eyes on any average mortal, they

68 |

would both have had a shock; and she would never again have had the innocence to meet anyone's eyes as she now met his.

He dropped his hand from her chin and turned away. He looked a little ashamed, she thought; and he said, "Forgive me," as if he meant it. But he looked more thoughtful than anything else, and, she realized with surprise, relieved, as if he had made—or had made for him—some important decision. What can be wrong with my face? she thought. Has my nose turned green? It has always been crooked, but it never astonished anybody before.

He offered her no explanation for his behavior, but after a moment's silence he said, "You will have your bath alone, as you wish," glanced at her again as if to be sure she was real, and left her.

She wrapped her arms around herself and shivered; and then thought, Very well, I do want a bath, the water's cooling off, and how long is a bath expected to take before someone else comes trotting in?

She took the fastest bath of her life, and was bright red with scrubbing but quite clean when she tumbled out again, dried off, and slithered into the white robe left for her. The sleeves came to her elbows, and the hem nearly to her ankles. There were long loose trousers to go underneath, but so full as to seem almost a skirt, and they rippled and clung as she moved. The clothing all was made from something adequately opaque, but when she had tied the golden rope around her middle she still felt rather embarrassingly unclad; Homelander garb for its women involved many more layers. She looked at her dusty dressing-gown, but was reluctant to put it back on; and she was still hesitating over this as she dried her hair on the second towel and tried to part the tangle with her fingers, when Corlath returned, carrying a dark red robe very much like his golden one—and a comb. The handle of it was wide and awkward in her hand, but it had familiar teeth, and that was all that counted.

While she watched through her wet hair, the bath was half-emptied as it had been filled, and the rest carried out still in the silver basin. The four men at its handles walked so smoothly the water never offered to slop up the sides. Then there was a pause and one of the men of the household—or so she supposed the forehead mark indicated—entered carrying a mirror in a leather frame and knelt before her on one knee, propped the mirror on the other, and tipped it back till she could see her face in it. She looked down, bemused—the man's eyes were on the floor. Did household servants of the Hills all take lessons in tipping mirrors to just the right angle, relative to the height and posture of the person to be served? Perhaps it was a specialty, known only to a few; and those few, of course, would be preserved for the royal household. She parted her hair gravely and shook it back over her shoulders, where it fell heavily past her hips. The deep red of her robe was very handsome; the shadows it cast were as velvety as rose petals. "Thank you," she said in Hill-speech, hoping that she remembered the right phrase; and the man stood up, bowed again, and went away.

Meanwhile a long table was being erected under the peak of the tent, next to the central pillar. It consisted of many square sections, with a leg at each corner of each square, set next to each other in a long single row; she wondered how they managed to stand so level on the whimsical layers of carpet. Corlath was pacing up and down the end of the tent opposite her, head bent and hands behind him. Plates were arranged on the table—each setting, she saw, was given a plate, one of the curious flat-bowled spoons, two bowls of different sizes, and a tall mug. The table was very low, and there were no chairs; some of the cushions scattered all over the tent were gathered up and heaped around it. Then large bowls of bread and fruit and—she thought—cheese were brought in, and the lamp that hung from the wooden rib over the table was lowered till it hung only a few feet from the plentiful food. It was just a little above her eye level as she stood watching. The lanterns that hung from the ceiling beams were suspended on fine chains which were attached to slender ropes looped around a row of what looked very much like belaying-pins on a ship lined up against one wall.

Corlath had stopped pacing, and his eyes followed the lowering of the lamp; but the expression on his face said that his thoughts were elsewhere. Harry watched him covertly, ready to look away if he should remember her; and as the lamp was fixed in its new position she saw him return to himself with a snap. He walked a few steps forward to stand at one end of the long table; then he looked around for her. She was not in a good position for judging such things, but she felt that he recalled her existence to his mind with something of an effort, as a man will recall an unpleasant duty. She let him catch her eye, and he gestured that she should take her place at his left hand. At that moment the golden silk door was lifted again, and another group of men filed in.

She recognized two of them: they were the men who had ridden with Corlath to assist at her . . . removal. She was a little surprised that she should recognize them so easily, since what she had mostly seen of them was the backs of their heads when they averted their faces, or the tops of their heads or hoods when they stared at the ground. But recognize them she did, and felt no fear about staring at them full-face now, for they showed no more inclination than they ever had for looking back at her.

There were eighteen men all told, plus Corlath and herself; and she was sure she could have recognized them as a group, as belonging together and bound together by ties as strong as blood or friendship, even if they had been scattered in a crowd of several hundred. They had an awareness of each other so complete as to be instinctive. She knew something of the working of this sort of camaraderie from watching Dedham and some of his men; but here, with this group of strangers, she could read it as easily as if it were printed on a page before her; and their silence—for none bothered with the kind of greeting Harry was accustomed to, any Hill version of hello and how are you—made it only more plain to her. Rather than finding their unity frightening, and herself all alone and outside, she found it comforting that her presence should so little disturb them. That instinctive awareness seemed to wrap around her too, and accept her: an outsider, an Outlander and a woman, and yet there she was and that was that.

She sat when everyone else sat, and as bowls and plates were passed she found that hers were filled and returned to her without her having to do anything but accept what was given her. Knives appeared, from up sleeves and under sashes and down boot tops, and Corlath produced an extra one from somewhere and gave it to her. She felt the edge delicately with one finger, and found it very keen; and was faintly flattered that the prisoner should be allowed so sharp an instrument. No doubt because any one of these men could take it away from me at my first sign of rebellion, without even interrupting their chewing, she thought. She began to peel the yellow-skinned fruit on her plate, as the man opposite her was doing. It seemed years since she had faced Sir Charles across the breakfast table.

She didn't notice when the conversation began; it proceeded too easily to have had anything so abrupt as a beginning, and she was preoccupied with how to manage her food. From the tone of their voices, these men were reporting to their king, and the substance of the reports was discussed as a matter of importance all around the table. She understood no word of it, for "yes" and "no" and "please" and "good" are almost impossible to pick out when talk is in full spate, but it was a language she found pleasant to listen to, with a variety of sounds and syllables that she thought would well lend themselves to any mood or mode of expression.

Her mind began to wander after a little time. She was exhausted after the long ride, but the tension of her position—I will *not* say that I am utterly terrified—served admirably to keep her awake and uneasily conscious of all that went on around her. She wondered if any of these men would give it away by look or gesture if the conversation turned to the Outlander in their midst.

But after a bath, and clean clothes, even these odd ones, and good food, for the food was very good, and even the company, for their companionship seemed to hold her up like something tangible, her mind insisted on relaxing. But that relaxation was a mixed blessing at best, because as the tension eased even a little, her thoughts unerringly reverted to trying to puzzle out why she was where she found herself.

Something to do with that abortive meeting at the Residency, between the Hillfolk and the Outlanders, presumably. But why? Why me? If I could be stolen from my bed—or my window-seat—then they could steal somebody from some other bed—and Sir Charles seems a lot more likely as a political figure. She repressed a grin. Though a very unlikely figure for riding across a saddlebow. There had to be a better reason than that of physical bulk for the choice of herself over . . . whoever else was available. She had been spirited out of her own house, with the doors locked and the dogs out, and Sir Charles and Lady Amelia asleep only a few steps away. It was as if Corlath—or his minions—could walk through walls: and if they could walk through the Residency walls and over the Residency dogs, probably they could walk through any other walls—at least Homelander walls—that they chose. It was uncanny. She remembered that Dedham, whose judgment she trusted above all others' at the station, and who knew more than any other Homelander about his adopted country, believed in the uncanniness of certain of the Hillfolk's tactics. Which brought her back to square one of this game: Why her? Why Harry Crewe, the Residency's charity case, who had only been in this country at all for a few months?

There was one obvious answer, but she discarded it as soon as it arose. It was too silly, and she was convinced that, whatever failings Corlath and his men might be capable of, silliness wasn't one of them. And Corlath didn't look at her the way a man looks at a woman he plans to have share his bed—and his interest would have to be very powerful indeed for him to have gone to so much trouble to steal her. He looked at her rather as a man looks at a problem that he would very much prefer to do without. She supposed it was distinction of a sort to be a harassment to a king.

She also swiftly, almost instinctively, discarded the idea that her Homelanders would mount any successful expedition to find her and bring her home again. The Hillfolk knew their desert; the Homelanders did not. And the Residency charity case would not warrant extraordinary efforts. She thought wryly: If Jack guesses where I am, he'll think I don't need rescuing . . . but poor Dick;

he'll manage to convince himself that it's his fault, he brought me out here in the first place. . . . She blinked hastily, and bit her lips. Her crossed legs were asleep, and the small of her back hurt. She was accustomed to sitting in chairs. She began surreptitiously to thump her thighs with her fists till they began to tingle painfully to life again; then she began on her calves. By the time she could feel when she wiggled her toes, the hot stiff feeling around her eyes had ebbed and she could stop blinking.

The men of the household entered the royal tent again, and cleared the table. The bread and fruit were replaced by bowls of something dark and slightly shiny. When she was offered a bit of it she discovered it to be sticky and crunchy and very sweet, and by the time she had eaten most of her generous serving, and what remained was adhering to her face and fingers, she noticed that a bowl of water and a fresh napkin had been placed at each person's elbow. There was a momentary lull while everyone sighed and stretched; and Corlath said a few words to the men of the household, which caused one of them to leave the tent and the other three still present to go around the walls extinguishing the lanterns, all except the one lamp that hung low over the table. The heavy woven walls shone in the daylight so the inside was palely lit; and the lamp over the table burned like a small sun, casting half-shadows in the quiet corners of the glowing white walls and in the hollows of eyes. None spoke.

Then the man returned, carrying a dark leather bag bound with brass in the shape of a drinking-horn. A thong hung from its neck and base, and this the man had looped over his shoulder. He offered it first to Corlath, who gestured to the man at his right. The man of the household handed it gravely to him, bowed, and left; there were none in the tent now but those twenty who sat round the table.

The first man drank—one swallow; she could see him letting it slide slowly down his throat. He balanced the bag on the table and stared at the burning lamp. After a moment an expression passed over his face that was so clear Harry felt she should recognize it immediately; but she did not. She was shaken both by its strength

74 |

and by her own failure to read it; and then it was gone. The man looked down, smiled, shook his head, said a few words, and passed the horn to the man sitting on his right.

Each man took one mouthful, swallowed it slowly, and stared at the lamp. Some of them spoke and some did not. One man, with skin sunburned as dark as cinnamon but for a pale scar on his jaw, spoke for a minute or two, and words of surprise broke from several of his audience. They all looked to Corlath, but he sat silent and inscrutable, chin in hand; and so the drinking-horn was passed on to the next.

One man Harry remembered in particular: he was shorter than most of the company, while his shoulders were very broad and his hands large. His hair was grizzled and his expression grim; his face was heavily lined, but whether with age or experience or both she could not guess. He sat near the foot of the table on the side opposite her. He drank, stared at the light, spoke no word, and passed the horn to the man on his right. All the others, even the ones who said nothing, showed something in their faces—something, Harry thought, that was transparent to any who had eyes to see beyond—some strong sensation, whether of sight or feeling— she could not even guess this much. But this man remained impassive, as opaque as skin and blood and bone can be. One could see his eyes move, and his chest heave as he breathed; there was no clue for further speculation. She wondered what his name was, and if he ever smiled.

As the leather bag rounded the bottom of the table and started up the other side, and Harry could no longer see the faces of the drinkers, she dropped her eyes to her hands and complimented herself on how quietly they lay, the fingers easy, not gripping each other or whitening their knuckles around her mug. The mug was still half full of a pale liquid, slightly honey-sweet but without (she thought she could by now conclude) the dangers of the gentle-tasting mead it reminded her of. She moved one finger experimentally, tapped it against the mug, moved it back, rearranged her hands as a lady might her knitting, and waited.

She was aware when the drinking-horn reached the man on her

left, and was aware of the slight shudder that ran through him just before he spoke; but she kept her eyes down and waited for Corlath to reach across her and take the waiting horn. This was not something an Outlander would be expected to join in—and just as well. Whatever the stuff was, watching the men's faces when they drank made her feel a little shaky.

And so she was much surprised when one of Corlath's hands entered her range of vision and touched the back of one of her hands with the forefinger. She looked up.

"Take a sip," he said. She reached out stiffly and took the brass-bound bag from the man who held it, keeping her eyes only on the bag itself. It was warm from all the hands that had held it, and up close she could see the complexity of the twisted brass fittings. It carried a slight odor with it: faintly pungent, obscurely encouraging. She took a deep breath.

"Only a sip," said Corlath's voice.

The weight of the thing kept her hands from trembling. She tipped her head back and took the tiniest of tastes: a few drops only. She swallowed. It was curious, the vividness of the flavor, but nothing she could put a name to. . . .

She saw a broad plain, green and yellow and brown with tall grasses, and mountains at the edge of it, casting long shadows. The mountains started up abruptly, like trees, from the flatness of the plain; they looked steep and severe and, with sun behind them, they were almost black. Directly in front of her there was a small gap in those mountains, little more than a brief pause in the march of the mountains' sharp crests, and it was high above the floor of the plain. Up the side of the mountain, already near the summit, was a bright moving ribbon.

Horsemen, no more than forty of them, riding as quickly as they could over the rough stony track, the horses with their heads low and thrown forward, watching their feet, swinging with their strides, the riders straining to look ahead, as though fearing they might come too late. Behind the riders were men on foot, bows slung slantwise over their backs, crossed by quivers of arrows; there were perhaps fifty of them, and they followed the horses, with strides as long as theirs. Beside them were long brown moving glints, supple as water, that slid from light to shade too quickly to be identified; four-footed, they looked to be; dogs perhaps. The sunlight bounced off sword hilts, and the metal bindings of leather arms and harness, and shields of many shapes, and the silver strings of bows.

The far sides of the mountains were less steep, but no less forbidding. Broken foothills extended a long way, into the hazy distance; a little parched grass or a few stunted trees grew where they could. Below the gap in the mountains by any other path but through the valley would be impossible, at least for horses. The gap was one that a small determined force would be able to defend—for a time.

The bright ribbon of horsemen and archers collected in the small flat space behind the gap, and became a pool. Here there was a little irregular plateau, with shallow crevasses, wide enough for small campsites, leading into the rocky shoulders on either side, and with a long low overhanging shelf to one side that was almost a cave. The plateau narrowed to a gap barely the width of two horsemen abreast, where the mountain peaks crowded close together, just before it spilled into the scrub-covered valley, and the rock-strewn descending slopes beyond.

The horsemen paused and some dismounted; some rode to the edge and looked out. At the far edge of the foothills something glittered, too dark for grass, too sharply peaked for water. When it spilled into the foothills it became apparent for what it was: an army. This army rode less swiftly than had the small band now arranging themselves in and around the pass, but their urgency was less. The sheer numbers of them were all the tactics they needed.

But the little army waiting for them organized itself as seriously as if it had a chance of succeeding in what it set out to do; and perhaps some delay of the immense force opposing it was all that it required. The dust beyond the foothills winked and flashed as rank after rank approached the mountains . . .

. . . and then time began to turn and dip crazily, and she saw the leader of the little force plunging down into the valley with a company behind him, and he drew a sword that flashed blue in his hand. His horse was a tall chestnut, fair as daylight, and his men swept down the hill behind him. She could not see the archers, but she saw a hail of arrows like rain sweeping from the low trees on either side of the gap. The first company of the other army leaped eagerly toward them, and a man on a white horse as tall as the chestnut and with red ribbons twisted into its long tail met the blue sword with one that gleamed gold . . .

. . . and Harry found herself back in the tent, her throat hoarse as if from shouting: standing up, with a pair of strong hands clamped on her shoulders; and she realized that without their support she would sag to her knees. The fierce shining of the swords was still in her eyes. She blinked and shook her head, and realized she was staring at the lamp; so she turned her head and looked up at Corlath, who was looking down at her with something—she noticed with a shock—like pity in his face. She could think of nothing to say; she shook her head again, as if to shake out of it all she had just seen; but it stayed where it was.

There was a silence, of a moment, or perhaps of half a year. She breathed once or twice; the air felt unnaturally harsh on her dry throat. She began to feel the pile of carpets pressing against her feet, and Corlath's hands slackened their grip. They stood, the two of them, king and captive, facing one another, and all the men at the table looked on.

"I am sorry," Corlath said at last. "I did not think it would take you with such strength."

She swallowed with some difficulty: the lovely wild flavor of the mad drink she had just tasted lingered in the corners of her mouth, and in the corners of her mind. "What is it?"

Corlath made some slight gesture—of denigration or of ignorance. "The drink—we call it Meeldtar—Seeing Water, or Water of Sight."

"Then—all that I saw—I really saw it. I didn't imagine it."

"Imagine it? Do you mean did you see what was true? I do not know. One learns, eventually, usually to know, to be able to say if

78 |

the seeings are to be believed or are . . . imagined. But imagined as you mean it—no. The Water sends these things, or brings them."

There was a pause again, but nobody relaxed, least of all herself. There was more to it than this, than a simple—*simple?*—hallucination. She looked at Corlath, frowning. "What else?" she said, as calmly as if she were asking her doom.

Corlath said, "There is something else," as if he were putting it off. He hesitated, and then spoke a few words in a language she did not recognize. It wasn't the usual Darian she heard the natives around the Residency speak, or the slightly more careful tongue that Dedham and Mr. Peterson used; nor did it sound like the differently accented tongue the Hillfolk spoke, which was still recognizable to those who were fluent in Darian. This was a rougher, more powerful language to listen to, although many of the sounds—strange to her Homelander ears—were common with the Darian she was accustomed to. She looked at Corlath, puzzled, as he spoke a little further. She knew nothing of this language.

"It is not familiar to you?" Corlath said at last; and when she shook her head, he said, "No, of course not, how could it be?" He turned around. "We might sit down again," and sat down with great deliberateness. She sat down too, waiting. The look she had seen before on his face, that of a man facing a problem he would far rather avoid, had returned, but it had changed. Now his look said that he understood what the problem was, and it was much more serious than he had suspected.

"There are two things," he said. "The Water of Sight does not work so on everyone. Most people it merely makes ill. To a few it gives headaches; headaches accompanied by strange colors and queer movements that make them dizzy. There are very few who see clearly—we nineteen, here tonight, all of us have drunk the Water of Sight many times. But even for us, most of us see only a brief abrupt picture—sometimes the scene lasts so little time it is hard to recognize. Often it is of something familiar: one's father, one's wife, one's horse. There is a quality to these pictures, or memories, that is like nothing else, like no voluntary memory you might call up yourself. But often that is all.

"Occasionally one of the people of our Hills sees more. I am one. You have just proven yourself another. I do not know why you saw what you did. You told us something of what you saw as you were seeing it. You may have seen a battle of the past—or one that never happened—or one that may yet happen; it may occur in Damar, or—in some other country."

She heard *may yet happen* as if those three words were the doom she had asked for; and she remembered the angry brilliance of the yellow-eyed Hill-king as he stood before the Residency far away. "But—" she said, troubled, hardly realizing she spoke aloud—"I am not even of your Hills. I was born and bred far away—at Home. I have been here only a few months. I know nothing of this place."

"Nothing?" said Corlath. "I said there were two things. I have told you the first. You told us what you saw as you saw it. But this is the second thing: you spoke in the Old Tongue, what we call the Language of the Gods, that none knows any more but kings and sorcerers, and those they wish to teach it to. The language I just spoke to you, that you did not recognize—I was repeating the words you had said yourself, a moment before."

CHAPTER SIX

S HE REMEMBERED little more of that day. She settled herself on a heap of cushions a little way from the long table while the king and his men talked; and if they spoke at all of her, she did not know it, but she did notice that none but Corlath ever allowed his eyes to rest on her. The feeling she had had earlier, before she had tasted the Water of Seeing, that the closeness among the king and his men in some way supported her, was gone; she felt lost and miserably alone, and she decided that when there were eighteen people pretending you didn't exist in a small enclosed area, it was worse than two people pretending you didn't exist outside under the sky. The shadows flickered strangely through the tent, and the voices seemed muffled. There was a ringing in her ears—a ringing not like the usual fear-feeling of one's blood hammering through one's body, but a real ringing like that of distant bells. She could almost discern the notes. Or were they human, the shifting tones of someone speaking, far away? The taste still on her tongue seemed to muffle her brain. And she was tired, so tired. . . .

When his Riders left, Corlath stood looking down at his captured prize. She had fallen asleep, and no wonder; she was smiling a little in her sleep, but it was a sad smile, and it made him unhappy. However much formal honor he showed her, seating her at his left hand, setting his household to serve her as they served him—he grimaced—he knew only too well that by stealing her from her people he had done a thing to be ashamed of, even if he had had no alternative—even if she and the *kelar* she bore were to do his beloved country some good he could not otherwise perform. Perhaps she could learn to see something of what made the Hills and their people so dear to him as a man, not as a king—? Perhaps her Gift would bind her to them. Perhaps she would hate them for her lost land and family. He sighed. Forloy's young wife had not wished to hate the Hills, but that had not helped her.

Harry woke in the dark. She did not know where she was; the shapes beneath her were not of pillow and mattress, and the odor of the air had nothing in common with Residency air, or Homeland air. For a moment hysteria bubbled up and she was conscious only of quelling it; she could not think, not even to decide why she wished to bottle up the panic—her pride automatically smothered her fear as best it could. Afterward she lay exhausted, and the knowledge of where she was reformed itself, and the smell was of the exotic woods of the carven boxes in the Hill-king's tent. But as she lay on her back and stared into the blackness, the tears began to leak out of her eyes and roll down her cheeks and wet her hair, and she was too tired to resist them. They came ever faster, till she turned over and buried her face in the scratchy cushions to hide the sobs she could not stop.

Corlath was a light sleeper. On the other side of the tent he opened his eyes and rolled up on one elbow and looked blindly toward the dark corner where his Outlander lay. Long after Harry had cried herself to sleep again, the Hill-king lay awake, facing the grief he had caused and could not comfort.

When Harry woke again, the golden tent flap had been lifted, and sunlight flashed across the thick heavy rugs to spill across her eyes and waken her. She sat up. She was still curled on and around a number of fat cushions; the back of the hand her cheek had lain against was printed with the embroidered pattern of the pillow beneath it. She yawned and stretched, gingerly pulling the knots of midnight fears out of her muscles. One of the men with a mark on his forehead approached her, knelt, and set a small table with pitcher and basin and towels and brushes before her.

She saw nothing of Corlath. The tent looked as it had when she had first entered it the day before; the low tables had been removed, and the peak lamp raised again.

When she had washed, she was brought a bowl of an unfamiliar cereal, hot and steaming like Homelander porridge, but of no grain she recognized. It was good, and she surprised herself by eating it all with good appetite. She laid down her spoon, and one of the men of the household approached again, bowed, and indicated that she should go out. She felt crumpled, in the same garments she had slept in; but she shook them out as best she could, observed that they didn't seem to wrinkle horribly as Homelander clothing would have done, raised her chin, and marched out—to be met by another man with a pair of boots for her, and a folding stool to sit on while she fumbled with the lacing. She felt a fool, let loose, however involuntarily, in a highly organized community which now wished to organize her too: like the grain of sand that gets into an oyster's shell. What if the grain doesn't want to become a pearl? Is it ever asked to climb out quietly and take up its old position as a bit of ocean floor?

Did she want to go back? What did she have to go back to?

But what was Dickie thinking of her absence? She had no more tears at present, but her eyelids were as stiff as shutters, and her throat hurt.

People were moving hastily across the open space before the king's tent; and as she watched, the outlying tents began to come down. They seemed to float down of their own accord; all was graceful and quiet. If anyone was doing any protracted cursing over the recalcitrance of inanimate objects, it was only under his breath. Her brother should see this. She smiled painfully.

She blinked, her eyes adjusting slowly to the bright sunlight. The sky overhead was a cloudless hard blue, a pale metallic blue. It was morning again; she'd slept almost a full day. To the left rose a little series of dunes, so gradually that she only recognized their height by the fact that her horizon, from where she stood, was the tops of them. Somewhere in that direction lay the General Mundy, the Residency, her brother—and farther, much farther, in that same direction, over desert and mountain, plain and sea, lay her Homeland. She felt the sand underfoot, nothing like the springy firm earth of Home, no more than the queer soft boots she wore were like her Homeland boots; and the strange loose weight of her robes pulled on her shoulders.

The king's tent was being dismantled in its turn. First the sides were rolled up and secured, and she saw with surprise that the rugs and lamps, chests and cushions, were already gone from inside; all that remained was the sand, curiously smoothed and hollowed from what it had borne. She wondered if they might have rolled her up like an extra bolster if she had not awakened; or if they would have packed up all around her, leaving her on a little island of cushions in a sea of empty sand. The corner posts and the tall central ones folded up on themselves somehow, and the roof sank to the ground with the same stateliness she had admired in the smaller tents. She counted ten of the household men rolling and folding and tying. They stooped as they worked, and the great tent in only minutes was ten neat white-and-black bundles, each a mere armful for one of the men. They walked to a line of horses who stood patiently as their high-framed saddles were piled with boxes and bundles such as those the king's tent made. She noticed how carefully each load was arranged, each separate piece secured and tested for balance before the next was settled. At the end all was checked for comfort, and the horse left with a pat on the nose or neck.

Horses were the commonest animals in the camp; there were many more horses than people. Even the pack horses were tall and elegant, but she could pick out the riding-horses, for they were the finest and proudest, and their coats shone like gems. There were also dogs: tall long-legged dogs with long narrow beautiful skulls and round dark eyes, and long silky fur to protect them from the sun. Some were haltered in pairs, and all were members of three or four separate groups. Sight-hounds, Harry thought. The groups roamed as freely as the untethered horses, yet showed no more inclination than they to wander from the camp. She noticed with interest that a few of the pack horses were tied in pairs, like the dogs, and reflected that perhaps it was a training method, a younger beast harnessed to an older, which could teach it manners.

There were cats too. But these were not the small domestic lap-sized variety; these were as lean and long-legged as the dogs. Their eyes were green or gold or silver, and their coats were mottled brown and amber and black. One animal looked almost spotted, black on brown, while the next looked almost striped, fawn-pale on black. Some wore collars, leather with silver or copper fittings, but no leashes, and each went its solitary way, ignoring any other cats, dogs, or horses that might cross its path. One came over to Harry where she stood; she held her breath and thought of tigers and leopards. It viewed her nonchalantly, then thrust its head under her hand. It was a moment before Harry recovered herself enough to realize that her hand was trembling because the cat was vibrating as it purred. She stroked it gingerly and the purr grew louder. The fur was short and fine and very thick; when she tried, delicately, to part it, she could not see the skin. The cat had very long blond eyelashes and it looked up at her through them, green eyes half closed. She wondered how all the animals got on together: were there ever any fights? And did the big cats ever steal one of the green-and-blue parrots that rode on a few of the Hillfolk's shoulders?

The tents were all down, and she was amazed at the numbers of beasts and people that were revealed. She wondered if the people were all men but herself, thinking of the attempt by the men of the household to wait on her at her bath the evening before. She could not tell, now, by looking, for everyone wore a robe similar to her own, and most wore hoods; and only a few wore beards.

"Lady," said a voice she knew, and she turned and saw Corlath, and Fireheart followed him.

"Another long ride?" she said, feeling a flush in her cheeks for being called *lady* by the Hill-king.

"Yes, another long ride, but we need not travel so quickly." She nodded, and a smile came and went on the king's face, so quickly that she did not see it, as he realized that she would not plead, nor ask questions. "You will need this," he said, and handed her a hood like the one he and most everyone else were wearing. She stood turning it over helplessly in her hands, for it was little more than a long tapered tube of soft material, and not too plainly meant as one thing or another to someone who had never seen one before. He took it away from her again and put it on her, then produced a scarf and showed her how to wrap it in place. "It grows easier with practice," he said. "Thank you," she said.

Another voice spoke behind them, and both turned; a man stood with another horse at his heels. This man was dressed in brown, and wore leggings and a tunic above his tall boots and bore a small white mark on his right cheek; and Corlath told her that so the men of the horse, the grooms, dressed; men of the hunt, who cared for the cats and dogs, were dressed similarly, but their belts were red, and they wore red scarves over their hoods and their white mark of office was on the left cheek.

"I—I thought all the Hillfolk wore sashes," Harry said hesitantly.

"No," Corlath answered readily enough; "only those who also may carry swords."

The brown-clad man turned to the horse he had brought them. "His name is Red Wind, Rolinin," Corlath said; he was another red bay, though not so bright as Fireheart. "For the present, you will ride him."

She speculated, a little nervously, about the *for the present*. She was pleased at the idea of not bumping on somebody else's saddlebow, but as she looked up at the tall horse, and he looked kindly down on her, she collected her courage and said, "I—I am accustomed to bit and bridle." She thought, I am accustomed to stirrups too, but I can probably cope without them—at least if nothing too exciting occurs. He looks like he'll have nice gaits. . . .Oh dear.

"Yes," said Corlath in his inscrutable voice, and Harry looked up at him in dismay. "Red Wind will teach you how we of the Hills ride."

She hesitated a minute longer, but couldn't think of anything further to say that wouldn't be too humiliating, like "I'm scared." So when the brown man went down on one knee and cupped his hands for her foot, she stepped up and was lifted gently into the saddle. No reins. She looked at her hands as if they should be somewhere else, rubbed them briefly down the legs, and then laid them across the rounded pommel like stunned rabbits brought home from a hunt. Red Wind's ears flicked back at her and his back shifted under her. She closed her legs delicately around his barrel and he waited, listening; she squeezed gently and he stepped gravely forward; she sat back and he stopped. Perhaps they would get along.

Corlath mounted while she was arranging her hands; I suppose they'll expect me to learn to mount without help too, she thought irascibly; when she looked up from Red Wind's obedient ears Fireheart moved off, and Red Wind willingly followed.

They traveled for some days. She meant to keep count, but she did not have the presence of mind immediately to find a bit of leather or rock to scratch the days on as they passed, and somewhere around four or five or six she lost count. The days of travel continued for some time after the four or five or six; every muscle in her body ached and protested from the unaccustomed exercise, after months of soft living at the Residency and aboard ship. She was grateful for her weariness, however, for it granted her heavy sleep without dreams. She developed saddlesores, and gritted her teeth and ignored them, and rather than getting worse as she had expected, they eased and then went away altogether, and with them the aches and pains. Her old skill in the saddle came back to her; she did not miss the stirrups except while mounting—she still needed someone to be a mounting-block for her every day—and slowly she learned to guide her patient horse without reins. She could bind her boots to her legs and her hood round her head as deftly—almost—as though she had been doing these things all her life. She learned to eat gracefully with her fingers. She met four women who were part of Corlath's traveling camp; they all four wore sashes.

She learned the name of the friendly cat: Narknon. She often found her keeping her feet warm when she woke up in the morning. Narknon also, for all her carnivorous heritage, had a taste for porridge.

Harry continued to eat at the king's table for the evening meal, with the eighteen Riders and Corlath; she still sat at the king's left hand, and she was still politely served and equably ignored. She began to understand, or at least to suspect, that Corlath kept her near him not only because the Hillfolk were not accustomed to dealing with enemy prisoners, but more because he was hoping to make her feel like a respected guest—he was quick to answer her questions, partly perhaps because she did not abuse the privilege; and there was often almost diffidence in his manner when he offered her something: a new cloak, or a piece of fruit of a sort she had never seen before. He wants me to *like* it here, she thought.

She still slept in the king's tent, but a corner was now modestly curtained off for her, and when she woke in the morning and put the curtains back, Corlath was already gone. One of the men of the household would see her, and bring her towels and water, and breakfast. She grew fond of the porridge; sometimes they made it into little flat cakes, and fried them, and put honey over them. The honey was made from flowers she had never seen nor smelled; the rich exotic fragrance of it set her dreaming.

She never asked Corlath why she was here, or what her future was to be.

In the mornings, after breakfast, while the camp was broken, or, if they were staying an extra day while messengers came from nowhere to talk to the king, she rode Red Wind and, as Corlath had told her, taught herself, or let the horse teach her, to ride as the Hillfolk rode. After her riding-lesson, if they were not traveling that day, she wandered through the camp, and watched the work going forward: everything was aired and washed or shaken out or combed, and the beasts were all brushed till they gleamed. No one, horse or dog or cat or human being, ever tried to stop the Outlander from wandering anywhere in particular, or watching anything in particular; occasionally she was even allowed to pick up a currycomb or polishing-cloth or rug-beater, but it was obvious that she was so permitted out of kindness, for her help was never needed. But she was grateful for the kindness. She spoke her few words of Hill-speech: *May I?* And *Thank you,* and the Hillfolk smiled at her and said, *Our privilege,* slowly and carefully, back to her. Sometimes she watched the hunts ride out; the dogs hunted in their groups, the cats alone or occasionally in pairs. There did not seem to be any order to those who rode with them, other than the presence of at least one man of the hunt; and she never saw any return without a kill: desert hares, or the small digging orobog—Corlath told her the names—or the great horned dundi that had to be hung on a pole and carried between two horses.

She was homesick in unexpected spasms so strong that Red Wind, who was a faithful old plug by Hill standards and could be trusted to children and idiots, would feel her freeze on his back, and toss his head uncomfortably and prance. She had not wept herself to sleep since her first night in the king's tent and she thought, carefully, rationally, that it was hard to say what exactly she was homesick for: the Homeland seemed long past, and she did not miss her months at the Residency in Istan. She recalled the faces of Sir Charles and Lady Amelia with a pang, and she missed her brother anxiously, and worried about what he must think about his lost sister. She found she also missed the wise patient understanding of Jack Dedham; but she thought of him with a strange sort of peacefulness, as if his feeling for his adopted country would transcend the seeming impossibility of what had happened to her, and he would know that she was well. That sickness of dislocation came to her most often when she was most at ease in the strange adventure she was living. She might be staring at the line of Hills before them, closer every day, watching how sharply the edges of them struck into the sky; Red Wind at Fireheart's heels, the desert wind brushing her cheek and the sun on her shoulders and hooded head; and suddenly she would be gasping with the thing she called homesickness. It would strike her as she sat at the king's table, cross-legged, eating her favorite cheese, sweet and brown and crumbly, listening wistfully to the conversation she still could not understand, beyond the occasional word or phrase.

I'm missing what I don't have, she thought late one night, squirming on her cushions. It's nothing to do with what I should be homesick for—Jack would understand, the oldest colonel still active, looking across the desert at the Hills. It's that I don't belong here. It doesn't matter that I'm getting burned as dark as they are, that I can sit a horse all day and not complain. It doesn't matter even that their Water of Sight works in me as it does in only a few of their own. It is only astonishing that it would work in one not of the Hills; it does not make that one any more of the Hills than she was before.

There was a certain bitter humor to lying awake wishing for something one cannot have, after lying awake not so long ago wishing for the opposite thing that one had just lost. Not a very useful sort of adaptability, this, she thought. But, her thought added despairingly, what kind of adaptability—or genius—*would* be useful to me? She traced her life back to her childhood, and for the first time in many years recalled the temper tantrums that she had grown out of so early it was hard to remember them clearly; but she did remember that they had frightened even her, dimly, still a baby in her crib, realizing there was something not quite right about them. They had scared two nursemaids into leaving; it had been her mother who had at last successfully coped, grimly, with her and them. That memory brought into focus another memory she also had pushed aside many years ago: the memory, or knowledge, of not-quite-rightness that grew up after the tantrums had passed; and with that knowledge had also grown an odd non-muscular kind of control. She had thought at the time, with a child's first wistfulness upon being faced with approaching adulthood, that this was a control that everyone learned; but now, lying in the desert dark, she was not so sure. There was something in her new, still inexplicable and unforeseeable life in the Hills that touched and tried to shape that old long-ignored sense of restraint; and something in her that eagerly reached out for the lesson, but could not—yet—quite grasp it or make use of it. There was, too, a reality to her new life that her old life had lacked, and she realized with a shock that she had never truly loved or hated, for she had never seen the world she had been used to living in closely enough for it to evoke passion in her. This world was already more vivid to her, exhilaratingly, terrifyingly more vivid, than the sweet green country, affectionately but indistinctly recalled, of her former life.

She did not have much appetite for breakfast the next morning, and fed hers to Narknon, who gave a pleased burp and went back to sleep again till the men of the household routed her out when they took down the king's tent. They were nearly to the foothills by the time they halted that evening. The scrub around them had begun to produce the occasional real leaf, and the occasional real leaf was green. For the first time, there was an open stream that ran past their camp, instead of the small secret desert springs; and Harry had a real bath in the big silver basin for the first time since her first evening with the camp, for there had been little water to spare since then. This time the men of the household left towels and a clean yellow robe for her, and left her, as soon as her bath was full.

They made camp behind a ridge that ran into what was certainly itself a hill. The tents were pitched around a clear space at the center, with the king's tent at one edge of it. That clear space always held a fire in the evenings, but tonight the fire was built up till it roared and flung itself taller than the height of a man; and as everyone's duties were completed, all came and sat around it till they ringed it. The dogs' pale coats turned red and cinnamon in the firelight; the cats' shadowy pelts were more mysterious than ever. The wall of the king's tent facing the fire was rolled up, and Harry and the king and his Riders sat at the open edge and stared at the fire with the rest.

After a time no more dark figures came to join the circle; the fire shadows fell and sidled and swam so that Harry could not guess how many people there were. The fire itself began to burn down till it was no more than the kind of glorious bonfire she and her brother had had now and again when they were children and the weather and their parents' mood had conspired together in their favor.

Then the singing began. There were several stringed instruments like lutes, and several wooden pipes for accompaniment and harmony. She recognized ballads even when she could not understand the words, and she wished again that she could understand, and fidgeted on her rug, and glanced at Corlath. He looked back at her, intercepting her frustration, and while there was nothing particularly encouraging about that look, still there was nothing particularly discouraging about it either—as was usual with the looks he gave her now; as was also usual, there was an edge of wistfulness, or sheepishness, in his glance. He had either lost or, as she thought more likely, learned to restrain the slightly resentful puzzlement she had seen the night she had drunk the Water of Sight. She stood up and went over to him and sat down beside him, and pulled up her knees and put her chin on them and stared at the fire, and listened to the words she could not understand. She knew that there had to be at least one more person in the camp who spoke Homelander, the man who had acted as Corlath's interpreter—and, as Peterson had guessed, unnecessarily—at the Residency: but she had never learned who that man was. Someone else who might have spoken to her, and taught her some more Hill words, that she might be able to talk to those around her— might be able to translate the words of the songs they were singing now. But someone who had chosen not to make himself known to her; someone who liked his skill so little that he felt no pity for her isolation: she, an Outlander, who did not belong to the desert and the Hills.

Corlath was watching her face as these thoughts went through her mind, and perhaps he read something of them there, for he said without prompting: "They sing of what is past, hundreds of years past, when the possession of *kelar* was so common it was hardly thought a Gift, any more than the length of your nose is a Gift.

"Those given the *kelar* are far fewer today than they were then.

I—we—believe that we are soon to learn at our gravest cost the worth of what we have lost."

He thought, wearily, looking at her and unable to read her expression, What does she see? What do we look like to her? And with a flash of anger he thought, Why is it so arranged that I must hope for the comprehension of an Outlander? Why must it be an *Outlander* who carries so precious a Gift? A Gift she may choose to repudiate or—or use against us, who need the strength so sorely?

Harry hugged her knees closer, and for a moment she saw again a bright narrow thread of riders trotting up a mountain way. So I have the Gift, she thought, but of what use is it to see uninterpretable visions? She came back to herself as Corlath said: "We sing because we have returned to our Hills; tonight is the first night we sleep again in their shadow.

"Listen. They will sing a ballad of Lady Aerin, Dragon-Killer."

Harry listened, listened hard, with the muscles of her back and of her thighs, as if the Hill-speech were a fractious horse she might tame; and out of the firelight came a figure, wavering with the leap and flicker of the flames, and with hair that was fire itself. A tall broad-shouldered figure with a pale face, and in its right hand it held a long slim blade that glittered blue. Harry stared till her eyes felt as dry as sand, and then the figure's face swam into focus, and it was a woman's face, and it smiled at her. But it didn't smile, it grinned, the wry affectionate grin of an elder sister; and Harry's head swam with love and despair. Then the woman shook her head gently, and her aureole of hair flamed and rippled about her, and she reached out her empty left hand, and Harry found herself on her hands and knees, reaching her hand back. But a gust of wind came from nowhere and whipped the fire as though it were an unruly dog, and the figure vanished. Harry fell where she had knelt, and pressed her face to the earth. One real dog sat up and howled.

Corlath picked her up as gently as if she were a baby, fallen down after its first steps; and she found there were tears running down her face. He stood up, holding her in his arms, and she cared nothing but that Lady Aerin, Firehair and Dragon-Killer, had come to her and then left her again, more alone than she had ever been before. She threw her arms around the Hill-king's neck and buried her face in his shoulder and sobbed. And Corlath, holding her, her tears on his neck, felt his resentment waver and dim and fall to ashes; and he felt pity instead for the Outlander, as he had felt pity when she tasted the Meeldtar. The Gift had been a hard enough thing for him, he who had grown up with it, had always known it existed and been trained from childhood in its use, or at least its acceptance. He had had his father to tell him what to expect, and his father had not scorned him when he wept as the Outlander now wept; had, in fact, cradled and comforted him and soothed the headaches the *kelar* brought. He would help this girl now, as much as he might, stranger and thief as he might be to her. He would do what he could.

Harry woke up the next morning in her usual corner, behind the usual curtains, her face still smudged with dirt and tears, and she remembered what she had done rather than what she had seen, and she went hot with shame and swallowed hard, wondering if she dared show herself outside her curtains, even for water to wash in. She could not think about seeing Corlath again at all. She thought, He must have laid the sleep on me again, as he did when he first took me away; put me to sleep like an unruly child because I behaved like an unruly child. Narknon didn't care; she walked up Harry's legs and rubbed her head against Harry's smudgy face, and Harry blinked hard and petted her fiercely.

She put back her curtains with an effort, and washed her face, and ate her breakfast as she might have eaten wood chips, silent and stony-faced. A voice broke in on her sorry reflections, and she looked up, surprised, and was still more surprised to see one of the Riders: the short square grim man she had noticed during her first meal in the king's tent: the one man who had tasted the Water and made no sign. He spoke to her again. Whatever the words were, they had the inflection of "Good morning," so she said, "Good morning." Some expression passed lightly over his face, and still he looked at her till she began to wonder if "Good morning" in their language sounded like a terrible insult and he was now considering whether to strike her dead on the spot or spare her ignorance. Maybe he was only musing on how best to handle an unruly child.

But he spoke to her again, slowly, patiently, and she was distracted from her shame of the night before. He broke his words down into syllables; so she took a deep breath and said them back to him. This time the flicker of expression was definitely kin to a smile, although she would never have seen it if she had not been watching his face so closely. He corrected her accent, and she said the phrase again, and this time apparently she said it properly; for next he bowed, laid a hand upon his chest, and said, "Mathin."

She said "Mathin" back at him, and she knew his name already from Corlath's speaking it and his answering. Then he stretched his hand out till the tips of his fingers did not quite touch her collarbone. "Harry," she said, thinking that the two-syllable version of her impossible name would keep them both out of trouble; and Richard wasn't there to disapprove. "Hari?" he said, a little taken aback; and she nodded, and made him a small bow.

It must have been a long day for Mathin. She knew he was one of the eighteen Riders, yet he did nothing till sunset but take her around the camp and touch various objects and speak their names. She also learned some useful all-purpose verbs, and the names—or at least she heard the names and tried to remember them—of about half of the men who sat around Corlath's table. She knew Faran and Innath already, for she had picked out their names from Corlath's calling of them, as she had Mathin's. They met her eyes as they were introduced, and quietly bowed, as if she had nothing to do with the awkward baggage their king had taken from the Outlander town in their company a few weeks ago; as if they were seeing her for the first time. Forloy was the man with the scar on his chin; Dapsim rode the black mare who won the horseraces often held in the evenings, till the other riders would no longer let her run.

She did not see Corlath that day, nor the next. The camp remained where it was, in the shadow of the Hills, though the evening fires were small again, and there was no more singing. The hunting-beasts went out every day, and returned laden with a far wider variety of wildlife than the desert had offered. Harry learned that Narknon hunted alone, and was famous for permitting no other beast near her; she occasionally made friends with a human being, but she was very choosy about such friendships. Harry felt flattered. As the days passed, lean faces and flanks grew a bit plumper on men and beasts; but Narknon still begged for her porridge.

Mathin came for Harry after breakfast each morning. By the end of the third day she was speaking in sentences, simple, painful, and ungrammatical ones; but she found that certain Hill words were creeping into her Homelander vocabulary and staying there; and the few people besides Mathin she tried to speak to stopped to listen to her and to answer. She was no longer invisible, and that was the best of all.

She was fascinated by the specialties of the language she was learning; there were, for example, a number of kinds of tent. The king's great tent, with its internal grove of poles to hold it up, was called a zotar, the only one in this traveling camp. The smaller tents, where most of the people were housed, were called the barkash; the stable tents were pituin. Then there were several terms she didn't have quite straightened out yet that referred to how the thing was made, how many corners it had, made of what material, and so on. A dalgut was a cheap, poorly made tent; there were no dalguti in the king's camp, and to refer to another man's tent as a dalgut, if it wasn't one, was a profound insult.

She woke up earlier than usual on the morning of the fourth day of Corlath's absence, and, despite Narknon's protests, went outside to stare at the eastern greyness that heralded the swift desert dawn. She heard the desert lark's song, a little speckled brown bird the Hillfolk called a britti. The camp was astir already; several of the men whose names she could recall hailed her as Hari-sol. She'd heard this the last two days and wondered if it was a term of respect, of definition, or a way of spinning out a name she could see did not meet with unqualified approval.

As the early light flowed down into the mountains, she saw the trees and rocky ridges pick themselves out of the shadows and assert their individuality. She didn't notice till they rode into the center of camp that Corlath and three companions had returned.

She turned around on her heel as she heard his voice, but her attention was distracted at once. Corlath still sat on Fireheart, who stood as still as a great red rock; and beside them stood another horse, riderless, as tall as Fireheart and a stallion like him, but golden, a chestnut as gold as the kicking flames of the bonfire three nights ago. She walked toward them silently, her bare feet in the still-cool sandy earth, but the chestnut horse turned his head and looked at her. She heard Corlath murmur something as she drew near, and at his words the horse took a step toward her, and lowered his head till she was looking into a calm, mahogany-brown eye. She raised her hands and cupped them, and she felt his warm breath, and his soft nose touched her fingers.

Corlath spoke aloud and a man of the horse appeared at once, carrying a saddle, golden leather only a few shades darker than the horse, with red stitching; and he set it delicately on the chestnut's back. The horse ignored him, not even shuddering his golden skin as the saddle settled into place; but he lipped Harry's fingers, and leaned his cheek against her shoulder.

"I brought him back for you," Corlath said, and she raised her eyes and found his resting on her; "I seem to have chosen well," he said, and he smiled.

The brown-clad man had girthed up the saddle and stood watching her expectantly. "Come, we will try his paces," said Corlath. It wasn't till she was tossed into the saddle and felt the great horse quiver under her as her legs found their places against the long supple flaps of the saddle that she realized that Corlath had spoken to her in the Hill tongue.

It was a glorious morning; more glorious than any she'd known since she had awakened as a disheveled huddle on the lee side of a scraggy little dune—more glorious than any since she'd set sail from the Homeland. "His name is Sungold," Corlath told her, and this he translated.

"Sungold," she said. "Tsornin."

Corlath sent Fireheart forward at a long-striding trot, as though they would leap into the dawn; and as soon as her legs closed against the big chestnut's sides he surged forward to follow. She was, for the first few minutes, fearful of her own lack of skill, and of the strength of the big horse; but she found that they understood each other. She felt half grateful, half ashamed, of the time and patience the good Red Wind had spent on her; and at the same time she felt almost uneasy that it was too simple, that she understood too readily. But she was too caught up in the beauty of it to wish to doubt it long. If she thought of it at all, she drove it out of her head at once: didn't she deserve something for all her bruises, of both body and spirit, over the last weeks? She could think of nothing better than the feel of Sungold's mane as it washed over her hands.

When the sun was almost overhead, and its rays were dazzling when they reflected off Tsornin's bright neck, and the emptiness of her stomach was beginning to force itself into her attention despite everything, Corlath said, "Enough," and wheeled Fireheart back toward camp. Sungold waited for her signal, and she stood a moment, first looking at Fireheart's quarters jogging away from them and then up, where a brown hawk swung on an updraft, high overhead. Just to test the magnificence of her power, she kneed her horse a half-turn to the left and shot him off at a gallop; and just as he reached the peak of his speed she brought him back to a gentle canter, circled once, and sent him after Corlath, who had paused and was watching her antics. They stopped beside Fireheart and his rider, and the two stallions nodded to each other. Harry expected a lecture on frivolity, or something, and lowered her eyes to Sungold's withers; but Corlath said nothing. She looked up again as she heard the ring of metal on metal; Corlath had drawn the sword that hung at his side.

She watched, surprised, as he held it, point up, and the sun glared fiercely on it. She remembered that this morning, as he rode into camp, he had been carrying it, the first time she had ever seen him armed with anything more ostentatiously threatening than a long dagger, or the slim short knives all the Hillfolk carried to cut up their food and perform any minor tasks where something with a sharp point was necessary. She'd forgotten about it as soon as she'd noticed Sungold; and now that she saw it more closely she decided she didn't much like the look of it. This was obviously a war-sword; it was much too unwieldy for anything but serious hacking and hewing.

Corlath took the deadly thing in his left hand and handed it to her, hilt first. "Take it." She grasped it, warily, and when Corlath let go it did not knock her out of the saddle, but it tried. "Lift it," he said. And as she tried, "You've never held a sword."

"No." She lifted it as if it were a snake that would crawl up its own tail and bite her. Corlath edged Isfahel out of harm's way as her arm and shoulder experimented with this new thing. She swung it in a short half-arc, and Tsornin came suddenly to life, and bounced forward on his hind legs, neighing. "Ouch," she said, as he came to earth again; his ears were tipped back toward her, and all his muscles were tense.

"Sungold's a war-horse," Corlath said mildly. "You're giving him ideas."

She turned to glower at him, and he rode up beside her and took the sword back. There was a gleam of humor in his eye as he returned her glower; and they turned back toward camp together. He said something that she didn't quite catch, and as she turned to him to ask him to repeat it, Fireheart leaped forward into a gallop that flattened out to full stretch at once. After a moment's shock she recognized the challenge, and Sungold bolted after them, and gained ground till her face was flicked by Fireheart's streaming tail, and then Sungold's nose drew even with Corlath's toe; and then they were sweeping into the camp, and the horses steadied down to a canter, and then a walk. Their nostrils showed red as they breathed, and Sungold turned away from the camp, asking for more; but Harry said, "I don't think so," and Sungold heaved a sigh and followed docilely at Fireheart's heels. It was only when she dismounted that she realized she was still barefoot.

Corlath and Harry had breakfast together, on one square of the long table. Harry did not speak, except to Narknon, who was inclined to be sulky; and Corlath's attention was for the men who came to speak with him, about the minor things that had gone wrong in his absence, and about messages they had received for him; and Harry understood much of what they said, and wondered if Corlath cared that it was no longer entirely safe to talk secrets around his Outlander. After they had eaten, a man of the household entered the zotar and handed the king a long thin bundle wrapped in linen. He bowed and retired; and Corlath shook the thing free of its covering and held up another sword. This one was appreciably smaller than the one he himself wore, but Harry still watched it with dislike. Corlath ran a quick hand over the scabbard with the linen cloth and then offered her, again, the hilt. She took it reluctantly, and rather than drawing it smoothly out, she backed up awkwardly, so that it rang free with a sullen *clunk*.

"You'll have to do better than that," said Corlath; and she was sure that he was amused.

"Why?" she said, anger beginning to uncoil itself somewhere deep inside her and make its way to the surface. "Why? What have swords and—" she gulped, for she loved Sungold already— "war-horses to do with me?"

He came a step or two closer to her as she stood with the point of the sword unhandily dug into the heaped carpets, and her arm out, as if to keep the undesired object as far from her as she could; and he looked, thoughtfully, into her eyes.

"It is because of what you have seen," he replied. "When you tasted the Water of Sight you saw a war-party coming to battle; I and all my Riders heard you cry out what you saw—in the ancient tongue of our forebears here, the tongue that was spoken when Damar was one land, a great and green land, before . . ."

Before my people came, she thought, but she was not going to say it aloud if he was not.

"And several days past the entire camp saw the Lady Aerin

come out of the fire to greet you, carrying the Blue Sword, Gonturan, with which she won back the Hero's Crown and defeated the armies of the North." He hesitated. "Aerin had not been seen since my father's father's day; and yet she has always looked after her country well, since she first rode out to face the Black Dragon, before Gonturan had come to her hand; and our dearest legends speak of her."

The bright bubbles of anger in her eyes burst and disappeared. She bowed her head; then bent her elbow and brought the sword under her eyes. The long wicked edge of it winked at her. It had a silver handle, nearly plain, with a few faint graceful scrolls on the underpart of the hand-guard, where it met the hilt. She stared at them unhappily: the sweep and arch of them seemed to her a more likely ornament for a church pew than a sword. Her wrist began to quiver with the unaccustomed weight.

He said, as gently as he could: "Here, anyone who is granted the Gift of Seeing is given to what they see; it is thought to be a guide, a direction, a help sent by the gods; or by the heroes of our past greatness, who still care what happens to their children's children. Children now sip the Water when they meet their tenth birthday, in the hope that they may be told what apprenticeship they are most fit for. Many see nothing, for, as I have told you, the Water does not work for many people; and then the simpler considerations of parentage and availability are allowed to decide. But all our priests were given Sight of the priesthood on their tenth birthday; each of my Riders saw himself carrying a sword . . . many of them will only choose a war-horse the color they saw themselves riding in the vision."

She broke out frantically: "But this is nothing to do with me. I am an Outlander, not of your Hills at all. If it is war I have seen, my people have feared war too; it is not strange that even I should feel it. This thing you have done to me, I—" She choked off, for she had heard herself speaking: *Outlander* she had instinctively said, and she was speaking swiftly in the Hill tongue that she had only—or so she had thought and now desperately was not sure— begun to learn, haltingly, a few days before. She heaved a breath that had she been a year younger might have been a sob; but it was not. She stood, trembling, holding the sword, waiting for it to speak to her too, to tell her her awful destiny.

Corlath took her right wrist in his hand and then turned her around till she was standing next to him; he rearranged her fingers on the hilt, curled her thumb under it for her. She felt at once, wearily, that this was the way it was supposed to be held; and wondered if swordsmanship, like riding a war-stallion and speaking a language strange to her, was suddenly going to awaken in her blood like a disease.

"Lady," Corlath said over her shoulder, his right hand still supporting her wrist, "I know it is difficult for you. Perhaps this may make it easier: you have given my people hope by your presence, by your visions, by your very foreignness. It is the first hope we have had since we knew that the Northerners would come. We need that hope, my lady. It is so nearly the only thing we have."

She pulled away from his hand on her arm so that she could turn and look up at him. She stared, appalled, and he looked gently down at her. A frown collected slowly on his brow. "What is it they call you—Hari? That cannot be your name."

She grimaced. "No. it's a—" She did not know the Hill term for nickname and her mysterious sixth sense didn't seem to want to provide it for her. "It's a short-name. I don't like my real name."

"And it is?"

There was a pause. "Angharad," she said finally.

He turned this over on his tongue a few times. "We will call you Harimad," he said. "Harimad-sol, for you are of high rank. Few See so clearly that others too may see, as all saw Aerin-sol come out of the fire.

"Try to have faith: even in these things that are strange to you. My *kelar* told me to bring you here, and your *kelar* speaks through you now. Lady, I know no more of your fate than that; but I believe, as do all the people in this camp, that your fate is important to us. And Aerin, who has long been the friend of her people, has given you her protection."

That does not make Aerin *my* friend, she thought sourly, but when she remembered the elder-sister grin Aerin had given her, she could not believe ill of her. And Corlath's *kelar* told him to bring me here. Oh dear. I suppose that explains something. Harimad. Mad Harry. I wish Aerin would stay long enough to talk to me—tell me what is going on. She looked up at him and tried to smile. It was a gallant effort; it was even almost a smile. But Corlath's gold-flecked brown eyes saw more than just the gallantry, and his heart went out to her; and he turned away from her and clapped his hands, and a man of the household brought the hot brown drink Harry had first tasted behind a scrubby small sand hill, barefoot and in her Homelander dressing-gown, and that she had learned since to call malak.

That evening Corlath and the Riders and Harimad-sol ate a great dinner of many dishes, and Harry made first acquaintance with the Hill mustard made of the jictal seeds, which burned out not only her mouth and tongue, but her throat and stomach lining; and the front of the zotar was rolled up, and outside much of the rest of the camp sat on rugs before small low tables and ate also, under the moon and the white stars. Harry began pulling nervously at her sleeves and twiddling the ends of her belt as the end of the meal approached; there was a tension hanging over the camp that she did not like, and she hoped that the tooled leather bag was not to put in an appearance tonight. It did not, but she suspected Corlath of eyeing her nervousness wryly.

The conversation went too quickly for her to catch all of it—or perhaps her sixth sense had overstrained itself and was resting— but she understood that the purpose of the journey they had been on was to discover how well, or ill, prepared the many small mountain villages, north, south, and east of the great central desert, were for holding off Northerners; and how many horses, arms and warriors, supplies and supply transport, each could provide. It had not been a very cheerful journey, not least for the western excursion into Outlander territory, where a stubborn and pompous old man had refused to listen to the truth; but Corlath had expected what he found and—she thought—saw no use in being discouraged. They were near the end of their trek now: in the Hills before them, although still several days' journey hence, was Corlath's city, where his palace lay, and where what there was of a standing army was quartered. Harry rather thought, from the way they referred to it, that "the City" was the only city in Corlath's realm; his people were not much interested in building and maintaining and living in cities, beyond the king's own, which had the advantage of being thick with *kelar*. But the Hillfolk were an independent lot; they preferred to hold their own bits of land and work them, and neither cities nor positions in a regular army appealed to them.

As she heard the word often, Harry was beginning to understand better what the word *kelar* indicated. It was something like magic; a Gift was the specific manifestation of *kelar* in a particular human being. *Kelar* was also something like a charm or a sorcery that hung in the air in a few places in the Hills; and one of those places was the City, where certain things might happen and other things be forbidden to happen, in ways quite unlike the usual physical laws. When all else was lost, the Hillfolk could retreat to the City; if the Northerners took or laid waste to all else, a few might live still in the City, for in it was some of the strength of the Damar of old.

She began to speculate about the City, to look forward to seeing it. Around her the Riders and their king spoke of repairs to be made, and new forging to be done, and the best blacksmiths— dhogos—and leatherworkers—parisi—in the Hills. Narknon had her front half in Harry's lap, and was purring to rattle the bones of them both.

It was very late. The Riders stared at their empty cups, the men outside stared at the stars; Harry was falling asleep, still listening to the hum in the air, and still unable to account for it.

"Mathin," said Corlath, and Harry twitched and woke up. Mathin looked up the table, and his eyes rested briefly on the golden-haired girl in the maroon robe before he looked at his king. "The laprun trials will be held six weeks from tomorrow on the plains before the City." Mathin knew this perfectly well, but out of the corner of his eye he saw the girl look up at Corlath, puzzled, and then glance down the table at her patient language teacher. "Harimad-sol will ride in them."

Mathin nodded; he had expected this, and, having taken some measure of Hari in the days past, was not displeased. Harimad-sol herself swallowed rather sharply, but found she wasn't too surprised either; and after a day of war-horses and swords could guess the sort of thing the trials (what was a laprun?) would prove to be. Poor Mathin. She wondered what he thought of the idea— six weeks to knock the rawest of beginners, even if *kelar*-guided, into shape—and resigned herself to not knowing.

"We will ride out two hours before dawn tomorrow," said Mathin.

Six weeks, thought Harry. How much can you learn in six weeks, even if Aerin is keeping an eye on you?

CHAPTER SEVEN

SHE WOKE AT ONCE when the man of the household pushed the curtains back from her sleeping-place and set a candle on the low bronze-top table beside her pillows. She stood up, stretched, creaked, sighed; and then changed quickly into her riding clothes and gulped the malak set beside the candle. Narknon protested all this activity with a sleepy grumble; then rewove herself into the tousled blankets and went back to sleep. Harry went outside and found Mathin's dark bay and her own Sungold there already. Tsornin turned his head and sighed at her. "I couldn't agree more," she whispered to him, and he took the shoulder of her robe gently in his teeth. Mathin appeared out of the darkness and a pack horse followed him.

He nodded at her, and they mounted and rode toward the Hills that reared up so close to the camp, although she could not see them now. As the sky paled she found that they had already climbed into the lower undulations of those Hills, and the camp they had left was lost to view. The horses' hooves made a sterner *thunk* now as they struck the earth of the Hills. She breathed in and smelled trees, and her heart rose up, despite her fears, to greet the adventure she rode into.

They rode all that day, pausing only to eat and pull the saddles off the horses for a few minutes and rub their backs dry. Harry had to find a rock to crawl up on before she could get back on her horse, far from the conveniences of brown-clad men who knelt and offered her their cupped hands, and Sungold obviously thought this ritual of his rider calling him over to her as she perched atop some rock pile before she mounted him very curious. Mathin said, "This is the first thing I will teach you. Watch." He put a hand at each edge of the saddle, and flung himself up and into it, moving his right hand, on the back of the saddle, gracefully out of his way as soon as he had made the initial spring.

"I can't *do* that," said Harry.

"You will," said Mathin. "Try."

Harry tried. She tried several times, till Sungold's ears lay flat back and his tail clamped between his hind legs; then Mathin let her find a small rock that raised her only a few inches, and made her try again. Sungold was reluctant to be called to her and put through the whole uncomfortable process again; but he did come, and braced his feet, and Harry did get into the saddle.

"Soon you will be able to do this from the ground," said Mathin.

And this is only the beginning, Harry thought miserably. Her wrists and shoulders ached. Sungold held no grudges, at least; as soon as she was on him again his ears came up and he took a few little dance steps.

They rode always uphill, till Harry's legs were sore from holding herself forward in the saddle against the downward pull. Mathin did not speak, except to force her to practice the saddle-vaults at each halt; and she was content with silence. The country they were crossing was full of new things for her, and she looked at them all closely: the red-veined grey rock that thrust up beneath the patches of turf; the colors of the grass, from a pale yellow-green to a dark green that was almost purple, and the shape of the blades: the near-purple grass, if grass it was, had broad roots and narrow rounded tips; but the pack horse snatched at it like grass. The riding-horses were much too well mannered to do anything but eye it, even after so many days of the dry desert fare. Little pink-and-white flowers, like Lady Amelia's pimchie but with more petals, burst out of rocky crevasses; and little stripy brown birds like sparrows chirped and hopped and whisked over the horses' heads.

Mathin turned in his saddle occasionally to look at her, and his old heart warmed at the sight of her, looking around her with open pleasure in her new world. He thought that Corlath's *kelar* had not told him so ill a thing as he had first thought when Corlath told his Riders his plan to go back to the Outlander station to steal a girl.

They camped at the high narrow end of a small cup of valley; Mathin, Harry thought, knew the place from before. There was a spring welling from the ground where they set the tents, two tiny ones called tari, so low that Harry went into hers on her hands and knees. At the lower, wider end of the valley the spring flattened out and became a pool. The horses were rubbed down thoroughly and fed some grain, and freed.

Mathin said, "Sometimes it is necessary, away from home and in a small camp, to tether our horses, for horses are more content in a herd; but Sungold is your horse now and will not leave you, and Windrider and I have been together for many years. And Viki, the pack horse, will stay with his friends; for even a small herd is better than solitude."

Mathin made dinner after the horses were tended, but Harry lingered, brushing Sungold's mane and tail long after anything resembling a tangle still existed. For all her weariness, she was glad to care for her horse herself, glad that there was no brown man of the horse to take that pleasure away from her. Perhaps she would even learn to jump into the saddle like Mathin. After a time she left her horse in peace and, having nothing better to do, hesitantly approached Windrider with her brush. The mare raised her head in mild surprise when Harry began on the long mane over her withers, as she didn't need the attention any more than Sungold had, but she did not object. When Mathin held out a loaded plate in her direction, however, Harry dropped the brush and came at once. She ate what Mathin gave her, and was asleep as soon as she lay down.

She woke in the night as an unexpected but familiar weight settled on her feet. Narknon raised her head and began her heavy purr when Harry stirred. "What are you doing here?" said Harry. "You weren't invited, and there is someone in Corlath's camp who

will not be at all pleased at your absence when the hunts ride out."
Narknon, still purring, made her boneless feline way up the length
of Harry's leg, and reached out her big hunter's head, opened her
mouth so that the gleaming finger-length fangs showed, and bit
Harry, very gently, on the chin. The purr, at this distance, made
Harry's brain clatter inside her skull, and the delicate prickle of
the teeth made her eyes water.

Mathin sat up when he heard Harry's voice. Narknon's tail
stretched out from the open end of the tent, the tip of it curling up
and down tranquilly. Harry, in disbelief, heard Mathin laugh: she
hadn't known Mathin could laugh.

"They will guess where she has gone, Harimad-sol. Do not trouble yourself. The nights are cold and will grow colder here; you
may be grateful for your bedmate before we leave this place. It is a
pity that neither of us has the skill to hunt her; she could be useful. Go to sleep. You will find tomorrow a very long day."

Harry lay down, smiling in the dark, at Mathin's courtesy: "Neither of us has the skill to hunt her." The thought of her lessons
with this man—particularly now that she knew he could laugh—
seemed a trifle less ominous. She fell asleep with a lighter heart;
and Narknon, emboldened by the informality of the little campsite
and the tiny tent, stretched to her full length beside her preferred
person and slept with her head under Harry's chin.

Harry woke at dawn, as though it were inevitable that she
awake just then. The idea of rolling out so soon did not appeal to
her in the least, rationally, but her body was on its feet and her
muscles flexing themselves before she could protest. The entire
six weeks she spent in that valley were much in that tone: there
was something that in some fashion took her over, or seized the
part of her she always had thought of as most individually hers.
She did not think, she acted; and her arms and legs did things her
mind only vaguely understood. It was a very queer experience for
her, for she was accustomed to thinking exhaustively about everything. She was fascinated by her own agility; but at the same time
it refused to seem quite hers. Lady Aerin was guiding her, perhaps; for Harry wasn't guiding herself.

Mathin was also, she found out, spiking their food with something. He had a small packet, full of smaller packets, rolled in with the cooking-gear. Most of these packets were harmless herbs and spices; Harry recognized a few by taste, if not by name. The ones new to her since her first taste of Hill cooking she asked about, as Mathin rubbed them between his fingers before dropping them into the stew, and their odor rose up and filled her eyes and nostrils. She had begun asking as many questions about as many things as she could, as her wariness of Mathin as a forbidding stranger wore off and affection for him as an excellent if occasionally overbearing teacher took its place. And she learned that he was in a more mellow mood when he was cooking than at almost any other time.

"Derth," he might answer, when she asked about the tiny heap of green powder in his palm; "it grows on a low bush, and the leaves have four lobes," or "Nimbing: it is the crushed dried berries of the plant that gives it its name." But there was also a grey dust with a heavy indescribable smell; and when she asked about it, Mathin would look his most inscrutable and send her off to clean spotless tack or fetch unneeded water. The fourth or fifth time he did this she said flatly, "No. What is that stuff? My tack is wearing thin with cleanliness, Sungold and Windrider haven't a hair out of place, the tents are secure against anything but avalanche, and you won't use any more water. What is that stuff?"

Mathin wiped his hands carefully and rolled the little packages all together again. "It is called sorgunal. It . . . makes one more alert."

Harry considered this. "You mean it's a—" Her Hill speech deserted her, and she used the Homelander word: "drug."

"I do not know *drug,*" said Mathin calmly. "It is a stimulant, yes; it is dangerous, yes; but—" here the almost invisible glint of humor Harry had learned to detect in her mentor's square face lit a tiny flame behind his eyes—"I do know what I am doing. I am your teacher, and I tell you to eat and be still."

Harry accepted her plateful and was not noticeably slower than usual in beginning to work her way through it. "How long," she said between mouthfuls, "can one use this . . . stimulant?"

"Many weeks," said Mathin, "but after the trials you will want much sleep. You will have time for it then."

The fact that neither Harry nor Mathin could hunt Narknon did not distress Narknon at all. Every day when lessons were through, and Harry and Mathin and the horses returned to the campsite, tired and dirty and at least in Harry's case sore, Narknon would be there, stretched out before the fire pit, with the day's offering—a hare, or two or three fleeks which looked like pheasant but tasted like duck, or even a small deer. In return Narknon had Harry's porridge in the mornings. "I did not bring enough to feed three for six weeks," Mathin said the third morning when Harry set her two-thirds-full bowl down for Narknon to finish. "I'd rather eat leftover fleek," said Harry, and did.

Harry learned to handle her sword, and then to carry the light round shield the Hillfolk used; then to be resigned, if not entirely comfortable, in the short chain-stiffened leather vest and leggings Mathin produced for her. As long as there was daylight she was put, or driven, through her steadily—alarmingly—improving paces: it was indeed, she thought, as if something had awakened in her blood; but she no longer thought of it, or told herself she did not think of it, as a disease. But she could not avoid noticing the sensation—not of lessons learned for the first time, but like old skills set aside and now, in need, picked up again. She never learned to love her sword, to cherish it as the heroes of her childhood's novels had cherished theirs; but she learned to understand it. She also learned to vault into the saddle, and Sungold no longer put his ears back when she did it.

In the evenings, by firelight, Mathin taught her to sew. He showed her how to adapt the golden saddle till it fit her exactly; how to arrange the hooks and straps so that bundles would ride perfectly, her sword would come easily to her hand, and her helm would not bang against her knee when she was not wearing it.

As she grew quicker and cleverer at her lessons, Mathin led her over more of the Hills around their camp in the small valley. She learned to cope, first on foot and then on horseback, with the widest variety of terrain available: flat rock, crumbling shale, and small sliding avalanches of pebbles and sand; grass and scree and even forest, where one had to worry about the indifferent blows of branches as well as the specific blows of one's opponent. She and Mathin descended to the desert again briefly, and dodged about each other there. That was at the end of the fourth week. From the trees and stones and the running stream, she recognized where the king's camp had stood, but its human visitors were long gone. And it was there on the grey sand with Tsornin leaping and swerving under her that an odd thing happened.

Mathin always pressed her as hard as she could defend herself; he was so steady and methodical about it that at first she had not realized she was improving. His voice was always calm, loud enough for her to hear easily even when they were bashing at each other, but no louder; and she found herself responding calmly, as if warfare were a new parlor game. She knew he was a fine horseman and swordsman, and that no one was a Rider who was not magnificently skillful at both; and that he was training her. Most of the time, these weeks, she felt confused; when her mind was clearer, she felt honored if rueful; but now, wheeling and parrying and being allowed the occasional thrust or heavy flat blow, she found that she was growing angry. This anger rose in her slowly at first, faintly, and then with a roar; and she was, despite it or around it, as puzzled by it as by everything else that had happened to her since her involuntary departure from the Residency. It felt like anger, red anger, and it felt dangerous, and it was far worse than anything she was used to. It seemed to have nothing to do with losing her temper, with being specifically upset about anything; she didn't understand its origin or its purpose, and even as her temples hurt with it she felt disassociated from it. But her breath came a little quicker and then her arm was a little quicker; and she felt Tsornin's delight in her speed, and she spared a moment, even with the din in her ears rising to a terrible headache, to observe wryly that Sungold was a first-class horse with a far from first-class rider.

Mathin's usual set grin of concentration and, she had thought recently, pride flickered a bit at her flash of attack; and he lifted his eyes briefly to her face, and even as sword met sword he . . . faltered.

Without thinking, for this was what she was training for, she pressed forward; and Windrider stumbled, and Sungold slammed into her, shoulder to shoulder, and her blade hit Mathin's hilt to hilt, and to her own horror, she gave a heave and dumped him out of the saddle. His shield clanged on a rock and flipped front down, so it teetered foolishly like a dropped plate.

The horses lurched apart and she gazed down, appalled, at Mathin sitting in a cloud of dust, looking as surprised as she felt. The grin had disappeared for a moment—quite understandably, she thought—but by the time he had gotten to his feet and she had slid down from Sungold's back and anxiously approached him, it had returned. She tried a wavering smile back at him, standing clumsily with her sword twisted behind her as if she'd rather not be reminded of its presence; and Mathin switched his dusty sword from his right hand to his left and came to her and seized her shoulder. He was half a head shorter than she was, and had to look up into her eyes. His grip was so hard that her mail pinched her shoulder, but she did not notice, for Mathin said to her: "My honor is yours, lady, to do with what you will. I have not been given a fall such as that in ten years, and that was by Corlath himself. I'm proud to have had the teaching of you—and, lady, I am not the least of the Riders."

The anger had left her completely, and she felt dry and cold and empty, but then as her eyes unwillingly met Mathin's she saw a sparkle of friendship there, not merely the objective satisfaction of a teacher with a prize pupil: and this warmed her more kindly than the anger had done. For here in the Hills, she, an Outlander woman, had a friend: and he was not the least of the Riders.

Lessons continued after that, but they were faster and more

| 113

furious, and the light in Mathin's face never faded, but it had changed from the sturdy concentration of a teacher to the eager enthusiasm of a man who has found a challenge. The heat and strength they expended required now that they stop to rest at midday, when the sun was at its height, even though the Hills were much cooler than the central desert had been. Tsornin would never admit to being tired, and watched Harry closely at all times, in case he might miss something. He took her lessons afoot very badly, and would lace back his ears and stamp, and circle her and Mathin till they had to yell at him to go away. But during the last ten days he was content to stand in the shade, head down and one hind leg slack, at noontime, while she stretched out beside him.

One day she said, "Mathin, will you not tell me something of how the horses are trained?" They were having their noon halt, and Sungold was snuffling over her, for she often fed him interesting bits of her lunch.

"My family raises horses," said Mathin. He was lying on his back, with his hands crossed on his chest, and his eyes were shut. For several breaths he said nothing further, and Harry wanted to shout with impatience, but she had learned that such behavior would shut Mathin up for good, while if she bit her tongue and sat still, hugging her irritability quietly, he would sometimes tell her more.

He told her more this time: how his father and three older brothers bred and raised and trained some of Damar's finest riding-horses. "When I was your age," he said bleakly, "the best horses were taught the movements of war for the fineness of control necessary in both horse and rider; not for the likelihood that they should ever see battle.

"My father trained Fireheart. He is very old now, and trains no more horses, but he still carries all our bloodlines in his head, and decides which stallions should be bred to which mares." He paused, and Harry thought that was all; but he added slowly, "My daughter trained Sungold."

There was a long silence. Then Harry asked: "Why did you not stay and train horses too?"

Mathin opened his eyes. "It seemed to me that a father, three brothers and their families, a wife, daughter, and two sons were enough of one family to be doing the same thing. I have trained many horses. I go home . . . sometimes, so that my wife does not forget my face; but I have always wished to wander. As a Rider, one wanders. . . . It is also possible that I was not quite good enough. None of the rest of my family has ever wished to leave what they do, even for a day. I am the only one of us for generations who has ridden to the laprun trials to win my sword."

Harry said, "Why is it that you are my teacher? Were you— Did Corlath order you?"

Mathin closed his eyes again and smiled. "No. On the day after you drank Meeldtar and saw the battle in the mountains, I spoke to Corlath, for I knew by your Seeing that you would be trained for battle. It might have been Forloy, who is the only one of us who speaks your Outlander tongue, or Innath, who is the best horseman of us; but I am older, and more patient perhaps—and I trained the young Corlath, once, when I was Rider to his father."

Forloy, thought Harry. Then it was Forloy. "Mathin—" she began, and her voice was unhappy. She was staring at the ground, plucking bits of purple grass and shredding them, and did not notice that Mathin turned to look at her when he heard the unhappiness. She had not sounded so for weeks now, and he was pleased that this should be so.

"Why—why did Forloy never speak to me, before I—before you began to teach me to speak your tongue? Does he hate Outlanders so much? Why does he know the—my—language at all?"

Mathin was silent as he considered what he could tell his new friend without betraying his old. "Do not judge Forloy—or yourself—too harshly. When he was your age, and before he was a Rider, Forloy fell in love with a woman he met at the spring Fair in Ihistan. She had been born and raised in the south, and gone into service to an Outlander family there; and when they were sent to Ihistan, she went with them. The second year, the next Fair, he returned, and she agreed to go to the Hills with him. She loved Forloy, I think; she tried to love his land for his sake, but she could not. She taught him Outlander speech, that she might remember her life there by saying the words. She would not leave him, for she had pledged herself to live in the Hills with him; but she died after only a few years. Forloy remembers her language for her sake, but it does not make him love it." He paused, watching her fingers; they relaxed, and the purple stems dropped to the earth. "I do not believe he had spoken any words of it for many years; and Corlath would not have asked it of him for any less cause."

Corlath, Harry thought. He knows the story—of the young foreign woman who did not thrive when she was transplanted to Hill soil. And she was Darian born and bred, and went willingly. "And Corlath? Why does Corlath speak Outlander?"

Mathin said thoughtfully, "Corlath believes in knowing his . . . rivals. Or enemies. He can speak the Northern tongue as well, and read and write it, and Outlander, as well as our Hill tongue. There are few enough of us who can read and write our own language. I am not one of them. I would not wish to be a king."

There were only a few days left to run till the laprun trials. Mathin, between their more active lessons, taught her more of the Hill-speech; and each word he taught her seemed to awaken five more from where they slept in the back of a mind that was now, she had decided, sharing brain space and nerve endings with her own. She accepted it; it was useful; it permitted her to live in this land that she loved, even if she loved without reason; and she began to think it would enable her in her turn to be useful to this land. And it had won her a friend. She could not take pride in it, for it was not hers; but she was grateful to it, and hoped, if it were *kelar* or Aerin-sol's touch, that she might be permitted to keep it till she had won her right to stay.

With the language lessons Mathin told her of the Hills they were in, and where the City lay from where their little valley sat; and he told her which wood burned best green, and how to find water when there seemed to be none; and how to get the last miles out of a foundered horse. And her lessons of war had strengthened her memory, or her ability to draw upon that other memory, for she remembered what he told her. And to her surprise, he also told

116 |

her the names of all the wildflowers she saw, and which herbs could be made into teas and jams; and these things he spoke of with the mild expression on his face that she had seen only when he was bending over his cooking-fire; and even these things she learned. He also told her what leaves were best for stopping blood flowing, and three ways of starting a fire in the wilderness.

He looked at her sidelong as he spoke about fire-making. "There's a fourth way, Hari," he said. "Corlath may teach it to you someday." There was some joke here that amused him. "Myself, I cannot."

Harry looked at him, as patiently as she could. She knew that to question him when he baited her like this would do her no good. Once, a day or two after Mathin's unexpected fall, she had let a bit more of her frustration show than she meant to, and Mathin had said, "Hari, my friend, there are many things I cannot tell you. Some I will tell you in time; some, others will tell you; some you may never know, or you may be the first to find their answers."

She had looked across their small fire at him, and over Narknon's head. They were both sitting cross-legged while the horses grazed comfortably not far away, so that the sound of their jaws could be heard despite the crackling fire. Mathin was rewiring a loose ring on his chain-encrusted vest.

"Very well. I understand a little, perhaps."

Mathin gave a snort of laughter; she remembered how grim and silent she'd thought him, he in particular of all the king's Riders. "You understand a great deal, Harimad-sol. I do not envy the others when they see you again. Only Corlath truly expects what I will be bringing out of these Hills."

This conversation had made it a little easier for her when he slyly told her of things, like the fourth way of lighting fires, which he refused to explain. She didn't understand the reasons, but she was a bit more willing to accept that a reason existed. It surprised her how much he told her about himself, for she knew that he did not find it easy to talk of these things to her; but she understood too that it was his way of making up, a little, for what he felt he could not tell her. It also, as he must have intended, made her feel as if the Hillfolk were familiar to her; that her own past was not so very different from theirs; and she began to imagine what it would have been like to have grown up in these Hills, to have always called them home.

One of the things Mathin would tell her little of was Aerin Dragon-Killer and the Blue Sword. He would refer to Damar's Golden Age, when Aerin was queen, but he would not tell her when it was, or even what made it golden. She did learn that Aerin had had a husband named Tor who had fought the Northerners, for the Northerners had been Damar's enemies since the beginning of time and the Hills, and every Damarian age had its tale of the conflict between them; and that King Tor was called the Just.

"It sounds very dreary, being Just, when your wife kills dragons," said Harry, and while Mathin permitted himself a smile, he was not to be drawn.

She did pry something else out of him. "Mathin," she said. "The Outlanders believe that the—the—*kelar* of the Hills can cause, oh, firearms not to fire, and cavalry charges to fall down instead of charging, and—things like that."

Mathin said nothing; he had marinated cut-up bits of Narknon's latest antelope in a sharp spicy sauce and was now frizzling them on two sticks over the low-burning fire. Harry sighed.

Mathin looked up from his sticks, though his fingers continued to twist them slowly. "It is wise of the Outlanders to believe the truth," he said. He dug one stick, butt-end, into the ground, and thrust his short knife into the first chunk of meat. He nibbled at it delicately, with the concentrated frown of the artist judging his own work. His face relaxed and he handed Harry the stick still in his other hand. But he spoke no more of *kelar*.

Mathin took no more falls, and by the middle of the sixth week Harry felt she had forgotten her first lessons because they were so far in the past. She could not remember a time when the palm of her right hand did not bear stripes of callus from the sword hilt; when the heavy vest felt awkward and unfamiliar; nor a time when she had not ridden Tsornin every day.

She did remember that she had been born in a far green country

118 |

nothing like the *kelar*-haunted one she now found herself in; and that she had a brother named Richard whom she still called Dickie, to his profound dismay—or would, if he could hear her—and she remembered a Colonel Jack Dedham, who loved the Hills even as she did. A thought swam into her mind: perhaps we shall meet again, and serve Damar together.

On the fourth day of the sixth week she said tentatively to Mathin: "I thought the City was over a day's journey from here."

"You thought rightly," Mathin replied; "but there is no need of your presence on the first day of the trials."

She glanced at him, a little reassured, but rather more worried.

"Do not fear, my friend and keeper of my honor," said Mathin. "You will be as a bolt from the heavens, and Tsornin's flanks shall blind your enemies."

She laughed. "I look forward to it."

"You should look forward to it," he said. "But I, who know what I will see, look forward to it even more."

CHAPTER EIGHT

O<small>N THE SEVENTH DAY</small> they left their valley. Harry felt a little sad, although she thought a bit of her nostalgia was apprehension for the future.

Just before they mounted, Mathin came and stood before her, with a long piece of maroon silk in his hand. Harry was wearing a long side-slashed red tunic over long full trousers of the same color, and a dark blue surcoat; she was accustomed to Hill dress now, and comfortable in it, unlike her first evening in the king's camp.

"Put this on, so," said Mathin. He gestured to his own waist; he wore a dark green sash. She looked down at herself. Mathin tossed the maroon strip over his shoulder, and pushed her hands away from her sides. He untied the brown cord she had used as a belt and dropped it as if it were trash, and wound the maroon silk twice around her waist, and tucked the ends of it away in some invisible fashion. She looked up: Mathin was wearing the fierce grin she was accustomed to seeing when they crossed swords. "One of the Hills must have a sash when she goes to the laprun trials, where it will be proved that she deserves to wear it." He turned away to mount Windrider.

Harry stood where she was a moment longer, feeling where the sash seized her lower ribs as she breathed. Then she put her hands on the pommel and cantle of the saddle and vaulted onto Sungold's back as she could now do easily; she had begun to consider if she could learn Corlath's way of mounting, which did not seem to require the use of the hands.

They jogged along steadily all that day, although the pack horse was inclined to complain. It had had a soft six weeks and was not entirely equal—even with its burdens much lighter than they had been six weeks before—to keeping pace with the flint-hard warhorses. Narknon loped along beside them, dashing off into the bushes occasionally on her private business, reappearing silently ahead of them, waiting by the trail for them to catch her up. They paused for lunch and a cold supper; but they continued on in the twilight. After the sunset was gone, Harry could see a glow in the northeast.

"It is a great bonfire on the plain before the City, to mark the opening of the trials tomorrow at dawn," Mathin told her. Harry wondered if any of the other trials riders were seeing things in the flames.

Her mind wanted to feel nervous and restless that night, but her well-trained body and that extra whatever-it-was sent her off to sleep before she had time to argue. At dawn when the trials were beginning, they were in the saddle again, riding easily and listening to the breeze, Harry half expecting to hear the distant clash and yell of combat. Slowly they rode all that day, that they might not arrive tired. The pack horse had given up complaining, and marched on resignedly.

They rode around the edge of a gaunt grey rockface at sunset and suddenly before her was a vast field, the Hills rising sharply at its perimeter. The plain was speckled with fires, and in the swiftly falling shadows she could make out the many-legged shapes of huddled horses and huddled men, and the angular silhouettes of tents. There were too many of them; her heart jumped out of its usual location and began beating frantically against the base of her throat. She raised her eyes to the watching Hills again: surely this great flat plain was not a natural phenomenon in this rugged land? And yet what labor could have flattened the Hills so?

Mathin was staring across the fires as if he would recognize the owners of the dark featureless tents even from here. She thought with his long eyes he might succeed. "Mathin, do you know how this plain came to be—has it always been here?"

Mathin, still looking out over the plain, said, "There is a story that Tor met the Northerners on this plain, and held them away from the City for nine days, and the heat of that battle melted the rocks of the Hills, which made a pool; and when the pool became hard again, it was this plain."

"What happened on the tenth day?" asked Harry. But Mathin put Windrider into a trot without answering. Sungold trotted obediently behind her, his ears pricked stiffly at the scene before him. He was ready for anything Harry might ask him to do; he gave her a little confidence. But the other riders here had known of the laprun trials perhaps all their lives; perhaps they had been training for them nearly as long.

Mathin glanced back at her. "We are opposite the gate to the City; you cannot see it from here. You will see it after the trials."

"Mathin."

His head turned warily back to her, anticipating a question he would not wish to answer. She saw his eyes glint in a yellow gleam of firelight.

"Are there other women at the trials?"

He grunted; she recognized it as relief that she wasn't going to nag him further about Tor the Just, who probably wasn't that boring if he could hold off the Northerners for nine days and melt a hole in the Hills, and Aerin and her dragons. He said gruffly, "A few. There are always a few. Once there were more." He put Windrider forward again, and in the click of hooves she had to strain to catch his last words: "It would be a great thing for us, and for our daughters—a damalur-sol."

Damalur-sol. Lady Hero.

They set up their own small and travel-stained tents not far in from the ring of Hills they had just left. She felt the drifting shadows of other Hillfolk as she rubbed Tsornin down, and when she came back to the firelight of the small blaze she had—rather efficiently, she thought, with the first of Mathin's three methods of fire-making, which simply involved the correct application of a tinder-box—started in front of their tari, there were four such shadows sitting on their heels around it. Mathin came into the light as she did, carrying his saddle. He joined the four, and after a moment's hesitation, so did she. She walked, pretending to be bold, toward a gap between elbows; and the owners of the elbows made room for her as they would for a comrade.

"How goes it, my brothers?" Mathin said, and she was startled by his voice speaking to someone other than herself.

One shadow shrugged. "As well as a first day ever does." Mathin had told her that the first day was reserved for those less highly trained, who did not seek to win their sashes; she had sighed. Mathin told her, "You would find it dull work, the first day. Believe me." Harry, after a moment, recognized the shadow as Innath, and relaxed slightly.

"And how does our prodigy?"

Harry blinked. It had taken her a second to remember the word *prodigy,* and then she was alarmed and heartened simultaneously by the *our.*

"Prodigiously," said Mathin, and he grinned at her. She smiled faintly back.

The shadows nodded and stood up; but each one touched her shoulder and then her head as he passed behind her. The last was Innath, and his hand lingered just long enough on her hair for him to have time to murmur, "Be of good courage, prodigy," and he too was gone.

The camp awoke before dawn; the tents were pulled down, and the fires, after heating the malak and the porridge, and singeing the breakfast bread—Someday, she thought, I will teach these people about toast—were tramped out. She gave Narknon less than her usual percentage of porridge, because she would doubtless need all of her strength, unenthusiastic as her appetite was at present. She mounted and waited to be sent to her fate. All over again she missed bridle and reins, and the scabbard of her sword looked strange to her, slung on the saddle, and the small shield banged awkwardly against her thigh. Mathin, with the pack horse reluctantly following, rode up beside her. "Your way lies there," he said, nodding in the direction of the invisible City gate. "You will find a man dressed all in red, a kysin, riding a black horse with a red saddle. Tell him your name—Harimad-sol," he added, as if she might need prompting. Maybe she did. "He'll know who you are." She surreptitiously hitched the shield an inch or so forward, and wiped her hands on her thighs. The leather felt clammy. Who would the kysin think she was? She couldn't even tie her own sash without help.

Mathin reached out to her, pulled her face toward him, and kissed her on the forehead. "The kiss of luck," he said. "You have no sash-bearing father or mother to give it you. Go as the Daughter of the Riders. Go."

She turned away. Innath was sitting his big grey stallion just behind her. He smiled at her, a friend's smile. "Be of good courage, Daughter of the Riders."

The morning was already hot, and the plain offered no shade; the ring of Hills seemed to hold the heat like water in a bowl. Harry found the man in red, and gave him her name; she thought he looked at her sharply, but perhaps he looked at all the laprun candidates sharply. He nodded and gave her a white rag to tie around her arm, and sent her off toward a milling mob of nervous horseflesh and even more nervous riders. She looked at them critically; there were some fine horses here, but none could outmatch her own mount, and very few could come near him. There was one big dark bay that caught her eye; she was ridden by a boy in blue who carried his shoulders and head well. Harry wondered what the other riders thought of the one in the maroon sash on the big golden chestnut.

There was little conversation. There were those who gave their names to the red man and joined the ever-increasing throng here at the City end of the plain; the rest—the audience, she supposed—crowded behind barriers she could not see, that stretched from the feet of the red man's horse to the far side of the plain. Around Harry, some of the trials riders moved their horses in fidgety circles, just to avoid standing still; some looked down at themselves often, as if checking to make sure they were all still there. Harry twisted strands of Sungold's mane between her damp fingers and tried to keep her teeth from chattering. There was the dull murmur of horses' hooves, and the rush of their breathing, and the squeak of leather, the hush of cloth; and the sun overhead gazing down. To try to take her mind off the trials for a minute, she looked up, searching for some sign of the City, some path to its gate, and saw nothing but rock. It's right before my eyes and I can't see it, she thought, and had a moment of panic. Tsornin, who could read many of her thoughts by this time, flicked one ear back at her: *Stop that.* She stopped.

Shortly before midmorning the trials began. First their weapons were taken away from them and replaced with flat wooden swords; and Harry discovered that she was much fonder of her own sword than she had previously supposed. Everyone else was settling helms on heads, so she fumbled hers loose from its straps and tied it on. It felt heavier than usual, and she didn't seem able to see around its cheek pieces clearly. Then the riders were divided into twos, threes, fives, eights. In these little groups they galloped hard to the end of that highway between spectators, wheeled, and came back. They met twos, threes, fives, eights rushing to meet them, swerved and collided; riders rolled in the dust, and horses bolted. She was not one of the former, nor Tsornin the latter. Neither was the young man in blue on the bay mare. She had a little trouble holding Tsornin back to the pace of the others; he was not over-pleased with crowds, but he did as she asked since she asked it. Those that remained mounted at each sweep galloped down and back again and again; and with each charge another obstacle had appeared along the highway that must be leaped or climbed over: a wall of rolled-up tents, stacked together; a fence of tentpoles; a banked heap of small stones with scrub piled on top. The first flecks of sweat broke out on Tsornin's shoulders as he gave her the slight heave she needed to hook a boot around a neighboring ankle and toss a rider to the ground.

There was a little troop of twenty left mounted when the last charge ended. Harry looked around her, wondering how many had been thrown or hurt; she guessed there had been several times twenty in the beginning. A few minutes passed while the uneasy twenty walked their horses, and breathed deep, and waited. Then it was the spectators who came toward them, huddled once again at the City end of the plain; some of them were mounted, and all were carrying long wooden poles. What? thought Harry; and then a pole descended on her helmeted head, and the horse in front of her stumbled and fell at Sungold's feet. Sungold leaped over the thrashing legs as carelessly as if they were blades of grass. Harry began laying about with her wooden sword. A pole thrust itself under her knee and attempted to remove her from her saddle. Sungold switched around on his forehand, giving her her balance, and she broke the offending pole with the hilt of her mock sword. She began to feel hot and annoyed. Sweat matted her tunic to her body, and her leather vest squeaked with it. The burning sunlight tried to push her out of the saddle even as the poles in human hands did. What is this nonsense? She used the flat and butt of her silly wooden stick and Tsornin reared and stamped and hurled himself forward. She broke a few more poles. She felt Mathin's grin pulling at her own lips. Someone thumped her sharply in the shoulder with a pole, but once again, as she lurched, Sungold slid sideways to stay under her; and she gave that pole a back-handed chop and saw it spin away from its wielder.

Tsornin leaped over another fallen horse. She saw abruptly that the audience hemmed the trials riders in; if one of them pushed too near the edge of the crush, he was set on with particular ferocity and turned back. She noticed this with interest, and began determinedly to get out; but there were several hundreds to twenty—and only a few of the original twenty were still mounted.

She began to feel that tide of anger she remembered from the day she had unseated Mathin—she caught somebody by the collarbone and knocked him off his horse with his own pole—and she felt that she would escape. Tsornin was backing up, mostly on his hind legs. Then he spun round, came down—one more whack with her wretched wooden blade; the hilt gave an ominous creak, but it didn't matter; she was . . . out.

The red man gave a shout. It was over.

The crowd dispersed instantly, as if the red man's shout had broken a cord that tied them all together. There were several loose horses standing clear, looking embarrassed for having behaved so poorly as to lose their riders; and several limping figures separated themselves from the others and went toward them. Harry sat where she was, the hot tide ebbing, leaving just a trace of headache behind, watching the others pass around her like grains of sand sifting around a boulder. She saw Mathin from a distance; he carried a pole across Windrider's withers and there was a shallow cut over one eye that had bled down his cheek. She saw none of the other Riders.

She squinted up at the sky. The Hills were black with shadows, but the sky was hard blue and she could feel the heat beating up again from underfoot. In the quiet—for, as it had been this morning, no one spoke and even the horses seemed to step softly—the heat seemed almost audible. She set Tsornin to walk himself as cool as possible. She patted his neck and dismounted, that they might walk together; he was sweating but not distressed, and he shook his head at her. She reclaimed her sword from the kysin, who saluted her. He had not saluted the laprun rider just before her.

Mathin reappeared and told her she could rest awhile. His cheek was washed clean and a bit of white cloth bound over his eyebrow. "The individual matches will go on all afternoon; you will be called late."

They found a spot of shade at the edge of the plain and pulled the saddles off the horses. Mathin gave her some bread and some wet white tasteless cheese. She sucked it slowly and let it trickle down her dry throat. She felt quite calm, and wondered what was the matter with her. "Mathin, are all the trials the same? Did you gallop and bash people with a wooden stick at your trials?"

"No and yes. They test your horsemanship in different ways; those who watch always have some chance to help—or hinder; and weapons of wood are safer. But the afternoon's matches are always the same, one rider against another, each with his own sword. If a kysin declares that a trials rider did badly in the general trials, he will not be permitted to ride in the individual sets."

They watched the dust clouds from the matches and the bright notches of color spinning in them; but Mathin made no move to return to that end of the plain, and Harry waited beside him, leaning on her elbows in spite of her sore shoulder.

The sun was halfway down the sky when they mounted again. Sungold, for the first time since she'd known him, refused to walk, and jigged along sideways, tossing his head. "Stop that, idiot," she hissed at him in Homelander, and he halted in surprise. Mathin turned his head and looked at her impassively.

They stood at the edge of the crowd now, and watched the combatants. There were five pairs, each the center of a private war; the red man had divided into ten red men on grey or black horses. There were two red men for each pair of fighters, and one man of each pair carried a small brass bell; when the bell rang out, that conflict was ended, and the horses fell apart, and riders and mounts panted the hot air. All the laprun riders were dressed in bright colors; there was very little white and no dreary dun or grey; with the scarlet kysin, it was a very vivid scene.

A bell sang out, a long gay peal, and she looked over at the finished pair. One of the riders held his sword up and shook it so the sunlight flickered on it. The other rider sat quietly, his sword on the ground at his horse's forefeet and, she noticed with a funny feeling in the pit of her stomach, his sash neatly sliced from around his waist and lying, part on his horse's croup and part on the ground.

Mathin said: "It is best to take your opponent's sash. The kysin mark each blow dealt, but to cut off the other rider's sash is best. This you will do."

"Oh," said Harry.

"You may, if you wish, unhorse him first," Mathin added as an afterthought.

"Thanks," said Harry.

"But you must not draw blood, for this is a sign of clumsiness. Baga, we call one who cuts his opponent during the laprun—baga, butcher. It is skill we look for. This is why no armor is allowed in the individual matches."

"Of course," said Harry.

Mathin grinned at her. "Of course. Is this not what I have been teaching you?" He watched the next pair of riders salute each other; and another bell from another pair rang; each of the five bells spoke a different note. "The trials go back many generations—once they were held every year, but there are no longer enough of us in the Hills to make up the number; we have them every three years now, since Corlath's father's day.

"The sash-cutting—churakak—is a duel of honor that is as old as Damar; far older than the laprun trials themselves, although few meet the churakak outside the trials any more.

"Aerin," he added thoughtfully, "met the churakak several times. Her red hair no doubt made her quick-tempered."

"Harimad," barked a kysin; and Tsornin jolted forward before Harry had registered her name. She was set facing a boy in a green robe and yellow sash; the kysin said, "Begin," and Harry feinted Tsornin to the left, back, forward, and the boy's sword fell to the ground, and his yellow sash fluttered down to cover it. A bell rang.

Harry was a bit taken aback. The kysin waved her aside. Tsornin flattened his ears; he was not interested in boys who did not know what they were doing. Next Harry removed a dark orange sash from around a sky-blue robe; and then a white sash from a purple robe. Harry began to feel as irritable as her horse, and with each cry of "Harimad" the two of them turned and stood and attacked and wondered when the real thing would begin. Harry began unhorsing her opponents before lopping off their sashes just to give herself something to do.

The Hills' shadows began to creep toward the feet of the charging dancing horses, and the lowering sun flicked dangerous gleams from the shining sides of swords and into opponents' eyes. Tsornin was dark with sweat, and foam streaked his sides, but he slowed not a whit, and it seemed to Harry that they were galloping down a long hall of statues with swords held stiffly in raised hands, waiting for her to lean languidly over Sungold's neck and knock their loose sashes off.

All five bells rang at once as the green sash fell off the point of Harry's sword to the ground, and she looked around and realized that she and her latest opponent were the last to finish. It was nearly twilight, and she was surprised that they had gone on so long. Now that she stopped to think about it, it was rather hard to see; it was as though dusk had fallen on them as soon as they stood still. Tsornin's nostrils were wide and red as he turned his head. She looked where he was looking. A big dark horse stood as if waiting for them. Harry blinked and stared; the other horse tossed its head. Was he bay or black? There seemed to be something wrong with her eyes; she raised one arm and rubbed them against her grimy sleeve, and looked again, but the horse and rider still, shimmered in her sight, a shimmer of darkness instead of light. The tall rider was muffled in a shadowy cloak that fell over his mount's shoulders and past his boot tops; he shrugged it back to show a white tunic and a red sash. The horse fidgeted sideways, and a bay glint showed along its dark flank.

The lapruni and the audience moved to form a ring around them, the shadowy bay and Tsornin. The silence after the pounding hooves, the grunts and thumps and crashes, was unearthly; and the sun sank farther behind the Hills. The first breath of the evening wind crept out of the Hills; its cool finger tapped Harry's cheek, and it felt like fear.

A torch appeared, held aloft by one of the ring, someone on horseback. Then another torch burst into fire, and another, and another. The beaten ground between Harry and the silent rider at the other end of the circle swam in the flickering light. Then the brass bells rang again, like the sound of Outlander cannon in Harry's ears, and Sungold came to life, and neighed, and the bay answered.

Harry did not know if the match lasted a long time or a short time. She knew at once that this swordsman, behind the scarf wrapped around his head and face so that only his eyes showed, could have dismembered her whenever he liked. Instead he drew her to attack him, opening his defense to attract each of the many moves Mathin had taught her, as if he were a schoolmaster hearing her lessons. It was so easy for him that Harry began to feel angry, began to clear a tiny space in her mind to think of some plan of her own; and her anger rose, and gave her a headache till the torchlight was red with it, but she did not care, for she knew by now that it gave her strength. Strength she needed, for she was tired, and her horse was tired, and she could see that the bay was fresh, and could feel up her arm as the swords met that the rider did not exert himself to resist her. But her rising anger lifted her and invigorated Sungold, and she began to harass the bay stallion's rider—if only a little, still a little. She pressed forward and the bay gave way a step or two, and the crowd gasped; and with a quick and merry slash the tip of her sword caught the scarf bound round the rider's face and tore it up from the chin. She misjudged by the fraction of a hair; a single drop of blood welled up from the corner of his mouth. She stared at it, fascinated, as she felt her sash slip down her legs in two pieces and lie huddled on the ground, for the face belonged to Corlath.

CHAPTER NINE

S HE FELT CAUGHT as she stared at the dark Hill-king astride his red horse, caught by the sky, by the stars winking into the new-fallen darkness, by the sand and encircling Hills; they seized her and held her down. She was a figure in some story other than her own—an embroidered shape in a Hill tapestry, a representation of something that did not exist in her Homeland. Then the crowd gave a roar and surged inward; she closed her eyes. But they were patting her ankles, her legs, her back, making her human again, with human bewilderment and human luck. She began to distinguish words in the roar: they were shouting, "Harimad-sol! Laprun minta! Minta—musti! Harimad-sol!" Tsornin and Isfahel were driven together, and they stood patiently while the crowd rose and foamed around them. Isfahel turned his head and Tsornin turned his, till their flared nostrils touched briefly in a salute.

Out of the corner of her eye Harry saw Corlath blot the drop of blood at his mouth with the back of his hand.

The crowd fell away from its center, breaking into smaller eddies that laughed and swung each other by arms and hands and shoulders. Sungold and Fireheart edged away from each other, their riders silent and motionless. Harry could not look at Corlath. He reached out one hand toward her, perhaps to touch her, but Tsornin sidled just one step farther and Corlath's hand dropped away.

Mathin appeared on Harry's far side and touched her elbow, and

Harry smiled gratefully at his familiar face. Mathin did not speak to her, but turned away, and she slid off Sungold and the two of them followed him, walking slowly, permitted their due of weariness at last. Mathin stopped where two taris were already set up, and knelt down to build a fire, companionably ignoring his two pupils; and Harry was glad to lay aside the glory of laprun-minta. The headache haze and sense of displacement began to ebb as she mechanically stripped off Sungold's saddle and rubbed him down. The smell of Mathin's cooking crept to greet her and cheer her, and remind her who she was, or who she had become. She was the Daughter of the Riders.

Harry ate too much that night. She ate till her stomach hurt—Mathin had kept them on strict rations during training—but she was only half aware of what she was eating. Many of the lapruni she had faced today came to her, to touch her hand and offer what seemed a sort of fealty; they materialized at the edge of the firelight, as indistinct as they had seemed to her that afternoon: they wore red robes and blue robes and brown robes and black, for none wore a sash, and their swords hung in scabbards by their sides instead of drawn against her. And they called her Harimad-sol, and laprun-minta, and their voices were hushed and reverent. Harry ate too much because it made her feel more real.

As the evening progressed other taris were set up nearby: she had noticed that Mathin was using a pot larger than the one for the two of them she had seen every night for six weeks. Soon she found they were sharing their fire and supper with Innath and Faran and Forloy and Dapsim, and others of the king's Riders. They watched without comment as the lapruni came to show themselves to the Daughter of the Riders, who kept putting more food on her plate as they appeared and vanished. Once when Harry looked up she saw Mathin handing Corlath a plate. The king slouched down, cross-legged, and began to eat. Harry would have liked to ask why the lapruni were saluting her, for it seemed beyond a simple acknowledgment of the loser to the victor, but she did not ask. Mathin had taught her patience, and she had known all her life how to be stubborn.

It seemed a bit unfair to complain, she thought, as it—or as I—have turned out; but couldn't I have been told a little more beforehand? She looked into the eyes of those who sought her and called her Harimad-sol, and tried to think of them as individuals, and not as robes and tunics and fallen sashes. The lapruni all went away without her having to speak to them, for they did not seem to expect her to answer them with anything but her presence. This was both restful and unnerving.

One laprun was a woman. For her Harry did have a question. "What is your name?"

The girl's robe was blue, and Harry suddenly recognized her as the rider on the bay mare. "Senay," she replied.

"Where is your home?"

Senay turned to face northwest. "Shpardith," she said. "It is there," and she pointed into the blackness. "Twelve days on a fleet horse."

Harry nodded, and the girl left to return to her own fire, and others came to speak to the laprun-minta who sat with the Riders and the king. When she looked around again she realized that there were eighteen dark figures besides herself and the king; all the Riders, from wherever they had been, had returned.

And Narknon reappeared, and Harry hugged her eagerly, for she felt in need of something to hug. She offered her bits of meat, which Narknon graciously accepted, although she attempted to nose through Harry's plate herself, to make sure Harry wasn't keeping back any of the best bits for herself.

Harry slept dreamlessly, her hand on the hilt of her sword; when she awoke and found this so, she stared at her hand as if it did not belong to her.

She crept out of the tari and looked around. The sky was light; yet most of the taris still had bodies in them, and there were more blanket-swathed figures motionless around banked or burned-out fires. Mathin's lips moved as he rebuilt their fire. She turned to look behind her. Corlath was gone; there was only a small ripple in the sand where he had lain, or it might be only the wind. Mathin handed her a cup of malak. It was reheated from last night, and bitter. Harry shrugged into her stiff grimy surcoat, hoping there would be bathing sometime today, and thinking wistfully of the little valley behind her, and its green pool. Her split sash lay beside her, where she had stuffed it through the tari's open flap the night before. She picked it up and, after a moment's thought, wrapped it around her waist again, tucking torn edges underneath till it would stay fixed. She did not do it very well, and she thought of asking Mathin for help, but chose not to.

After the wildness of the night before, this morning everyone went quietly about the business of packing up and returning, it seemed, to where they had come from. A few lingered: Harry and several of the Riders, for many of them had vanished with Corlath, and perhaps a dozen riders she did not recognize, and a few of the lapruni. She looked for Senay hopefully, but did not see her. The wind whispered over the bare land. But for the black hollows of dead fires, there was nothing to show that several hundred people had spent the last three days here.

Mathin turned Windrider east, east where the City lay just beyond one of the enigmatic rockfaces before them. Tsornin fell into step beside Windrider; Viki came along behind them, still grumbling to himself; and the others, some thirty riders, strung out behind them. Harry peered over her shoulder several times, watching the procession winding behind her, till she caught Mathin's expression of restrained amusement when he glanced over at her. After that she looked only straight ahead. Narknon padded softly among them all. There was another big hunting-cat with them, a handsome spotted-mahogany male an inch or two taller than Narknon; but she scorned him.

Tsornin strode out like a yearling having his first sight of the world beyond his paddock. Harry tried to keep her back straight and her legs quiet. Yesterday she had been glad of her perfectly fitted saddle, for it gave her suppleness and security; today she was glad of it because it told her where her legs were supposed to be even when they felt like blocks of wood. Her shoulder hurt, and her head felt woolly, and her right wrist was as weak as water, and she had a great purple bruise on her left calf. My horse is ignoring me, Harry thought. Or maybe he's trying to cheer me up. She had gone over him with great care the evening before, and again this morning, and applied salve to the few small scrapes he had collected. He had no suspicious swellings, no lameness, and his eyes were bright and his step buoyant. He made her feel woollier. "Are you trying to cheer me up?" she said to his mane, and he cocked a merry ear at her and strutted.

They had just begun to step upward off the plain into the Hills when they rounded another abrupt shoulder of rock like the one she and Mathin had passed for her first view of the laprun fields; and here was a wide highway mounting steeply to massive gates not far away. There lay the City.

They passed through the gates, borne beneath an arch two horse-lengths thick, their horses' hooves echoing hollowly. There was a cold grey smell, as if of caves, although the gates had stood for a thousand years. They walked down a broad avenue where six horsemen might walk abreast. It was stone-paved, laid out in huge flat cobbles, some grey or white or red-veined black; it had edges of earth where slender grey trees grew. Behind them were stone walkways where children played; and beyond them were stone houses and shops and stables and warehouses; stone flower-pots stood in doorways and on window ledges. The green-and-blue parrots Harry had seen in the traveling camp were perched on many shoulders, and some of them joined, gay and noisy, in the children's games. Often with a flirt of wings one would carry off the stone counter or mark a group of children was using, while the children shrieked at them, and occasionally threw pebbles at them, but only very small ones.

"Is there *no* wood?" said Harry. "Nothing but stone?" She looked up at the roof and walls and gables mounting up the hillside behind the gates, tiers of stone, multi-colored stone, no shingles or slats or carved wooden cornices, or shutters or window frames.

"There is wood here," said Mathin, "but there is more stone."

Innath rode up on Harry's other side. "Mathin cannot see the strangeness of this place," he said; "his village is just as stony as the City, only smaller. Where I come from we cut down trees and plane them smooth and slot them together, our houses and barns are warm and weathered, and do not last forever and haunt you with the ghosts of a thousand years."

"We use wood," said Mathin.

Innath made a dismissive gesture. "The grand receiving-rooms here have wooden paneling—you'll see some of them at the castle—and parlors, where people really live, often have wooden screens as ornaments."

"There are wooden chairs and tables and cupboards," said Mathin.

"There are more stone chairs and tables and cupboards," said Innath. "They don't often rearrange the furniture here."

Harry looked around. She saw doors so well hung on their hinges that they were opened and closed by a child's touch, yet made of stone slabs so heavy she wondered how they had been wrestled into their places to begin with. Free-standing walls, she saw, were often as wide as the reach of her two arms; yet often too the inner wall facing on a courtyard encircled by tall houses was so fine and delicate, cut into filigree work so complex, it looked as though it must tremble in the lightest breeze; as if one might roll it up like a bolt of silk and store it on a shelf.

"To be either a stonemason or a carpenter is to be respected," Mathin said. "The best of them are greatly honored."

"Hear the horse-breaker," said Innath.

Mathin smiled.

The children began calling: "The lapruni are here! And the Riders—and the laprun-minta!"

"Harimad-sol," Innath called to them, and Harry blushed.

"Harimad-sol," agreed the children; and people came out from the houses and down the narrower ways off the wide central way to look. Harry tried to look around her without catching anyone's eye, but many of the onlookers sought hers; and when one succeeded, he—or she—would touch right wrist to forehead and then hold the flat empty palm out toward her. "Harimad-sol," she heard, and eagerly they added, "Damalur-sol." The children danced in front of Tsornin's feet to make her look at them, and clapped their hands; and she smiled and waved shyly at them, and Tsornin was very careful with his hooves.

They rode on. At first the Hills rose up behind the low buildings, but as they went farther in, the buildings grew taller and taller and seemed part of the Hills themselves; and the trees that lined the way grew larger, till the shade of them could be felt as one passed beneath. Then another gate rose up before them, the wall around it running into the flanks of the mountains as if wall and gate had been formed with the mountains at the beginning of time. They went through this gate too, and entered a wide flat courtyard of polished stone. This stone was mirror-white, and it blazed up fiercely in the morning sunlight, and Harry felt as if she had emerged from underground. She blinked.

Before her stood Corlath's castle; no one had to explain to her what this huge stone edifice must be. She tipped her head back to see the sharp points of the turrets, brilliant as diamonds. It was itself a mountain, proudly peaked, seated among its brothers; its faces glittered dangerously. The shadows it threw were abrupt and absolute; one wall reflected white, another black. The central mass was taller than the Hill crests here; the road they had climbed had reached near the summit of the dark Hills, and like an island in the crater lake of an extinct volcano, the castle stood in its stone yard that shone as bright as water in the sun.

Harry sighed.

Men of the horse were approaching them in the swift but un-hurried way she remembered from the days on the desert in the traveling camp; and she felt a sudden sharp stab of memory, as if that were a time many years past, and the present were sad and weary. She slipped down from Tsornin's back and he suffered himself to be led away when one of the brown men spoke to him gently by name and laid a hand in front of his withers. Narknon sat down neatly at Harry's feet; Harry could feel her tail twitching at her ankles.

Those who had ridden with her began now to go purposefully in their own individual directions. Mathin said to her, "It is here I am to leave you. Perhaps it may be permitted that we ride against each other again and you may practice your skills upon me, Daughter of the Riders." He smiled. "We will meet again at the king's table, here in the City."

Harry looked up toward the castle when Mathin left her, feeling a little forlorn; and it was Corlath himself who walked to meet her. She swallowed rather hard, and blessed the sunburn that would prevent her fierce blush from showing as clearly as it would on an Outlander's pale skin.

"We meet again, Harimad-sol," Corlath said. There was a tiny scab at one corner of his mouth; he looked down at her with a cold dignity, she thought; he is the master of this place, and what am I? Even Daughter of the Riders could not comfort her as Corlath stood before her with his castle shining savagely behind him.

But then he spoiled the effect—or perhaps the effect was all in Harry's eyes to begin with—by saying, "So *that's* where the thrice-blasted cat disappeared to. I should have guessed it."

He did not look very majestic while glaring at a cat; so Harry said crossly, "I wish I knew what was going on."

Corlath looked at her thoughtfully, and Narknon, with customary feline charm, stood up and went to twine herself around Corlath's legs. Corlath's face softened and he rubbed her ears. Harry could hear her purr; she could almost feel it through the soles of her boots on the white stone. Narknon was a champion purrer. "And don't tell me that no one knows what is going on and that it is for the gods to decide, either."

Corlath's face wavered and then broke into a smile, although whether at Harry or the big cat, Harry didn't know. "Very well," he said. "I won't. I will tell you that you are the First of the laprun trials, laprun-minta, which you already know, and as such the most important of the lapruni, the untried." Corlath's hand lay motionless on Narknon's head. "The army marches, to do what it can, in less than a fortnight's time. You and the best of the lapruni will ride with us." Narknon bumped Corlath's hand violently and the fingers stirred and began scratching again.

In a lighter tone Corlath continued, "In other years that the laprun trials are held, there is a week's celebration at their end, and a great many songs are sung, and lies about one's own prowess told, and all the minta of past years claim that their year was the best, and much wine and beer is drunk, and it is all very cheerful. This year we have not the time, and many of those who would be part of it are far away, and those who are here are busy, and the work they do is melancholy." He paused as if hoping she would say something, or at least raise her eyes from Narknon's sleepy face and look at him; but when she did finally look up, he immediately squinted up at the sky. "But tonight there will be a feast in your honor. You are not the least of those who have been laprun Firsts. There are many who will come tonight merely to look at you."

Harry stopped smiling at the cat. "Oh," she said.

"Come. I will show you where you will stay till we leave the City."

She followed him across the smooth courtyard and around one wing of the castle; as they rounded the tip, set back from the edge and guarded by the castle's great bulk was a wall that at first seemed low; but it was fully ten feet high as they approached. It curved back on itself as if it protected something within that was very precious. In the wall was a door, the height of a tall man. Corlath opened it, and looked around for her. She stepped in first, Narknon crowding at her heels, with the odd feeling that he was watching her anxiously for her reaction.

It was very beautiful. Here the courtyard was not stone, but green grass, and a stream ran through it from one end to the other, with a fountain at the center, and a stone horse reared in the midst of the falling spray. On either side of the stream was a path of paving-stones, grey and blue, that went all the way around the fountain. There were curved stone seats on either side of the fountain, with the stream running between them. Beyond all this was what Harry thought of instantly as a palace, for all its diminutive size; it was no bigger than the gateman's cottage on her father's—now Richard's—estate, back Home. But this cottage had slender peaked towers at each of its five corners, and a cupola at the center of the slanting roof, with a delicate fence surrounding it. But for the cupola, it was only one story high, and the windows were tall and thin. The walls and roof were a mosaic of thousands of small flat blue stones, with colors from aquamarine to turquoise to sapphire, but Harry had no idea what these stones might be, for they were opaque, and yet they gleamed like mother of pearl. She sighed, and then to her horror she felt her eyes filling with tears; so she ran forward. It seemed as though even her leather riding-boots made no sound on the stone here, and she plunged her hands into the water of the fountain, and put her face under the spray. The coldness of it quieted her, and the drops danced around her. Narknon climbed up on one of the benches and lay down.

Corlath followed them through the door in the wall and then went on to the little mosaic palace. There was no door in the arched entrance. Harry stepped slowly inside. Here the stream had slipped around behind and entered by some back way, for in the center of the front room was another fountain, and the stream ran in under the rear wall; but here the stone horse stood on all four legs and bowed his head to drink from the pool at his feet. There were tapestries on the walls, and rugs and cushions on the floor, and one low table, and that was all. Corlath opened the stone door beside the place where the stream came under the wall. She looked in. The stream entered over a tiny falls of three stone steps under the far wall, to run under the near wall and out to the fountain in the front room. The water tinkled as it fell. The floor of this room was thick with carpets, and against the wall opposite the stream was the long bolster-like object she had learned to recognize in the traveling camp as the Hill idea of a bed, although she had entertained higher hopes of the furnishings of the City. There were pillow-sized cushions at one end, and body-sized rugs folded up at the other end.

She went back into the bigger room and looked around again. There was another door between two long blue-and-green tapestries. She walked over to it and opened it, wondering if she would find a dragon breathing fire from a heap of diamonds, or merely a bottomless chasm lined with blue stones, but instead it was only a bit more of the grassy courtyard, and a few steps away was a door in the wall surrounding this magic place into what she thought vaguely must be the castle itself.

She closed the door and turned back; Corlath was dangling his fingers in the pool just in front of the horse's stone nose. He looked as if he were thinking very hard about something. Harry leaned back against the door behind her and stared at him, wondering what he was looking at, and waited for him to remember her.

He looked up finally, and met her eyes. She didn't think she flinched. "Do you like it?" he said.

She nodded, not quite sure of her voice.

"It has been a long time since this place sheltered anyone," he said; she wanted to ask how it came to be here at all, who had built it so lovingly and why; but she didn't. Corlath left her there. He walked out past the fountain of the rearing horse, and at the door where they had first entered he paused and turned back toward her. She had followed him from the small jeweled cottage, and stood next to the low bench where Narknon lay at her ease. But he said nothing, and turned away again, and closed the door behind him. She went to the little back room with the bolster and took off her surcoat. Her hands met her torn sash; her fingers curled around it and then she pulled it off in her two hands and tossed the pieces away from her. They fluttered to the floor. She lay down by degrees, leaving the lower half of her left leg hanging over the edge of the bolster, where the bruise need not come in contact with anything, and carefully arranged her sore shoulder.

A young woman woke her, but she was dressed as the men of the household were dressed, in a long sashless white robe, and had the same mark they did on her forehead. "The banquet will begin soon," said the girl, and bowed; and Harry nodded and sat up stiffly, and yawned, and contemplated her bruises, which seemed to be spreading. She unfolded herself, and weaved to her feet. She put on her blue robe but left the sash lying, and followed the girl out of the mosaic palace and through the castle door into an antechamber. She looked to the left and saw a room with tables, high tables, and real chairs: not chairs like the ones she had known at Home, but still chairs, with legs and backs, and some with armrests. The girl guided her to the right and into an immense bath-room, with the bath itself sunk into the floor, the size of a millpond, and steaming. The girl helped her out of her clothes, and Harry sat for a moment at the edge of the lake and dabbled her tired feet in it. Her attendant hissed with sympathy over the bruises.

Once she was fairly in and wet all over, two more young women appeared, and one of them presented her with a cake of white soap. The third young woman unbound her wet hair—now that it was wet, it smelled terribly of horse—and started rubbing shampoo into it. The shampoo smelled like flowers. She thought, I bet Corlath's shampoo doesn't smell like flowers. She would rather have climbed out of her own clothes—in spite of the aches and pains—and washed her own hair. The young woman who had given her the soap washed her back with a scratchy sponge, and Harry repressed the urge to giggle; she hadn't had anyone wash her back for her since she was five years old.

She was clean at last and wrapped in towels, and sat quite patiently while the young woman who had washed her hair now tried to work the tangles out of it. It was long and thick and hadn't been combed properly smooth for weeks. Better her than me, Harry thought cheerfully; there are advantages to servants, perhaps; and this girl is very gentle. . . . Harry caught herself dozing. I'm going to be less than a success at my own banquet if I can't even stay awake, she thought. I suppose the last six weeks are all catching up with me now, and Mathin's grey dust.

She tumbled off her stool at last, the towels removed, and a heavy white shift dropped over her head. They put velvet slippers on her feet and a red robe around her shoulders, and twisted a gold cord around her hair but let it hang down behind her so she had to flick the end of it aside when she sat down. At Home, one never wore one's hair loose when one was no longer a child; at night it was braided, during the day it was tied up. Harry shook her hair; it felt funny. These last weeks she had tied and pinned it

fiercely under her helmet, where it couldn't get caught in anything, like the branch of a tree, or Mathin's sword, or under her
own saddle. The young woman who had awakened her had
rubbed salve into her shoulder and leg before they dressed her,
and Harry found that she could move more freely, and the weight
of the robe didn't bow her down, nor the sleek surface of the shift
rub her like sandpaper.

The three girls ushered her across the anteroom to the room
with the chairs, and they all three bowed, and looked shyly at her
with smiles hovering in their eyes, so she grinned at them and
flapped the edges of her clean scarlet robe at them, and they
smiled happily and left.

Harry sat down tentatively in one of the queer crook-legged
chairs, and leaned back luxuriously. Rugs and cushions and stools
can be very comfortable, but they are inevitably backless, and it
was apparently not done to lean against a tent wall; no one else did
it, at least, so she hadn't tried. The shift billowed around her as
she shrugged farther into the chair: No sash, she thought.

There was a long hall she could see through an open door; and
after a few minutes Mathin appeared through another door at the
far end of it and came toward her. In his hand was a bit of maroon
cloth; and when he came through the door, the air that swept in
with him smelled of flowers. Harry smiled.

"Well met, Daughter of the Riders," said Mathin, and unrolled
what he had in his hand. It was her old sash, washed clean. The
smile left Harry's face, and when Mathin held the sash out to her,
still in its two pieces, as if he would tuck it around her waist, she
backed up a step.

He stopped, surprised, and looked at her face, white under the
tan. "I think," he said slowly, "that you do not understand." He
held his arms out to his sides, and the hand indicated a line on his
own dark green sash. "Look here."

Harry looked and saw a similar tear, but carefully mended, with
tiny exact stitches of yellow thread. "All the Riders wear them so.
Many of us won the slash at the hand of the king after being First
at the laprun trials—as I did, many years ago. It was Corlath's

144 |

father gave me this cut. Two or three of us have won them at other times. Any one lucky enough to have a sash cut off by a sol or sola will wear the mended sash ever after."

Harry, faintly in the back of her mind, heard Beth saying: "They come in those long robes they always wear—over their faces too, so you can't see if they're smiling or frowning; and some of them with those funny patched sashes around their waists."

Mathin said: "I will teach you to mend yours; you must do it yourself, as you clean your own sword and pay your own homage." He looked at her slyly and added: "All those sashes you lopped off their owners you may be sure will be saved and mended; and the cuts will be bragged of, given by the damalur-sol whose prowess was first seen when she was First at the laprun trials."

Harry suffered Mathin to put the maroon sash around her waist again. He did not tuck it together, as she had, so that the slash did not show; instead it went in front, proudly—Harry gritted her teeth—and was fixed by a long golden pin. Then she silently followed him down the corridor.

There were pillars reaching up three stories to meet the arched ceilings; the floors were laid out in great squares, two strides' length, but within each black-and-white border were scenes drawn in tiny mosaic tiles. Harry tried to look at them as she walked over them, and saw a great many horses, and some swords, and some sunrises and sunsets over Hills and deserts. She had her eyes so busily on the floor that when Mathin stopped she ran into him.

They stood under one of the three-story arches the pillars made, but on either side of them the spaces between the tall columns were filled in, and tapestries hung on these walls, and they stood in the doorway to an immense room. It too was three stories high, and a chandelier was let down from the ceiling on a chain that seemed hundreds of feet long. Mathin and she went down six steps, across a dozen strides of floor, and up nine steps to a vast square dais; around three sides of the square was a white-laid table. At the one edge of this dais where there was no table were three more steps up to a long rectangular table on a smaller dais;

and around this table sat Corlath and seventeen Riders. There were two empty seats at Corlath's right. Chairs, Harry thought happily. Chairs seem quite commonplace in the City, even if they don't understand beds.

They sat, and the men and women of the household brought food, and they ate. Harry cast a sharp eye over those bearing the dishes; it seemed that those of the household here in the City were about equally divided, men and women. Harry turned impulsively to Mathin and said, quietly so that Corlath would not hear, "Why were there no women of the household with us in the traveling camp?"

Mathin smiled at his leg of fowl. "Because there were so few women riding with us."

Corlath said, "There will be some to go with us in ten days' time, if you wish it; for even an army on its way to war needs some tending."

Harry said stiffly, "If this wish of mine is not a foolish one, it would please me to see women of the household come with us."

Corlath nodded gravely; and Harry thought of that first banquet she had attended, still dizzy and frightened from her ride across the desert, bumping on Corlath's saddlebow. She was still dizzy and frightened, she thought sadly, and touched the gold pin in her sash; it was cold to her fingers.

There was talk over the food of the laprun trials just past and of how so-and-so's son had ridden well or poorly; all the Riders had been watching the trials with an attention made more acute by the nearness of the Northerners. Mathin mentioned that a young woman named Senay had done well; a place should be offered to her when the army was ready to march. The kysin had ranked her high, and so she was still in the City, hoping for such a summons.

"Where is her home?" Corlath asked.

Mathin frowned, trying to remember.

"Shpardith," Harry said.

"Shpardith?" Mathin said, surprised. "She must be old Nandam's daughter. He always said she'd grow into a soldier. Good for her."

146 |

"Mathin's growing into a billitu, do you think?" said Innath, and a ripple of laughter went around the table. Harry turned to look at Mathin, and thought he was looking even more stolid than usual. "I choose only the best," said Mathin firmly, and everyone laughed again. A billitu is a lady-lover. Harry smiled involuntarily.

No one mentioned the brilliant performance of the youngster on the big chestnut Tsornin who had had the luck to carry off the honors, and Harry began to relax as the meal progressed, although, she thought, staring into her goblet, the wine was probably helping.

All was cleared away at last, and then came a pause so measured and expectant that Harry knew before she saw the man bearing the leather sack that they would bring out the Water of Seeing. This time she could understand when the Riders spoke of what they saw: war was in almost everyone's eyes, war with the Northerners, who were led by someone who was more than a man, whose sword flickered with a light that was the color of madness, and terror filled the heart of anyone who rode against him.

Faran laughed shortly and without mirth and said that what he saw was no use to anybody; Hantil saw his own folk riding grimly toward the City bearing a message he did not know. Hantil came from a village in the mountains that were the northern border of Damar. "I do not like it," said Hantil; "I have never seen my father look so stern."

Innath sighed over his Sight. "I see the Lake of Dreams," he said, "as if it is early spring, for the trees are in bud. The Riders ride along its edge, but our number is only fifteen."

Mathin tipped a swallow of the Water into his mouth, and stared into the distance; and it was as though he were turned to stone, a statue in the stone City; but his face broke into a sweat, and the drops rolled from his forehead. Then he moved, became human again, but the sweat still ran. His voice was rough when he spoke: "I am on fire. I know no more."

As soon as Harry's hands closed around the neck of the flask, a picture swam before her; in the brown leather of the bag, among the fine tooling, there was another image placed there by no leather worker. She saw Tsornin standing on the desert, and his rider carried a white flag, or a bit of white cloth tied to the end of a stick. "What do you see?" asked Corlath gently, and she told him. She could not see the rider's face, for there was a white cloth pulled over nose and chin; but she shivered at the thought of seeing her own face so eerily: and worse yet, what if it were not her face? Tsornin broke into a canter and then a gallop, and Harry saw what he approached: the eastern gate of the General Mundy. Then the picture faded, and she was looking at the curiously tooled leather of the Water bag again. She raised it to her lips.

Something like an explosion occurred in her head as she tasted the Water. She shuddered with the shock. Her right arm was numb to the shoulder, and it was her left hand's grasp on the neck of the bag that prevented her from dropping it. Then she felt another shock like the first, and realized that Tsornin was between her legs, and he screamed with rage and fear. The sky seemed to be black, and there were shouts and shrieks all around her, and they echoed as in a high-walled valley. One more of those shocks and she would be out of the saddle. She felt it poised to fall on her—and her vision cleared, and there was the table again. She looked at her right hand; it was still there. She looked up. "I don't—I don't know exactly what I saw. I think I was in a battle and—I seemed to be losing." She smiled weakly. Her right arm was still not working properly, and Corlath lifted the bag out of her left hand.

He took a sip in his turn; and Harry, watching, saw his eyes change color till they were as yellow as they had been the first time she had seen him in the Residency's courtyard. Then he closed them, and she saw the muscles in his face and neck and the backs of his hands tense till she thought they would burst through the skin; and then it was all over, and he opened his eyes, and they were brown. They moved to meet hers, and she thought she saw something of his vision still lingering there, and it was something like her own.

"I have seen our enemy's face," Corlath said calmly. "It is not pretty."

148 |

Then the man came to carry the Water away, and the wine was brought back, and the shadows were chased away for a little. The Riders began looking expectantly toward Corlath, but this was a happier expectancy than that which had predicted the Meeldtar, and Harry caught the eagerness herself, though she knew not what it was for, and looked around for clues.

They had eaten their meal alone in the vast hall, and their few voices ran up into the ceiling like live things with wills of their own. But after the Water bag had been taken away, people had begun to appear around the small dais where the king and his Riders sat; they entered from all directions and settled on cushions or chairs. Some of them mounted the lower dais and sat around the great table that surrounded the Riders. More of the folk of the household appeared, some bearing trays and some low tables, and set out more food, or passed it among the increasing audience. There was a murmur of talk, low but excited. Harry rubbed her fingers up and down the length of the gold pin in her sash till it was no longer cold.

One of the men brought Corlath his sword, and he stood up and slung the belt of it around him. Harry wondered sourly how many years it took to learn to sling oneself into a sword as easily as yawn; and then wondered if she wanted to spend so many years that way. Or if she would have the choice. She had not liked waking up to find herself clutching her sword hilt as a child might clutch a favorite toy. Perhaps it was as well to have to think of shoulder and waist, belt and buckle. Another man came in, carrying another sword. Corlath took this one too, and held the scabbard in his left hand, letting the belt dangle; and he pulled it free and waved it, gleaming, under the light of the candles in the great chandelier. There was a blue stone set in its hilt, and it glared defiantly in the light. This was a shorter lighter sword than Corlath's, but the suppleness of it, and the way it hung, waiting, in the air, gave it a look of infinite age, and sentience, as if it looked out at those who looked at it. "This is Gonturan," said Corlath, and a murmur of assent and of recognition went around the hall; the Riders were silent. "She is the greatest treasure of my family. For a few years in his youth each son has carried her; but she was not meant for a man's hands, and legend has it that she will betray the man who dares bear her after his twentieth year. This is the Lady Aerin's sword; and it has been many a long year since there has been a woman to carry it."

Harry was staring at the blade, and barely heard Corlath's words; she was watching a flame-haired woman riding in a forest that seemed to grow against the flat of the shining sword; in her hand was another sword, and the hilt sparkled blue.

All the other Riders were standing up, and Corlath reached down and seized her wrist. "Stand up, disi," he said. "I'm about to make you a Rider." She stood, dazed. A disi was a silly child. There was another who rode with the woman who carried the Blue Sword; he rode a few paces behind her.

"A Rider?" Harry said.

"A Rider," Corlath replied firmly.

She dragged her eyes away from the winking sword edge and looked at him. Another man of the household set a small flat pot of yellow salve at Corlath's right hand. The king dipped the fingers of that hand in it, then drew them to smear the ointment across his palm. He had shifted Gonturan to his left hand; now he seized the blade near the tip with his right, and gave it a quick twist. "Damn," he said, as the blood welled between his fingers and dripped to the floor. He picked up a napkin and squeezed it. "Take my sword, Harimad-sol," he said, "and do the same—but not so enthusiastically. I think, though, that Katuchim has not the sense of humor that Gonturan does, so do not fear him."

She dipped her fingers in the salve, and touched them gently to her palm; reached out and, as awkwardly as if she had never learned one lesson from Mathin, dragged Corlath's sword from its scabbard. It was so long she had to brace the hilt against the table to get a reasonable angle on the edge. She closed her fingers around it, thought about something else, and felt the skin of her palm just part. She opened her hand, and three drops of blood only sprang from the thinnest of red lines across her skin. "Well done!"

said Mathin over her shoulder, and the Riders cheered; and the whole hall picked it up, shouting.

Corlath grinned down at her, and she could not help smiling back. "There have been more graceful kings and Riders since the world began, but we'll do," said Corlath to her, quietly, below the roar around them. "Take your sword, and mind you treat her well. You will have Aerin's shade to answer to, else."

Harry's fingers closed round the blue hilt and she knew at once that she would handle this sword very well indeed—or it would handle her. For a moment she found herself wishing that she had been carrying Gonturan the day of the trials, and at this a slow sly smile spread across her face. She raised her eyes to Corlath's face—he had taken his own sword back and sheathed it, and one of the Riders was tying the napkin around the wounded hand and saying something sardonic; but Corlath only laughed, and turned back to watch her. Such was the slow sly smile he offered her in return that she rather thought he knew just what she was thinking.

"Damalur-sol!" the people cried. "Damalur-sol!"

| 151

H ARRY HAD TROUBLE FALLING ASLEEP that night; she listened to the gentle sound the water made walking down the three stone steps, and often she stretched out her hand to touch the hilt of the blue sword that lay beside her, carefully laid upon a small carpet of blue and green and gold that she had found in a corner of a hall on her way back to her mosaic palace after the feast. She had appropriated it, rolled it up, tucked it under her arm, and glared at the woman of the household who was conducting her. The woman dropped her eyes, but did not seem unduly disturbed. Who would grudge a damalur-sol a little rug? Harimad-sol thought airily.

But each time she touched the blue sword it was as if a shock ran through her, and she listened to the quiet night, hearing the echoes of sounds that had rung themselves to silence hundreds of years ago. Her restlessness made Narknon grumble at her, although the cat did not offer to leave the bed and sleep elsewhere. At last Harry tucked her hands firmly beneath her chin and fell asleep, and in her sleep she saw Aerin-sol again, and Aerin smiled at her. "Gonturan will do well for you, I think, child, as she did well for me. You can feel it in the way she hangs in your hand, can you not?" Harry, in her dream, nodded. "Gonturan is far older than I am, you know; she was given me with the weight of her own years and legend already upon her. I never knew all she might lead her bearer into—and as it was, I learned more than enough.

"Gonturan has her own sense of honor, child. But she is not

human, and you must not trust her as human; remember it. She is a true friend, but a friend with thoughts of her own, and the thoughts of others are dangerous."

Aerin paused, and the dream began to fade; her face was pale, and half imagined, like a cloud on a summer's dawn, with her hair the sunrise. "What luck I had, may it go with you."

Harry woke up, and found the sword gleaming blue in a light that seemed to come from the blue mosaic walls, from the blue stone in the hilt, even from the silver water of the stream.

Several days passed, while some of the Riders went forth on errands; but the newest Rider did not. She spent long hours in the mosaic palace, staring at the air, which hung, or so it seemed to her, like tapestry around her; and in that tapestry was woven all of history—her own, her Homeland's, as well as Damar's. Sometimes she saw a little bright shimmer like someone tossing back a fire-red mane of hair; and sometimes she saw the glint of a blue jewel—but that was no doubt only some chance reflection from the glossy walls around her.

But most of all, she slept. Mathin had been right about the sorgunal. For several days she was content to sleep, and waken to do nothing in particular, and sleep again. Narknon enjoyed it as much as she did. "I'm sure Mathin did not put any of that stuff in the porridge," Harry said to the cat; "there's no excuse for you."

On the fourth morning Mathin came to her, and found her pacing from fountain to fountain and from wall to wall. "This is not a cage to enclose you, Hari," he said.

She turned, startled, for she had been deep in her thoughts and had not heard his approach. She smiled. "I have not felt caged. I have . . . slept a great deal, as you warned me. It is only today I have begun to . . . think again."

Mathin smiled in return. "Is it so ill, this thinking?"

"Why am I a Rider?" she replied. "There is no reason for Corlath to make an Outlander girl, even the laprun minta, a Rider. Riders are his best. Why?"

Mathin's smile twisted. "I told you, long ago—long ago, more than a week since. It is a good thing for us to have a damalur-sol.

It is a good thing for us to have something to look to, for hope. Perhaps you do yourself too little honor."

Harry snorted. "Has a laprun ever been made a Rider before?"

Mathin took a long time to answer. "No. You are the first to bear that burden."

"And an Outlander at that."

"You Outlanders are human, for all of that—as the Northerners are not. It is not impossible that some Outlander might have . . . a Gift, *kelar,* like ours, as you do—for you do. There is something in you we recognize, and we know it is there, for Lady Aerin has chosen you herself. Corlath makes you a Rider to . . . to take advantage of whatever it is you carry in your Outlander blood that has made you Damarian, even against your will."

Harry slowly shook her head. "Not against my will. At least not any more. But I do not understand."

"No; nor do I. Nor even does Corlath. He—" Mathin stopped.

Harry looked sharply at him. "Corlath what?"

The faint smile drifted across Mathin's face again. "Corlath did not steal you of his own free will. His *kelar* demanded it."

Harry grinned. "Yes; I had guessed, and once he told me—something of the sort. I saw dismay on his face often enough, those early days."

Mathin's face was expressionless when she raised her eyes again to his. "You have not seen dismay there for a long day since."

"No," she agreed, and her eyes went involuntarily to the mosaic walls around her.

Mathin said, "You are a token, a charm, to us, Daughter of the Riders and Rider and Damalur-sol."

"A mascot, you mean," Harry said, but without bitterness; and still she looked at the mosaic walls. She asked timidly, not certain of her own motives, "Does Corlath have no family? I see here, in the castle, the people of the household, and the—us—Riders, but no one else. Is it only that they are cloistered—or that I am?"

Mathin shook his head. "You see all there is to see. In Aerin's day the king's family filled this place; some had to live in the City, or chose to, for privacy. But kings in the latter days . . . Corlath's father married late, and Corlath is his queen's only surviving child, for she was a frail lady. Corlath himself has not married." Mathin smiled bleakly. "Kings should marry young and get heirs early, that their people may have one thing less to worry about. There has been no one in generations whose *kelar* is as strong as Corlath's; it is why the scattered folk along our borders and in the secret hearts of our Hills, who have acknowledged no Damarian king for many years, rally now to Corlath. Even where he does not go himself his messengers are alight with it."

After Mathin left her, Harry thought of taking another nap, but decided against it. Instead she rode out on Sungold, Narknon deigning to accompany them. She found at the back of the stone castle and beyond the stone stables a practice ground, stepped into the sides of the Hill, for those wishing to practice horsemanship and war. It was deserted, as though the menace of the Northerners was too near to permit of practice. But she jogged slowly around the empty field, Sungold stepping up or down as they came to each edge, and decided to practice anyway: she who was laprun victor, who had never held a sword till a few weeks ago, who was suddenly a Rider: she felt, a little wildly, that she needed all the practice she could get.

She was wearing Gonturan, a little self-consciously, but she had felt somehow that it would be impolite to leave her behind. She unsheathed her and wondered if the ancient sword had ever been used to hack at straw figures and charge at dangling wooden tiles. She galloped Tsornin over poles laid on the ground, piles of stone and wooden logs, and up and down turfed banks, and over ditches. She felt a little silly; but Tsornin made it plain that he enjoyed it all, whatever it was and however humble, and Gonturan always struck true.

Harry took Tsornin back to his stable and put him away with her own hands, studiously ignoring the brown-clad groom who hovered near her. Hers was the first human face she had seen since she rode out. The stables were on the same scale as the castle: large and grand, the loose-boxes the size of small fields. There were over a hundred stalls—Harry lost count when she tried to multiply them out in her head—in the barn Sungold was quartered in, and two other barns as big stood on either side of it. Sungold's stable was nearly full; sleek curious noses were thrust out at them as they left and returned. Harry saw no other men or women of the horse; they must reappear at some point, she thought, to tend the horses. Unless Hill horses can be trained to take care of themselves—it wouldn't surprise me. The silence was uncanny. Tsornin's hoofs had echoed around the practice field; and when she thanked the brown woman and said no, she needed nothing, her voice sounded strange in her ears.

Over the next few days she rode out again and again, and spent some hours slaying straw men with the Dragon-Killer's sword, and then some hours riding out from the stone ring of the castle, and into the stone City, down the smooth roads. She saw mostly women and young children, but even of them there were rarely more than a few. The women watched her timidly, and smiled eagerly if she smiled at them first; and the children wanted to pet Sungold, which he was good enough to permit, and Narknon, who usually eluded them; and sometimes they brought her flowers. But the City was as empty as the castle was; there were people, but far fewer than its walls might hold. Some of this, she knew, was because the army was massing elsewhere—on the laprun fields, before the City; messengers came and went swiftly, and the gathering of forces hung heavily in the air. But most of it was because, as the king's family had dwindled, so had the king's people; there were few Damarians left.

She thought again of the mounting strangenesses of her recent life; and she wished, if she was to be given to Damar, as apparently she was, that she would be given no more long pauses of inaction in which to brood about it all.

One of the young women who had assisted her at her bath brought her food, in the blue front room with the fountain, or outside in the sunshine where the other fountain played; and she managed to convince her and the other women sent to wait upon her that, at least as long as there were no more banquets requiring special preparations, she might bathe herself. For three more days she slept and watched the shimmering of the air and rode Tsornin and played with Narknon. There was a friendship between the horse and the hunting-cat now, and they would chase one another around the obstacles of the practice field, Narknon's tail lashing and Sungold with his ears back in mock fury. Once the big cat had hidden behind one of the grassy banks, where Harry and Sungold could not see her; and as they rode by she leaped out at them, sailing clean over Sungold and Harry on his back. Harry ducked and Sungold swerved; and Narknon circled and came back to them with her ears back and her whiskers trembling in what was obviously a cat laugh.

And Harry polished Gonturan and tried not to brood, and looked often at the small white scar in the palm of her hand. But with all her inevitable musings she found that a certain peace had come to her and made its way into her heart. It was not like anything she had known before, and it was only on that third day that she found a name for it: fate. Yet she wished that the business of war were not so all-consuming, that she might have someone to talk to.

On the fourth day when the woman came with her afternoon meal, Corlath came with her; and evidently he was expected, although not by Harry, for there were two goblets and two plates on the tray, and far more food than she could eat alone. She was sitting on the flagstones beside the fountain in the sunshine, watching the prisms that the falling drops threw into the air; and Narknon was washing Harry's face with her razored tongue, and Harry was trying not to mind. She was trying not to mind with such concentration that she did not realize till she looked up, still dazzled by tiny intricate colors, that he was there; and she remained sitting, blinking up at him, as the woman set down her tray and retired.

"May I eat with you?" he said, and Harry thought that he seemed ill at ease.

"Of course," she said. "I would—er—be honored." She pushed Narknon's head away and started to scramble to her feet, but Corlath dropped silently down beside her, so she settled back again, grateful that her bones decided not to creak. He gave her a plate and took his own; and then sat staring into the fountain much as she had done, and she wondered, watching him, if he felt any of the queer peacefulness that crept into her with the same looking; and if he would call it by the name she had discovered.

"Eight days," she said, and his eyes drew back from the water spray and met hers. "Eight days," she repeated. "You said less than a fortnight."

"Yes," he replied. "We are counting the hours now." He made a swift sweeping motion with his right hand, and Harry said suddenly: "Show me your hand."

Corlath looked puzzled for a moment, but then he held his right hand out, palm up. There was one short straight pale mark across it, obviously new; and many small white scars; she didn't have to count them to know there would be eighteen of them, the still-fresh—and longest—cut a nineteenth. She studied the hand a moment, cupping it in her own, not thinking that she was poring over a king's hand; then she looked at her own right palm. One tiny straight line looked back at her.

He closed his hand and rested it on his knee. "They don't fade," Harry said. "The old ones don't disappear."

"No," said Corlath. "It is the yellow salve, before we make the cut; it is made of an herb called korim—forever."

She studied her own palm again for a moment. The scar cut through the lines a fortune-teller would call her life line and her heart line; and she wondered what Damarian fortune-tellers might see in her hand. She looked up at Corlath, who absently put a piece of bread in his mouth and began to chew; he was staring into the fountain again. He swallowed and said: "There is a story of one of my grandfather's Riders: the Northern border was restless then—but only restless, and this man had gone North to see what he might learn. But they caught him, and recognized him as from Damar; but he knew they would find him a little before they did, and he slashed his hand that they might not find the mark and hold him for ransom—or torture; for the Northerners, if they wish, can torture with a fine prying magic that no mind can resist."

Harry thought: If the Northerners know about the Riders' mark, they must be a bit slow not to wonder about a spy caught with a cut-up hand.

Corlath continued after a moment: "He had traveled dressed as a merchant, so when he knew they would find him he freed his horse and sent it home, and took off his boots, and began to climb the near-perpendicular face of one of the Hills that is the boundary between our land and theirs. When they found him he was half mad with sunstroke and his hands and feet were as tattered as autumn leaves. They decided they had not caught a prize at all, and after they had beaten him a bit, they let him go. He finished climbing the mountain with his hands and feet, because he remembered that much of what he was doing; and just over the summit, just inside the border of Damar, his horse was waiting for him, and she took him home. He recovered from the sunstroke, but he never held a sword again."

Harry swallowed a lump of bread that didn't want to go down, and there was silence for a bit. "What happened to the mare?" she said at last.

"Your Tsornin's dam is a daughter of his mare's line," Corlath said, but it was as if he were tracing some thought of his own. "The mare lived till she was almost thirty, and dropped a foal every year till the last. Many of our best riding-horses are descended from her." Corlath looked at her, coming back from wherever he had been.

"That mare's line is called Nalan—faithful. You can see it in Tsornin's pedigree."

Harry asked lightly: "And is there a name for the line of the kings of Damar?"

Corlath said, "My father's name, and his father's, and mine, is Gulkonoth: stone."

Harry looked at his right hand resting quietly on his knee. He paused and added as if inconsequentially, "There are other names for the king. One of them is Tudorsond. Scarred hand."

"Does the korim scar the foreheads of the household, and the faces of the hunt and the horse as well?" And Corlath said, "Yes."

There was a silence again, and Harry wondered how many other questions she might be able to gain answers for. She said, "Once in the mountains before the trials, Mathin said to me that he could teach me three ways of starting a fire, but that you knew a fourth. He would not tell me what the fourth was."

Corlath laughed. "I will show you one day, if you wish. Not today. Today it would give you a headache."

Harry shook her head angrily, her feeling of contentment gone. "I am *tired* of having things only half explained. Either I am damalur-sol, when it is convenient, or I am to be quiet and sit in a corner and behave till it is time to bring me out and show me to the troops again. Did you choose Mathin to teach me because he is close-mouthed?"

Corlath looked a little abashed, and Harry guiltily remembered how much Mathin had told her, although—she defended herself— it was not enough. Never enough. But she could not help remembering his answer when she had asked him why he had been chosen for her training.

"I chose Mathin because I thought he would teach you best; there are none better than he, and he is patient and tireless."

And kind, thought Harry, but she would not interrupt when she might learn something.

"We of the Hills—I suppose we are all, as you say, close-mouthed; but do you think you have learned so little of us?" And Corlath looked at her—wistfully.

"No," she said, ashamed of herself. There was a pause, and she said, "Could you perhaps, please, tell me why Mathin would not tell me any of the legends about the Lady Aerin? They are a part of your lives that all of you share—and it is her sword you have given me—and the legends, why, there are a few sung even at the spring Fairs in the west, where Outlanders can hear them."

Corlath tapped his fingers, one-two-three, one-two-three, on the brim of the fountain. "Aerin is a part of your destiny, Harimad-sol. It is considered unlucky to . . . meddle with destiny. Mathin would feel that he was doing you a disservice, speaking much of Aerin to you, and I—I find, now, that I feel the same." Tap-tap-tap. "If you had grown up . . . here, you would have heard them. But you did not. And if you had, perhaps you would not now be what you are.

"I am sorry." He turned and looked at her. "If—after we have met the Northerners, and the gods have decided between us, if you and I are left alive, I will tell you all the stories I know of Aerin Dragon-Killer." He tried to smile. "I even can sing a few."

"Thank you."

Corlath's smile became more successful. "There are a very great many of them—you may not wish to hear them all."

"I *do* wish to hear them all," said Harry firmly.

Corlath took his hand away from the stone brim and began to shred a chunk of bread into fragments on his plate. "As for the first question," he said, "watch." He blinked a few times, closed his eyes, and a shudder ran through him; then he opened his eyes again and gave a hot yellow glare to the little heap of bread crumbs, which burst into flame, crackled wildly for a few minutes, and subsided into black ash.

"Oh," said Harry. Corlath looked up; his eyes were brown. They stared at one another. Harry found herself saying hastily, in a voice that was a little too high-pitched, "What is this place— here—?" and she jerked her eyes away, and waved to the mosaic walls. "I have seen nothing else like it anywhere in the City."

Corlath shook his head. "Nor will you." He got slowly to his feet, and looked around, and cupped his scarred hand under the fountain, and drank from it. "My father built it for my mother just after he married her. She was fond of the color blue—and I think he wanted to tell her that he did not mind that she would never carry the Blue Sword, the greatest treasure of his family, the woman's sword." He looked down at her inscrutably, but his eyes did not focus on her. Then he turned and left her, going through the door into the castle.

Two days later the army rode away from the City. Corlath and his Riders rode together down the highway from the castle to the gates of the City, with men and women of the household and the hunt and horse, and pack horses behind them; and the people of the City lined the streets and silently watched them go, although many raised their hands to their foreheads and flicked the fingers as they rode by. Harry had not seen so many before; some were refugees from northern Damarian villages, and farmers from the green lands before the Bledfi Gap. And they rode down to the plain where the army Harry had not seen, for she had not left the City since she rode into it, lay before them; and behind her she heard a sound no Damarian had heard in generations: the City's stone gates closing, heavily, mournfully.

Tsornin was restless. Now, with the ranks upon ranks of the Hill army drawn up upon it, the plain looked like some other place than the plain where Harry and Tsornin had fought with blunt staves and sword points. Tsornin was too well bred to do more than fidget slightly in place; but his shoulder, when she ran her hand down it, was warmer than the morning air deserved. The muscles under the golden skin were hard; she felt that if she rapped her knuckles against his shoulder ridge it would ring like iron.

She stood, a little awkwardly, in the group of Riders, only a little way into the plain from the end of the City highway. They were on a little rise of land, so they looked out and down over the rest of the company, and Harry felt unnecessarily conspicuous. "Why couldn't you be liver chestnut or something?" she whispered to Tsornin, who bowed his golden head. A new helm fitted closely down over her bound-up hair, and there were new boots on her legs, with tops that rolled up and lashed into place for battle; and she felt Gonturan hanging expectantly at her knee. Ten days were not enough to accustom herself to being a Rider, however hard she had driven herself and Tsornin round the lonely practice fields with their stiff wooden silhouettes of enemy swordsmen; and while the Riders themselves—particularly one or two: Mathin, and the merry (for a Rider) young Innath—closed ranks around her and accepted her as one of them, she could not believe that they did not themselves wonder, a little, about her presence among them.

Sungold blew impatiently and began to dig a hole with one front foot. She booted his elbow with her toe and he stopped, but after a moment he lowered his head and blew again, harder, and she could feel him shifting his weight, considering if she might let him dig just a small hole. She looked around: the other horses were showing signs of stress as well. Mathin stood next to her; Windrider, although rock still, unlike the younger Tsornin, wore a dark sheen of sweat down her flank. Corlath's Fireheart was standing on his hind legs again; the king could bring him down as he chose, but Harry rather thought the horse was expressing the mood of both of them. Narknon, so far as Harry could see, was the only one of their company who remained undisturbed. She sat in front of Sungold, just beyond the reach of pawing forefeet, and washed her chest and combed her whiskers.

They marched west. They crossed the low but steep ridge of mountains between the City and the desert plain that stretched far away, up to the back door of the Outlander Residency in Istan. They retraced Harry and Mathin's route, going in single endless file through the narrow paths; and they came to the desert edge at the end of the second day. Beyond the ridge they turned north.

All the spies—those still living, for the North had caught a few—that Corlath had sent out in the last several years had come back in the last few months, in a rush, all with the same word: the waiting was over, the Northerners were moving. The last man of them had returned not six days before; it had taken him so long because they knew about him, and he had dodged and fled and scrambled to get away from their creeping tracking magic. His tale was that their army was only days behind him, and that it was many thousands strong. He had delayed and delayed to take a fairer tally of the total; and yet, he said, even as the army marched south, hundreds and more hundreds appeared as if out of the air to march with it. Out of the air, Harry thought, and wondered if the phrase was more than just a manner of speaking. She had been included in the council of Riders that heard the man's tale; and the candlelight seemed to cast more shadows when he was through. Yet there was nothing to be done; the army that would stand for Damar was already gathered; the plans to face the Northerners were already laid.

Of the Northerners' dread captain no spy was sure; no Damarian dared get that close, for the uncanny way he was said to smell foreign blood.

There were hundreds of mounted men and women now following Corlath's word; and as they rode with the eastern Hills at their right hand, they looked a great many. A few hundreds more would join as the southern army made its way to the wide plain before the Gap. But that was all.

Innath, riding at her elbow, said conversationally, "Less than half of the Northern army will be mounted; and not many of them will be riding horses; and very few of their horses will match the poorest of ours. One can double our tally at least, just for our horses; for they are Damarians and will fight for Damar as fiercely as we human beings, for all that we are the only ones who talk about it."

"Yes," said Harry, her voice only a little muffled.

Noontimes they stopped briefly, loosening girths to let the horses breathe, and eating bread and dry meat and water. At night they camped behind ridges of shale and scrub, and lit fires enough to boil the terrible dry meat to a slightly more edible consistency, and rolled up in their blankets to sleep where they sat. A few of the hunting-cats and a dozen dogs were with them; but they could not spare the time at present to use them. Narknon continued at Harry's heels and, as she had done once before, began hunting on her own, and brought back some of her grisly victories to lay at Harry's pillow. As the days passed and Mathin's stew pot became generally known as the only one reliably containing fresh meat, it grew very popular.

The nights were clear and quiet, and the weather-casters among them promised no sudden windstorms; the edges of the Damarian Hills were known for their unpredictable weather, where mountain storms bottled up by the steep slopes might suddenly find

164 |

their way to the flatter lands where they could rage and riot as they chose.

Corlath was not trying to strike at once for the center of the northern mountains and the Bledfi Gap. After the Hill army crossed the narrow range behind which the City lay, they worked their way around the curve of the mountains, trotting through the sandy sour grass and broken rock at their feet. At first this made them ride almost due north, then in an increasing arc to the west; and the sun moved across the sky before them. Often in the mornings when the mist was still lying around them, trailing from the mountains' shoulders into their camp, a little group of riders, or even a solitary figure on horseback, would loom up at them from nowhere; but Corlath always seemed to be expecting them, and they always knew what to say to the guards that they might pass; and in this way the army a little swelled its ranks. Occasionally Harry heard a woman's voice among the strangers, and this made her glad; and often she'd rub a finger over the blue gem in the hilt of Gonturan and think of the sword no man could carry. Mathin said to her once: "We did not think to see so many women—few have fought with us within any man's memory, although in Aerin's day it was different. But I think many fathers are letting their daughters join us who had not thought to till they heard of Harimad-sol, and that Gonturan went to war again."

Many of these women she met; particularly after Mathin had spoken to her, for then she began to feel a little uneasily responsible for them. Senay she saw several times—and saw too that she was wearing a sewn-together sash as if she were proud of it. Harimad-sol asked the names of the women when she had a chance, and they answered gravely; and they often gave her the back-of-hand-to-forehead gesture of respect, and none ever asked her her name, even when she was not carrying Gonturan and ought to look—she thought—like any other disheveled soldier.

Most of those who came thus late to join Corlath's army did not carry a sword, and wore no sash; these were men and women who had spent their lives in their own villages, on their own farms and in their own shops, and had never attended laprun trials, nor felt the lack that they had not.

One evening they rode into a hollow where nearly a hundred strangers, all mounted, and with several pack horses and hunting-beasts besides, waited for them; and Corlath rode forward with a great hearty cry of welcome, a sound nearer happiness than any Harry had heard from him since they began their march north. A rider at the head of the group rode to meet him, and they seized each other by the shoulders while their horses bumped uneasily together and rolled their eyes at each other. A third man then de-tached himself from the new group and joined Corlath and his friend. "Murfoth and his son, Terim," said Mathin in Harry's ear. "Murfoth was one of the old king's friends, though he's not much more than ten years older than our king. He might have been a Rider, had he wished, but he chose instead to stay at home and look after his lands; and a good job he's made of it too. Some of our best horses now come from him, and grain to feed many more."

"We Riders," said Innath from her other side, "as you may have noticed, tend to be fourth sons or otherwise penniless—or incura-ble wanderers like Mathin here—but Murfoth now, when he comes to ride with his king, can bring eighty men with him." In-nath's voice, for all its careless pride, sounded almost wistful. Harry found herself remembering her father's words to her—it seemed decades ago: "You haven't a penny, you know."

Terim was Harry's age, and when he and his father came to sit at the king's fireside he came to her and sank down beside her, folding up his long legs as all the Hillmen did. She looked at Terim and he looked at her; his look was eager and a little, to her embar-rassment, reverent. "I was First at my laprun trials three years ago," he said; "but when I took my turn against Corlath my sash was on the ground before I had a good grip on my sword." He thumped the hilt of his sword, which jangled as it bit into the ground. "My father gave me Teksun here anyway, he said no one ever got a grip on a sword against Corlath. You did, though." His eyes shone in the firelight.

Harry ran a meditative finger over the careful seam in her sash,

166 |

which she had put in under Mathin's promised tutelage. "I didn't know it was he—I never thought. And he *allowed* me to cross swords with him; and when I realized how much of it was allowing, I got . . . mad." She paused. "I was surprised too." She frowned, remembering the awful headache she'd had for most of that day, and then the more awful sick lurch that seemed to start behind her eyes, where the headache was, and quiver all the way through her body, when she saw the face behind the scarf she had just removed. No one had called her baga for the cut at the corner of Corlath's mouth, though. She met the boy's eyes somewhat ruefully and said, "It wasn't as pleasant an experience as you might think."

Terim gave a little snort of laughter and said, "Yes, I believe you," and Harry looked across to where Corlath sat with Terim's father ar.d found him watching her. She wondered if he had heard what she had just said.

CHAPTER ELEVEN

I N THE HOLLOW WHERE THEY MET Murfoth they set up their first proper camp. The hunting-beasts all went out that night, and everyone, not just a few Riders, had good fresh meat for dinner. The king's zotar was put up, and it was obvious that it was the king's, for it was the biggest, but this one was plain, a dull dun color, and the door was just a tent flap, and inside there were a few carpets, and hooks on side poles for lanterns, but that was all; although the black-and-white banner still flew bravely from the peak of the roof. She and the king and Murfoth and most of the Riders—Innath and Mathin among them—slept within it; but she lay awake a long time listening to the others breathe. You didn't hear the person next to you breathing if there wasn't a ceiling over you to keep the noise closed in. She missed the stars.

The next morning there was breakfast at a long table similar to the one where she had first met the Riders; they were all there again, with a few others of those who had joined them over the last few days. Corlath explained what was immediately ahead of them: how they would climb into the mountains again—the range was widest where the curve west was sharpest—to meet the high plateau where the Lake of Dreams lay, and where Luthe lived. Luthe? thought Harry. Most of the army would not climb all the way to the meeting-place, but fade into the forest in little groups and pretend to be invisible; for, so far at least, Corlath and the outriders believed they had not been sighted. Harry blinked and wondered if the morning mists that seemed to continue all day long every day as a kind of dull haze had after all been more than a curious local weather pattern. Luthe himself—Mathin told her this during an interval while the household folk brought in hot malak—had ways even Corlath did not understand of seeing things, and Corlath wished to see and speak to him. But Luthe never left his lands, and so it was necessary to seek him there. "Luthe claims that lowland air confuses him," Mathin said, and shrugged the uneven Hill shrug. "It is not for us to know." He picked up his cup.

"Yes, but who *is* Luthe?" said Harry.

Mathin regarded her with his inscrutable expression. "No one knows," he said. "Luthe is . . . someone who lives in the mountains, who sees things—things something like what some of us see when we taste the Meeldtar. He has been there a very long time. No one can remember when Luthe came, or when he has not lived on his mountain."

"And the Lake of Dreams?"

Mathin stared into his cup. "There is a spring that runs into the Lake of Dreams, and it is where the Water of Sight is found; but sometimes the water from the spring is only water, and no one knows why; although it is believed that Luthe knows. Water drunk from the Lake of Dreams does not give the Sight, as the true Meeldtar does; but it is not quite like drinking . . . water."

Harry sighed.

Corlath explained briefly for the newcomers what the army was proposing to do. The Northerners must, perforce, choose the one wide pass in the mountains that led into the great central plain and then the bare desert of Damar, for it was the only gap large enough to accommodate an army's numbers. The gap was a bit west of the midpoint of the length of the mountains from the curve where the north-south mountains, the Ildik range, became the east-west Horfel Mountains. When the last of Corlath's little army had collected in the hollow at the elbow of the two ranges, they would ride as quickly as horseflesh would allow to the mouth of that pass, and prepare to engage the enemy among the empty villages and deserted fields of Damar.

Then there was a silence, for all in the king's tent knew that Corlath's force could not win a victory from the Northerners; nor were they likely able to resist them to the point that the invaders would decide Damar wasn't worth the trouble and return home. The best the defenders could hope for, and this they did hope for, was to cause enough trouble and loss that the Northern army would not have the strength left to seize all of Damar in quite so tight and effective a grip as Thurra would wish; and that pockets of renegade Hillfolk might hide in the Hills, or under the *kelar* of the City. If they succeeded so much, the battle would be worth what it would cost them, for they would have preserved themselves a future.

Harry swallowed uncomfortably. She heard, a little dizzily, what Corlath was saying about the foothills the mountain pass gave into, and where the army would stand; and she cast in her mind for her best memory of Damarian geography, for she had the unpleasant sensation that something was being ignored, something that shouldn't be. Corlath was saying that they would decide more exactly once they arrived, but he seemed to know every stone and clump of grass there, the exact location of every farmhouse, as did those who listened; no one fell so low as to seek recourse to a map. She frowned in concentration. She could almost see the Residency map of Daria; it was very poor at the eastern end; it barely admitted to the existence of the mountains where the king's City stood—the City itself was one of Jack Dedham's native legends—but about the west it was pretty accurate. . . . Ah!

Corlath had fallen silent. Murfoth said something and there was another silence, and Harry put in, timidly but stubbornly: "Sola, what of the pass just northwest of the . . . of the Outlander station? It is narrow, but not so narrow that the . . . the Northerners could not send a line through to come up behind us."

Corlath frowned. "Let them take the Outlander city—it will keep them amused long enough to delay them, perhaps. Even the Outlanders will try to stop them when they are on the threshold."

There was a silence so rigid that Harry felt that speaking words into it was like chopping holes in a frozen lake. "They would do a better job trying to stop them if they were warned," she said. Her words didn't make much of a hole; the ice thickened visibly. She didn't want to do anything so obvious as put her hand on her sword hilt; but she did press her elbow surreptitiously against it, and stiffened her spine.

"They *were* warned," said Corlath, and Harry raised her eyes to his and saw the golden tide rising in them; and wondered what that fruitless conversation in the Residency must have cost him. Yet he hadn't burned the Residency down with that golden glare of his, as she suspected he could have; and so she blinked at him now and said, "Colonel Dedham would listen to you. You did not know the Northerners were on the march . . . then; you know for certain now. The pass is narrow; he could hold it for you indefinitely—but not if they have had time to come through and go where they will." Her voice was rising with fear and perhaps anger: was there anything but stubborn pride, the offended majesty of the absolute ruler of his small land, working in Corlath, that he should waste a chance to gain a little more time? How little she knew him after all, and how little she knew Damar, she who could not visualize every yellow blade of korf before the great pass in the mountains. And yet she could see—did she not truly see?—the threat that this second, narrow pass presented; a threat that the king and the commander of the army was choosing to overlook. She did not understand; she was born of a different people and she understood different things.

"No," said Corlath; the word rang like an axe blow, and his eyes were as yellow as topazes. Harry stared back at him—*you great bully*—even knowing what he could do to her, even as the sweat broke out on her skin with the effort of holding his eyes. Her elbow clamped desperately on Gonturan, and the hard edge of the blue gem dug into her ribs and encouraged her. Then he snapped his gaze from her and pointed it at the tent flap and shouted, though he rarely shouted, and fresh malak was brought in and fruit with it. The ice began, nervously, to break up, and Harry glowered at her cup and refused to be drawn into conversation, and listened to her heart beating, and wondered if she were a traitor; and if so, to whom?

The next morning thirty-five chosen horsemen, with Corlath at their head and Harry, still somewhat sulky, among them, started up the track to Luthe's holding. The rest of the army broke camp first, and melted into the scrub of the mountains' feet, taking the hunting-beasts and the pack horses with them. Corlath and the little band with him waited till last, watching them go, judging if their disappearance was effective; looking to see if there were any too obvious paths broken in the undergrowth. A few fleeks broke cover, but that was the only sign of their passage. Corlath and whoever else might have a weather talent must have been satisfied, and Harry watched, with a few cold fingers working their way up her spine in spite of the heat: for the loyal fog over them was blandly breaking up. The sky was blue and clear. A britti burst into song, and Harry raised her eyes to watch the little brown speck zigzagging madly overhead. Corlath sent his big bay forward, and thirty-four riders, and one obstinate hunting-cat, followed.

Harry hung near the back. She had not slept the night before for thinking of the northwest pass and Jack Dedham; Dedham's face watching Corlath as he stormed out of the Residency; and Corlath's face as he said, "Let them take the Outlander city—it will keep them amused."

Surely there was a reason none of the Hillfolk thought that gap into Damar worth consideration? But if there was a reason, what was the reason? Perhaps this Luthe would show some sense. Perhaps his crystal ball or what-have-you would say, "Beware the northwest pass! Beware!"

And then again maybe it wouldn't. So, Harry, what do you propose to do about it then?

She didn't know. She concentrated on Sungold's ears, slender and pricked, framing the trail in front of her, and the dark grey haunches of Innath's horse going on before. The scrub gave way to trees, and the trees to greater trees, till they were walking in a forest heavy with age, where even the air tasted old. By the end of the afternoon all the riders were on foot, walking with their sweat-dark horses up a steep uneven incline. Harry was panting, but she tried to do it quietly. Corlath probably never breathed hard. Tsornin's nostrils showed red, but his ears were as alert as ever, and occasionally he would rub his nose gently against the nape of her neck, just in case she was momentarily not thinking about him. Narknon ranged beside them like a dappled shadow. The trees were so tall and grand that Harry, watching her, could believe that she was no bigger than a housecat; that when she came up to be petted, she would twine around Harry's ankles, and Harry would pick her up with one hand and put her on her shoulder.

The trees were so high overhead that the twilight beneath them might have been sunset, but might only be leaf shade; and they were a silent company, for no one spoke and the footfalls were muted by leaves and moss. Harry allowed herself to wonder about the trail, as an alternative to her endless mental circles about northwest passes: that it stayed clear enough that no one had to duck under low-hanging branches, or fight a way through an encroaching bush, but so little used that the moss underfoot was thick and smooth. And still smooth after thirty horses and thirty human pedestrians have tramped over it, the thirty-first pedestrian thought, scuffing it curiously with one foot. Sturdy moss. Maybe Luthe is a botanist in his spare time.

By nightfall Harry was still walking only by dint of holding a large handful of Sungold's mane in one hand. She had tried resting an arm across his back, but his back was too high for comfort; and her sweaty hand kept sliding through his fine hair. Even his head was hanging a little low, and Harry knew she was still in company only by the soft creaking of other saddles and the occasional flicker in the gloom immediately ahead that was Innath's horse flipping its tail.

As she walked her eyes closed and the colors of exhaustion twinkled across her eyelids. Then to her dismay they began to sort themselves out into patterns, but she was too tired even to open her eyes and disperse them. She saw a red-haired rider on a white horse. The horse was old, white with age, the bones of its face very clear and fine; she thought it went just a bit short with its right hind foot, but its neck was arched and its tail high. The rider's shoulders were set grimly, the legs against the horse's sides were determined, not eager. There was a smoky redness to the horizon beyond them, scarlet that did not look like dawn or sunset; they were going toward it, and the light flashed off a chain around the rider's neck and the helm tied to the saddle, and the rider's hair, and the horse's flanks. Harry wondered where they were going, where they had come from. The countryside could have been Damar. It could have been almost anywhere.

She realized there was light shining through her eyelids; it was setting the white horse on fire. The horse broke into a canter, a shining glistening wave of motion. . . . Harry dizzily opened her eyes. They were approaching a clearing set with torches; she could see Corlath halted, talking to a man as tall as he was, but narrower; the man's hair was yellow. Innath broke into the lighted circle, and Harry came after, trying not to stumble, too tired even to take her hand out of Sungold's mane for pride's sake. She looked around a little, and the faces she could see near her were haggard and drooping. Perversely, this gave her strength; she dropped her hand and straightened her shoulders. Sungold turned his head to rest his chin on her shoulder. "Who's reassuring whom here?" she murmured, and Narknon immediately sat on Harry's feet and bumped her hand with her head as if to say, *I am.*

Someone knew the way, for while Corlath finished speaking with the yellow-haired man the rest of the Riders were following someone else to . . . someplace to lie down, Harry wished fervently. She stole a glance at Corlath as she passed him, and was comforted by the hollows under his eyes and cheekbones. It might have been only the torchlight.

When Harry woke up the sun was high, and for a minute she had no idea where she was. Her first thought was that she had missed breakfast and her father would tease her about burning midnight oil. Then she remembered, with the old lurch of the heart, that she was in Daria with Richard—no, Damar, with Sungold, and Narknon, who sprawled across her feet. And Corlath, and Gonturan. Her hand had rested lightly on her sword hilt again as she slept, and through the first upheaval of waking; now her fingers recognized what they touched. She shivered, sighed, sat up.

She was in a long narrow hall with a dozen or so low beds in it; high overhead, narrow but close-spaced windows let in a flood of sunlight. She only dimly remembered coming here, having seen Tsornin stabled and unsaddled and happy with a manger of grain and a heap of hay; and falling into her bed, asleep before she touched it. Most of the other beds in the room were still occupied. The hall was built of large blocks of undressed grey-and-white stone; the same sort of stone, she thought, as much of Corlath's City. The room was cool, but it smelled clean and sharp, like young leaves.

There were doors at each of the narrow ends of the room, and as she stood at the foot of the bed she could look through either of them. The flagstones were cold underfoot. She sat back down on the edge of the bed—It's even a real bed, she thought—and regarded her pillow a moment. Then she sighed regretfully and pulled on her boots. Narknon opened one eye and closed it again. The rooms on each side looked much like the one she was in, and full of still-sleeping bodies rolled in dark blankets. There was another door midway in the wall opposite the windows. This she went through.

Here was a vast hall, taller than the ancient trees of the forest she had just walked wearily through, with windows cut at the very heads of the walls to open above the lower roofs of the sleeping corridors. At one end of this space was a fireplace that in any room less immense would have been itself enormous; here it looked insignificant. There were several massive wooden chairs before it, and a long trestle table beyond these; the rest of the chamber was empty. Opposite the fireplace wall were doors, thrown open to admit sunlight and birdsong and the rustle of leaves. She looked up at the ceiling. Curiously, there was no sense of oppression built by the stone and space; rather there was peacefulness, the quiet of repose.

Contented simply to be less tired than she had been the night before, she stood a moment, drinking in the sense of relaxation. For the first time since the confrontation with Corlath, the thought of the northwest pass left her freely, without her straining to push it aside; even the knowledge of the coming war, of her part in her first battle, did not trouble her at present. Of the latter she did know it would trouble her later—soon; but she would attend to it later. For now she smiled. Her mouth felt stiff.

She brought her gaze down from the ceiling and directed it again toward the fireplace. Sleep and peace were all very well, but she smelled food, and she was hungry.

The man with yellow hair who had stood talking with Corlath the night before was sitting in one of the great wooden chairs; she did not notice him till she was quite near. Her footfalls dropped gently to silence; no sullen echoes ran up the walls to disturb the birdcalls. She stopped. There was a tiny fire, barely two hands' breadth, burning at the front of the cavern of the hearth. Over it hung a large silver pot on a chain, and on a stool nearby were a stack of deep silver bowls, and a heap of shining silver spoons.

"Breakfast," said the man with yellow hair. "I've had mine; eat as much as you like. I flatter myself it's quite good, although I admit I'm not much accustomed to cooking for so many, and one begins to lose count of how many potatoes one has already put in after the first armful." She sat down with her bowl, feeling that formal introductions were not wanted and that he would be amused if she tried to be conventionally polite; and she was so hungry. As she sat, he brought up a leather bag from the far side of his chair and poured into a flagon discovered at his feet. He handed it to her: "Goat's milk," he said. There were brown flecks of spices floating in it. She smiled, not so stiffly this time.

She looked at him as she ate; and while she was sure he knew she watched him, he kept his eyes on the small leaps and dance steps of the flame beneath the pot, as if letting her look her fill was a courtesy he did her along with filling her belly.

He was tall, she knew; sitting, he looked even taller, for he was so slender. His arms were spread wide from his sides to rest on the

176 |

arms of the chair; but his long fingers reached well over the curled fronts of the armrests, and his knees were several inches beyond the long seat of the chair. He wore a dark green tunic, and a brown shirt beneath it, with long full sleeves gathered at the wrists with gold ribbons. He wore tall pale boots that reached just above his knees, where the tunic fell over them. The tunic was slit up the side to his waist, and the leggings beneath it were the gold of the ribbons. He wore no sash; rather a narrow band of dark blue cloth made a cross over his breast, and wrapped once thinly about his waist. The ends of it were tassels, midnight blue shot with gold. A huge dark red stone hung on a chain around his neck.

His face was thoughtful as he stared at the fire. His nose was long and straight and his lips thin; his eyes were heavy-lidded and blue. His hair was curly as well as bright gold, and it grew low over his collar and ears although he was clean-shaven. He should look young, Harry thought. But he did not. Neither did he look old.

He turned to her as she set down her bowl and cup, and smiled. "Well? Did I know when to stop adding potatoes?"

Hill potatoes were golden and far more flavorful than the pale Homelander variety that Harry had eaten obediently but without enthusiasm when she was a child, and here they blended most satisfactorily with the delicate white fish that was the basis of the stew. It was the first time she had eaten fresh fish since she had left her Homeland, where she had often brought supper home after a few hours beside a pool or stream on her father's estate; and she was pleased, now, to notice that remembering this fact caused no nervous ripples of emotion about her past or her future. "Yes," she said peacefully.

Their eyes met, and he asked, as though he were an old friend or her father, "Are you happy?"

She thought about it, her gaze drifting away from his and coming to rest on the tip of Gonturan, as she leaned against her sol's chair; for she had, without thinking about it one way or another, slung Gonturan around her as soon as she stood up from her bed. "No, not precisely," she said. "But I don't believe I wish to complain of unhappiness." She paused a minute, looking at the thoughts that had been with her constantly for the weeks since she had left her old life as a bundle across Fireheart's withers. "It is that I cannot see what I am doing or why, and it is unsettling always to live only in the moment as it passes. Oh, I know—one never sees ahead or behind. But I see even less. It is like being blindfolded when everyone else in the room is not. No one can see outside the room—but everyone else can see the room. I would like to take my blindfold off."

The man smiled. "It is a reasonable wish. No one lives more than a few moments either way—even those fortunate or unfortunate ones who can see how the future will be cast; and perhaps they feel the minute's passing the most acutely. But it is comforting to have some sense of . . . the probability of choices, perhaps?"

"Yes," she sighed, and tapped a finger on Gonturan's hilt, and thought of the red-haired rider on the white horse. He had looked as though he knew where he was going, although she had to admit that he had also looked as if the knowledge gave him no joy.

"Not he," said the man with yellow hair. "The Lady Aerin. You should begin to recognize her, you know; you have seen her often enough."

She blinked at him.

"You carry her sword, and ride to a fate not entirely of your own choosing. It is not surprising that she in some manner chooses to ride with you. She knew much of fate."

Not surprising. It continued to surprise her. She would prefer that it surprise her, in fact. She permitted herself—just briefly—to think about her Homeland, with the wide grassy low hills and blue rivers, when the only sword she knew was her father's dress sword, which was not sharp and which she was forbidden to touch; and where the only sand was at the seaside. She rediscovered herself staring at a silver pot over a tiny fire.

"I'm afraid I can't comfort you very much with predictions; it is pleasant when I can comfort anyone with predictions, and I always enjoy it as much as possible because it doesn't happen too often. But I can tell you even less than I can usually tell anyone, and it hurts my pride." His hand closed around the dark stone at his neck; it glowed through his fingers like fire.

She looked at him, startled.

"You have already begun to see the hardness of the choices that you will soon be forced to make; and the choosing will not be any easier for your not knowing why you must choose." His voice took on a singsong quality, the red light of the stone pulsed like a heart, and the heavy eyelids almost closed.

"Take strength from your own purpose, for you will know what you must do, if you let yourself; trust your horse and the cat that follows you, for there are none better than they, and they love you; and trust your sword, for she holds the strength of centuries and she hates what you are learning to hate. And trust the Lady Aerin, who visits you for your reassurance, whether you believe it at present or not; and trust your friendships. Friends you will have need of, for in you two worlds meet. There is no one on both sides with you, so you must learn to take your own counsel; and not to fear what is strange, if you know it also to be true." He opened his eyes. "It is not an enviable position, being a bridge, especially a bridge with visions. I should know."

"You're Luthe, of course," she said.

"Of course. I told Corlath in particular to bring you—although he has always brought his Riders if he brings anyone. And I knew you had been made a Rider. I don't ask for anyone often; you should be pleased."

"I can see the two worlds I am between," she said, unheeding, "although why the second one chose to rise up and snatch me I still don't understand—"

"Ask Colonel Dedham the next time you see him," Luthe put in.

"The next—? But—" she said, bewildered, and thrown off her thought.

"You were about to ask me a question important to you, for you were trying to put your thoughts in order, when I interrupted you," said Luthe mildly, "although I won't be able to answer it. I told you I am not often comforting."

"What are your two worlds?" she said, almost obliterating the question as she continued: "But if you can't answer it, why should I ask? Can you hear everything I'm thinking?"

"No," he replied. "Only those arrow-like thoughts that come flying out with particular violence. You have a better organized mind than most. Most people are distressing to talk to because they have no control over their thinking at all, and it is a constant barrage, like being attacked by a tangle of thornbushes, or having a large litter of kittens walking up your legs, hooking in their claws at every step. It's perhaps also an effective preventative to having one's mind read, for who can identify the individual thorn?"

Harry laughed involuntarily. "Innath said you lived where you do, high up and away from everything, because lowland air clouds your mind."

"True enough. It is a little embarrassing to be forced to play the enigmatic oracle in the mountain fastness, but I have found it necessary.

"Corlath, for example, when he has something on his mind, can knock me down with it at arm's length. He's often asked me to come stay in his prison that he calls a city, saying that I might like it as it is made of the same stone as this—" He gestured upward. "No thank you." He smiled. "He does not love the stone walls of his city, and so he does not understand why I do love my walls; to him they look the same. But he knows me better than to press it, or to be offended."

"If it is only within arm's length you find Corlath overwhelming, I have no sympathy for you," Harry said ruefully, and he laughed.

"We soothsayers have other means of resistance," he said, "But I shall be sure to tell him you said so."

She sobered. "I'd rather you didn't, if you don't mind. I'm afraid we're—we're not on the best of terms just now."

Luthe drummed his fingers on the wooden armrest. "Yes, I did rather suspect that, and I'm sorry for it, for you need each other." He drummed some more. "Or at any rate he needs you, and you could do a lot worse than to believe in him." Luthe rubbed his forehead. "But I will grant you that he is a stubborn man at times."

180 |

He was silent a moment. "Aerin was a little like that; but she was also a little like you. . . . Aerin was very dear to me." He smiled faintly. "Teachers are always vain of the students who go on to do great things."

"Aerin?" said Harry. "*Aerin?* Lady Aerin of this sword?"—and she banged the hilt of Gonturan.

"Yes," said Luthe gently. "The same red-haired Aerin who troubles you with visions. You asked me about my two worlds: you could say that they are the past and the present."

After a long cold moment Harry said, "Why did you ask Corlath to bring me here?"

"I told you that, surely. Because I knew he needed you; and I wanted to find out if you were the sort of vessel that cracks easily."

Harry took a deep breath. "And am I?"

"I think you will do very well." He smiled. "And that is a much more straightforward answer than anyone consulting an oracle has a right to expect. I shall stop feeling guilty about you."

Corlath and his Riders spent two days in Luthe's hall; the horses grazed in a broad meadow, the only wide stretch of sunlit green within a day's journey of the tree-filled valley where Luthe made his home. Harry found Sungold tearing across the field, head up and tail a banner, on the first morning, the toilsome way up the mountain apparently forgotten. He galloped over to where Harry leaned on the frame of the open stable, where a few of the horses still lingered inside, musing over their hay. "You make me tired," said Harry absently, thinking of her conversation with Luthe. "You should be recuperating, not bounding around like a wild foal." Tsornin thrust his nose under her chin, unrepentant. "You realize we will have to do the whole thing again shortly? And then go on—and on and on? You should be harboring your strength." Sungold nibbled her hair.

The other Riders and the fifteen other horsemen slowly seeped out of the tall stone house. Harry tried to decide, watching them, if any had had bewildering conversations with their host; but she couldn't guess, and it did not seem the sort of thing one might ask. They all looked only semi-awake, as if the journey so far—this was the first real halt since they left the City—combined with the sweet peacefulness of Luthe's domain prevented the lot of saddle-hardened warriors from feeling anything but pleasantly drowsy. They smiled at one another and leaned on their swords, and even tended their precious horses nonchalantly, as though they knew that the horses did not need them here. Narknon, so far as Harry could tell, never moved from her bed; she merely stretched out when Harry left it, and reluctantly permitted herself to be shoved to one side when Harry re-entered. Harry, although she felt the same gentle air around her, was surprised; whatever it was, it had less effect on her.

Corlath himself strode around in his usual high-energy fashion; if any sense of ease was trying to settle on him, it was having a hard time of it, for he was no different than he ever was, although he did not seem surprised at the condition of his followers. Harry stayed out of his way, and if he noticed this, he gave no sign. Mostly he spoke to Luthe—Harry saw with interest, on the occasions she saw them together, that Corlath seemed to do far more talking than his companion—or muttered to himself. The mutterings couldn't have been pleasant, for he was often scowling.

The two days were fine and clear; warm enough during the day to make bathing in the pool at the edge of the horses' meadow pleasant, cool enough at night to make the blankets on the beds in the sleeping-chambers of comfort. The torches that formed a ring outside the front gates of the hall were not lit again; Luthe was willing to welcome his guests, but did not deem further illumination necessary.

On the second afternoon Harry followed the stream that spilled out of the bathing-pool, and after a certain amount of fighting with curling branches and tripping over hidden hummocks she burst out of the undergrowth to a still silver beach bordering a wide lake. The Lake of Dreams. The stream stopped its chattering as it left the edge of the woods, and slid silently over the silver sand and slipped into the waters of the lake. Harry went to the edge of it and sat down, looking at the water. There was a step at her side; she looked up and it was Luthe. "There is a path," he said. "You should have asked." He bent down and detached a twig from her hair, and another from the back of her tunic. Then he sat down beside her. "I will show you the way to return."

"Do you live here alone?" Harry said, extracting a leaf from the neck of her undershift.

"No," he replied, "but my housemates are even shyer than I am, and have a tendency to retreat into the undergrowth when visitors are anticipated. There are quite a number of visitors, now and again."

"The oracle is a popular one," said Harry, smiling.

Luthe smiled back, but sidelong. "Yes; I think it may be private dismay that sends my companions away at such times; they have something of *kelar* and the Sight themselves."

He did not seem disposed to go on, so Harry said: "Does everyone who comes here behave as though they're half asleep?"

"No again; I and my friends are generally quite sharp. But yes, most visitors find it a sleepy sort of place—a reputation I, um, encourage, as it makes their thoughts sleepy too, and thus easier to dodge."

Harry said, "Encourage?"

Luthe said, "You are not a sleepy one, are you? The source of the Meeldtar taints all the water here; and the air that passes over the Lake of Dreams carries something of sleepiness with it. Only those bearing much *kelar* of their own do not find that faintest touch of the Water of Sight a little drowsy. Like you. And Corlath."

Harry, at that, caught a thought just as it was streaking out, and stuffed it back behind her eyes.

"Very good," said Luthe. "I thought you might prove apt. I didn't catch a glimpse of that one."

Harry smiled faintly.

"I suspect, however, that it might make you more comfortable to ask me it nonetheless," Luthe said, looking into her face; but she turned away.

"Corlath, eh?" Luthe said gently.

Harry shook her head, not denying it, but as though she could shake herself free of her anxieties; but Luthe said no more. At last she stood up, gazing across the lake; she could not see its farther shore. "It is so large," she said.

Luthe rose to stand beside her. "No, not so large," he said, "but it is a private sort of lake, and hard to see. Even for me." He was quiet a moment, looking across the water. "I think perhaps the reason I stay in this particular uninhabited valley of all the uninhabited valleys in the Hills is that it comforts me by reminding me of things I cannot do. I cannot see the farther shore of the Lake of Dreams." He turned away. "Come; I will show you the path. Unless you prefer fighting your way through the poor trees, which are accustomed to being undisturbed."

CHAPTER TWELVE

T HE THIRD MORNING DAWNED as bright and valiant as the two before; and still slightly bemused but cheerful, Corlath's entourage made itself ready to follow its leader back down the mountain. Harry contrived to be the very last of the file, and she looked around her as the penultimate horse and rider left the clearing before the hall and disappeared down the close-grown trail. She had been standing where she was standing now when Corlath had stepped into the clearing before the hall, Fireheart at his heels, to bid farewell to the man he had come to see. They spoke a few words, too low for her to hear as she skulked in the background, as well as anyone on a tall bright chestnut horse with a hunting-cat at its feet could skulk; and then she saw Corlath hold out one hand, palm down and fingers spread, toward Luthe. They held each other's eyes for a long moment, and then Luthe reached out two fingers to touch the back of Corlath's hand. Corlath turned away and mounted, and the Riders began following him into the mouth of the trail.

Narknon was yawning hugely, leaning against one of Sungold's forelegs. She had been grumbling to herself all morning, although she seemed to know they were leaving, since she had at last deigned to climb out of bed and follow Harry as Harry took her saddle and gear and went to fetch Sungold. Harry thought with surprise that in just two days she had grown fond of her surround-ings and was sorry to leave. This place felt like home; not her home perhaps, but someone's home, accustomed to shelter and keep and befriend its master. Its emptiness did not have the hollow ring of Corlath's castle, for all that the proud City castle was more richly furnished. She told herself straitly that her affection for this place could too easily be only that she dreaded what the path away from this haven was leading her toward. She found Luthe standing beside her, with a hand gently laid on Sungold's crest—a familiarity Sungold rarely permitted any stranger.

"Harry," he said, and she blinked; no one had called her by her old nickname since that last day at the Residency, and it gave her a disconcerting flash of homesickness, for the Hillfolk could not say it as a Homelander would: Mathin called her *Hari.* "I believe all will go well with you: or at least that you will choose to stay on the best path of those you are offered, and that's the most any mortal can hope for. But I don't see so beautifully that I have no doubts, for you or anyone; and I am afraid for you. The darkness coming to Damar will not temper itself for a stranger. If you should need a place to come to, you may always come here. You will find it quite easily; just ride into these mountains—any Damarian mountains will do, although the nearer here the better—and say my name occasionally. I will hear you, and some guide will make itself known to you." There was a sparkle of humor in his hooded blue eyes, but she understood that she might take his words seriously nonetheless.

"Thank you," she said, and Sungold walked forward, into the trees. Narknon, with a last stretch and tail-lash, bounded off before. Harry did not look back, but her peripheral vision told her how the sunlight dropped back, and the trees closed in behind her, and Luthe's clearing was only a spot of gold, a long distance away.

The road down was much easier than the road up had been, for all the uncertainty of stepping downward and downward, Sungold's hocks collected under him, his hoofs delicately feeling the safety of the footing; but some cloud of foretelling, or chance, had been left behind them in the pleasant vagueness of the three days in Luthe's hall. Whatever doom lay before them now, it was a definite doom of definite shape, and the swifter they rode, the more swiftly they might meet it and have done with it, for whatever result.

They camped at the edge of the foothills that night, and the army rematerialized around them; and everyone looked easier, and more relaxed, even obscurely comforted, by their few days' break, loitering in the forested feet of the mountains, listening to the birds, and catching hares and antelope for the cooking-pots. It was not all idleness, however, for Corlath's army on that morning after leaving Luthe had swelled by a few hundreds more.

Terim rode up beside her as they set out, and stayed near her all day; they rode at the front, with Corlath and the Riders, and Murfoth, and the few other chieftains who led more than fifty riders to Corlath's standard. Harry saw Senay once, not many horse-lengths distant—for the riding was close—and she caught her eye and began a smile; but suddenly uncertain how the winner of the laprun trials was expected to behave to one of those defeated, and one who besides wore a sash with one's own slash mark in it, dropped her eyes before the other had a chance to respond. In the evening, however, when Harry dismounted, she found herself staring at a bay flank she did not recognize for a moment; its rider dismounted also, and was found to be Senay. This time the two young women looked at each other directly, and both smiled.

So several more days passed, and Corlath's little force made a glorious and frightening thunder when it galloped; and even as Harry thought that her Outlanders did not guess there were so many in all the Hills, she thought too of what each of the Hillfolk knew: of the Northerners there were many more. Harry rode now with Terim and Senay on her either side, and the three of them ate together. Harry noticed that while the Riders as a group stayed in the same area, all seemed to have friends or blood kin from the army outside who came closer to stand by them, as Terim and Senay, for whatever reason, had chosen to stand by her. Corlath's small force would fight shoulder to shoulder and friend to friend; it was a little comforting.

Mathin found her once, head against Sungold's neck and brush hanging limply in one hand. "Hari—" he said, and she started and snapped upright, and began to brush Sungold's shoulder. "Hari," he said again, "it is only your old teacher, and there is no shame to your thoughts. We all have them; but it is the worst for you, and for all those riding with us fresh from the trials, but worst of all for you as laprun-minta and bearer of the Blue Sword. Do not be too hard on yourself."

Harry said, "I am not too hard on myself."

Mathin smiled grimly. "I don't believe you. Even young Terim, who worships the ground you walk on—" Harry snorted—"has spent the past three years riding the borders, under his father's wise and watchful eye, that he might strike his first angry blow and draw his first blood with his newly earned sword before the great battle of the Bledfi Gap. You do not have three years. It is not your fault."

"It does not matter that it is not my fault, does it?" Harry tried to smile, but Mathin's dark face was too worried, and she gave it up. "Thank you, my old teacher; I will try to remember what you say."

Mathin said softly, "You are still the keeper of my honor, Harimad-sol, and I have faith in you, whatever happens. If you forget all else, do not forget that."

"I will not," Harry said.

They had left the slight shelter of the mountains now, and rode northwest across the plain to come to the great gap in the northern range as soon as they might, where the Northern invaders would pour through. They rode quickly but without driving, for the horses and their riders needed to have the strength to engage the other army; and Corlath further hoped to arrive enough in advance of their enemy that he might choose the ground where they would meet. They had ridden over little true desert; soon after they left the foothills' border the scrub fringe of desert began turning green, and they passed the occasional carefully irrigated small-holding, now silent and empty.

In three days' time they would arrive at the Gate of the North, the Bledfi Gap, and Corlath called a meeting again of his Riders and the chieftains. Terim and Senay waited outside the zotar by a little fire, guarding Harry's saddle and baggage, and Harry went to hear what her king would have to say; and she remembered Luthe's words to her: "You could do worse than to believe in him."

They counted themselves. There were some foot soldiers who would meet them at the end of their ride, but only a few; there were few of the Hills who did not feel better, more useful, more real, on horseback. Barring them, they were full strength. Few of the Hillfolk came from any farther west, for the taint of the Outlanders was oppressive to them. Harry stared at her hands, burned a cinnamon-brown as dark as any Hillman's. Aerin's hair was red, she thought, and pushed back her hood; and I am a Rider.

The muster came to a little shy of two thousand; and there was silence as everyone considered the Hills black with Northerners, and the width of the mountain pass. Corlath, without making any face-saving remarks about its not being as bad as it looked—For Hillfolk, thought Harry, don't seem to like that sort of thing: what would poor Sir Charles do here?—began to describe their options; but Harry, to her horror, found her mind wandering. She yanked it back, pointed it at Corlath, and it promptly ducked out again. Is this the first symptom of failure of nerve? she thought, feeling cold and clammy in spite of the dry heat.

Various of the new men had questions or comments; and then the meeting broke up; and while Riders' councils always ended quietly, there was a subdued feeling to the air in the king's tent that was not pleasant. Only a few people were left when Harry stood up and faced Corlath and said, tiredly, as if she couldn't help herself: "Why do you persist in ignoring the northwest pass? I cannot believe the Northerners may not give us an unwelcome surprise by its use."

"I ignore it because it does not require my attention," said Corlath, and while his voice was a low rumble, there was as yet no lash of anger in it.

"But—"

"You know nothing of it."

The flatness of his tone goaded her and she said: "The Outlanders make maps none so ill, and I have seen the maps of that area— and I can read maps too! And they tell me that a force, not so small as to be ignored, could slip down the northwest pass very easily, and follow the mountains east, and catch us on the plain from behind, and then your earthworks will be mounts to fall on when we are set on from our backs!"

"Enough!" roared Corlath. "You I will place in a hollow in the side of the hill, so you may see from all directions, and I advise you to look overhead as well, for eagles that might be carrying rocks!"

Harry turned and ran out. She noticed, without registering it, that Innath and Faran and Mathin stood listening; and she did not see the troubled looks they sent after her.

The night air was cool with the sudden coolness of the desert when darkness falls, and she took a few deep breaths. Then she went to her fire, and sat down, and tried to make her face calm; and if her mind had been calm, she might have thought it strange that Senay and Terim asked her no questions; but she was relieved at their silence and wrestled as best she could with her own demons. Mathin came and sat near her also, and he too was silent, and she did not notice how he looked at her.

The fires burned down, and everyone lay down to sleep. Harry chose not to sleep in the zotar that night; and Mathin stayed by her little fire as well, though he still said nothing. Harry turned on her back and stared at the sky. She let the stars swing above her for a time, and then she stood up quietly, and picked up her bedding and her saddlebag, and made her way to the horses; and she remembered what Mathin had taught her of stealth. Narknon made none of her usual protest at being disturbed, and meekly followed her. Sungold rubbed his head against her but made no sound, for war-horses are trained to silence; and she mounted him and jogged away slowly. She had a terrible headache; it had been building all evening, and now it seemed to stand out around her like a cloud. Perhaps it was a cloud indeed, for no one challenged her as she set Sungold's head west.

They covered many miles before morning, for Sungold was of the best of the Hill horses, and the speed the army traveled was to him slow. Harry remembered a little spur of hills running down to the central plain that she should meet before morning broke too clearly for watching eyes to see a lone chestnut horse with a Hill-man on his back working his way quickly west. She hoped, because the hills had looked overgrown on the Outlander map, and because Dedham himself had ridden so far and drawn the chart himself, that she would be able to lose herself in them; and she hoped that the stream that flowed through them would be easy to find.

She was tired by the time she felt the sun on her back, and she knew Sungold was weary too, although his stride was as long and elastic as it had been hours ago. Narknon loped along beside them, keeping pace. But the hills were at hand: rough outcroppings of grey and rust-red rock, with little but lichen to meet the traveler's first look; but as Sungold picked his way around a tall grey standing stone, suddenly grass appeared before them, and Sungold's feet struck good dark earth, and then they heard the stream. Narknon reached it first; she had none of most cats' aversion to water, and leaped in, sending water in all directions, and splashing Harry playfully when she followed. "I should not have let you come with me," Harry said to her; "but I don't suppose there's any way I could have prevented you. Thank the gods." Sungold was laying his ears back in mock anger and striking with his forefeet as Narknon splashed him too. "And besides, I daresay Sungold would miss you, and I had to bring him."

It was after they had all soggily climbed out of the water again that she heard the hoofbeats; and she whirled around to face them. The faces of her four-footed companions remained undisturbed, and Sungold turned his head mildly to look over his shoulder at whoever approached, but this was no comfort, for they did not understand the awfulness of what she had done, or that the friends who had followed her were friends no longer.

It was Senay and Terim. Their horses showed the pace they had kept worse than Sungold; but they were well mannered and stood quietly, waiting hopefully for their riders to tell them they might stop and rest, and drink and graze, as their brother was doing already.

"Why did you follow me?" said Harry. "Did Corlath send you?

I—I won't come back. If you take Sungold away from me, I'll go on foot."

Terim laughed. It wasn't a very good laugh, but there was some weary humor in it nonetheless. "I don't think anyone could take Sungold away from you, unless perhaps by cutting him in pieces; and we are not sent by anyone. We followed you . . ."

"We followed you because we chose to follow you," said Senay. "And Mathin sat up and watched us go, and said nothing; and you will not send us back, for we shall follow you anyway, like Narknon." Senay dismounted deliberately, and sent her grateful horse to the water; and Terim followed her.

Harry sat down where she stood. "Do you realize what I've done? What you've done by following me?"

"More or less," said Terim. "But my father has other sons; he can afford to disinherit one or two."

Senay was pouring water over her head. "There are a few who will come to me; we will pass near my village, and I will tell them, and they will follow. There are not many left in the western end of the Horfels; but most of those there are owe allegiance to my father. The best of them, I fear, rode to join Corlath after I left for the trials; but there are some—like my father himself—who chose not to desert the land they've loved for generations."

"That will not help you when he disowns you, like Terim's father," said Harry.

Senay shook her wet hair back and smiled. "My father has too few children to lose one; and I am the only child of his first wife, and he raised me to make up my own mind. The way he did this was by yielding to me when I asked, even when I was foolish. I lived through it; and I know my own mind; and he will do what I ask him."

Harry shook her head. "Do you know where . . . we're . . . going?"

"Of course," said Terim, surprised. "Besides, Mathin told us, days ago."

Harry was beyond arguing; and, she realized in the back of her mind, she didn't want to argue. She was too warmed and heartened by having two more friends with her in her self-chosen exile; and unlike Sungold and Narknon she could not feel she had compelled this man and woman. "And we brought provisions," Terim said matter-of-factly. "You shouldn't go on desperate missions without food."

"Narknon would take care of me, I think," Harry said, trying to smile.

"Even Narknon can't bake bread," said Terim, unrolling a twist of cloth that held several loaves of the round pot-baked bread the army ate in vast quantities.

They unsaddled their horses in companionable silence, and rubbed the sweat marks with grass, and the horses waded into the stream again and splashed their bellies, and then found sandy patches on the shore to roll in, scratching their backs and withers and grunting happily. Horses and riders together rested in the shade of some thin low-branching trees, till the sun was low on the western horizon; and then the riders brushed their horses till they gleamed in the twilight. And they saddled and rode out with the sunset blinding their eyes, with a long lean cat-shadow following behind.

Mathin could not sleep after he had silently wished Senay and Terim speed and luck. He lay down again, and his thoughts roved back over the last weeks, and his memories were so vivid that dawn was breaking and other bodies were stirring before he thought to rise himself. Innath joined him at the fire that Senay and Terim and Harry had sat around the night before; and neither of them was surprised when they saw Corlath leave the zotar and come directly to them. They remained seated, and gazed up at him as he towered over them; but when he looked down they found they could not meet his eyes, or did not want to recognize the expression in them, and they stared into the fire again. He turned away, took a few steps, and paused; and bent, and picked something up. It was a long maroon sash, huddled in a curve in the ground, so that it looked like a shadow itself. He held it over his hand, and it hung limp like a dead animal; and the small morning breeze seemed unable to stir it.

CHAPTER THIRTEEN

I T WAS TWO DAYS LATER when, as the morning sun shone down on them, Harry first saw Istan again; and she altered their course a little to the north, for it was not the town she was aiming for, but Jack Dedham's garrison. She prayed to anything that might be listening that he would be there, not off on some diplomatic sortie or border-beating. She could not imagine trying to explain her errand to anyone else; she did not think Jack would conclude that she was mad. She did think that anyone else—even Dickie; especially Dickie—would. But even if Jack were at the fort, and believed her story, would he help her? She didn't know, and didn't dare make guesses. But she and Terim and Senay, even with Senay's father's reinforcements, would not be very effective by themselves.

Rather more effective than I would have been by myself, though, she thought.

The first evening, after Senay and Terim had joined her, and after the animals were settled and the other two human beings were asleep, Harry had cut herself a long straight slender branch from a tree, and stripped it with the short knife she kept in one boot. When they set out that evening she tied it lengthwise to Sungold's saddle, so it rubbed against her right leg as she rode, but at least it did not threaten either of her companions, who rode close at her sides. They eyed it, but said nothing. When she first recognized Istan looming out of the dawn light at them, she paused, took out her knife again, and deliberately ripped several inches of hem from her white tunic, unlashed her branch, and tied the raveling bit of cloth to one end of it. She tucked the other end just under one leg, and held it upright with one hand. "It is a sign that we come in peace," she explained, a little sheepishly, to her friends; their faces cleared, and they nodded.

It was still very early. The town was silent as they skirted it; nothing, not even a dog, challenged them as they rode toward the fort. Harry found herself watching out of the corners of her eyes, looking for any odd little wisps of fog that might be following them. The dogs ought to bark. She didn't see any fog. She didn't know if either of her companions was a fog-rouser; and she knew only too well that she did not know what she herself was capable of.

They rode up to the closed gate of the fort, the horses' hooves making small *thunks* in the sandy ground, kicking up small puffs of grit; she thought of the fourposter pony, who was no doubt drowsing in his stall now, dreaming of hay. Harry looked at the fort gate in surprise; as she remembered, and she was reasonably sure that she remembered correctly, the gate was opened at dawn, with reveille, and stayed open till taps at sunset. The gate, wooden and iron-barred, in a wall of dull yellow brick, was higher than her head as she sat on Sungold, looking up; and its frame was higher yet. They rode right up to it, and no one hailed them; and they stood in front of it, at a loss, their shadows nodding bemusedly at them from the grey wood before them and Harry's little flag limp at the end of its pole. Narknon went up to the gate and sniffed it. Harry had never thought of the possibility of not being able to get inside the fort in the first place. She rode up next to the gate and hammered on it with her fist. As her flesh struck the solid barrier it sent a tingle up her arm, and a murmur of *kelar* at the base of her skull told her that she could walk through this wall if she had to, to pursue her purpose. In that instant she realized exactly how Corlath had stolen her from the bedroom that at present was not so far from where Sungold stood; and she understood as well that the *kelar* must see some use in her errand at the Outlander fort to back her so strongly; and for that she did not know whether to be glad or sorry or fearful. And if fearful, for the sake of whom? Her new people—or her old friends? And she had a quiver of wry sympathy for how the Hill-king must have felt, walking up the Residency stairs in the middle of the night; and then she tipped her head back to stare at the Outlander wall, and touched her calf to her Hill horse's side, to move him away from that wall.

"Since when is this gate closed during daylight?" she shouted; and Homelander speech tasted strange in her mouth, and she wondered if she spoke the words as a Hillwoman might.

With her words, the spell, whatever spell it might be, was broken; and the three Hill riders suddenly blinked, as if the sun had grown brighter; and a small panel shot back, beside the gate and above their heads; and a man's face glared down. "Where did you come from, Hillman, and what do you want of us?" He looked without pleasure at the white rag.

"We came from the Hills," Harry said, grinning, "but I am no Hillman; and we would like speech with Colonel Dedham."

The man scowled at her. She suspected that he did not like her knowing Jack's name. "He does not speak to Hillfolk—or those who ride like Hillfolk," he added disagreeably. By now there were several faces peering over the wall at them; Harry did not recognize any of them, and found this strange, for she had known at least by sight nearly all of Dedham's men. She had not been gone for so many months that it seemed likely the entire complement of the fort could have changed. She squinted up at them, wondering if her eyes or her memory was playing her tricks.

She frowned at her interlocutor's tone. "You could bear a message to him, then," she said, trying to decide if it was worth the possibility of some kind of uproar if she said her name.

"Hillfolk—" began the man at the window, and his tone was not encouraging.

"Oh, Bill, for the love of God, the new orders say nothing about rudeness," said one of the faces at the fence. "If you won't carry a message as requested, I will—and I'll be sure to mention why an off-duty man had to do it."

"Tom?" said Harry hesitantly. "Is that Tom Lloyd?"

There was a tense and breathless silence, and the man at the open panel hissed something that sounded like "witchcraft." The voice from the fence came again, slowly but clearly: "This is Tom Lloyd, but you have the advantage of me."

"True enough," said Harry dryly, and shook back her hood and looked up at him. "We danced together, some months ago: my brother, Di—Richard, collected favors from all his tall friends to dance with his large sister."

"Harry—" said Tom, and leaned over the fence, his shoulders outlined against the light, his face and hands as pale as the desert sand. *"Harry?"*

"Yes," said Harry, shaken at how strange he looked to her, that she had not recognized him before he spoke. "I need to talk to Colonel Dedham. Is he here?" Harry's heart was in her mouth.

"Yes, he is: reading a six-months-old newspaper from Home over a cup of coffee right now, I'd say." Tom sounded dazed. "Bill, you wretch, open the gate. It's Harry Crewe."

Harry's legs were tight on Sungold's sides, and the big horse threw his head up and shivered.

"He don't look like Harry Crewe," Bill said suddenly. "And what about the two with him—her? And that funny-colored leopard?"

"They're my friends," said Harry angrily. "Either open the gate or at least take my message."

"I can't leave my post—another man'll have to take the word. I won't open the gate to Hillfolk. It's Hillfolk it's closed for. Tom's too easy. How do I know you're Harry Crewe? You look like a bloody Darian, and you ride like one, and you can't even talk right."

Harry's pulse began to bang in her ears.

"For pity's sake—"

"Not you, Tom," said Bill; "we already know as how you're off duty. Get another man what's on."

"Don't bother," said Harry, between her teeth; "I'll take the message myself. I know where Jack's quarters are." She dropped her pole in the dust, and, conscious she was doing a supremely stupid thing, she brought Sungold a few more dancing steps away from the gate, turned him, and set him at it.

He went up and over with a terrific heave of his hindquarters, and Harry had reason to be grateful for the perfect fit of her saddle; but once in the air he seemed to float, and look around, and he came down as lightly as a blown leaf. He trotted two steps and halted, while Harry tried to look calm and lofty and as though she had known what she was doing all the time. The leap was over in a few seconds, and no one had expected anything so incredible, even from a Hillman; now men were shouting, and there was a crowd all around her. She thought no one would shoot her out of hand, but she wasn't quite sure, so she waited, instead of going in search of Jack Dedham as she had threatened. Sungold stretched his neck out and shook himself. Narknon flowed over the gate behind them—there was a howl of fear and wrath from Bill—and the cat trotted to Sungold and crouched under his belly.

But she did not have to look for Jack after all, because the row at the gate brought him at a run scant seconds after Sungold's leap. He rounded the narrow corner of some dark building opposite the place where Sungold stood. The horse lifted first one foot and then another, unaccustomed to such noisy reckless human beings, but still obedient to his rider's wishes. He replaced each foot in just the print it had left.

Jack came to a halt, barely avoiding running into them. Sungold pitched his ears toward the balding grey-haired Outlander who stood now, stock still, staring: his eyes traveled from the big chestnut horse down to the laconic cat, up to the horse's rider, and his jaw visibly dropped. Harry's hood was still back on her shoulders, and her bright hair flamed in the young sunlight; he recognized her immediately, although he had never seen such an expression on her face before. A moment passed while he could think of nothing; then he strode forward with a cry of *"Harry!"* and raised his arms, and she, a young girl again with a young girl's face, ungracefully tumbled off her horse and into them. He thumped her on the back, as he might have one of his own men back from an impossible mission and long since given up for lost;

and then he kissed her heartily on the mouth, which he would not have done to any of his own men; and Harry hugged him around the neck, and then, embarrassed, tried to back away. He held her shoulders a minute longer and stared at her; they were much of a height, and Tom Lloyd, looking wistfully on, found himself thinking that they looked very much alike, for all of the girl's yellow hair and Hill clothing; and he realized, without putting any of it into words, that the girl he had danced with months ago, and thought about as he blacked his boots, and lost sleep over when she disappeared, was gone forever.

Harry drew a hasty sleeve across her eyes; and then Tom, emboldened by his commander's behavior, hugged her too, but backed away without meeting her eyes; and Harry, even preoccupied as she was, was briefly puzzled by Tom's air of farewell, and she guessed something of what her brother had never told her.

The whole fort was aroused; there were dozens of men standing around staring, and asking questions of one another; some were in uniform, and some looked like they had fallen out of bed a minute before; a few carried rifles and were looking around wildly. A few of those rifles were pointed at Narknon, but the cat had sense enough not to move, or even yawn and display her dangerous-looking fangs. The Outlanders asked each other questions, and there was a lot of shrugging; but while their colonel's evident delight in their sudden Hill visitor allayed any immediate fears they might have, Harry thought they looked tense and wary, as men may who live long under some strain.

"What should I ask first?" said Jack. "Why are you here? Your horse tells me where you've been these months past—God, what an animal—but I am totally awestruck by the intelligence . . . although, come to think of it, I don't seem to be surprised. Do you know that the entire station turned out to look for you when you vanished? Although I doubt in fact that you know anything of the sort; I flatter myself I searched as painstakingly as anyone, but what the Hills take, if they mean to keep it, they keep it, and I rather thought they meant to keep you. Everyone was sure the Hillfolk did have something to do with your evaporating like that—

although it was more a superstition than a rational conclusion, as nary a trace of anything did we find; no rumors in the marketplace either. Amelia, poor lady, had well-bred hysterics, and Charles chewed his mustaches ragged, and Mrs. Peterson took her girls south to Ootang. And your brother stopped talking to everybody, and rode three horses to death—and he takes good care of his horses, usually, or I wouldn't have him here. I don't think he even noticed when Cassie Peterson left."

Harry blushed, and looked at her feet.

"So you see, he does care—you've wondered, haven't you? He wasn't too fond of his commanding officer there for the weeks that it lasted, for I couldn't somehow work up the proper horror—oh, I was worried about you, but I was also . . . envious."

He looked at her, smiling, wondering what her reaction would be to his words, wondering if he had said the right thing, knowing that the truth was not always its own excuse; knowing that his relief at seeing her made him talk too much and too freely—a reaction that had, often enough in the past, gotten him into trouble with his superior officers. And Harry looked back at him, and she smiled too, but she remembered the vertigo of the Outlander girl alone in a camp of the Hillfolk, surrounded by a people speaking a language she could not speak, whose hopes she did not understand, whose dreams she could not share.

The people of the Hills had been her own people's foes for eighty years and more, for she was born and bred a Homelander; how could Jack—even Jack—speak of envy?

Her smile froze, and her tunic flapped against her back and hips, for she had, somehow, lost her sash, and she had hung Gonturan from Sungold's saddle, so as to look, she hoped, a little less like immediate war. Lost her sash. A Hillman would never lose his sash. What was she? Dama!ur-sol. Ha. She laid a hand on Sungold's shoulder, but when he turned his head to touch her with his nose she was not comforted, for he had lived all his life in the Hills. She wished bitterly that her brother had told her of Tom Lloyd, months ago. That was something she might have understood, and Tom was kind and honest.

She swallowed and looked at Jack again, and he saw memory shining in her eyes, and he smiled sadly at her, and was sorry for any further pain his thoughtless words had given her. "Child," he said quietly, "choices are always hard. But do you not think yours is already made?"

Harry's fingers combed through her Hill horse's mane, and she said, "There never was a choice. I ride the only way open to me, and yet often and again it seems to me I am dangerously unfit for it." She laughed a little and shakily. "It seems to me further that it is very odd that fate should lay so careful a trail and spend so little time preparing the one that must follow it."

Jack nodded. "It is not the sort of thing that is recorded in official histories, but I believe that such thoughts have come not infrequently to others—" he smiled faintly—"ensnared as you are."

Harry's hand dropped back to her side and she smiled again. "Colonel, I shall *try* not to take myself too seriously."

"And I shall *try* not to talk too much." They grinned at each other, and knew that they were friends, and the knowledge was a relief and a pleasure and a hope to each of them, but for different reasons. Then Jack looked her over again, as if noticing the travel stains for the first time and said in a deliberately bright tone: "You look like you could use a bath. . . . My God, that sword: you're carrying a king's ransom casually across your pommel."

"Not casually," said Harry somberly.

"Questions later," Jack said, "but I will hope that you will answer them. First food and rest, and then you will tell me a very long story, and it has to be the true one, although I don't promise to believe it."

"I am not quite alone, " said Harry, smiling again. "Will you let two friends of mine past your formidable gate as well?"

"Not so formidable," said Colonel Dedham. "I wish I'd arrived a minute earlier and seen that jump. I don't believe it."

"It's true, sir," said Tom.

"I believe it's true, I just don't believe *it*," said Jack. "No doubt all of your story will be just as impossible. And just to start with, what is that?" he said, pointing at Narknon, who still had not moved.

"She's a hunting-cat, a folstza. She adopted me soon after . . . I left here."

Narknon, deeming the moment right, stood up slowly, and opened her big green eyes to their fullest extent, batted the long golden lashes once or twice at Jack, and began to pace toward him, while he gamely held his ground. Narknon paused a step away and started to purr, and Jack laughed uncertainly; whereupon the cat took the last step and rubbed her cheek against the back of his hand. Jack, with the look of a man who throws dice with the devil, petted her and Narknon redoubled the purr. "I think I'm being courted," said Jack.

"Narknon has an excellent sense of whose side it is most expedient to be on," said Harry. "But—"

"Yes, we will let your companions come in in the traditional fashion. Unbar the gate, there, Shipson, and be quick about it, before anything else comes over it. I don't like the new standing orders, and they obviously aren't much good besides." Jack looked up from Narknon, who was now leaning her full weight against his legs and tapping her tail against the backs of his thighs, to gaze again at Sungold. "A real Hill horse. Can they all leap over Outlander forts before breakfast?"

"No. Or they may, but most of their riders have more sense than to try it. Particularly after a journey such as we've had." The excitement of seeing Jack again, and the reassurance of the warmth of his welcome, drained away from her, and she remembered that she was exhausted, and the sense of coming home to a place that was no longer home oppressed her further. "I'd like the bath and the food, and we all have to have sleep. But most of the story will have to wait; I'll tell you what I must, but . . . we don't have much time."

"You are here for a purpose, and I can guess some of it. I'll try not to be stupid."

The gate opened, and Terim and Senay rode quietly through and stopped by Sungold's flank and dismounted. Harry introduced them, and they bowed, touching their fingers respectfully to their foreheads, but without the last flick outward of the fingers that indicates that the one addressed is of superior rank. When she said in Hill-speech, "And this is Colonel Dedham, whose aid we are here to seek," she was pleased with the way her Outlander friend in his turn bowed and touched his fingers to his forehead, only glancing at her with mild inquiry.

"I am sorry," said Jack as he led the way to his quarters, "but I speak only a little of your Hill tongue. I must ask you to tell me what I need to hear in my own language, and apologize to your friends for the necessary rudeness of excluding them." This was spoken in heavily accented but perfectly adequate Hill-speech, and Terim and Senay both smiled.

"We understand the need for speed and clarity, and it would not have occurred to us to take offense," said Terim, who had a king's son's swiftness for turning a diplomatic phrase; and Senay simply nodded.

So Jack Dedham cleared off the table in the second of the two small rooms that were his, the table in question accustomed to duty as a dining-table and writing-desk, as well as a convenient surface to set any indeterminate object down on; and his batman brought breakfast for three. The three ate their way through it with enthusiasm, and the man, grinning, brought second breakfasts for three. "Make it four, Ted," said Dedham. "I'm getting hungry again."

When they were finished, and Harry was staring into her teacup and realizing with uneasy chagrin that she'd rather be drinking malak, Jack filled his pipe and began to produce thick heavy clouds of smoke that crawled around the room and nosed into the corners. "Well?" he said. "Tell me in what fashion you have come to seek my aid."

Harry said, staring at the worn tips of her Hill boots, "The Northern army will be coming through the mountains . . . soon. Very soon. Corlath's army is camped on the plain before the wide gap—the Bledfi Gap, we call it—the Gate of the North, you know, in the Horfel Mountains—"

Jack said from a cloud of smoke: "The Gambor Pass, in the Ossander range. Yes."

"We want to plug the northwest leak, the little way through the mountains above Ihistan—where an undesirable trickle of Northern soldiers could come through and—"

"And raze Istan, and go on to harass Corlath."

Harry nodded. "Not just harass; there are not many Hillfolk to fight."

"That explains, no doubt," said Jack, "why there are only three of you—and a cat with long teeth—for the northwest leak, as you call it."

Harry smiled faintly. "It was almost one of me, alone."

"I would hazard, then, that you are not precisely here under Corlath's orders."

"Not exactly."

"Does he know where you are?"

Harry thought about it, and said carefully, "I did not tell him where I was going before I left." Her ribs missed the pressure of a sash.

Dedham blinked a few times, slowly, and said, "I assume I am to conclude that he will be able to guess where you've gone. And these two poor fools decided to throw their lots in with an outlaw? I am impressed."

Harry was silent for a minute. For all her brave words to Jack at the fort gate, she felt that the path she had thought she was following had blurred and then lurched underfoot as soon as Sungold had jumped the wall. It was difficult for her now to remember who she was—damalur-sol and sashless—and why she was here, and where she was going; her thoughts ambled around in her head, tired and patternless. She remembered Luthe saying to her: "It is not an enviable position, being a bridge, especially a bridge with visions"; and she thought that in fact a nice clear vivid vision would be a great boon. She sighed and rubbed her eyes. "Corlath did not take at all kindly to Sir Charles that day, did he?"

Jack smiled without humor. "Not at all kindly, no."

Harry scowled. "He's still cutting off his nose to spite his face, ignoring the northwest pass."

"Ritger's Gap," said Jack. "He probably doesn't look at it that way, though. He came to us offering an alliance of mutual support, true, but he was doing us a favor by giving us the benefit of his spies' work in the north—which Sir Charles, in his less than infinite wisdom, chose to disbelieve. I would assume that your Corlath will now simply wipe out as many Northerners as he can, and what's left of his Hillfolk in the end will retreat to those eastern mountains of his. Whether or not the western plains are overrun with unchecked Northerners is not, finally, of great interest to him one way or another. Our decision not to help only means a few more divisions of the Northern army to harry them in their Hills: unfortunate but not of the first importance."

"If the Homeland got behind the attempt to throw back the Northerners—"

"There was never any chance of that, my dear, believe me," replied Jack. "You are attempting to be logical, I suspect, and logic has little to do with government, and nothing at all to do with military administration.

"You are also still thinking like a Homelander—an Outlander, if you wish—for all you've learned to ride like a Hillman," and his eyes settled on Gonturan, hanging by her belt over the back of Harry's chair. "You know Istan is here, and it seems like a waste to you that we should be obliterated without a chance; and you were also fortunately absent that day, and did not hear Sir Charles being insufferable. Sir Charles is a good man in many ways, but new things disconcert him. The idea of an alliance between Hill and Outlander is blasphemously new."

You are also still thinking like a Homelander—an Outlander, if you wish—for all you've learned to ride like a Hillman. The words hung before Harry's eyes as if sewn on a banner and then thrust into the ground at her feet as her standard. She looked at nothing as she said, "You are working up to telling me that there is nothing that can be done."

"No; but I am working up to telling you that there is no possibility of there being done what ought to be done—I agree with you, our, or at any rate my, country should get serious about the threat from the North. It is a real threat." He rubbed his face with his hand, and looked momentarily weary. "I am glad you have put this chance, little as it is, in my hand. My orders, of course, forbid me to go skylarking off to engage the Northerners at Ritger's Gap or anywhere else—the official, illogical attitude is that this is a tribal matter, and if we stay quietly at home with our gates closed the wave will break and flow around us. I know this is nonsense, and so do a few of the men who've been here more than a few years. I've been brooding for months—off and on since Corlath's unexpected visit; I believed what he told us that his spies had brought back from the North—whether or not it's worth my pension to go try and do anything about it. I rather think it is, as we're sure to be killed if we stay at home and I'd rather be killed out doing something than have my throat slit in bed. You're just the excuse I've been looking for; it's been a bit hard to determine which dragon a solitary St. George should take on, when there seem to be dragons everywhere."

Harry looked at Jack, conscious of Terim and Senay at her elbow, and a furry shoulder pressed against her feet under the table. The sense of dislocation was almost a physical thing, like a stomachache or a sore throat; but Jack's words now eased the sore place a little. The bridge could stretch to cross this chasm, perhaps, after all. She was still alone and still scared, but for the first time since she had ridden away from Corlath's camp she felt that her errand was not necessarily a mad one; and so her conviction that she was doomed to it was therefore a little less terrifying. And perhaps it did not matter in what world she belonged if both worlds were marching in step.

And now that Jack believed her, she could depend on him; for Harimad-sol was still laprun, and while she was glad of Terim and Senay, they looked up to her, and she didn't entirely like the sensation. The old friendship with Jack had taught her what kind of man he was, and he would not be embarrassingly awed by Harimad-sol and her legendary sword. The literal-minded pragmatism of the Outlander psyche had its uses.

But as the weight of solitude eased, his words laid a new weight on her: Were her perceptions so wrong then? Was she in fact thinking like a Homelander—and had she, then, betrayed her new allegiance? She opened the palm of her right hand, and looked at the small white scar that lay across it. What did Corlath think of her desertion? Had Luthe's fears for her been correct, and had she not been able to see the right way when the ways divided before her?

"*Harry.*" Jack reached across the table and pulled her right hand toward him. "What is that?"

She closed her fingers till what she suddenly felt was her brand of Cain disappeared. "It's a . . . ritual I went through. I'm a king's Rider."

"Good Lord. How the—excuse me—how did you manage that? Not that I ever doubted your sterling qualities, but I know something of that tradition—king's Riders are the, um, the elite. . . ."

"Yes," said Harry. Jack only looked at her, but her mouth went dry. She swallowed and said, "They thought it would be . . . useful . . . to have a damalur-sol again."

"Lady Hero," said Jack.

"Yes." She swallowed again. "Cor—Corlath said that this war had no hope, and something like—something like a damalur-sol was a little like hope. I—I have seen Lady Aerin—do you know about the Water of Sight?—and so they think I must be someone important too."

Jack studied her as a botanist might study a new plant. "Blood calls to blood, evidently. Although Richard is the straightest arrow I've ever seen: maybe it only runs from mother to daughter."

Harry brought her head up sharply and stared at her old friend. "*What?*"

"Surely you know," Jack said, frowning. "Your great-grandmother—mother's mother's mother—was a Hillwoman; one of rank, I believe. That was before we'd gained a proper foothold here, or we were at least still struggling to keep what we'd got. It was a terrible scandal. I don't know much about it; it makes Richard quite green even to think about it. Young Dick turns green rather easily about some things: but some curious sense of honor compelled him to tell me, as his commanding officer, so that I could make allowances if he went off screaming into the Hills of his ancestors, I suppose. The blood taint that Fate has seen fit to hand him seems to prey on his mind." Jack had been watching her closely as he rattled on, and broke off abruptly. "My dear, you must have known of this?"

Harry sat still in her chair, where she was sure she would sit forever, gazing in amazement at the story Jack had just told her. She must have looked very queer, for Terim said to her anxiously, "Harimad-sol, what is wrong? You look as if you have seen your father's ghost. Has this man said aught of ill to you?"

Harry roused and shook her head, which felt thick and heavy. "No; he has just told me something that bewilders me even as it makes all plain."

Senay said softly: "Sol, might we know what it is?"

Harry tried to smile. "He has said that my mother's grandmother was a Hillwoman, and thus the blood of your Hills runs in my veins."

The two looked back at her with the sort of surprise and consternation she was sure was still plain on her own face. Terim said: "But we know you must be one of us, or the king's madness would not come to you, and everyone knows that it does: already there are tales told of Harimad-sol at the laprun trials. The Water of Sight shows you things, and Lady Aerin speaks to you, and your eyes turn yellow when you are held by some strong emotion. In fact, they are yellow now."

Harry laughed: a little laugh and a weak one, but still a laugh, and she said to Jack, "My friends are not the least surprised by this intelligence, for all that it shakes me to my soul and makes my heart beat too fast—with fear or joy I am not quite sure. They say they have known me for a Hillwoman all along."

"I've no doubt that's true," Jack said dryly. "You may be sure

208 |

Corlath would have made no Outlander his Rider, even if the Lady Aerin ordered him to."

"But why was I never told?" Harry mused, still trying to collect her thoughts together in one place so that she could look at them. Perhaps she was a better-constructed bridge than she had realized; and she thought of beams and girders, and almost laughed; how Outlanderish an image that was, to be sure. And as she labeled that bit of herself Outlander she then was free to label some other bit Damarian; and she felt a little more like herself all over, as though she were fitting into her skin a little more securely. She still was not sure what she was, but at least she need not be unhappy for not knowing: and now, perhaps, she had the missing pieces she needed to begin to learn.

"I think," Jack said slowly, "that I have an idea about that. I had assumed that you did know, but I remember now how Richard and I talked about you when you were to come out here—he seemed to think it would be bad for you in a particular way—" He frowned, trying to remember clearly. "You were evidently a little too, um, bohemian for him, and he obviously thought living in the land of your grandmother's mother was going to aggravate the tendency. But I never thought he would, er . . ."

"Protect me from myself by keeping me in ignorance?" Harry smiled ruefully. "Well, I didn't know, but I'm not surprised. Angry maybe—how *dare* he?—but not surprised. He takes the man's responsibility toward his frail female relations very seriously, does Dickie. Drat him. Where is my inestimable brother? Here?"

Jack was smiling at her, as she sat with her sword hilt touching her shoulder when she gestured. "No," he said, "he's off being diplomatic, which is something he shows some brilliance at, for me and Sir Charles. We'd like some extra men here, just in case this silly tribal matter gets out of hand, and I would only get red and froth at the mouth, while Richard can look earnest and beseeching, and may even have some effect." He looked gloomily at the table. "I torment myself, now and again, wondering whether, if Corlath had given us a bit more warning about what he had in mind, if Peterson and I could have brought Charles around—even a little—this mess we're in might have been, even a little, less of a mess. But it is not, as we say when we are being diplomatic, a fruitful source of inquiry."

Harry was thinking, For that matter, why didn't Mummy or Father tell me about my mysterious inheritance? They must have known, to tell my wretched brother—indeed, it must have been generally known to some extent; that explains why we were never quite the thing—I always thought it was just because we didn't give the right sort of dinner parties and spent too much time in the saddle. She went hot and cold, and her last shred of doubt about whether she had chosen wisely when she chose the Hills over the country that had raised her dissolved; but she had loved her family and her home, and she was without bitterness.

She yanked her attention back as Jack began to speak again: "It's been a little anxious here lately. There is something, or there are somethings, hanging around the town and the fort; and twice my men have gone out scouting and found signs of battle; and once there was a corpse." His face was drawn and old. "It wasn't quite human; although from a distance it would probably look human enough."

Harry said softly: "I have been told that much of the Northern army is not quite human."

Jack was silent for a little, then said: "In simple numbers I can't promise much. I don't want to risk forcibly anyone's neck but my own, as we will be going against orders, but there are a few men here I know who have the same attitude toward the Northerners that I do. I will put it to them."

Harry said, "So, how many and how quickly?"

"Not very and very. Those of us who will go have been quivering like so many arrows on so many bowstrings for weeks; we'll be grateful for the chance to snap forward. Look: you and your friends can have a bath and a nap; and we should be able to march at sunset."

There had been something obscurely troubling Harry since she entered the fort so precipitously; and at first she had put it down to the confusion, to her first sight of Outlanders since she had ceased to be one herself; and the troubled reflections that this recognition had brought her. But the sense of not-quite-right, of a whiff of something unpleasant, or a vibration in the air, increased as the rest of her relaxed. She looked around her now, able to think about this specific disturbance, to focus on its cause if her *kelar* would point the way. She turned her head one way and another; it was much worse in the small closed space that was Jack's rooms. It was as she put her hand over the blue stone on Gonturan's hilt that she finally understood what it was. "One last thing," she said.

"Yes?" said Jack, but it took Harry a little time to put it in words. "No . . . guns. Rifles or revolvers, or whatever it is you use. They'll only, um, go wrong." And she shivered in the proximity of Jack's hunting-rifles hung on the wall, and two revolvers on belts hooked over the back of an unoccupied chair.

Jack tapped his fingers on the table. "Not just rumors, then?" he said.

Harry shook her head. "Not just rumors. It's not something I've seen, about guns—but I know. I know something of what the Hillfolk do, or are—and even if we could stop whatever it is we do, and I can't, because I usually don't know what I'm doing in the first place—I know too that, whatever it is, it will ride with those that we will be facing. And—and the presence of yours in this room," and she waved her hand, while the other one still rested on the blue gem, "is making me feel . . . edgy. It's the sort of thing I'm learning to pay attention to."

The room was suddenly smaller and darker than it had been before Harry spoke; Jack stared at her, seeing his young friend and seeing almost clearly the outline of the thing she had taken on in the Hills; and then an unexpected ray of sunlight fell through the window and the blue gem of her sword hilt blazed up as her hand slipped away from it, and her cheek and hair were lit blue. But the outline of her burden was gone. Jack thought, I am going to follow this child, to my death perhaps, but I am going to follow her, and be proud of the opportunity.

"Very well. I believe you. It's rather pleasant to have one's favorite old-wives'-tales borne out as truth. You'll not want infantry anyway; and our cavalry is accustomed to its sabers."

"Now, about that bath?" Harry said. Ted was told to provide the baths and beds required; she and Senay were led to Jack's bathroom first, and Harry sank gratefully into the water in the tall tin tub, sliding down till the water closed over her face and she looked up at a wavering circular world. She had to come up at last to breathe, and the world opened out again. Senay unbraided and combed her long dark hair, which fell past her knees in well-ordered waves; Harry watched with envy. Her own hair was nearly so long, but it liked escaping whatever it was put into, and bits were always getting caught in things and snapped off; so while Senay's hair smoothly framed her face and smoothly twisted into a knot at the nape of her neck, Harry always had unrepentant tendrils launching themselves in all directions. Senay bound her sleek mane up again as Harry climbed, dripping, out of the tub. Senay slipped into the water with her own grateful sigh, and Harry put on the oversized nightshirt Ted had laid out for her and stumbled into Jack's bedroom, where two cots had been set up by the bed. Narknon finished investigating all the corners of Jack's rooms, while Jack and Ted eyed her warily, soon after Harry finished her bath; but when the cat tried to squeeze herself next to her sol on the bed, Harry was so deeply asleep already that she refused to make room and Narknon, with a discontented yowl, had to sleep humped over her feet.

CHAPTER FOURTEEN

S HE WOKE UP WITH A JOLT, hearing her name, "Harry," and for a moment she did not know where she was, but was convinced she was a prisoner. It was only Jack, standing in the doorway of the bedroom. She sighed and relaxed, conscious that much of her panic was caused by the fact that her right hand had closed only on bedclothes. Jack was looking at her quizzically; the white-knuckled right fist was not lost on him. "It's right here," he said, nodding to his left, where Gonturan hung from a peg on the wall, next to silver-hilted Dalig and long Teksun. She unbent her fingers one by one, and with her left hand smoothed the bedding. Senay and Terim sat up and quietly began pulling on their boots, and Narknon lay down with an offended grunt over the pillow Harry had just vacated.

There was food on the table again, and silent Ted stood to one side, poised and waiting to fill a plate or a cup. Harry came into the front room with her left arm close to her side and her hand across her stomach; Gonturan was hanging over her right shoulder. "Jack," she said, "do you suppose I could borrow a—a belt from you? I seem to have . . . lost mine."

Jack looked at her and then at the saffron- and blue-sashed waists of her two companions. "Lost?" he said, knowing something of Hill sashes.

"Lost," said Harry firmly.

Ted put down his coffee-pot and went off to search for a leather Outlander belt.

The sky was red when two dozen grim Outlanders set out beside three Hillfolk, one wearing a brass-buckled Outlander belt, heading north and west away from the Outlander fort. "We include one first-rate bugler," said Jack cheerfully. "At least we'll know whether we're coming or going." His men were dressed in the Homelander uniform of dull brown, with the red vertical stripe over the left breast that indicated Damarian duty. Harry permitted herself a twinge of nostalgia for her first sight of those uniforms, in the little clattering train, sitting opposite her brother. She asked, "Is it indiscreet, or merely putting a good face on it that you're wearing your proper uniforms?"

Jack replied, staring toward the mountains, "It is that most of us have little useful clothing that is not of army issue." He turned to her and smiled. "And besides, familiarity also breeds comfort. And I think, just now, we might do well to think of morale whenever we can."

They jogged steadily, with much jingling of tack from the fort horses; Harry had forgotten how noisy bits and chains and stirrups were, and felt that the Northerners would hear them coming from behind the mountains. They stopped just before dawn, in a valley at the beginning of the foothills. "Tonight," said Senay, "we must go east into these hills, for there my village is." Harry nodded.

Jack looked uneasy. "Harry," he said, "I'm not sure my lot will be very welcome in Senay's home town. If you like, we can ride a little farther along the way, so as not to lose time, and meet you near the pass—at the foot of the final trail to it, perhaps."

"Mm." Harry explained this to Senay, who looked at Jack and then Harry with surprise. "We will all ride together," she said. "We are comrades."

Harry did not need to translate. Jack smiled a little. "I wonder if Corlath would approve."

Terim had caught the king's name, and asked Harry what was said. "He would say the same, of course," Terim replied. "It is true we are often enemies, but even when we are enemies, we are

214 |

nearer each other than we can ever be to the Northerners, at least so long as only human blood runs in our veins. It is why this war is so bitter. We cannot occupy the same land. It has always been thus."

"We don't occupy the same land particularly well ourselves, however human we may be," said Jack, and when Terim looked inquiringly at him, Jack put it in Hill-speech.

Terim chewed his lip a minute. "Yes, we fight, and usually we do not love each other; but we are still the same. The Northerners are not. You will see. Where their feet step, it will be as if our land were sown with salt."

Jack looked at Harry, and Harry looked at Jack. "I am not sure of this," she said. "I know the wizardry their folk produce is different than the Hillfolk's, and . . . I know that any possibility of a part-blood Northerner is looked on with disgust and . . . fear. You call someone half-North, thidik, and they may be forgiven for trying to kill you. Evidently," and Harry's voice was very even, "Hill and Outlander blood is supposed to cross more gracefully."

As Jack stared at his horse's neck, Senay leaned toward him, and touched his horse's mane. "We are like enough, Jack Dedham; we all follow Harimad-sol."

Jack smiled. "We all follow Harimad-sol."

Harry said, "Jack, you are *not* following me. Don't *you* start."

Jack looked at her, still smiling; looked up, for his stolid gelding Draco was a hand and a half shorter than Sungold. But he did not answer.

They rested most of the day and started off again an hour before sunset, following Senay's directions. The desert was behind them now, and so neither the sun nor the conspicuousness of traveling through empty country would force them to march only by night. It was near midnight when two men stepped into the path before them, and held up torches that suddenly burst into fire. Everyone blinked, and the Outlander horses tossed their heads. Then a voice behind one torch said sharply, "Who are you, who travel to the town of Shpardith?"

Senay replied, "Thantow, have you forgotten me so quickly?"

Thantow walked forward, holding his torch high, and Senay dismounted. "Senay you are," he said, and those near behind could see him smile. "Your family will be pleased to see you return to them," although his eyes wandered over them, and the jingling of bits was very loud in Harry's ears.

"These are my comrades," Senay said simply, and Thantow nodded. He muttered a few words to his companion, who turned and trotted off, the light of his torch bobbing dizzily till he disappeared around a bend of the rocky way.

Harry dismounted, and Narknon reappeared from the darkness to sit under Sungold's belly and watch the goings-on, and make sure she wasn't being left out of anything interesting. Senay turned to Harry and introduced her reverently as "Harimad-sol," whereupon Thantow swept her a very elegant Hill bow, which included the hand gestures of respect, and Harry tried not to shuffle her feet. They all moved forward again, and after a few minutes the narrow path opened up. It broadened slowly till it turned into a round patch of grass encircled by a white path that gleamed mysteriously in the torchlight. A little breeze wandered around them, and the smell was like roses.

Thantow led them around the white path, and at the end of the circle opposite was a tall building of brown and grey stone, built into the mountainside, with moss and tiny, carefully cultivated trees bordering its roof. In the windows of this building lights were appearing. As they approached nearer, the wooden door crashed open, and a child in what was probably a nightgown came flying out, and unerringly sprang into Senay's arms. "You've been gone weeks and *weeks*," the child said accusingly.

"Yes, love, but I did tell you I would be," said Senay, and the child buried her face in Senay's diaphragm and said, "I *missed* you."

Three other people emerged from the still-open door. First was a tall old man carrying a lantern, and limping on one leg; a younger woman strode behind him, then hurried forward to say, "Rilly, go *inside*." Senay gently disengaged the reluctant Rilly, who backed up, one foot at a time, toward the house, not caring whom she might run into, till she bumped into the doorframe, fell through it, and disappeared from view. The young woman turned back to Senay, and embraced her long and silently. When the old man came up to them, he called Senay daughter. Harry blinked, for this man was certainly the local lord, the sola, of this place; but then, to be able to send his daughter so far to the laprun trials, perhaps it was not surprising.

The third person was a young man, Senay's brother, for they both looked like their father; and he patted her arm awkwardly and said, "How was it?" He looked about sixteen.

Senay smiled at him. "I was well defeated," she said, in the traditional phrase, "and I wear my sash so," and her fingers touched the torn rent. Harry sighed. "This is Harimad-sol," Senay said, "who wielded the sword that cut my sash. She took the trials."

The old man turned to look at her sharply, and Harry met his gaze, wondering if he would comment on her obviously Outlander cast of features under the Hillman's hood; but he looked at her a moment, the lantern light shining in her eyes, and then bowed himself, and said, "My house is honored." Only then did his eyes drop to the blue hilt just visible beyond the edge of her cloak. He turned to look at the rest of them, and his quiet face gave nothing away as he looked at two dozen Outlander cavalry standing uneasily at his threshold. "These are my comrades," Senay said again, and her father nodded; and the woman, Senay's stepmother, said formally, "They are welcome."

Terim and Jack followed Harry and Senay into the house, while Jack's men and horses were led along the stone ridge of mountainside that the sola's house was built against, to a long low hall. "It is the village meeting-place," Senay explained. "Many of our Hill towns have them, near the sola's house, for there we can all come together to talk or to celebrate; and when it is necessary we can shelter our friends and stable their horses."

Harry nodded slowly. "And if you must . . . defend?"

The old man smiled without humor. "There are caves, and twisting paths that lead pursuers to walls of stone or cliffs; and we can disappear if we must. You would not have come easily to this place if Senay had not guided you. The Hills are not good country for conquerors; there are too many holes in them."

"Yes," murmured Jack.

The room they entered was a large one; there were rugs on the floors and walls, and a long low table beside a long window, although it was closely curtained now. "Rilly," said her mother firmly, "you may stay up for a short while, but you must put your robe and your boots on." Rilly disappeared again.

Servants entered the room bringing malak and small fat cakes, and Rilly reappeared and snuggled down by Senay, who put an arm around her. Harry waited, wondering if she would have to explain their errand; but Senay said with the same simplicity as she had explained the Outlanders as her comrades: "We go to stop the Northerners who come through the Madamer Gate. Who is there that can come with us?"

Sixteen riders joined them in the morning when they set out once more, and Harry began to feel a trifle silly riding at the head of what was becoming at least a company if not an army. But it was obviously expected of her to ride first, chin in the air, staring forthrightly ahead. It's better than one mad Outlander on a Hill horse, she thought. What would I have done if Senay and Terim hadn't followed me, if Jack hadn't been at the fort?

"Jack," she said.

"Mmm?"

"Have you ever seen Ritger's Gap?"

"No. Why?"

"I am wondering, in a foresightful commanding sort of way, how ridiculous a few dozen of us strung out across it are going to look when—if—the Northerners do in fact decide to use it."

Jack grimaced. "Not very—silly, I mean. I believe it's a very narrow place; there's a valley spread out on the far side of it, but the gap itself we should be able to bottle up for some time, even the few of us."

Harry expelled her breath. "I do keep thinking how much of a fool's errand this is."

Jack smiled. "A noble and well-meaning fool's errand at least."

218 |

That night Harry dreamed: Ritger's Gap, the Madamer Gate, was a thin cleft of rock, no more than two-horse width; on the south side was a small rocky plateau, which then fell away abruptly into the forested mountainside. On the north was a wide bowl of valley with some dull brush and loose rock covering it; uneven footing, she thought in her dream, and no protection. Not a battlefield of choice. The valley led slowly up to the final narrow gap in the rock. She turned in her dream, and saw a little string of riders, the leader on a tall chestnut horse that gleamed like fire in the sun, striding up the path to the rocky plateau. She had seen these riders before, toiling up that mountainside. The familiarity of the vision comforted her; perhaps she had, after all, made the right choice when the path had forked. Perhaps she would justify Luthe's faith in her.

And Corlath?

She woke with a start. There was the greyness before true dawn in the sky, but she arose nonetheless and began to stir the fire. She noticed, with a flash of fear and anger, that her hand trembled; and then the fire burned up, and in its red heart she saw two faces. First was Corlath's. He stood quietly, staring at something she could not see; and he looked sad, and the sadness wrung her heart as though she were the cause of it. Then his face became the flames of a campfire again, but they flickered and rearranged themselves and became the face of Aerin, who smiled wryly, and it came into Harry's mind that perhaps Aerin had something to do with Senay and Terim following her, and Jack having sent Richard alone to argue for the General Mundy. Harry smiled a little, weakly, herself, at the face in the fire. Aerin looked away, as if something had caught her attention, and there was a blue glint at her side, which might have been Gonturan's hilt, or only the snapping of a small fire.

"Do we ride out early, then?" said Jack, his voice rough with sleep.

"Yes," said Harry. "I don't like my dreams—and I . . . suspect that I am supposed to pay attention to some of my dreams."

Their voices caused other sleepers to stir, and by the time the sun rose up over the crest of the Hills on their right, they had ridden some miles. "We will be there by tomorrow," said Harry at their midday halt; and the grimness of her own voice surprised her. She was sitting on the ground as she spoke, and Narknon came to her, and wrapped herself around her shoulders and back like a fur cloak, as if to comfort her.

There was a scuffle, suddenly, to one side, and Harry whipped around, one hand on Gonturan. A tall woman strode out from the trees, two of Jack's soldiers, looking tousled, slightly annoyed, and slightly afraid, standing on her either side. One of them held half a loaf of bread and the other a drawn dagger; but he held it like a bread knife. The woman was dressed in brown leather; there was a woven blue belt, sky blue, a color that comforted the eye, around her waist, and a dull crimson cap on her head; and she wore a quiver of arrows over her shoulder and carried loosely in her hand a long bow, with blue beads the color of her belt twisted just below the handgrip.

"I am Kentarre," she said. "Forgive the abruptness of my arrival."

"The filanon," breathed Senay, standing stiffly at Harry's side.

"The who?" muttered Harry; and then to the tall woman, "You have just proven to us that we need to post sentries, even to eat a mouthful of bread. We thought outselves alone here, and our haste to our own ends has made us careless."

"Sentries, I think, would not have stopped me, and you see—" and Kentarre held up her bow—"I come in peace to you, for I cannot notch an arrow before any of your people might stop me."

She spoke Hill-speech, but her accent was curious, and the inflections were not predictable. Harry found she had to listen closely to be sure she heard correctly, for she was not that accustomed to the Hill tongue herself. Perhaps it was her attention that caught the unspoken *"even"* before "I cannot notch an arrow," and she smiled faintly. Kentarre stood quite still, smiling in return. Narknon came to sit, in her watch-cat disguise, at Harry's feet. She gave Kentarre one of her long clear-eyed looks and then, without moving, began to purr.

One mark in your favor, thought Harry, for Narknon's judgment is usually pretty good. "What do you wish of us?" she said.

Kentarre said, "We have heard, even in our high Hilltops, where we talk often to the clouds but rarely to strangers, that she has come who carries the Lady Aerin's sword into battle once more; and we thought that we might seek her, for our mothers' mothers' mothers followed her long ago, when Gonturan first came to Damar in the hands of the wizard Luthe. So we made ready for a long journey; and then we found that Gonturan, and the sol who carries her, were coming to us; and so we waited. Three weeks we have waited, as we were told; and you are here; and we would pledge to you." In the last sentence Kentarre's lofty tone left her, and she looked, quickly and anxiously, into Harry's face, and color rose to her cheekbones.

Harry was doing some rapid calculations. Three weeks ago she had sat in a stone hall and eaten breakfast with a tall thin man who had told her that he had no clear-cut fortune for her, but that she should do what she felt she must do.

Harry met Kentarre's gaze a little ruefully. "If you knew so well when we would be here, perhaps you know also how pitifully few we are and how heedless an errand we pursue. But we would welcome your help in holding the Northerners back for what time we may, if such is also your desire."

The last finger of the hand holding the bow gently spun one of the blue beads on its wire; and Harry thought that Kentarre was not so much older than herself. "Indeed, we do wish it. And if any of us remain afterward, we will follow you back to your king, whom we have not seen for generations, for in this thing perhaps all of what there is left of the old Damar must come together, if any of it is to survive."

Harry nodded, thinking that perhaps Kentarre's people would be convinced to go without her when the time came, for Corlath was likelier to be pleased to see them without his mutineer in their midst; but such thoughts were superfluous till they found out if any of their number would survive a meeting with the Northerners. Kentarre turned and stepped briskly back into the woods.

"The filanon," Senay murmured again.

"The which?" Harry said.

"Filanon," she repeated. "People of the trees. They are archers like none else; it is said they speak to their arrows, which will turn corners or leap obstacles to please them. They are legends now; even my people, who live so near their forests, have believed that they no longer exist, even if the old tales are true, and once the filanon, with their blue-hung bows, did live high in the mountains where no one else went." She paused a moment, and added, "Very rarely one of us has found one of the blue beads; they are thought to be lucky. My father has one that his father found when he was a little boy. He was wearing it the day the gursh—boar—gored him, and he said that it would have had him in the belly, and killed him, if the blue bead had not turned the beast at the last."

Jack said, "Tell me, Captain, do you always take in the loose wanderers you find in the woods if they offer to fall in with you?"

Harry smiled. "Only when they tell stories that I like. Three weeks ago I was talking to a . . . wise man who told me that . . . things would happen to me. I am inclined to believe that this is one of them. Besides, Narknon likes her."

Jack nodded. "I prefer to believe you. Although I have my doubts about your tabby's value as a judge of character." He blinked at her once or twice. "You're different, you know, than you were when you still lived with us Outlanders. Something deeper than the sunburn." He said this, knowing its truth, curious to see its effect upon the young woman he had once known, had once watched staring at the Darian desert.

Harry looked at him, and Jack was sure she knew exactly what was passing through his mind. "I *am* different. But the difference is a something riding me as I ride Sungold." She looked wry.

Jack chuckled. "My dear, you are merely learning about command responsibility. If you were mine, I'd promote you."

They finished their noon meal without seeing anything more of Kentarre; but as they mounted, many of them looking nervously around for more tall archers to burst from the bushes upon them, the materialization suddenly took place. Kentarre stood before

222 |

Harry with a dark-haired man at her elbow; he carried a bow too, but among the blue beads at its grip was one apple-green one; and his tunic was dun-colored. Then Harry without turning her head saw that the path was lined with archers; she nodded blandly as if she had expected them to appear like this—which in fact she rather had—and moved Tsornin off. Kentarre and the man fell in with her and Jack and Senay and Terim, and the rest of the archers followed after the last horses had passed. Kentarre walked with as free and swinging a pace as Sungold.

There were about a hundred of her new troop, Harry found, when they stopped again. With them were about twenty hunting-cats: bigger-boned, with broader flatter skulls than Narknon's, and more variety of color than Harry had seen among Corlath's beasts. Narknon herself kept carefully at Harry's heels: even the indomitable Narknon seemed to feel discretion was the better part of valor when faced with twenty of her own kind, and each of them a third larger than herself.

Harry and her company found a little rock bowl, sheltered from the northwest wind that had begun to blow that afternoon, and all of them clustered in it, around several small fires. The archers unstrung their bows and murmured to or over their arrows, and the others watched them surreptitiously. Bows seemed as outlandish to the sword-bearers as feathers on one of their horses. Jack's men felt absently for revolvers that weren't on their hips.

At dawn they set off again, and now Harry felt that she rode into her dream; perhaps she would wake up yet and find herself in the king's tent, with unknown words on her lips and Corlath's hands on her shoulders, and pity in his eyes. They rode, the archers striding long-legged behind them, up a narrow trail into the mountain peaks; up the dark unwelcoming slopes to the border of the North. The cold thin air bit at their throats, and the sun was seen as scattered falls of light through the leaves. The ground underfoot was shaly, but Tsornin never stumbled; his ears were hard forward and his feet were set firmly. Harry tapped her fingernail on the big blue stone in the hilt of Gonturan and thought of a song she'd sung as a child; the tune fluttered through her mind, but she couldn't quite catch the words. It made her feel isolated, as though her childhood hadn't really happened—or at least hadn't happened as she remembered it. Perhaps she'd always lived in the Hills; she'd seen Sungold foaled, and she had been the one first to put a saddle on his young back, and had trained him to rear and strike as a war-horse. Her stomach felt funny.

They reached Ritger's Gap, the Madamer Gate, before sunset, spilling out across the little plateau that lay behind it, with trees at its back and only bare rock rising around it to the mountaintop, a few bowlengths above them. There was a long shallow cave to one side, where the mountain peak bent back on itself, and low trees protected much of the face of it. "We'll sleep in something resembling shelter tonight," said Jack cheerfully. "At least as long as the wind doesn't veer around and decide to spit at us from the south."

Harry was listening to the northern breeze; it sneered at her. "It won't," she said. Jack cocked an eyebrow at her, but she said no more about it. The plateau was loud with the panting of men and horses; they had hurried to arrive, just as her dream had told her they would, or must; the last hour, men and horses had had to scramble up, side by side. Harry leaned against Sungold's shoulder, grateful for the animal solidity of him; he turned his head to chew gently on her sleeve till she petted him. After a minute of staring around her she slowly followed Narknon as the cat paced up to the Gap itself and stared into the valley beyond. Even Narknon seemed subdued, but perhaps it was the day's hard miles.

Two riders abreast could pass the narrow space in the rock, perhaps, but their knees would touch. On this side of the Gap, the plateau sloped up to the shoulders of the narrow cleft and down the other side, where men and clever-footed horses might climb. Harry stared through, and became conscious of Sungold's warm breath on the back of her neck. Narknon leaped down from her perch beside the cleft, turned her back on it, and began to wash. Harry stood in the Gap itself, and leaned against the spot Narknon had vacated. A pebbly slope dropped down away from her to a scrub-covered valley between the mountain's arms; there was a lower valley wall on the far side, but it fell away into foothills. Harry felt her sight reaching away, into the harsh plain beyond the dun-colored valley and scattering of low sharp hills; and on the edge of the plain she saw a haze that eddied and drifted, like a tide coming in, exploring the shore before it, reaching out to stroke the little hills before it swept over them.

Harry turned and went back to her company. She said to no one in particular, "They will be here tomorrow."

It was a silent camp that night; everyone seemed almost superstitiously afraid to polish a dagger one last time in too obvious a fashion; much quiet checking of equipment went on, but it was a shadowy sort of motion. No one met another's eyes and there was no bright ring of metal on metal. Even footfalls were muffled.

Jack's bay gelding Draco and Harry's Sungold had become friends over the days of carrying their riders side by side. The Outlander horses were always set out on a picket line while the Hill horses wandered where they would, never far from the human campsite; and Sungold and Draco stood nose to nose often, murmuring to each other perhaps about the weather and the footing of the day past; perhaps about the eccentricities and preoccupations of their riders. Tonight they stood near together with their heads facing the same way—watching us, Harry thought, looking back at them; or watching that awful northwest wind. Sungold flicked one ear back, then forward again, and stamped. Draco turned his head to blow thoughtfully at his companion, and then they both settled down for a nap, one hind leg slack, their eyes dim and unfocused. Harry watched enviously. The north wind gibbered.

"Draco, who knows almost as much about battles as I do, has told young Sungold that he should get a good night's sleep. I, world-weary warrior that I am—that's hard to say after too many hours in the saddle—am about to say the same thing to you, my brilliant young Captain."

Harry sighed. "Do stop calling me Captain. Carrying Gonturan is enough; and she's not *your* legend."

"You'll get used to it, Captain," said Jack. "Would you deny me one small amusement? Don't answer that. Go to sleep."

"Perhaps if I could stand on three legs and let my eyes glaze over, it would help," she replied. "I do not feel like sleeping and I . . . dread dreaming."

"Hmm," said Jack. "Even those of us who aren't compelled to believe in what we dream aren't happy about dreams the night before a battle, but that's . . . inevitable."

Harry nodded, then got up to unroll her blanket and dutifully laid herself down on it. Narknon couldn't settle either; she paced around the fire, wandered over to touch noses with Sungold, returned, lay down, paced some more. "I'll send Kentarre and her people into the woods on either side of the Gap, looking down on the valley; we can all mob together here—and see what comes."

"Splendid," said Jack from his blanket, as he pulled off his boots. "I couldn't arrange it better myself."

Harry gave a breathless little laugh. "There isn't much to be organized, my wise friend. Even I know that."

Jack nodded. "You could send us through that crack in the rock two at a time, to get cut in pieces; I would then object. But you aren't going to. Go to sleep, General."

Harry grunted.

Harry's eyes stayed open, and saw the cloud come across the moon, and heard the whine of the north wind pick up as the clouds strangled the moonlight. She heard the stamp of a horse from the picket line, and an indeterminate mumble from an uneasy sleeper; and Narknon, who had finally decided to make the best of it by going to sleep, snored faintly with her head on Harry's breast. And beyond these things she heard . . . other things. She had set no sentries, for she knew, as she knew the Northerners would face them tomorrow, that they were not necessary. It was a small piece of good fortune that every one of her small company might have the chance of sleep the night before the battle, and it would be foolish not to accept any good fortune she was offered.

But as she lay awake and solitary she heard the stamp of hooves not shod with iron, the shifting of the bulk of riding-animals that were not horses, the sleeping snores of riders that were not human. Then her mind drifted for a few almost peaceful minutes;

but she heard a rustle, and as her drowsy mind slowly recognized the rustle as a tent flap closing she heard Corlath's voice say sharply, "Tomorrow." She sat up in shock; Narknon slithered off her shoulder and rearranged herself on the ground. Around her were the small dead-looking heaps of her friends and followers, the red embers of campfires, the absolute blackness of the curve of rock and the shifting blackness that was the edge of the trees. She turned her head and could faintly see the silhouette of horse legs, and she heard the ring of iron on a kicked rock. Jack was breathing deeply; his face was turned away from the dying fire glow, and she could not see his expression; she even wondered if he were feigning sleep as a good example for her. She looked at Narknon, stretched out beside her; her head was now over Harry's knees. There was no doubt that she was sincerely asleep. Her whiskers twitched, and she muttered low in her throat.

Harry lay down again. The wind sniggered around the rocks, but overhead it flung itself, laughing shrilly, through the mountains, into the quiet plains of Damar, bearing with it the inhuman whispers and moans of the Northern army. Harry shivered. A finger of breeze touched her cheek and she recoiled; it ran over her shoulder and disappeared. She pulled the blanket over her face.

She must have slept, for when she pushed the blanket away from her face again the mountain was edged with dawn and her mouth tasted sticky. She sat up. Narknon was still asleep. Jack's eyes were open. He was staring grimly at nothing; she watched his eyes pull into focus to look at her. He sat up, saying nothing, and put his elbows on his knees, and rubbed his hands over the grey stubble of hair on his head. Other bodies were stirring. There was a small spring-fed pool in a fist of rock where the front of the shallow cave was sheltered by the trees; one of Jack's men filled a tin at it and brought it to one of Kentarre's archers, who had produced a slender tongue of flame from last night's ashes. Harry stared dreamily at the little fire till something black came between her and it, which proved to be Jack, kneeling down at their own bed of embers. Harry got up, kicking her blankets off, and went to fetch another tin of water.

Jack smiled at her when she returned. She tried to smile back; she wasn't sure how successful she was.

While they waited for the water to boil, Harry walked to the Madamer Gate and stared through it. The top of her head stood above the rock cleft, and the north wind howled down on her; her scalp felt tight and cold. The haze still hung where she had seen it the evening before, at the beginning of the foothills; but this morning she felt she could see flashes of color and motion within it. The color was the color of fear.

The wind chewed into her and she went back to the cave. They were all sitting, hunkered down around their tiny fires; and they were all watching her; or all but Jack, who was shaving. She admired the steadiness of his hand as he bent over a ragged bit of mirror propped against a rock on the ground. She stopped just before the shadow of the cave began. "Stay out of the wind while you can," she said. "It's not . . . the right sort of wind."

Terim looked up, as if he could see the shape of the wind itself, and not only the way it shook the leaves and bounced pebbles from the rockfaces. "The Northerners send their wind to chill us," he said.

Harry remembered the creeping touch on her face the night before. "Yes," she said slowly. "To chill us—but I think also to discover us. I prefer that we tell it no more than we must."

At midmorning Harry saddled Sungold, unrolled the tops of her boots and lashed them to her thighs, settled her leather vest with particular care across her shoulders, and Gonturan against her hip. Shield and iron-bound helm hung ready from the front of the saddle; Sungold turned to look at her. The saddle looked strange, unbalanced, without the bulky knapsacks strapped around it. Draco chewed his bit, and Tsornin pointed an ear briefly at the sound.

Shortly before noon Harry sent Kentarre and her archers and their big soft-footed cats out beyond the Gate, into the last trees on the mountains' shoulders rising above the haggard valley. Harry watched anxiously, for the covering of stunted trees was not good, and she felt that every blue bead would be visible; but the archers

228 |

disappeared as if they were no more than thrown pebbles. Harry was sure that whatever approached them knew the Gate was held against them—knew and smiled at the tale the wind brought; but she could do no more.

Jack saw them for the first time just before Kentarre led her archers away. He was staring through a narrow black spyglass; his hands were as steady as they had been with his razor. Harry could keep hers from chafing and plucking at each other only by thinking about it constantly; she clamped them on her sword belt. They felt damp. Harry had been watching those coming toward them all morning and it took her a moment to understand Jack's sudden grunt of comprehension. The fog had flowed into the mouth of the valley, and now it resolved itself into a mass of dark moving shapes which still seemed to cast more shadow than they should, for they were very near.

"Mount," said Harry.

The wind chuckled wildly as it tore at their hair, and pinged madly off metal as helms were settled in place, and dragged at the fingers of gloves, and sword tips, and horse tails. Sungold stood with his nose in the Gate; Draco stood at Harry's knee, stolidly, ears pricked. Harry could feel Tsornin tremble, but it was impatience; and she bit her lip in shame for herself and pride for her horse. Terim's horse tossed its head anxiously and switched its tail; Terim's face beneath the helm was unreadable. Narknon reappeared from wherever she had spent the morning, licking her chops; she hadn't been satisfied with porridge this morning. She polished her whiskers carefully, then came to the head of the column, to sit between Tsornin and Draco. "Narknon, my dear," said Harry, "why don't you go sleep by the fire for now, till . . . till we come back? This isn't your sort of hunting."

Narknon looked up at her, perfectly aware that she was being addressed; then she lowered her gaze again and stared out across the valley.

"The filanon's cats went with them," said Jack. "You'll hurt her feelings if you try to leave her behind."

Harry said fiercely, "This is not the time to make silly jokes."

| 229

"On the contrary, Captain," replied Jack. "This is exactly the time."

Harry swallowed and looked out at the Northerners again. At the front of the army before them was a rider on a white horse. The horse was magnificent, as tall as Sungold, with the same proud head and high tail; red ribbons fluttered from its forelock and crest. His reins were golden glints against its snowy neck; and the rider's heavy sword was a great golden bar at his side. Beside him a dark rider on a mud-colored beast carried a banner: white, with a red bird on it, a bird of prey with a curved beak.

"No army can move that fast," said Jack.

"No," said Harry.

The white horse screamed and Sungold answered, rearing; Harry punched his neck with a closed fist, and he settled back, but his haunches were tensed under him, waiting to hurl them forward.

"Very well," said Harry. "We will go to meet them now."

A rain of arrows fell from the sky into the dark sea at their feet, and some of the dark many-shadowed shapes fell, and weird cries drifted up to the watchers at the Gate. "At least arrows pierce them," Harry heard Terim say. Sungold's ears lay flat to his head, and he pranced where he stood. Harry could hear the horses moving up close behind her; Senay and Terim stood with their horses' front feet half up the rock slope on either side of the Gap.

"Jack," said Harry. "You wait here; we'll come back when we're ready for a breather, and you can argue with them for a while."

"As you say, Captain," said Jack. And he whispered, "Good luck, Harimad-sol."

Harry gestured to Jack's trumpeter, and they sallied out under a banner of bright brass notes, for they carried no other.

Sungold leaped down the slope, and the white stallion reared and neighed; his rider turned him and galloped to one side, and the lightless mass of the army surged up the sides of the valley. War-cries rang in harsh throats, twisted by ill-shaped tongues.

The ground before the Gate was in Harry's favor, for there was little room to maneuver, and no room for the overwhelming numbers of the Northerners to sweep around their small adversaries and crush them. Each side must fight on a narrow front; it was a question merely of how long the Hillfolk had the strength to fight, for there were always replacements for any Northerner who fell or grew weary. Harry pulled Gonturan from her scabbard and swung her once, shrilling through the air, splitting the northern wind into fragments that fell, crying, under Sungold's feet. "Gonturan!" yelled Terim. "Harimad-sol and Gonturan!" called Senay, not to be outdone; and then the Hillfolk met the Northerners.

Sungold plunged and struck with teeth and hooves as Gonturan cut and thrust; and Harry felt the yellow wave rising in her mind and was glad of it, for her intellect was of little use, and that the wrong sort, just now; and she noticed that Gonturan was wet with blood, but that the blood seemed an odd color. Clouds massed to cover the sun, but they kept breaking up and drifting away again, and the Hillfolk fought more strongly for this proof that the black army was not all-powerful.

Harry was dimly aware that Draco's head was at her knee again, and there was a momentary lull when her right arm could drop and her small shield rest heavily on her leg, and she said, "Where did you come from?"

"It looked as if you never would come back and give us a chance, and we got tired of waiting," said Jack; and then the battle swelled around them again, and the clank of metal and the bash of blows rose up and smothered them. There was a smear of blood along Sungold's neck, and as he tossed his head, foam flew backward and ran down Harry's forearm.

Those they fought were hard to see clearly, even from as close as a sword stroke. Harry saw better than most and still she could not say why she was sure that those she faced were not all human. Some glittering eyes and swift arms were human enough; but others seemed to swing from curiously jointed shoulders and hips, and the eyes were set oddly in odd-shaped skulls—although perhaps the skulls were all right, and the helms were deliberately misshapen. Some of the horses too were true horses; but some had hides that sparkled like scales, and feet that hit the ground unlike hooves, and teeth that were pointed like a dog's.

Minutes passed and Gonturan had a life of her own; and the next time Harry saw Jack, Draco crashed into them from one side and Jack's stirrup caught at her ankle; and he yelled, "You might think of retiring for a few mintutes, Captain; we've upset them, and we deserve it."

Harry looked around puzzled, but it was true; her handful had driven the dark army back; they were halfway down the valley again. "Oh," she said. "Umm. Yes."

"*Back!*" shouted Jack, standing in his stirrups. "Back to the Gap!" The trumpeter picked it up, for he had followed Jack when the colonel struggled to reach Harry, as he had followed Colonel Dedham often before in years and battles past; and never yet had he received a wound that hindered his playing, although the border skirmishes he was acquainted with had little prepared him for this day. He was tired and bloody now, and it took him a moment to fill his lungs to make his trumpet speak; but then the notes flew out again, over the heads of the combatants, and Harry's company collected themselves to fall back to the Gap. Harry saw Senay near at hand, and then the others, one at a time, turning, half aware, in their saddles, hearing the notes of the retreat; some picking up the cry and throwing it farther; the filanon had a long clear singing note that they passed among themselves. As the Hill and Outlander horses wheeled to gallop away and Harry prepared to follow them, suddenly the white stallion was before her.

This one almost looked like a real horse, she thought; but its teeth were bared, and they were the sharp curved fangs of a flesh-eater. Its bit came to a sharp point on each side of its jaw, so it could slash an opposing horse with a sideways twist of its head. Its long ears were flat to its skull, and its blue eyes rolled. It reared and screamed its stallion scream again, and Sungold answered; but when her horse's front feet hit the earth again, he leaped forward; and Harry saw the other stallion's rider sweep his golden sword up in challenge. Gonturan glittered in the sunlight; but when they met, the blow was of more than physical strength. The other rider's sword drew no blood, but Harry reeled in her saddle; the noise the sword had made against her fresh-stained and pitted shield sent waves of fear through her, and her yellow war-rage went grey and dim. Sungold reared and shrieked; the white stallion was not quick enough, and when the chestnut swerved away there was blood on the other's neck and shoulder and rein.

This seemed to drive the white horse mad, and it came again; Harry heard through the deadening thunder in her ears that the other rider laughed. She raised her eyes to where his should be, under his blazing white helm, and saw spots of red fire; below that, teeth were bared in a grin in a jaw that might once have been human. The power that washed over that face, that rolled down the arms and into the sword and shield, was that of demonkind, and Harry knew she was no match for this one, and in spite of the heat of Gonturan in her hand her heart was cold with fear. The two stallions reared again, and reached out to tear each other; the white stallion's neck was now ribboned with blood, like the real ribbons he wore in his mane. Harry raised her sword arm, and felt the shock of the answer; the hilts of the swords rang together, and sparks flew from the crash, and it seemed that smoke rose from them and blinded her. The other rider's hot breath was in her face. His lips parted and she saw his tongue; it was scarlet, and looked more like fire than living flesh. Her arm was numb. The contact lasted only a moment; Sungold wrenched himself and his rider free, and Harry's legs held her on his back from habit, while she struggled only not to drop her sword. Sungold bit the white stallion just above the tail, and the horse kicked; too late, for Sungold again twisted out of the way and bit him again on the flank, and the blood flowed from the long wicked gash. The white stallion threw up his head and lunged forward, away from his enemy. Harry heard the rider laugh again, although he made no attempt to rein his horse around for another attack; an attack that Harry knew would be her last defense. He could wait. He knew the strength of his army and the size of the force that chose to try and block it, for the wind he sent had told him.

But it was then, as the white stallion ran from them, and the banner-bearer turned to follow its leader, that from the black ground-swell a long stripy body rose and flung itself snarling at the mud-colored beast. Sungold was leaping forward again before Harry was aware of her legs closing around him; for it was Narknon. The cat slashed at the rider, and dropped away again, and then sprang at the beast's face and seized its nose in her teeth; purple blood welled out and poured down Narknon's matted sides. The beast reared, trying to tear at the cat with its clawed forefeet, but Narknon twisted in mid-air. The beast came to the ground again as its rider made a sword cut at the cat, but it missed, for Gonturan got in its way. And the beast reared up once more, mad with pain, and flung itself over backward; and neither beast nor rider rose again, and the red-and-white banner was trampled underfoot.

CHAPTER FIFTEEN

SUNGOLD TURNED AND RAN UP THE VALLEY to the Gate, and leaped lightly through the cleft, and Harry was aware of Narknon shooting past her as she slid or fell out of the saddle and into Jack's arms. Gonturan clattered to the ground. "Brandy," said Jack, and put something between her teeth; she drank a mouthful, gagged, and shoved the thing away.

"Good for you," said Jack, but the lightness of his tone was forced, and they both knew it. "Are you hurt?"

Harry shook her head dizzily. "No. You?"

"No."

"But—?" Harry looked around. Narknon was beside her, covered with blood, but little of it seemed to be her own. Her flanks heaved and her green eyes were glassy, but she sat in her usual precise manner and, as Harry watched, slowly, stiffly, began to try to lick herself clean. The archers stood with empty quivers on their backs, cleaning their long daggers. There were fewer of them than there had been when she sent them into the valley's forested sides less than an hour before; and more than half of their cats were gone. She saw Kentarre, who had a rag wrapped around one forearm, but was on her feet. She saw Senay and Terim. Terim's horse was bleeding from a tear on its side, and Senay stood at its head, a hand on its crest, whispering to it, and Terim spread some pale ointment on the wound. The only wounds she saw were minor ones; none who were worse hurt had returned to the Gate.

"Is this all of us now?"

Jack nodded. "I'm afraid so."

There was barely half the tally of the defending southerners that had stood at the Madamer Gate in the morning; and there was an ashen cast to the faces that remained, for the northwest wind was not good to breathe. Unwounded limbs were numb and slow, and brains were clouded with a nagging dread that had little to do with the mortal risk of battle.

Kentarre said, as she bound up another archer's arm, "Thurra is known to love slow bloodshed, and he can afford not to hurry, for nothing can stand against him. But you have done him a blow he did not expect, for you tore down his standard."

"Thurra?" Harry said in disbelief.

Kentarre nodded, and Terim and Senay both stopped what they were doing and looked at her. Kentarre said: "I recognized him at once. He laughs during battle, and he always rides a white stallion who loves bloodshed as much as he does.

"Why do you think there are so few of us left after so brief a meeting? We are strong fighters, and we fight with the strength of despair besides, for we are terribly outnumbered. But anyone who is struck by the white rider dies on the first blow."

"Not everybody," said Terim. "Not Harimad-sol."

Kentarre nodded solemnly. "Why do you think we follow her?"

Harry said, with her left arm across Sungold's saddle to help hold herself up, "I did not die only because he chose not to kill me. I cannot match him, even for one blow." Sungold turned his head, and Harry reached stiffly out to put her fingers on his soft muzzle. She rested them there for a moment, and a little warmth crept into her nerveless hand. "And, perhaps, a little because I ride a better horse than his."

There was a commotion then, somewhere behind them, near the mouth of the trail; and then one of Jack's men laughed, and the commotion subsided. Harry looked inquiringly in the direction of the laugh, and saw a tall slim figure stride forcefully into the clearing, leading a tired horse.

"Dickie!" she said; and blushed uncomfortably, because she

236 |

knew how he hated the old childhood name. "Richard—" she began, humbly, but he had reached her by then and threw his arms around her. She hugged him back, although her right arm was still not functioning very well and the left was weaker than it should be. He let her go at last, and her eyes blurred, and she couldn't tell if the brightness in his eyes was her own tears, or his.

He said to Jack, although he was staring at his sister, and his hands were closed on her arms as if she might disappear if he let her go, "I returned two days after you had left, sir. I had gotten no satisfaction on my mission, as you anticipated."

Jack grunted.

"They told me what had happened, and where you were going—and who was with you—and I took a fresh horse and followed you." He smiled at last. "Harry, damn you, we all thought you were *dead*."

She shook her head. "I'm not, you see." She smiled back. "Not yet, at least."

Richard let his hands drop. The shadowed army lay spread below them, and the north wind, which had quieted a little after Tsornin beat back the wizard's stallion and Narknon pulled down the red-and-white standard, began to howl around them again, and sting their eyes and throats.

"Took another horse?" said Jack musingly. Richard had dropped his reins when he reached for Harry, and the animal stood, weary and patient, where it had halted. "This looks like Bill Stubbs' horse."

Richard turned back to his commander and grinned. "It is. It always was too good for him; and I needed something fast, to catch up with you before it was all over."

"You've just blighted a spotless career with horse-stealing?" Jack said mildly.

Richard sobered. "If you like. You know that all of us who have come here—thrown in our lot with the old Damarians—are finished as far as Her Majesty's Government is concerned. You knew that when you decided to come."

Harry stared at Jack, although in the back of her mind she had known this all along. "Is this true?"

Jack shrugged. "Yes, it's true. That's why the two dozen of us who came are all grizzled old veterans—we don't have much to lose. But Richard, you—"

Richard made an abrupt gesture with one arm. "I knew what I was doing. Blood calls to blood, I suppose—for all that I've resisted it the last few years." He glanced at his sister. "It was your coming out here to Daria—Damar—and loving it, loving the desert, even though you knew nothing of it—I could see it. You were as bad as Colonel Dedham—begging your pardon, sir—by the end of the first month. It made me ashamed. I—I couldn't talk about it. . . ."

Harry realized she was being offered an apology, and nodded. It didn't matter any more. He was here, and that was what mattered.

"Then, after you disappeared," Richard went on slowly, "these last long months, I've thought a lot—I even thought that you weren't dead—and the thought felt like betrayal. . . . You know, I came here, to the Gap, without ever having to think about it. I knew which way to turn, all those mad little trails on the way up here. I always knew."

"Blood calls to blood," Harry said. "Why didn't you ever tell me there was Hill blood in us?"

Richard looked surprised. "Father told me. I—I assumed he'd told you. I didn't want to talk about it. There was a lot I didn't want to talk about."

Harry said, "I found out a week ago, when Jack told me."

There was a silence, and Richard began to laugh. "My God. Then becoming a king's Rider must really have been a shock to you. It was shock enough to me, when Tom Lloyd told me." He took her right hand and turned it over to look at the palm. "I was proud of you. That's when I knew I had to follow you—not only to see my sister again. To—reclaim something. Or admit to owning it all along."

The north wind snapped at their hair and eyelashes, listening to their conversation. Harry wondered idly if it understood Homelander speech.

238 |

Kentarre had left them; she returned now and said, "My lady. The North prepares to move against us again."

Richard turned to face his sister; he put his shoulders back as if bracing himself for a blow. "Command me, sol," he said awkwardly, in Hill-speech. Then in Homelander he went on: "As I came late, perhaps you'd like me to commit a daring single-handed raid."

Jack snorted.

Harry smiled in spite of herself. "No; that won't be necessary. We'll arrange ourselves across the Gap, here, and on the plateau." She paused. "I can't risk what's left of us going into the valley again. . . ."

She raised her voice: "We're here to slow the Northerners down. We'll do the best we can. But we're overmatched—vastly more overmatched than I expected. I don't expect any of you to fight to the . . . last. The day is half over; if we can hold them till this evening, they'll have to wait till morning to try again." Harry closed her eyes and thought, I hope. Even demons see better by the light of day—or do they? Swimming through the mist behind her eyes then, she saw Corlath and his army; they were beating back a horde of Northerners that outnumbered them by no more than three to one. The black mass that filled the valley below the Madamer Gate was twice the size of the army that sought to pass the Bledfi Gap. Corlath's stallion ran red from its nose as it leaped and struck; Corlath's sword was dull with blood. She recognized Fireheart first; it took her a moment to recognize his rider, for Corlath's sash was the wrong color. She saw Mathin, who grinned fiercely as he fought at Corlath's heels. "If we have gained a day, we have gained . . . something. Tonight, those of you that remain . . . may scatter. Fade into these Hills; make your way back to Corlath if you can."

Senay said: "Why do you say those of *you*, lady? Do you not come with us? Are you so certain of death?"

Terim, very low, said, "Do you seek it?"

Harry sighed. "I can't leave. This defense, here, was my great idea. I can't leave. But what's-his-name, out there, will take care of that, when next we meet." She tried to speak lightly.

"Very noble of you, my dear," said Jack, "but we will, I think, stand with Harimad-sol. We can hold here . . . perhaps three days, if Thurra is so fond of slow death. Three days might give your Corlath a breathing-space; and it's always remotely within the realm of possibility that Sir Charles will believe the letter I wrote him, and the Northerners will find the Outlanders a little more troublesome than they expected for a few more days of preparation. We will stay." The last three words he said in Hill-speech, and Senay and Terim and Kentarre repeated, "We will stay."

Terim said, with his usual buoyancy, "Harimad-sol, you cannot ask us to give up so easily, after we have come so far."

Harry blinked. She looked out over the valley; the Northern mass was beginning to shift forward again. "Very well," she said gruffly. "I suggest everyone eat something and take a few minutes' rest; for Thurra is moving. And . . . thank you." She smiled. "Perhaps we will hold out three days."

"And think of the songs they'll sing about us," said Jack.

He handed her a bit of meat in a hard roll, and she began absently to chew it. Her right arm was still nearly useless, but her left hand closed and opened when she told it to, the elbow bent, and the shoulder swung. She squinted up at the mountains around her. The peaks that surrounded the Gate were perhaps four times a man's height from the shallow plateau where she stood; then beyond them the mountains sloped up again, and a little distance from the stony Gate some small trees covered the steep ground and spilled out toward the valley below them. She looked around, toward the forested arm where the archers had stood.

She found she had finished her roll. "I'll be back in a moment," she said. Jack and Richard looked at her questioningly. "In plenty of time to stand against our friends." She picked up Gonturan and awkwardly wiped and resheathed her, and began to clamber slowly up the western side of the Gate. She could only use her left hand, and even its grasp was not strong.

Jack said sharply, "Harry, what have you done to your arm?"

She waited till she was standing on the low crest to answer: "Strained a muscle, I think," she said. "Don't worry." She turned away as Jack opened his mouth; and from where her little band stood, disappeared around a spur of rock.

Richard started after her, but Terim moved in front him as Jack said, "No. If she wants to be left alone, we'll leave her alone. I don't like it either, but she—or the thing that's riding her—still knows a little more about this than the rest of us. Or so I believe."

Richard shrugged, but his eyes stayed on the spot where his sister had disappeared.

"She did promise that we could die together," Terim said cheerfully.

Jack rubbed his face wearily. "I'm not thinking about dying yet." He looked out into the valley, and slowly he brought his glass to his eye. More figures, some riding on strangely jointed steeds and some lumbering along on their own heavy feet, were pouring into the valley; there was no end of them. They roiled up the slope toward the Gate, the slope Harimad-sol had so laboriously pushed them down less than an hour before. He could no longer see the lower half of the rocky bowl at his feet for the creatures that walked upon it. He dropped the glass. "However foolish that may be."

Richard took the glass from Jack's hand and gazed through it. He saw Thurra's white stallion near the front; but there was no standard-bearer.

Harry stumbled up, and up farther; and then her feet found something like a path or a deer track, and she gratefully followed it. She came above the trees again, and looked down. Below her was the valley, full of tiny crawling things; nearer her, but still far away—I hadn't realized I'd come so far, she thought, startled—was a small flat space behind a cleft in the rock, where her people waited. She looked down dispassionately; the thought flickered through her mind that she was too far, and should return at once; but there seemed to be something she should do first. Her numb right hand crept its way up the scabbard of Gonturan till it felt over the hilt to rest on the stone at her peak; Harry found that she was panting for breath. "Lady Aerin," she murmured; and the scene before her wavered, and she blinked, and suddenly she could see as an eagle sees: she recognized the white stallion that Thurra rode, with the red ribbons in its mane and the red blood dried on its neck and flank, and saw the red- and green- and black-eyed faces of those who followed him, and the queer beasts many rode instead of horses, that had clawed feet and forked tongues. She saw the north wind pluck at her brother's hair and realized abruptly she felt no wind on her bare mountaintop; and with that there was a stab of pain from the base of her neck down her right arm, and her hand grasped the hilt of the sword and drew her. She raised her slowly above her head, point upward, as if to cut the clouds that Thurra had brought, and throw them down on his head in knife-edged fragments. The pain in her neck rose and flooded her brain; "Corlath, help me," she said to the air.

The small knot of people on the plateau behind the Gate looked up suddenly as a blaze of light fell over them and splattered like water; and they saw Harimad-sol on a peak behind them, where no peak had stood before; and around her head and shoulders was blue-and-white fire. She raised her right arm, and Gonturan sparkled so fiercely they could not look at her; and Harimad-sol stabbed skyward once and again and shouted words that each felt they heard distinctly but could not repeat or understand; but Kentarre and Jack recognized the Old Tongue of the Hills, the Language of the Gods. Blue fire began to run down from the stone on the hilt of the sword and splash to the ground, where it seemed to eddy around Harry's feet, and bits of it flaked off and floated into the air, and the bits spun and glittered like prisms, and tossed tiny rainbows down the sides of the mountains, although the rainbows had more blue in them than most rainbows.

In the valley they heard hoarse cries, but the voices did not seem to reach the Blue Sword or the woman who held it, but fell back into the valley like fish who had leaped too high, gasping for their lives. They heard the white stallion scream, and heard an awful voice they knew to be Thurra's, but no one turned to look;

everyone stared upward. Even the horses stood with raised heads and pricked ears, facing as their riders faced; and Narknon, who had not followed Harry although she could have, stood stone still but for her lashing tail; Sungold pranced, looking up the rocks he could not climb. The blue light fell into his eyes and mouth and nostrils till he looked like a ghost horse.

The hillside began to move. Pebbles, then larger pebbles, then rocks and boulders began to tumble into the valley. The woman's clear voice went on, and the incomprehensible words poured over the Hillfolk and the Outlanders with the brilliant blue light; then the noise of the mountains falling grew louder, and many fell to their knees and bellies because they could not keep their feet. They could no longer see with their eyes, though the light burned into their brains, and they no longer heard with their ears, for the roaring of falling earth blocked them, yet they heard in their minds the blue-lit words going on and on.

And then it was over. The horses shook themselves; some had to haul themselves, sweating, to their feet. The human beings turned over where they lay, and looked up at the sky, which was blue and cloudless; and shivered, and cautiously stood up. Jack looked up first; there was no sign of Harry. At first he thought it was because his eyes were still blind from the light, but he could pick out the shape of the mountain peaks around him, and he could work out where Harry had been standing; but where Harry had been was there no longer. He was sure he was looking in the right direction. Puzzled, then, he looked around for confirmation; his eyes crossed Richard's; he was going through the same bewilderment. They turned together to look out over the valley.

But there was no valley. There was a smoking rubble of broken stones and uprooted trees; the cliff face beyond the Gate itself had sheared clean away, and the Gate would be a pass through the mountains no more. They stood at the edge, looking down, and then out and across; there was no sign of life anywhere. The only things that moved were clouds of dust. The dust was curiously blue-edged, and twinkled in the sunlight. A little breeze began. It came through a wide breach in the mountain that had not been there before; surprised, it began to investigate the new landscape. The weary anxious people and beasts on the ridge that was once a Gate turned a little to face it. It smelled good, of young green things.

"The north wind is gone," said Jack.

"Yes," said Richard. "This wind blows from the south and east."

They stood for a moment, collecting their thoughts.

"We should look for Harry," said Richard. "Shouldn't we?" He sounded very young.

"Yes," said Jack.

"That *was* Harry, wasn't it?" Harry's brother said, a little uncertainly.

Jack smiled a small smile. "Yes. Or it was Harry as much as it was anyone. Terim," he went on in Hill-speech, "we would like to look for Harimad-sol. She might be too . . . exhausted to return to us. Will you come?"

Terim said, "Yes," and Senay joined them, while the rest would wait for word. Sungold followed them to the foot of the rock wall Harry had disappeared beyond, and whinnied anxiously after them, and reared and pawed the rock behind them as they climbed away from him. "We'll bring her back," Jack said to him. "Be patient." Narknon came with them.

The four of them seemed to move very slowly; or perhaps their feet moved at a reasonable pace, but their minds could not keep up. Narknon, instead of ranging around them as she usually did, trotted at their heels and paused when they paused. Jack felt that he was grinding out thoughts that moved as grudgingly as centuries, and when he shook his head, his brain seemed to turn over uneasily, like a bad swimmer in deep water. His eyes hurt in their sockets, and he still saw Harry with her sword raised and the blue fire around her, although the picture was memory now, and his eyes focused on scrub and dirt and rock and blue dust.

They all stopped as they came to a slope with trees growing above them. "This can't be right," said Richard; "we saw her on bare rock."

Jack peered up at the sun. "It is right, though; or at least this is

244 |

the right direction. If the sun hasn't moved, which I don't guarantee . . . perhaps these trees grew while the mountains were
falling."

Jack began to climb again as if he were sure he knew the way;
Terim and Senay followed, for they were less shocked by Harimad-
sol's performance than Jack or Richard, and did not expect the
landscape near such a piece of sorcery and *kelar* to conform to the
usual physical rules. They had looked at the sun too, and knew
they were heading in the right direction. Richard was last. He felt
old, and his bones creaked, and Narknon made him uncomfortable. He knew of the Damarian hunting-cats, but he had never
before met one.

There was a tiny path, as if made by small hoofed animals, up
the slope, and Jack followed it hopefully; and after only a few minutes they broke through the trees and into a small glade, with
fresh green grass in it, the first good grass they had seen since
they left Senay's village. Harry lay crumpled near one edge of the
glade, with Gonturan, dull as pewter, the blue stone of her hilt
opaque, lying on the grass beside her. Harry lay on her side, curled
up, and both her hands touched the sword; the left awkwardly fell
over the hilt, the right grasped the blade just below the guard.
Jack came into the clearing first, and he was the only one who
saw—or thought he saw—a figure in the trees just behind Harry;
he thought he saw a glint of red hair. But he blinked, so he could
stare again harder, feeling for his saber; and when he looked
again, the figure was gone. He was never sure afterward if he had
seen anything but an odd fall of leaf shadow, although he knew
the Hill legends, and knew who had carried Gonturan before his
young friend.

"Harry," said Richard, and ran forward, and dropped to his
knees beside her. The others, who had a little more faith in Hill
magic—or who understood a bit better that whatever had happened was finished now, for good or ill—followed more slowly.
Jack looked around. There was nothing like the stone knoll where
Harry had stood anywhere near them; the trees—real trees, not
the grey and stunted things they had seen around the Gate, and in

the valley that was no more—stood high overhead, rustling softly in the green breeze from the east; and beyond the little glen there was nothing but more trees, more sweet greenness, for however far the eye could reach, no sunlight-glint of a clear space anywhere.

Harry was dreaming something, but Dickie was calling her. Aerin was leaning over her, smiling the wry smile Harry knew well by now; it was a smile of affection, but more of understanding. Aerin spoke to her, for the second time; she had a low rough kind voice. "This is what one mad Outlander on a Hill horse would have done; rather like something I once did. But it's not fair that the heroes get all the adventures and all the glory alone; your band will be sung of for centuries to come, and Jack's great-great-grandchildren, and Richard's and yours, and Senay's, and Terim's will remember the Madamer Gate and how the mountains fell and crushed Thurra's army. I found out that those at home don't like having no part in adventures—I didn't learn very much, but I did learn that; and it's as well if someone can learn by my mistakes. . . ."

"Corlath," said Harry miserably; and Aerin answered her gently: "Corlath is waiting for you." Harry wanted to say, That's what I'm afraid of. But Dickie was calling her. It couldn't be Dickie, she hadn't seen him since . . . She opened her eyes. Her memory of the immediate past was not good, but she knew she had called on Aerin, and asked Corlath for help in whatever Gonturan's past master might send her, and that something had happened; and that Aerin had spoken to her about it . . . and Corlath . . . Her head hurt. "Richard," she said.

The other three sat down with a sigh beside her, and there was a silence that no one seemed to know how to break. Narknon put a paw on Harry's chest and began licking her face; a hunting-cat's tongue is much harsher than a housecat's. Harry thought her skin would crumble and peel off, but she didn't have the strength to push her away. At last Harry said, and her voice sounded low and hollow, "Not that I feel much like moving just now, but don't we have some fairly urgent business in the valley? Or have three days gone by while I . . . and . . ."

Richard said, "There is no valley."

Jack said, "The Northerners are now lying under a very large pile of rock, which used to be a mountain range. You appear to have pulled it down around their ears, and, Harimad-sol, I salute you." He touched his forehead and flicked the fingers out in the particular curl that is the Hillman's gesture of respect to his king.

Harry smiled weakly. "That's blasphemous, you know. I'll have you court-martialed."

"By Homelanders or Hillfolk?" Jack inquired blandly. "Can you stand?"

"I am gathering my courage to find out," replied Harry. She had flopped over onto her back—Narknon was now nibbling lovingly on her hair—and then hauled herself up on one elbow; now Senay and Richard propped her up on both sides, and she reeled to her feet. Her leather vest seemed as stiff as iron. "I feel like a potato that's recently been mashed," she said. Narknon leaned against her knee and purred madly.

"Shall we carry you?" Terim said, hovering anxiously, torn between respect and caution.

"Not yet, thank you," said Harry. "But you could hand me Gonturan. I don't quite feel like bending over just now."

This was said in Hill-speech, so it is possible that Richard did not understand. But of the other three there was a brief but obvious moment when no one moved, and everyone thought of the blue fire on the mountaintop, and everyone's palms prickled. Then Jack took a step forward and bent and picked up Harimad-sol's blade, flat silver now, glinting faintly in the sunlight, and offered the hilt to her. One narrow gleam of white fire ran up the edge of the blue sword, and outlined Jack's fingers. Jack's and Harry's eyes met, for it was only when it was too late to stop her words that she realized what she was—or might be—asking. "Thank you," she said. "I probably should have bent over myself, to find out if I could." She resheathed the sword. Jack looked at his glowing white hand, and rubbed his palm along his thigh. There was a tingle in that hand that buzzed up his arm and fluttered for a moment in his brain. It was not an unpleasant sensation.

As her fingers closed on Gonturan, Harry realized that her body was functioning; that she would be able to walk. She kept her hand on the hilt of Gonturan and took a step forward. "We'll stop where we are tonight," she said. "Tomorrow we ride back to find Corlath." She shut her eyes a moment; the world spun, then steadied. "They're farther west than they expected to be. Six days, if we hurry. If we *can* hurry." She frowned, her eyes still closed. "They are beating the Northerners back; they are winning." She opened her eyes again. "They're *winning*," she repeated, and the color rose in her cheeks, and her three friends smiled at her.

Harry concentrated on walking, and by the time they came to the rockface at the Gate she had gotten pretty good at it; she still kept her eyes on her feet, but she slid and scrambled down by herself, while Jack and Richard, who had gone before her, tried very hard not to reach up and help her. When she got to the bottom, and her people were standing around her, and Tsornin was bumping her shoulder angrily, asking her why she had gone anywhere he couldn't come too, and her Hillfolk were flicking their finger salute at her, Kentarre very deliberately touched her forehead too and flicked the fingers out, and all the archers followed suit. And Jack's Outlanders stared and bowed and pointed saber hilts at her, and she realized how quiet they were. Too quiet. She turned to look at the valley.

She turned white, and then Jack and Richard did put out hands to steady her. "My God," she said. "That was a bit of . . . something, wasn't it?" The dust still swirled in clouds over the desert of rubble they looked at, and it hung thickly enough that they could not see beyond it. There were threads of blue woven through and over it, as if there were a webbing holding it in place. The sun burned brightly over the blue-shot fog, and hurt the eyes. The dust got into eyes and noses and throats as they breathed, and mouths as they talked, and their voices grew hoarse with it.

"Kentarre," said Harry. "Will a lot of rock simply falling on him stop someone like Thurra?"

Kentarre shrugged. "My sol, I don't believe it has been tried before."

Harry smiled wanly.

"It will at least have stopped his army," said Terim; " few of them have any *kelar* of their own."

"They have never needed it," said Senay, "for Thurra has always been stronger."

Jack said, "There's more than rock out there. There's something holding the rock down." He stared out, the flecks of blue teasing the corners of his eyes.

Kentarre and Senay and Terim, who knew the legends of the Northern mage, were silent. "It is possible that he will rest here," said Kentarre at last. "But we can say that today is ours."

"Today is Harimad-sol's," said Terim firmly, and Senay's face lit up, and she cried, "Harimad-sol!" Kentarre drew her dagger and tapped herself on the chest with the hilt and then shook the point over her head. "Harimad-sol!" she called, and "Harimad-sol!" the other archers echoed, drawing their daggers in the same gesture; and Senay's people picked up the shout next. Jack's men, shaken out of their half-fearful amazement, began to applaud and stamp, as if they didn't know what else to do; and it was Richard who yelled, *"Angharad!"* whereupon the Outlanders shouted *"Angharad!"* too, and a few whistled, as though Harry had just sung an aria at the opera. When at last they stopped, everyone was smiling and easy again, as if individually inspired landslides and earthquakes were quite a normal feat of warfare, or at least of leadership. Then everyone heaved a sigh and settled down, and supper fires were lit; and Narknon appeared, dragging a brown deer larger than herself, and looking terribly pleased with herself. The sunset that evening over the mountains was violet-blue.

CHAPTER SIXTEEN

T HE NEXT MORNING THEY LEFT the Madamer Gate, to go back down the mountain as they had come. The little troop was less than half what it had been the morning before, and it moved more slowly, from weariness, wounds and . . . a slight feeling of anti-climax, Harry thought. She had a foul headache. Every step Sungold took struck like a mallet behind her eyes, and her vision sparkled with it. "Does one always feel a bit lost, the day after a battle?" she asked Jack, who was riding somewhat stiffly at her side. Draco had suffered a cut over his poll, and the headpiece of the bridle was paddled with a bit of blue cloth.

"Yes," he said. "Even when you win."

They rode gently but steadily all that day. That evening Harry said to Kentarre: "You may leave now, if you wish, to go home. I— we're all grateful for your help. It's very likely we would not have held them off even long enough for—for Gonturan to drop the mountains on them, without you. And," Harry said more hesitantly, "it is also good to find another friend and ally."

Kentarre smiled. She smiled much more easily now than she had when she and her archers first stepped out of the trees to pledge to Harimad-sol; and Harry didn't think it was only because the threat of the Northerners had been halted. "It is good to find a friend, lady, as you say, and it is ill to lose one too soon. We would follow you still, and see your king, and give you a little more glory at your return. I think perhaps we filanon have held alone in our woods too long; and without you, Harimad-sol, we would have no homes now to go back to. We were Damarians not so very long ago, and our fathers called Corlath's fathers king. We would go with you." Four of her archers had materialized out of the firelight to stand beside her when she began to speak, and they nodded. One wore a white rag around his forehead, and it covered one eyebrow, which gave him a puzzled uncertain look; but there was no uncertainty in his sharp nod.

Harry looked unhappily at her hands. "I—I'm not sure it would be wise of you to come to Corlath on my heels, calling me sol. I came here—left him and his army and his battle plans—expressly against his wishes, and I think it more than likely that I'm riding into trouble, as I choose to go back. I—er—applaud the idea that you should declare yourselves as Damarians again, but I—well—highly recommend that you make your own path to Corlath, without me."

Kentarre did not seem surprised by Harry's words; but then Terim or Senay must have told her the story. "Your Corlath I think is not a fool, and it would be foolish to treat with less than great honor the one who buried Thurra and thousands of his army. We will come with you, and if he turns you away, we will still come with you. You are welcome here," Kentarre said with a wave of her hand and a faint musical clatter of the blue beads around her wrist. "You need not go into exile homeless."

Harry said nothing. She found that she was too tired to argue, and too grateful for their loyalty, for she was simply afraid of what she was returning to—afraid mainly because she realized how desperately she wanted to be able to go back. It was true, Corlath would be forced to honor her as the cause of Thurra's downfall, for he was no fool and he was a very honorable king; but she did not want him forced. "Very well," she said at last; "let it be as you wish." Kentarre bowed, a brief graceful sweep. "Thank you," said Harry.

"It is my honor to follow Harimad-sol," said Kentarre.

Jack smiled at Harry as she knelt down again by their fire, and was swarmed over by Narknon, who seemed in her own way to be as shaken by the mountains' falling as the human beings had been. "We cling to you like leeches," he said, and she looked at him in surprise. "Or so I believe was the gist of your conversation just now."

Harry nodded.

"So perhaps this is a good time to warn you that Richard and I and our lot are planning to come too—throw ourselves at the mercy of your Hill-king. There's nothing at home for us. And um—" he turned his hands over to warm the backs of them by the fire, and stared at his callused palms—"we'd like to."

"But—"

"You'll only be able to talk us out of it with an extraordinary amount of effort, because any reason you may come up with we will immediately assume has to do with your praiseworthy desire to spare us pain or trouble, and we are quite selfishly set on riding east on your heels. And we none of us have the strength for protracted arguing anyway, yourself included. And I may be old and stiff and sore, but I'm wonderfully stubborn."

There was a pause. "Very well," said Harry.

Richard, at Jack's left hand, poked the fire with a stick. "That was easier than I was expecting," he said. Jack smiled mysteriously.

They came to Senay's village the next day, and they were met with a feast. Senay's father explained: "We felt the mountain fall three days ago, for the earth shook under us and ash blew over us. The air felt brighter afterward, and so we knew it had gone well for you."

"The dust was *blue*," said Rilly.

"And it is a three days' ride to the Gate from here, so we expected you," the young woman, Rilly's mother and Senay's father's second wife, explained; and Senay's father, Nandam, said: "Hail to Harimad-sol, Wizard-Tamer, Hurler of Mountains."

"Oh dear," said Harry in Homelander, and Jack snorted and coughed, and Richard demanded to be let in on the joke. But when the platters, heavy and steaming, were passed, she decided that fame had its advantages. She had not eaten so well since she had sat at the banquet that made her a Rider . . . with Corlath. . . .

The next morning, to her dismay, Nandam appeared with a tall black horse with one white foot. "I will come with you," he said. "This leg has made me useless in battle, but I am not without honor, and Corlath knew me of old, for Senay is not the first to ride to the king of the City from my family and my mountain. I will ride in your train too, Wizard-Tamer."

Harry winced. "But—" It was her favorite word of late.

"I know," said Nandam. "Senay told me. It is why I will come."

They avoided the fort of the Outlander town, lying peacefully in the sun, untroubled by the tiresome tribal matters of the old Damarians. The Outlanders had known all along there were too few of the Hillfolk to make serious trouble; and if the earth had shivered slightly underfoot a few days ago, it must be that the mountains were not so old as they thought, and were still shifting and straining against their place upon the earth. Perhaps a little volcanic activity would crack a new vein of wealth, and the Aeel Mines would no longer be the only reason the Outlanders went into the Ramid Mountains.

Jack looked rather broodingly toward the iron-bound wall inside which he had spent most of the last eighteen years. He caught Harry looking at him and said: "Anything there waiting for me is something on the order of 'Confine yourself to quarters while we decide what to do with you—poor man, the desert was too much for him and he finally went bonkers.' I'm not going back."

Harry smiled faintly. "I botched it, you know. If I'd known what I was doing, I could have gone alone, quietly dropped half a mountain range where it would do the most good—"

"And ridden off into a cloud, never to be heard of again," said Jack. "I sometimes think the blind devotion—or the press of numbers—of your loyal followers is all that is sending you back to your king at all."

Harry stared unseeingly at the horizon of her beloved Hills, and she remembered Aerin's words, and that Dickie had called her back to this world just a little too soon.

"Is he really such an ogre?" Jack went on. "Don't you want to go back?"

Harry turned and looked back at the smudge on the golden-grey sands that was Istan. "No, he is not an ogre. And, yes, I want to go back—very much. That is why I am afraid."

Jack looked at her; she could feel his gaze on her, but she would not meet his eyes.

The trip back, Harry thought unhappily less than three days later, seemed a lot shorter than the trip away; and this in spite of the fact that they were moving slowly for the sake of their wounded, who had resisted staying in Nandam's village to be healed and demanded to come with them. "They don't want to miss out on any of the fun," Jack said apologetically, as if it were all his fault.

"*Fun?*" she said, exasperated.

"Your attitude is perhaps a little unnecessarily rigorous," suggested Jack.

Harry muttered something that was better not said aloud, and added, "They take honor and loyalty very seriously here, you know, you Damarian-mad Homelander."

Jack shrugged. "And if they throw us out on our collective ear—even that is fun of a sort, I believe." He paused, and looked at her out of the corner of his eye. "But I'm afraid I have the same optimistic outlook as the rest of Harry's bandits."

Harry protested, "But I know more about it!"

"Ignorance is bliss," replied Jack.

They had no difficulty finding their way to the camp of the Hill-king. Harry never thought about it, beyond the simple word "east." But although "east" covers a great deal of territory, she had pointed Sungold's nose as surely as if she were a route-rider, covering the same path she had traveled for years. She wished now she weren't quite so accurate. She could see the king's tent looming in the twilight before them, the sunset fading behind them, and their long shadows beginning to dissolve in the ripples of the grey sand underfoot. She knew that they were marked by the king's guard, but no one hailed them. She could well believe that she and Sungold and Gonturan were immediately recognizable, but she was surprised that even if she were not to be taken prisoner on sight the very obvious presence of twelve armed Outlanders in her train was exciting no comment.

Since she did not know what else to do, she rode reluctantly but directly to the king's tent; it rose from the center of the other tents, the black-and-white banner flying from its peak. Still no one stopped or questioned her; but several offered her silent hand greeting, the kind a king's Rider might expect, and this comforted her a little. But she wished she would see someone she knew well enough to talk to—Mathin or Innath by choice—to ask what sort of welcome she might expect.

There was little sign that this army had fought a desperate battle against the odds only days before; and she suddenly realized that it had never occurred to her that Corlath might lose. She was learning to believe what the backs of her eyelids told her. The tents were all neatly and precisely pitched, and the horses she saw were sleek and fit. There was a hum of tension about the camp, though, which she could feel; the silence had a stretched quality to it, and those people she saw hurrying from tent to tent looked as though their errands might be about life and death.

Sungold's steps fell too quickly. She saw no other Rider, and at the door to the king's tent she paused, and her company came up behind her, and fanned out into a little court around their captain. The gold-sashed guard saluted her, just as he had done half a year ago; she thought it was even the same man, although he looked much older, almost as old as she felt. She stayed in the saddle; she wanted to stay there forever; at very least it made her taller than a man on foot—even Corlath. What was she to say? "The prodigal has returned? The mutineer wishes to be reinstated? The subordinate, having gone to a great deal of trouble to prove her commander wrong, has come back and promises to be a good little subordinate hereafter, or at least until the next time?"

Then Corlath put back his golden silk door and stood before her, and she stared down at him, and she could not have gotten out of the saddle then even if she had wanted to. She realized why, when her *kelar* had shown him to her in battle some days ago, she had not at first recognized him, that his sash was the wrong color. He was wearing her sash.

"Hari," he said; then "Harimad-sol," as he walked to Sungold's side; stiffly he moved, she thought, and her heart failed her at the thought that he might have been wounded. She stared down at him still, and could not move, and then, shyly, he put his hand around her dusty leather ankle and said, carefully, *"Harry."*

She pulled her leg over the withers and slid down Sungold's shoulder as she had once slid down Fireheart's, and put her arms around her king and hugged him fiercely; and his arms closed around her and he murmured something, but her blood was ringing in her ears, and she could not hear what it was.

It is not very comfortable, holding someone close who is wearing a sword and various unyielding bits of leather armor, and it is less comfortable yet if both parties are so accoutered. Harry and Corlath dropped their arms after a short time and looked at each other, and each distantly thought that the other one was wearing a rather silly smile, and Harry noticed that Corlath's eyes were the color of gold.

"You are unhurt?" she said; her voice sounded tinny in her hot ears.

"I am unhurt," he said. "And you?"

"Yes," said Harry, still looking at his golden eyes. "Or no. I am not hurt."

"I am glad," her king said, and his voice was still low and shy, "to see you—here—and still—" he hesitated—"still of the Hills?"

Harry took a deep breath. "I will be of the Hills till I die, but what are you going to do to me for going off like that? And it's not their fault," she went on hurriedly, gesturing behind her, "but they would come with me even though I warned them how it was with me. Whatever you say, I will obey, but—what is it?" She stopped, for as she tried to make her apologies, or her amends, or whatever they were, she remembered that she and Corlath were not alone, and that she was a deserter. She looked up and around, but her company were only dark figures to her, dim in the fading light.

"I will return to you your sash," Corlath said, but his hands did not move to untie it from around his waist. "You should not have lost it—for I assume you lost it. If you had not, but flung it away deliberately, it would be a sign that you denied me, and Damar, and were making yourself an exile forever."

"Oh *no*," said Harry, horrified; and the slightly foolish and uncertain smile on Corlath's face grew into a real smile, one unlike any Harry had ever seen on the Hill-king's face before. "No," he said. "I hoped not."

Harry whispered: "You have done me much honor—since the beginning."

Corlath replied: "I did only what I must, for the *kelar* gave me no choice; but I—I came to believe in you, and I did not care what the *kelar* said."

"Did you believe in me then, when I rode away and left you, my king, and I a king's Rider, against your orders?"

The smile faded, but his eyes were still bright yellow. "I did," he said. "Luthe . . . warned me you would do something mad—and I . . . feared something else, for thus a man makes a fool of himself, and will not accept the wisdom the gods send him. I did not realize what Luthe had told me—I had forgotten what the *kelar* had told me—till you had gone."

"Something else?" said Harry. "What did you fear?" Her heart beat more rapidly as she waited for his reply, and she hoped he would ask her such a question, that she might answer it as her heart bade her.

But Corlath looked around them. "The Outlanders you bring to my camp are not your escort home?"

Harry shook her head violently. "They are my escort home only insofar as they would bear me company in my home, in the Hills, if you will have them."

"I will have them, and be honored," said Corlath, and his eyes lingered on Jack, who sat Draco quietly between Richard and

| 257

Terim, "they who stood at Madamer Gate and watched the mountain fall on Thurra. This tale they will tell, I hope, and tell often."

"And I hope I will never have to do anything like that again," said Harry, and for a moment she could not see Corlath's yellow eyes, but a demon-thing that had once been human on a white stallion with the teeth of a leopard.

Corlath looked down at the top of her bent head. "For you I hope that you do not either; the *kelar* strength is not a comfortable Gift.

"I saw—I watched the mountain fall. I heard you call me and knew then who it was you faced—and thus why it was that I had not seen him before me: why we were able to throw the Northerners back, for all that they outnumbered us. They did not, I think, expect us to be so strong, or Thurra would not have divided his army as he did; for Thurra's demon blood had told him that only the demon Gifts are strong.

"I was proud of you—and I was glad that it was I you called upon." His voice died away to a murmur, but then he spoke loudly: "There is a tradition that goes back hundreds of years, to Aerin and Tor, that we do not often see today, for there have been few women warriors of late, till Gonturan rode to battle again. But tradition is that a betrothed pair may exchange sashes, and thus they pledge their honor to each other, for all to see. I will return you your sash if you choose, for I have no right to wear it, as you have not granted me the right. But I have been honored to wear it, in my people's eyes, till you returned—for as I had had so little faith in you despite Luthe's words to me, so I decided to have faith that you would return, to the Hills and to me, and to hope that your answer might justify me."

Harry said clearly, that all might hear: "My king, I would far rather you kept my sash as you have kept it for me in faith while I was gone away from you, and gave me your sash to wear in its place. For my honor, and more than my honor, has been yours for months past, but I saw no more clearly than did you till I had parted from you, and knew then what it would cost me if I could not return. And more, I knew what it would cost me if I returned only to be a king's Rider."

Then a cheer went up from many throats, and not only from those of Harry's company; for many of the camp had gathered in the center court before the king's zotar to hear how this meeting would go, for they had seen Harimad-sol's sash around their king's waist, and those who remembered the tradition had told of it to those who did not. And there was no surprise, in those who had followed Harry or in those who had fought with Corlath, and there was much joy; and the echoes of those cheers must have come even to the city boundaries of the Outlander town called Istan, and the barred gate of the General Mundy. And the Outlanders who had followed Jack Dedham when he decided to follow the young Harry Crewe, who had become Harimad-sol and the Hill-king's Rider, and who did not know the Hill tongue, looked around them, and at the two tall figures before them standing beside the chestnut stallion, and they cheered too; and Jack, in a lull, said to them: "In case you would like to be sure what you're cheering, our Harry is going to marry this chap. He's the king, Corlath."

Under the cover of the shouting Corlath drew Harry closer to him and said: "I have loved you long, though at first I did not know it; but I knew it when I sent you into the Hills with Mathin and Tsornin for your teachers, for I saw then how I missed you. And when in the City I found that Narknon had followed you, I was jealous of a cat, who could go where she wished."

Harry said, softly, that only his ears might hear: "You might have spoken."

Corlath smiled wryly. "I was afraid to tell you, for I had stolen you from your people, and the awakening of your *kelar* might make you hate me, for she whose blood gave you the Gift left the Hills long ago. When you knew what it was that this heritage gave you, it might drive you back all the more strongly to your father's people, to a fate the Hills had no part of. The Gift is not a pleasant burden.

"But when I saw you were gone I looked to the west, for I knew where you must be going, and I vowed that if we both lived, when we met again I would tell you that I loved you, and ask you to stand by me not as Rider but as queen; for suddenly it seemed worth the risk, and I could not bear it that you might never know."

Harry said: "I love you, and it has haunted me that for my disobedience I would be exiled, not from the people I have claimed as my own, though this were punishment enough, but from you that I loved best of anything and best of all. I think I knew you could not exile me, for the victory Gonturan had won for you and your Hills; but I knew that for you to have turned against me for leaving as I did, it would have been the bitterest exile, even if I sat at your left hand as Rider all my life."

It was Innath who grabbed her away at last and danced her around, for Innath had no dignity, and Corlath and Harry seemed able to ignore the tumult around them indefinitely. Then Jack took her away from him, and then she was embraced and knocked about and swung back and forth till she was dizzy; but she laughed and was happy, and thanked everyone who touched her. But there was one face in particular that she looked for and could not find, and its absence troubled her. At last they let her go to Corlath again, and her happiness was shaken for the face she could not find, and she seized his arm anxiously and said, "Where is Mathin?"

Corlath, who had been dancing too, went very still.

"He is not dead?" she said, and her voice rose till it broke; but when he shook his head it gave her no comfort. He took her hand in his and said, "Come," and led her away, through the tents. Now she could see the traces of battle, for by lantern light she saw blood-stained gear and unidentifiable bits and tatters moving mournfully in the evening breeze, and some few people, bandaged, limping, or lying by campfires, gently tended by those who were unhurt. Corlath led her to a long low tent and drew her inside, and the smell of death struck her at once, although the figures lying on rugs and blankets and cushions were well cared for and cleanly bandaged, and their chests still rose and fell with breathing, and there were many nurses watching over them and bringing drink and thin invalid food. Corlath brought her to the far end of the narrow tent, and the figure there turned its head toward them. Harry threw herself on her knees, weeping, for here was Mathin.

"I knew you would return," said Mathin, and one hand moved a few inches to close weakly around Harry's; and Harry gulped and nodded, but still her tears flowed and she could not stop them. "And you will marry our king?" he went on, in what would have been a conversational tone if it had not been so faint, and Harry nodded again.

"I wanted you to toast us at the wedding, my old friend and horse-breaker and teacher," she said.

Mathin smiled. "I leave my honor in good hands, best of daughters," he said gently.

"No," said Harry, and while her tears still fell her voice gained strength. "*No.*" As she knelt, Gonturan dug a hole between her ribs, and she stood up impatiently and unbuckled her and let her fall; and as she bent down again a few of her tears fell on her own hand, and they were hot, scalding hot, and left red marks where they touched the skin; and she realized that her eyes and cheeks burned with them. She drew the blanket away from Mathin's chest and belly, where a long mortal wound oozed through its wrappings; the blood was almost black, and green-tinged, poisoned, and there was an unhealthy smell.

"In Aerin's day," murmured Harry, "*kelar* was good for things. It didn't only hurt things, and make trouble."

Corlath came to stand behind her. Mathin looked up at his king and said, "Aerin—"

Harry felt Corlath's hands on her shoulders, and twisted where she knelt, and seized his hands. "Help me," she said. "You helped me on that mountaintop. It was as though you held me up, held me by the shoulders as you did the first evening when I tasted the Water of Sight." Her eyes, wide open, were going blind; it was like the golden war-rage, only worse; it would split her skin, she would wither and blacken in the heat of it.

Corlath said, as if against his will, "Mathin fell, guarding me, while I was far away on a mountaintop; if it had not been for him, I would have had no body to return to."

Harry shivered and the heat plucked at her nerves and ate up her strength, and blindly she reached out one hand to touch Mathin, and her fingers touched the bare skin of his upper arm, and she felt him shudder, and his breath hissed between his teeth. Whatever it was thundered through her veins and filled her lungs and stomach, her hands and mouth; and she let go of Mathin and turned to the next bed, and scrabbled with the bedclothes, for she could see nothing but the golden storm and feel nothing but one of Corlath's hands tight in one of hers, and she touched the throat of the occupant of the pallet next to Mathin. She groped her way down the long length of that tent, stumbling, almost crawling but for Corlath, touching foreheads and hands and shoulders, and the nurses turned back the bedding, and the eyes of the dying looked into her blind eyes and hoped for her touch but feared it, and none but Corlath who were themselves whole came near enough even to brush the hem of her tunic, for it was hard just to breathe if she, with the power that was in her, was too near. The fire rose through her and crackled in her ears, so that she was deaf as well; but at last they came to the door, and Corlath led her out, her feeble feet not sure where they would find the earth with each step; and she felt the evening breeze, and the fire began to subside, reluctantly at first. But as it drained out of her, back to where it had come from, it took with it the marrow of her bones and the elastic of her muscles, for such was the fire's fuel, and she leaned against Corlath. He put his arms around her, and when the fire flickered at last and went out and she crumpled, he picked her up and carried her back to his zotar, and she lay in his arms as limp a burden as when he had put the sleep on her, the night he stole her from the Residency.

Harry woke up feeling as if she had been sick for a year and was now approaching convalescence. She stared at the peaked roof of the zotar and slowly realized where she was. Even her thoughts were too weak to entertain the idea of moving. Narknon, by some extra feline sense, knew when she opened her eyes, and without moving from her sprawl across Harry's legs, began to purr.

With the purr came Corlath, who had been sitting just beyond the curtain that had been hung by Harry's bed to give her peace from the comings and goings of the king's tent. He put back the curtain when he heard Narknon. He was himself weary, for much of the strength Harry had used the evening before was his; and he had not been able to sleep that night for watching her. He watched her sleeping, hoping only that she would awaken and still be Harry. His heart was in his mouth as he dropped down beside her.

The look on his face brought Harry more strongly back to herself; and she sat shakily up; and he put an arm around her shoulders, and she was happy to rest her head against his chest and be silent.

She did not want to ask, but she could not help herself, so at last she said: "Mathin?"

His voice sounded deeper than ever with her ear against his chest when he spoke. "He will carry a handsome scar, but he will carry it lightly, and he will be strong enough to sit on Windrider when we leave this place to return to the City, in a few days' time; although his right arm still pains him somewhat, from the long raw burn near the shoulder, as though a fire had scorched him."

Harry remembered how she had known the fire was eating her, that it would leave nothing of her; and she opened her right hand, the hand that had touched Mathin. It looked as it always had, but for the small white mark across the palm, which was only two months old.

"And the others?"

"None will die, and while none is as quick to recover as Mathin, none either bears the mark of where Harimad-sol touched them."

"And—my people? Jack, and Kentarre, and those who follow them? And Nandam, and—and Richard? Have you met my brother Richard?"

"Your Jack has introduced us." Corlath had remembered Colonel Dedham when he saw him standing in the twilight behind Harry; remembered him as the one man who had seemed to listen to what Forloy said, and believe that the men of the Hills might be speaking the truth, even to Outlanders. It was that sight of the man who had offered the Hill-king his loyalty while standing on the Residency verandah that had given Corlath the courage to declare his love for Harry the night before. It had seemed a fine bold thing to him at the time to bind her sash around himself and wear it openly; it hadn't occurred to him till he saw her with her company at her back, and her pale eyes fixed on him with an expression he could not read, that it would force him to face *her* with it and what it meant immediately, whenever he saw her again—if he saw her again. It would doubtless have been kinder or more courteous—and less dangerous—to choose his time and place; and not make such a public display of it. But then, without the sash around his waist and his people watching eagerly for the outcome, it was also extremely possible that his courage would have failed him again, for all his noble words about risk-taking. All these things he would tell Harry later. "But Richard has the face of your family, though he has not the eyes, and I would have guessed who he must be."

"Jack would like better than anything in the world to ride a Hill horse." Harry heard the beginning of his laugh far inside him before it burst out into the air; and she raised her head and looked inquiringly into his face. He shook his head at her and said, "My heart, your Jack shall have a hundred of our horses, and welcome," and then he bent his head and kissed her, and she drew him down beside her. A few minutes later Narknon, with an offended growl, climbed off the bed and stalked away.

Mathin was a trifle paler than usual when Corlath's army mounted and set their faces to the east, but he sat easily on Windrider and looked all around him as if reminding himself of what he thought he had lost; but most often he looked at Harimad-sol, riding at the king's right hand. The army moved slowly, for there were litters to carry, and they need not hurry. Even the desert sun overhead seemed glorious rather than relentless, and their king was to marry the damalur-sol who bore Gonturan the Blue Sword, and the Northerners had been defeated, at least for their time, and probably for their children's time, and perhaps even their grandchildren's; and Damar was still theirs. And it was as well also that the army was moving slowly for the sake of Jack Dedham and Richard Crewe, who were riding Hill horses, and finding Hill horsemanship a little more difficult than Harry had, and were dismayed at the idea of being able to stop a horse at full gallop simply by sitting down a little harder in the saddle. Harry, when she was not with Corlath, rode circles around them and teased them, and made Sungold do all sorts of fancy passes and turns, not really to annoy them but only because she could not contain herself for happiness. Sungold bucked and bounced till even Harry had to clutch at his mane to stay on—Jack had the temerity to laugh—and behaved not at all like a well-schooled war-horse, and seemed just as happy as she.

CHAPTER SEVENTEEN

W HEN THEY REACHED THE CITY a fortnight later, the City gates were open again, for what the people's *kelar* had told them was confirmed by messengers that Corlath sent; and on the laprun field there were thousands of the Hillfolk waiting to cheer their king and his bride, for the messengers had taken it upon themselves to tell more than Corlath had charged them with. All those who had come to the City for safety had stayed, and most of those who had elected to stay in their own land in spite of the Northerners now exultantly left those lands to hasten to the City and see their king's marriage; for somehow the news flew over the mountains and across the desert in all directions, and all of Damar knew of Harimad-sol, and that she would be queen; even into the fastnesses of the filanon, and a hundred of Kentarre's folk traveled to the City in the company of the people of Nandam's village—including Rilly, who was beside herself with excitement, and her mother, who was beside herself with Rilly—to attend the wedding.

The City was decked with flowers, and long trailing cloaks of flowers had been woven which were thrown around Corlath's shoulders and Harry's, and over Tsornin's withers and Isfahel's, and the ceremony was performed in the glassy white courtyard before Corlath's palace. People were hanging from windows and balconies, and clinging to the stark mountainside where there was not purchase for a bird's claws, and lining the walls, and crowded into the courtyard itself till there was barely space for the king and queen to walk from the palace door to the courtyard gate, where they waved and smiled and threw kaftpa, the traditional small cakes that were good luck for anyone who could catch one and eat it. And they threw armfuls and armfuls of them, that anyone who wanted one might have one, and everyone wanted one. Then they retreated again. Their wedding night they spent in the little room with the waterfall, in the blue mosaic palace. Before they slept Corlath began the long task of telling Harry all the tales of Aerin, as he had once promised he would. The telling stretched over many of their evenings together, for Harry never wavered in her desire to hear them all—and when she had heard them all, her patient husband was required to teach them to her; and when she had learned all he had to teach, she made up a few of her own, and taught them to him.

Gonturan was hung on the wall of the Great Hall, where Harry, like all Riders before her, had cut her hand on the king's sword and been made another of the company. The king's sword hung opposite, for only the king's and queen's own swords could hang on display in the Great Hall. Gonturan had spent many years wrapped in cloths in an old wooden chest, black with age, since the last time she hung in the Great Hall. And after the wedding feasts everyone went home, because there would be no traveling in the winter rains.

The filanon stayed in the City till the rains were gone, partly to pay the respect due to the City and the king they had turned away from many years before; and partly for reasons that became obvious—although everyone already knew what was happening—when in the spring Richard Crewe married Kentarre, and returned with her and the filanon to the western end of Damar, although he carefully avoided the Outlander station. Thus the filanon became once again well known to the king and his City, for the Damarian queen often visited her brother, and he her. Richard was never entirely happy riding as the Hillfolk rode, but he had a talent for woodcraft and archery that might almost have been a Gift.

He taught his sister to hold a bow properly and to put an arrow more or less where she wanted it to go, but Harry failed to rise above the merely competent.

"*Do* you talk to your arrows, and tell them to find the stag that has to be in that brush up ahead somewhere and stick him?"

"Did you *tell* Gonturan to knock down the mountains on Thurra's ugly head?"

This conversation took place almost a year after Gonturan had been hung on the wall of the palace, and Harry could laugh.

Kentarre's first child was a daughter with blond hair and grey eyes, and she was born before the rains came again. Harry's first child was born a fortnight later—"Ah, bah," Harry said, with her hand on her belly, when the messenger came from the west with the word, and the winter's first rains fell over them, and dulled the stone of the City; "I did want to be first." The child was a son, with black hair and brown eyes.

Jack grew as skilled on horseback as any Hillman, for all that he had come to it so late; and Mathin took him to his home village, where he learned how the Hills trained their young horses. He was good at this too, and Mathin's family liked him, but always he found himself returning to the stone City, where Corlath seemed more content to stay since Harry now stayed with him. And the year that young Tor Mathin was two years old, Jack was called to a banquet in the Great Hall, where he had attended many banquets before, and to his own amazement he was made a queen's Rider, to sit with the fifteen king's Riders, for Corlath had made no more since the war with the North. Gonturan, which Jack had held once before on a mountaintop, lightly and kindly drank three drops of his blood, while he stared at the cut and for once had nothing to say.

"We Outlanders must stick together," said Harry, smiling.

Jack looked up at once and shook his head. "No—we who love the Hills must stick together."

The year after Jack was made a Rider, Harry bore another child, and this one was a daughter, and she had red hair and blue eyes, and a wry whimsical smile even in her cradle. "You're calling her

Aerin, of course," said Jack, tickling her with the end of his sash while she giggled and clutched at it.

"I'm calling her Aerin Amelia, and Forloy and Innath and Mathin and I are riding west as soon as she's six months old, to invite Sir Charles and Lady Amelia to the Naming, here in the City. Will you come with us?" Harry was holding her baby, and as Jack, startled, stopped looking at her and instead looked up at her mother, Aerin grabbed the sash and stuffed as much of it as would fit into her mouth.

"Yes, of course I'll come. Don't I have to, anyway? As the only queen's Rider, I have a reputation to maintain." Harry's anxious look relaxed into a smile.

And so six months later five Riders set their faces west from the City; and as they were about to leave the City gates, Harry, who was lagging behind as if unhappy about something, heard hoof-beats behind her and turned around to see Fireheart bearing down on her. There were traveling-bundles hanging from his saddle, and Harry's face lit up and she said: "Oh, you *are* coming with us after all."

And Corlath sighed, and reached over Sungold's withers to take her hand and said, "Yes, I'm coming. I don't want to, you understand. Perhaps you should just think that I cannot bear to be parted from you for so many days; which is true enough."

"I don't care," said Harry.

Corlath looked at her and smiled in spite of himself. "Perhaps you are right, my heart. I am inclined to forget that there is still some Outlander blood in your veins; and perhaps this mad scheme of yours will work."

The six of them stopped and set up camp where a much bigger traveling camp had stopped several years before, to wait upon another visit to the Outlander town. Forloy and Innath rode in alone, early in the morning, with a written message for the District Commissioner and his wife; none of them knew what to expect, but least of all did the four who remained behind expect to see a cloud of dust hurrying back toward them a bare few hours later. "Hill horses never kick up so much dust," Jack said thoughtfully. Harry stood up and took a few steps in the dustcloud's direction; she could see two figures on horseback within it, and behind them the grey and brown that were Innath's and Forloy's horses.

Lady Amelia reached Harry first; Harry's hood was back, her hair shining in the sunlight, but in her Hill dress and with her skin burned to the color of malak, she was astonished when little Lady Amelia climbed or fell off her horse just in front of her, said, "Harry, my *dear,* why did you never send us any *word?*" burst into tears, and threw her arms around her former houseguest and foster child.

"I—" she said.

"Never mind," said Lady Amelia; "I'm so glad to see you again. I'm glad you didn't quite forget us. You don't have to name the baby after me, you know—" her voice was muffled, because it was buried in Harry's shoulder—"but if you meant the invitation, I shall certainly come. And Charles too."

Harry looked up, and Sir Charles was ponderously dismounting. Lady Amelia let her go, and Sir Charles said nothing as he embraced her in his turn; and his silence she thought was a bad omen till she looked into his face and saw the tears in his eyes. He snuffled through his mustache once or twice, and then his eyes opened wider as they looked over Harry's shoulder, and she heard Jack's voice saying: "Good to see you again, old friend."

The meeting between Sir Charles and Corlath was a trifle constrained. Sir Charles, forgetting himself in an attempt to get off on the right foot this time around, put out his hand; and Corlath looked at it, and looked at Sir Charles, and Harry gritted her teeth; and then Corlath seemed to remember a description, from her perhaps, or from Jack, of this curious Outlander ritual; and he put out his hand, tentatively, and Sir Charles shook it heartily. After that things went more or less smoothly; and Sir Charles spoke the Hill tongue, not nearly so badly as Corlath had privately been expecting—he's been practicing, the Hill-king thought in surprise, and felt almost warm toward him—and Corlath spoke Homelander, and Sir Charles tactfully refrained from remarking on how fluently he knew it.

Sir Charles wanted to insist that they all return to the Residency while he and Lady Amelia packed up for their journey, and Jack could see how he was trying to restrain himself, so he spoke to Harry and Harry spoke to Corlath. And Corlath eyed his wife and thought dark thoughts; but eight riders rode back toward Istan together.

And so diplomatic relations between Outlander and Damarian began, for the first time since the Outlanders had come over the sea and seized as much as they could. Jack discovered that Sir Charles had taken his letter, written while Harry and Senay and Terim and Narknon lay asleep in his bedroom, very seriously indeed; and had, in fact, put his own career in jeopardy by insisting that the colonel of the General Mundy had not gone desert-mad at last, but had answered a real threat to Outlander security in the only way he could. It was because of Sir Charles' efforts that Jack himself and the men who had gone with him were honorably listed in the military rolls as missing in action at the Border and presumed deceased. Sir Charles had further had one of the unhuman corpses found near the fort—for two more were discovered after Jack disappeared—bundled up and sent off to be analyzed by Homelander physicians in the south of Daria, where the biggest Homelander cities were, and the best medical facilities. The physicians had nervously announced they didn't know what the thing was they were looking at, but, whatever it was, they didn't like it. Sir Charles also dug out all the reports of irregular and belligerent activity on the Northern border, gathered more, and sent them off to where they might do the most good; and such was his reputation as stolid, conservative, and unflappable—and such was his skill at treading a very narrow line—that he was listened to, if reluctantly.

So when he returned from the Naming, leaving Lady Amelia behind for an extended visit with her name-child in the stone City, and began writing dispatches about the time being ripe for the opening of formal diplomacy between the Homeland and Damar— for so he called it—he was permitted to pursue the role he had chosen. It is true that only he and Lady Amelia were ever invited to the City in the Hills; but specially chosen Damarians did begin regularly to visit Istan, and eventually the cities in the south; and to exchange gifts, and speeches of good will, and to receive official administrative notice, even from the Queen and her Council, over the sea in the Homeland.

And Harry and Corlath attended to their administrative duties as earnestly as they had to, but no more; and much of their time they spent wandering alone together through the City, or across the plains before the City; or they rode to Mathin's village, or Innath's; and as often as they could they slipped away north through the Hills to Luthe's valley. They took the children with them—Aerin was followed by Jack, and Jack by Hari, as the years passed—for Luthe was fond of children.